We All Have Secrets

A Novel

Florence Love Karsner

SeaDog Press, LLC

This book is a work of fiction. Any references to historical events, real people, or real places are used fictitiously. Other names, characters, places, and events are products of the author's imagination, and any resemblance to actual events or places or persons, living or dead, is entirely coincidental.

Cover Design: Dar Albert, Wicked Smart Designs
Ship Logo: © Dn Br | Shutterstock
Editor: Elizabeth A. White

"First, do no harm . . ."

Excerpt from the Hippocratic Oath
Circa 500 BC

Chapter 1

Baltimore, September 1962

A miracle would occur this day. A tragedy would occur this day. But not necessarily in that order. After all, a miracle is oftentimes a response to a tragic event.

Tragedies occur more often than miracles, but even if a miracle does occur it can't remove the scars the tragedy leaves behind . . . occasionally physical ones . . . always psychological ones.

~ ~ ~

Run feet run! I must help her!

Molly's brain was far ahead of her feet that felt like they were encased in concrete galoshes.

She might have a chance if I get there quickly.

Traffic was stopped and pedestrians were gawking at the body—the one in the bright red coat with matching red hat—the one lying in a pool of blood.

Molly heard the wailing of a siren in the distance. The paramedics would be on the scene shortly. She scurried across the street.

"Let me through! Move!" Pushing her way through the crowd, she bent down and placed her fingers on the woman's carotid artery.

No pulse.

Then she made a quick head-to-toe assessment: Elderly female, bleeding from the mouth, impossible position of right foot indicating a tibial fracture, and most telling of all, clear fluid flowing from her ears and nose.

Fluid is most likely cerebrospinal. Brain injury. Still no pulse. Think Molly. You know what to do now. Help her!

Molly knelt and closer inspection revealed a massive contusion on the woman's left frontal lobe, and when she placed her hand behind the woman's head, her fingertips entered the base of the skull. A skull that felt like a melon that has been left to ripen—and has rotted instead.

For an instant, Molly found herself trying to staunch the bleeding with her scarf, knowing she couldn't.

She was gone before I even got here. Heaven help her.

A few moments later the paramedics arrived and removed the body as Molly looked on. There had truly been nothing she could have done. The woman had died instantly.

When she had left her apartment earlier, she was headed to a most important ceremony. Graduation for interns, like herself, who had completed their Internal Medicine Residency Program at Johns Hopkins Hospital.

Since she was already late for the ceremony, she took another few moments and made a quick trip to the restroom and attempted to clean her now blood-splattered dress. But she quickly realized this was a hopeless endeavor as blood leaves a stain that is all but impossible to remove.

Molly hurried into the last row of seats in the auditorium. The graduates were squirming by now, having endured long speeches by their professors extolling the virtues of the medical profession. Finally, the moment the graduates had waited for arrived.

The final speaker, Dr. Luis Cajina, Dean of the Internal Medicine Residency Program, stood at the dais and in his pleasant, accented-English began to speak.

"One last reminder before I get to my most important task. First, do no harm. These words are your mantra. Keep them in your heart. They will serve you well. Now, let me complete my task." He smiled and pushed at his thick glasses that forever slid down his nose.

"It is with great pleasure that I present the Nora Adeline Johnson Award for Clinical Excellence to a most deserving graduate."

A palpable hush fell over the group. This award was much coveted as it was a "medal" so to speak, that a new graduate could attach to their job applications, which they would all be submitting to the various medical institutions where they hoped to find employment.

After another moment filled with shuffling feet and quiet whispering, Dr. Cajina put them out of their misery.

"Dr. Molly McCormick, please come forward."

Applause broke out and a cheer erupted from the back corner. But Molly didn't go forward. She was glued to her seat.

He can't mean me . . . surely. He's called the wrong name.

She was aware she excelled in the academic arena, but this award signified much more than that. In simple terms it meant the recipient had demonstrated abilities in many clinical areas, not just those he or she was particularly interested in. In other words, this student was exceptional.

Molly's desire was to help people, which in her case meant working in research as her interpersonal skills were not her forte. A research position would also mean she could become self-sufficient, in charge of her own destiny. A long-wished-for goal.

More applause broke out and Dr. Charlie Watts, a fellow graduate and friend, clapped and cheered loudly, "Way to go, Molly!"

He wasn't surprised she'd been selected. Yes, she was an introvert with a quiet personality, but Charlie saw the raw intelligence lurking beneath that meek-as-a-mouse exterior.

Molly stood and looked about as if to make sure there wasn't another Molly McCormick somewhere . . . the one they were *really* calling for.

As she made her way toward the dais, her blood-spattered dress revealed how she'd spent her earlier hour. If Dr. Cajina noticed, he did not comment. He continued, "Your life will change today and tomorrow. Change is inevitable. Don't fight it. Embrace it. It's how we move forward."

This message wasn't one Molly particularly wanted to hear. She didn't deal well with changes and certainly didn't plan to embrace any. She liked her life just the way it was. Ordered, with no surprises. Predictable.

The ceremony and festivities lasted into the early evening, and Molly now walked along the waterfront which was blanketed in the first snowfall of the year, a rare occurrence in September. A bitter cold wind seared across the harbor bringing shards of ice, like razor blades, that sliced at her cheeks. Even so, she smiled as she strode along, her award tucked inside her bag.

A sudden blast of arctic air whipped at her face and tentacles of ice wove their fingers into her hair. Cramming her hands inside her pockets, she pulled her coat tighter. Perhaps she should have taken the local shuttle instead of braving the cold, but when she left the hospital she was floating on a cloud and needed to walk off the rush of adrenaline that had come with the award.

As she walked along, she recalled the face of the elderly woman this morning—the one that was dead before she arrived—and filed it away in a sacred place she reserved for those she'd been unable to help but would remember.

Her day had begun with a few glorious last moments snuggled beneath her duvet, remembering days on Cayo Canna. Then her evil alarm clock broke the spell. Now, at the end of her exciting day, she stepped along quickly, anxious to get home before too terribly late.

As she approached her apartment, she heard Glenn Miller's band blaring from the other half of her duplex. Mrs. Jennings, her landlady, was hard of hearing and Glenn Miller was her favorite. The music would soon come to a halt, however, as Mrs. Jennings would be in bed by eight o'clock, and she would put Glenn to bed too.

She walked up the steps of the apartment with keys in hand. "A young woman living alone can't be too careful. Leave your radio on and have your key in hand, ready to lock the door behind you," Papa Jack had said. And if he had suggested it, Molly knew it was important.

She stomped on the porch, dislodging snow from her boots, inserted the key in the lock, stepped over the threshold and heard her own radio playing. Elvis was warning anyone who might be listening to stay off his blue suede shoes.

She entered, locked the door, then removed her gloves and scarf, tossing them over the large armchair. She hung her coat in the foyer closet then pushed the door closed behind her. Or attempted to. The warped closet door never stayed closed without a lot of effort, so Mrs. Jennings had her handyman install an old-fashioned steel lock that slides from left to right to lock or unlock. Simple but effective.

The apartment was charming. It had a chintz-covered sofa and armchair, a small black and white television, an antique dining table for two, and a poster bed. Molly loved it.

Elvis made his final plea for his shoes and the news began. Molly didn't listen to the news often as her time was spent studying, preparing for the next exam. But the mention of Fidel Castro grabbed her attention as Cuba was just a short distance from the island of Cayo Canna where Papa Jack lived.

The reporter continued, "The White House is in daily communication with Cuban officials. Fidel Castro has been ramping up his defense capabilities, but President Kennedy and his Cabinet are confident that negotiations with the Cuban leader will produce agreements that will satisfy both countries. Now back to your regularly scheduled program."

The Kingston Trio took the stage now and Molly turned them down a notch. She'd take a warm shower, then share her exciting news with the most important person in her life, Papa Jack.

After much argument, Molly had convinced Papa Jack that he did not need to attend this ceremony. He'd come to her college graduation and her graduation from medical school. She assured him she would see him shortly as she was planning a trip to Cayo Canna before she began whatever new position she was able to attain.

She walked through the living area to her bedroom, then stopped abruptly, turned around, and stared back at the front door. Her thoughts rushed like blood from a severed artery.

I never turned the key . . . it was already unlocked . . . but I always . . . lock . . .

She caught a fleeting glimpse of a looming, dark shadow as it leaped out from the bathroom behind her. Before her brain could process this visual input, her keen nose recoiled when it detected the odor of an unwashed body and fetid breath. Then she felt hot air breathing down her neck and a cold, metal instrument was jammed against her temple. She tried to order her thoughts, but found it most difficult as the metal item was pressed even harder against her head.

A gun? Is that a gun?

Her pulse raced wildly, her heart pounded, and she raised her arms to ward off the impending shadow. Too late. Her right arm was quickly twisted behind her back, and she cried out in pain as she was shoved into the dining area and pushed against the wall.

"Wha . . . what are you doing?" she cried.

6

"Something I've waited several weeks to do, Dr. McCormick," a deep voice said, twisting her arm even harder.

"Stop! My shoulder!"

He was close behind her. She'd heard that voice before.

Is this someone I know?

"You're hurting me! Please stop!" she screamed through her tears. The pistol was still shoved against her temple. She didn't dare move a muscle.

"You think that hurts? That's not pain. But pain will come. Soon. First, we've gotta have a little chat. Become better acquainted. You know a lot about me but I need to learn a few things about you. Then we can begin our relationship." He released her arm, then stood facing her, the gun pointing at her chest.

"Sit here. In front of me." He pulled a chair from the small table. Molly was relieved when he released her arm and she had no doubt her shouldered had been dislocated. It was on fire with pain. She sat on the edge of the chair, her heartbeat now pounding in her head as well as her chest.

Her internal thoughts were giving her instructions again. *Adrenaline. Too much adrenaline. Take a deep breath, Molly. Remain calm.*

"Who are you? Why are you doing this?" she sobbed.

"Take a good look, Dr. McCormick. Still don't recognize me?"

Molly stared at him. Young, late twenties, early thirties. Tall, thin. Too thin. Dirty jeans barely hanging on his bony hips. Dark, lank hair. Two-three-day-old beard. Stained teeth, one broken canine. Eyes dilated. Slight tremble in hands. Reeking of alcohol. No, beer. Yeasty.

She took a deep breath and looked at him, struggling to keep her voice calm even though her insides were screaming for her to run, escape, flee.

"You look vaguely familiar," she whispered.

7

"Vaguely familiar? Really? Not a clue? Even though you screwed up my whole life, tried to play God? And you don't remember me? Well, guess what? You're going to remember me after today, bitch!"

He stood quickly then, causing his chair to overturn. He towered over her and leaned down, his face only inches from hers.

"Who do you think you are? Galen? By the time I'm finished with you, you'll remember everything. This event— the one you have no recollection of—it was your way of showing how much power you, a female doctor, had over me."

Molly kept her gaze on him. *Stay calm, Molly. Don't agitate him.*

"As I recall, one of the first things a physician must do is 'assess and observe' their patient. Am I right?" he asked.

Molly squirmed in her chair, the pain in her shoulder excruciating. She nodded.

"Yes, and that's what we're going to do today, doc. I'm going to 'assess and observe' you. Then I'll record each reaction to various stimuli. That's only fair, don't you think? To treat you as I was treated?"

Still pointing the gun at her, he reached behind his chair, retrieved a large canvas bag and threw it at her feet. "Feel inside. Get one of the ropes. Tie it around your ankles."

Molly reached inside the bag and found a thick rope. She tied it around her ankles, all the while her shoulder screaming at her to stop moving.

"Not good enough, doc. Do it again. This time make sure it's tight. Let's have it biting into your ankles." He beamed at her as if enjoying this event. Molly retied the rope and pulled it tight, snug enough that her ankles were turning red.

"That's better. Now reach in and bring out the roll of tape."

Molly's fingers found the tape, but her shaking hands dropped it and it rolled over close to his feet.

"Pick it up, doc. Tear off a strip and place it over that lovely mouth of yours. That mouth that got you into this trouble. If you'd kept it shut, you could have had a long, prosperous career. And being a doc, you'd have lots of money.

"Yeah, I know about money. And I know what it's like to not have any. My father died early. Cardiac arrest. Then my esteemed mother went on to live a very comfortable life. She had loads of money. Money my father left her. More than she needed. But she refused to share it with me, her only child, her son. Thought I should 'earn' it. Thought I should get my life in order, become a responsible human being. Idiot woman. Like you, she wanted to show her power over me. Well, that's one problem that's been solved already."

Molly's mind raced, ignoring her pleas for it to slow down. If he was telling the truth, then he was obviously from a well-to-do family. He appeared to be a homeless person, but his vocabulary belied that thought. He knew about Galen, an early Greek physician who served several Roman emperors. That spoke of an educated person.

Think, Molly. Think. It's what you do best.

"That's duct tape. It's quite abrasive." Molly knew that was a lame statement, but was desperate to say anything that might help.

He threw his head back and cackled, "Ha! Abrasive? You think I care? You forget. I'm assessing and observing here. I'll record what happens when I rip it from your tender kisser."

He picked up the roll and threw it, striking her cheek. "Put it on." Molly tore off a piece and placed it over her lips.

"That's better. Now I'll talk and you'll do what I tell you. The others from the psych center will get their assessment and observation treatment also.

"I've followed you for two weeks, waiting for the right moment. When I saw you leave the hospital today, walking alone, I knew the day had arrived. Getting here before you took some doing, what with the snow. But your unlocked door was a pleasant surprise I hadn't expected. Now, for the next step. Remove that sweater. Let's see what's beneath it."

Molly hesitated then began to lift her sweater, bringing agony to her shoulder. "Please, my shoulder hurts!" she cried out, unable to restrain herself. She was wearing a thin pink camisole underneath her sweater and quickly felt the chill.

He raked his eyes from her head to her toes, then ran his tongue across his lips. "Nice. Nice. I've been picturing this scene for two weeks now. But we'll take our time. There's no hurry. Not likely anyone will come out in this weather."

Molly shivered. Whether from the cold or the fear within, she didn't know.

"Cold doc? No problem. You'll be hot soon." He took her chin in his hand, forcing her to look at him.

"I think we'll put you in restraints. Isn't that the proper word? Restraints?" He took another piece of rope and tied her arms to the chair, turning her wrists upward.

"Now, let's proceed with the first phase of our research project. Shall we see how long it takes to elicit a response after a lighted cigarette has been applied to the skin of a young, female physician? Correction. A young, *beautiful*, female physician."

He reached in his shirt pocket, pulled a cigarette from his pack of Marlboros, lighted it and inhaled deeply, blowing the smoke in Molly's face. He took the cigarette from his lips, leaned forward and lightly touched it to the upper portion of Molly's left breast, just above the lacy edge of her camisole.

With the tape covering her mouth, Molly could only utter a long groan. He ripped the tape from her mouth, causing her to gasp.

"I think I'd enjoy hearing your screams. No one around to hear you anyway. Let's try that again." He proceeded to press the cigarette to her breast again.

With her hands tied to the chair, she could only scream, knowing it was to no avail. "No! Stop, please!" But that response only seemed to excite him more.

"That didn't take long at all. Perhaps two seconds? I'll record that." He smiled broadly as if pleased with her response.

Molly's body began to shake involuntarily. She knew exactly what was happening. *Fight or Flight Response. Hyperventilation. Constriction of peripheral blood vessels. Vasodilation of the central vessels. Increasing muscle tension. Piloerection.*

Her brain dashed through a litany of autonomic nervous system responses to pain and trauma, but no matter how many medical terms she came up with, she was just plain out scared to death.

"Just the beginning of the branding process. Soon you'll belong to me. That's right. Me," her attacker sneered.

Molly watched in disbelief as his eyes sparkled and he again licked his lips. He stood then and took a step in her direction. Kneeling next to her chair, he whispered in her ear and once again his foul breath—that reeked of beef jerky—assaulted her nostrils.

"The next experiment will be even more exciting. Let's see how long it takes you to respond when I slit your wrists. You know, kinda like I did mine.

"I'll be very careful as I don't want to go too deep. Why, if I cut too deeply, you could bleed to death in a matter of minutes."

Molly's hands and body trembled and she sobbed with every breath. He laid the gun down by his feet. Taking her left hand into his, he traced the blue veins of her wrist with his forefinger.

"Such small wrists. So delicate. And those tiny blue veins." He then drew a small item from his bag, held it in his hand, then lifted it for her to see.

Molly shivered when she saw the item—a small utensil with a handle and a convex edge—a surgeon's scalpel.

"It's a little toy I borrowed from my father. He has no more use for it. It'll do the trick."

Slowly, with the precision of a surgeon, he drew the blade across Molly's left wrist. With the dull side of the blade. She drew in a short, quick breath racked with sobs.

"You've done this, doc. You know how precise one should be." Once again—now with the sharp side—he pulled the scalpel across her wrist, bearing down slightly. She winced and could no longer contain the scream tearing at her throat. It echoed off the walls.

"No! Oh please stop!" she screamed.

Her attacker grinned. "Ah, just like the cigarette. An immediate response. Perhaps even less time than I recorded for the first experiment. No problem, though, with your wrists. These wounds are superficial. You'll not bleed to death . . . yet."

He took her chin in his hand and placed a kiss on her mouth. "Ah, sweet. I knew you would be."

With blood flowing from her left wrist, he took her right hand in his and brought the blade closer. "Now the other wrist. Let's do this properly. Take our time."

In spite of herself, she screamed again . . . even before he sliced. "Stop it! You're a madman! Stop!" She leaned forward in the chair and pleaded with him. "Please! Don't do this!"

The unexpected ringing of the telephone—such a jarring interruption—brought hope. Molly prayed it would keep ringing. Maybe if she didn't answer it someone would check on her. Surely, they would, wouldn't they?

Her brain brought forth a conversation from earlier today. *Maybe that's Charlie. He said he might drop by!*

Her eyes widened and, as if reading her thoughts, her captor grinned. "The fop from the hospital? Really? I don't think so."

The scream of a siren pierced the air. Molly knew that sound was from a police squad car. Then a second, higher-pitched screeching noise joined the first one. That was the Fire Department.

"I smell smoke! There's a fire close by!" Molly was certain he would see through her pitiful effort, but she had to try.

"I don't smell anything. And neither do you," he snickered.

Then the slamming of a door got their attention. Was that coming from next door?

Maybe Mrs. Jennings will come to see about me, Molly thought. Or maybe just hoped.

The attacker considered the situation for a second. Perhaps there was a fire close by. Was a possibility. The last thing he needed was to have the Fire Department come pounding on the door. He'd been careful so far and his plan for retribution was working. There were others he still needed to "treat" also. So he'd not take the chance of getting caught.

He stood, then dragged his finger down Molly's cheek gently. As a lover might. "It appears I must curtail this 'observation session' more quickly than I'd planned. But we're not finished, doc. We'll meet again."

He leaned over and yanked her gold necklace—the one Papa had given her—from her neck. "I think I'll keep this as a souvenir."

Molly's body continued to shake. She could no longer think. Pain and fear were paralyzing her brain. She watched in terror as her torturer picked up the pistol and, with his other hand, reached up to her neck again.

"I prefer brunettes with long legs and a bit of flesh. But something about your small, thin body is appealing, and I love your soft skin that begs for my touch."

He looked down at her. "Oh, almost forgot. Need to finish the branding process. Leave you with a little souvenir of me, also."

Molly's paralyzed brain quickly became alert again and she was more frightened than ever before in her life. *He's going to kill me now!*

"Please, don't! I can . . . "

The butt of the pistol came crashing down on her skull, and her words were lost somewhere in her brain, a brain that could no longer process any information whatsoever.

Using his scalpel, he slashed through Molly's wrist restraints and laid her on her side on the floor. Then he began to make an incision on the left side of her face, carving deftly. As if he had done this before. He grabbed her scarf from the back of the chair and held it on the incision. Soaking up blood. Admiring his handiwork.

"Ah, well done my good and faithful servant," he smiled.

The letter "S" now covered a three-inch area of Molly's face, beginning at her temple and coming down the side of her cheek. The incision was rather deep. As the carver had intended.

"S is for Sam. You're mine now."

With his task completed, he picked Molly up and placed her inside the foyer closet, then packed the scarf about the incision. He bent down and whispered in her ear, "You'll never be able to get out of here and no one will hear you if you call out. I'll be back, doc."

He closed the closet door, slid the old-fashioned latch into place and crawled out a kitchen window, leaving all doors locked. The sirens were quickly moving away from the area. In search of their next assignment. And so was Molly's attacker.

Chapter 2

*B*lood. *Smells like blood. Only blood smells like blood.*
Tastes like blood. Only blood tastes like blood.

The sense of touch—feeling—was the first sense to awaken as evidenced by excruciating pain that racked her body.

The sense of smell was sniffing at its heels, informing her that blood was present. Both these senses, touch and smell, returned with a vengeance.

Taste tongued its way to the surface next, only to confirm the findings of the first two senses. Pain and blood were definitely present.

The remaining senses, vision and hearing, were still blind and deaf. Absent from the scene. It was pitch black and the only sound Molly could hear was the deafening beat of her heart.

Finally, the three pounds of gray matter that processed this input clamored for attention. It issued a thought. Just one.

Physician . . . that blood you smell and taste? It's
yours.

Molly lifted her hands and searing pain rushed through her shoulder. Moving upward, her fingers waded through the thick, sticky wetness oozing from her scalp, streaming down the side of her face. Not only could she smell the blood, but she could also taste it as rivulets pooled in the corners of her mouth.

Yes, that blood is mine. Oh, dear God, my head hurts so!

The unrelenting pain throbbed in perfect union with her heartbeat. Each beat reinforced the agony, making it difficult to put together a cohesive thought. She discovered she was lying face down on a hard surface in a place that was darker than Hades. In fact, maybe it was Hades.

I'm alive. Alive.

Some lobes of her brain were functioning, but even those were slow to get their act together. She may not like the messages that were getting through, but at least they were being sent and received . . . sort of.

Moving was painful. Using her good arm, she pushed herself up on her elbows. Something soft brushed against her face.

What is that? Soft. Like clothing. Feels like wool.

Lifting her head, she again brushed against something soft, and her nose caught a whiff of an unmistakable and unpleasant smell. Mothballs.

The closet. The foyer closet had mothballs when I first moved in. I threw them out but that awful smell is still present. I must be in the foyer closet.

She eased herself to a sitting position, which caused the pounding in her head to intensify. Blood oozed from her wrists but not profusely. As her attacker had said, the cuts were only superficial.

The most pressing problem was the agonizing pain coming from her head wound and the side of her face was on fire. She touched her cheek, then jerked her fingers away as she felt the blood streaming down.

Taking their own sweet time, all cranial lobes began to come to life. But this was not necessarily a positive development as only bits and pieces of memory surfaced.

But enough information seeped through to allow fear to take precedence over pain.

Once again her body was flooded with adrenaline, epinephrine, norepinephrine and a host of other hormones. The fight or flight response was in high gear, and this déjà vu moment was crippling to an already-wounded victim.

Someone put me in here. Who? A man. Yes. He smelled. Is he still out there? Do I dare make a sound? I'm bleeding and my head is going to explode any minute. Oh, Papa, I need you!

She sat up straighter. *Okay. I'm in the foyer closet. Unless I've been locked in, I can get out of here. I'll call the police. They'll help me.*

Getting to her knees was difficult. The minute she moved the slightest bit her pounding head shuddered in agony and the wound to her temple came alive again, sending a new stream of blood flooding down her face.

I've got to get help. I'll die in here!

One attempt to turn the doorknob told Molly she was locked in. That lock the handyman had installed was impossible to break through. She could not get out of this closet, and Mrs. Jennings would never hear her even if she screamed to high heaven. She sat down again, this time facing the opposite direction.

"Oh!" she gasped, as the slightest inkling of hope filtered through to her foggy brain.

"No! No! I'm not alone!"

She burst into sobs as she inched her wounded body to the back corner of the closet where she let her fingers be her eyes.

"Where? Oh where?" she called out.

On the right side, Molly. It's on the right side.

She felt in the darkness for another moment. Her hands trembled and struggled to obey her brain's instructions. Then her fingers latched on to their prey.

19

One click later and a yellow-eyed monster glared at her in the darkness. It had been lurking in the corner all along. Crouching beneath her hanging clothes.

Molly sobbed, then began to laugh. With blood dripping from her wrist, she reached out to the monster and felt its warmth, its vibrations. She needed to get closer. With a final sob, she embraced it and cried out, "Oh, Nancy, I forgot you were in here. I can't get out, but *you* can!

Chapter 3

Cayo Canna

After rapping for the second time on the pitted, salt-encrusted ship's anchor that served as a door knocker, Patrick opened the door, walked in, and called out.

"Hey, anyone home? Jack? Are you here?"

From somewhere up high a deep, gravelly voice echoed down the stairwell. "Up here, Patrick. Come on up."

Patrick sighed, then mumbling under his breath, began the long hike up the spiral staircase that would bring him to the top of the lighthouse. To the lantern room. He detested this spiral staircase. It was quite narrow and Patrick's big feet barely fit on the steps. He was sure he was going to tumble down them one day.

He bent his head to one side to keep from whacking it on the ceiling, then began his now-expected diatribe.

"For God's sake, Jack, do you have to stay holed up here all the time? I know the light's better in your ivory tower, but it would be all right for you to hang out in that cozy little downstairs den occasionally. I might drop by more often if you did."

The older man standing at the easel removed his pipe from his mouth, poked at it with a yellow-stained finger, and looked over his half-glasses at his friend.

"Ever occur to you that might be the reason I don't?" But the statement was accompanied by a quirky little smile that never failed to please whomever he was inclined to bestow it on.

"Ah, you old seadog. You'd be lonely if I didn't stop at least once a day. What are you working on this morning? Another seascape?"

"Nope. Not this time. Something I've been working on for a while. I bring it out, work on it for a few weeks, then put it away again. May finish it now. But then, may not."

"If it's not a seascape, then what?" Patrick asked, peering over the top of the canvas on the easel.

"Not for your eyes, my friend. Don't show my work 'til it's finished," Jack responded as he placed his long brush into a jar of linseed oil and walked across the room, taking a moment to look out one of the open windows.

He reached down and lifted Chica, an old calico cat that had free roam of the lighthouse. Most of the time she could be found sprawled on top of the humming Frigidaire. He rubbed her head between her ears, then placed her on the floor, and she disappeared down the stairs.

The sun was still blazing even though it was late afternoon, and the aqua ocean was just a few knots from white capping. And far out, dark ominous clouds were gathering on the horizon.

Jack looked out the window and down at his old 24-foot Chris Craft Cobra tied at his dock. "Looks like weather coming. Better check on my girlfriend down there. She's yanking at her lines already."

Patrick picked up a large, battered, old brass lantern laying on the work table in the corner. "This old relic has seen better days," he remarked as he returned it to the table.

"Nah. It stopped working a few months ago. I've been trying to repair it, but need a couple of parts before I can get her working again."

"Why don't you just get a new one?"

22

"Can't do that. When Molly was young, I would tell her if she'd look out her window in Connecticut—where she went to boarding school——she might just see my lantern far in the distance.

"Of course, she always swore she saw it. 'Papa's light' she called it. Gotta get it repaired before she comes. If she ever finds time again, that is."

Patrick looked out across the choppy water. "Wish it would come a storm. It's hot as hell at the moment. Sometimes I really would like a cold, dreary, New England day."

"Had enough of those myself," remarked Jack. "This drenching humidity and warm days and nights suit me fine. And just think, if you were in New England, huddled inside out of that cold, dreary weather, you'd be wishing you were here with me playing a round of golf over on Sanibel."

"I didn't say I wanted a month of it, Jack. Just a day or so would do. If we could have one or two days of freezing temperatures maybe those damn mosquitoes would find a new home. I've even resorted to netting over my bed. You know, like you see in those movies set in Africa or India."

"Huh. Bet that's a sight to see. Does it work?"

"No. Those pesky devils still manage to squirm through the netting and latch their nasty little suckers onto my body. I fully expect they'll drag me off to the Mosquito Lagoon any day now."

Jack laughed. "They're probably no-see-ums, not mosquitoes. Let's go down. See if we can talk Solana into making a pitcher of sangria. Never thought I'd drink that concoction, but it's too early for the hard stuff."

As they started down the staircase, Patrick tilted his head again as early on he'd had a couple of bumps that left an impression on him.

His thick, dark hair, a bit shaggy around his neck at the moment, was beginning to show a sprinkling of white around the temples. His dark penetrating eyes completed the look.

"You look menacing, Patrick. A right brooding Irishman, my lad," Mum had often told him, but always with a smile. Patrick was the oldest and whether she'd admit it or not, her favorite.

Jack called out, "Solana! Would you take a moment from your work and make a pitcher of sangria for the good father and me? Painting stirs up a mighty thirst."

A soft, accented voice floated up the stairs. "You do not have to shout, Captain. I hear very well." The housekeeper sauntered out from the kitchen, without so much as a hint of "hurry" in her step.

Tall and thin as a reed, Solana was regal with her full length, printed skirt, a long tunic blouse, and her ever-present satin ribbon holding back her abundant, raven-colored hair. And, unless she was forced to, she never wore shoes.

Her large dark eyes twinkled as if she knew something you didn't . . . but wish you did. She was striking and somewhere between forty and seventy years old. Jack couldn't tell her age and certainly didn't plan to ask her.

Solana had been the housekeeper at the lighthouse when the U.S. Coast Guard was responsible for its maintenance. But once it became a non-working lighthouse, they didn't want the expense of keeping it up.

When it went up for auction a number of years ago, Jack had jumped at the chance to buy it. He "inherited" Solana then, which had been a fortunate thing. She'd been there ever since and had stepped in when he needed someone to help care for his wife, Margaret, in her final days.

Solana kept her thoughts to herself, especially when it came to how she felt about some of the Captain's friends.

Good father, my foot. Never met a priest yet who wasn't hiding something behind that collar. Handsome as he is, there's probably a woman in his closet somewhere.

Drinking that Irish whiskey and talking nonsense about stuff nobody else ever talks about. Wearing his sandals and shorts, then putting on that black shirt and white collar and dishing out Christ's blood to the heathen. Can't be right.

Solana had her own ideas about how a spiritual man ought to dress and behave, and Father Patrick O'Brien didn't fit that picture.

The lighthouse stood on the edge of the Gulf and a breeze constantly blew through the open windows. Two rattan chairs, upholstered in a bright, tropical-print fabric, were placed near the open window and a large rattan table was nestled between them.

Solana waltzed in and deposited a cold pitcher of sangria on the table, along with two chilled mugs and a small plate of what she called *tapas*.

She noticed the Captain appeared to be thinner lately. Perhaps she'd start making his favorite dishes so he'd eat a little more.

"Now you two eat those *tapas* and my supper, too. Don't just sit here drinking that wine concoction. It'll fill you up and when I get here in the morning my jerk-chicken dinner will still be sitting there."

The young priest nodded, and Captain Jack saluted her. He poured their drinks, then made his way to the table in the corner where he'd positioned several pieces of electronic equipment. The most important item on this table was his ham radio. A fine, Viking Ranger model that he'd had for many years.

"Better switch Drew on. Molly usually calls around eight o'clock. Don't want to miss her." He flipped a switch on the radio then went back to his chair at the window.

"Drew?" asked Patrick.

Jack chuckled. "Yeah, that's what Molly named my ham radio. She was taken with that radio years ago when she was a kid. Nothing would do except for me teach her to use it. She was quick with anything I threw at her, so I eventually got one for her.

"She passed her licensure exam the first time around and for the longest time she had ham radio friends everywhere. Of course, the last few years she's been in medical school and had no time for such. Now she just calls me on it. Before Tom went missing, they communicated on it from wherever he was stationed."

He stared out the window, lost in memories for a few seconds. Patrick knew the story of Jack's son, Tom, and asked no questions.

"Anyway, now we talk once a week, sometimes more if she's got something important to tell me. The radio's much more reliable than the telephone system on the island. Half the time you get cut off if you're even able to get a call through. And the electricity is no better. Irritates the shit out of me."

Patrick smiled. When Margaret was alive, Jack had kept his "salty" Navy tongue in check. But now, he would occasionally toss out some colorful phrases and words. But, then, so did Patrick.

"I don't even have a phone in my place. Fine by me. Done enough talking during my time at St. Mark's. Don't want to talk to most folks anyway these days. Especially not ones from there."

"If you ever need one, you can come here. And Agnes, at Bailey's Grocery, will let you use hers. Now, I think we better eat these *tapas* and a few bites of that jerk chicken, else Solana will never stop nagging me."

They consumed the plate of *tapas* and Patrick downed his share of the chicken and some of Jack's portion as well. Both men were tall, but Patrick was a bit heavier, just as his Irish father and brothers. Jack still had broad shoulders, but as Solana had noticed, he'd gotten a bit thinner lately.

"I'll take these plates to the kitchen. Don't want Solana after me, too," Patrick laughed.

"Just put them on the counter. Solana doesn't like it if I try to wash up. Says I just make a bigger mess for her."

Patrick returned, reaching for a last sip of sangria. "Think I'll find my way home. It's almost nine o'clock."

"Really? Nine o'clock? I wonder why . . ."

The blaring static of the radio got his attention. "Late for Molly. Probably one of my pals on the East coast. Old Navy buddies."

"K4ELD! K4ELD! Please answer!"

Jack's call sign. A female voice, high pitched and strained. The caller was upset and crying. Who was it? Surely that wasn't Molly, was it?

In his deep, resonating voice, Jack answered quickly.

"K4ELD here. Over." He'd answered the call all the while feeling the hair on his neck standing on end.

"Oh, Papa! Help me! I'm trapped in Nancy's closet. Help ...I can't..." A burst of scratchy static blared out. Then nothing. Silence.

"W3CYY, W3CYY. Molly talk to me!" The transmission was over. The connection was lost. She was gone.

"Jaysus, Mary, and Joseph! Was that Molly?" asked Patrick.

"Yes, that was Molly."

"Trapped in Nancy's closet? Is that what she said?"

Jack grabbed his pipe and stuck it in his mouth as though chewing on it would speed up his thought processes. He nodded. "Yes. Sounds like she's trapped in the closet in her apartment. Somehow, she's gotten locked in. But it's more than that. I could hear it in her voice. She's in trouble."

"Are you sure she's in her apartment? Sounded like she must be at a friends' place. Nancy?"

"Nancy's the name she gave *her* ham radio. It comes from those Nancy Drew mysteries she read when she was young. She found it entertaining for her to have a radio named Nancy and me to have one named Drew. She was quite clever as a young girl. When she relocated to Baltimore to complete her medical residency, she had me set the radio up in her foyer closet. She still likes using that thing."

After a moment of silence, his head reeling with thoughts, Jack began issuing orders. "I'll call the Baltimore police. Hopefully, they can get there quickly and help Molly."

Patrick piped up, "The ferry will leave at 8:00 tomorrow morning. You can be ready to go. And I'll look out for your place."

"No, I'll leave tonight. I'll take the Cobra to the mainland and catch the red-eye flight out of Page Field in Fort Myers. This situation can't wait until morning."

"But it's night, Jack. It's kinda hard to see out in that ocean at night."

The old seadog looked at the young priest. "I believe I can find my way, Patrick."

Realizing what an idiotic statement he'd just made to a retired Navy Captain who had spent his life aboard ships, Patrick shook his head. "Oh, of course you can. Sorry."

"While I'm making the call, you go down to the dock and get the boat ready. Make sure I've got enough fuel. I'll be going wide open. And would you take care of Ensign 'til I get back? Solana's afraid of anything with four legs. She'd make him stay outside the whole time."

"Right. I'll go to the boat now. See you down there."

Chapter 4

J ack's old Cobra had run hot on him the last time he had her out. But tonight he pushed the throttle forward to its stop. He needed to get to the mainland. To Page Field. If he hurried, he'd make the red-eye flight and be in Baltimore in a few hours.

As he stood at the helm with salt spray splashing over the bow, his brain was traveling as fast as the Cobra. He was certain Molly was in trouble. He heard it in her voice and could feel it in his bones. She'd been such a part of his life that he refused to let his mind go to that dark place where it wanted to drift . . .to wonde111ring if she had been hurt, or worse, killed.

A kaleidoscope of pictures had been etched in Jack's memory and now came forward in a rush. Pictures of his son, Tom, decked out in his Tropical White Long uniform, standing next to a beautiful young woman holding an infant. Such a wonderful picture. But that picture brought its own set of memories. Some which were painful, and this one particularly—from 1944—

Soothing music—Bing Crosby harmonizing about a blue moon—filled the air. With a quick turn of a knob, the music came to an abrupt halt.

"Papa Jack, really. A ham radio? What in heaven's name is she going to do with that? Young ladies don't need

a ham radio. They need pretty dresses, make-up, jewelry. What were you thinking?"

Cathy, Miss Rhode Island 1934, had snagged herself a handsome young naval officer, Ensign Thomas (Tom) McCormick, in the spring of that same year. They met at the Officer's Club in Quonset Point, Rhode Island, and engaged in a whirlwind courtship followed by a wedding in the chapel at Naval Station Newport.

All was well until nine months later when a baby girl arrived. They named her Margaret (Molly) after her paternal grandmother. Tom was delighted with the child but he quickly discovered Cathy was not happy with the motherhood scene.

"I'll never have another baby! Do you hear me? Look at me. Since having her I have no waistline whatsoever. Instead, I have stretch marks . . . and that child never stops crying!"

The marriage continued, with Tom at sea much of the time. Then one cold blustery day in Norfolk, Virginia, where Tom was stationed and Cathy and Molly resided, the doorbell rang.

Cathy opened the door to a Navy Commander who stood there in his Service Dress Blue uniform. He removed his cover and nodded.

"Ma'am. I'm Commander Hardee. I have a special message from the Secretary of the Navy." He said nothing more, but instead, handed her a typewritten letter. Actually, only about a half page.

Cathy slowly read the letter. "The Secretary of the Navy extends his deepest sympathies. Lieutenant Commander Thomas McCormick failed to return from a mission two weeks ago and has been officially declared Missing In Action . . . "

Months passed, then a year, and Tom was still MIA. Molly was now eleven years old. As was evident from day one, she was exceptionally bright. Very much an introvert,

30

she preferred a trip to the library over going shopping with Cathy. But more than anything, she loved spending time with Papa Jack and Mimi, her grandparents.

Papa Jack and Mimi lived on an island off the west coast of Florida and Molly spent her summers with them. Papa taught her to swim, to snorkel, to read Morse Code, to fly a kite, ride a bike, and—her most favorite thing of all— how to use a ham radio. He loved her inquisitive nature and encouraged her to use her very agile brain.

Cathy never understood her daughter. Quite different from herself. So now, less than two years after Tom had been listed as MIA, she made a decision. One Molly was not happy with.

"But, why can't I go to California with you? I don't want to go to boarding school. I'll have nothing in common with those girls. I'd rather go with you," Molly cried.

"Molly, you can't go with me, I don't even know what I'm going to do just yet. Maybe I'll find a job, I don't know. But it will be some time before I'll be able to bring you out."

"Then, why can't I go live with Papa and Mimi in the lighthouse? They have room. I know they would let me."

"There's no school on that island, Molly. And that old seadog may not be the best influence for a young girl. He's too indulgent where you're concerned and thinks he knows more than everyone else. Boarding school in Connecticut is the answer for you."

Though he kept his thoughts to himself, Papa Jack believed Molly getting away from Cathy would be a blessing. That idiot woman had convinced Molly that looks were more important than brains and had suggested Molly keep her intellectual prowess in hiding.

Boarding school wasn't terrible. At least there were other "brainiacs" like her. But Molly treasured her time on the island with Papa and Mimi and visited them during her school breaks.

Then, when Mimi succumbed to the cancer that had already taken so much of her life, it was just the two of them, she and Papa Jack.

Jack was glad to see the lights from the marina on the mainland. He pushed his painful memories to a distant corner of his brain and concentrated on his task. His only task. He had to get to Molly. And come hell or highwater, he would do just that.

Chapter 5

Baltimore, 1962

The police kept sirens quiet as they streaked towards their assignment. The caller had pleaded with them to hurry. He'd stated his granddaughter was locked in a closet and he feared she was in trouble.

Was it just an accident that she'd been trapped? Or had someone put her there? If that was the case, the intruder could still be on the premises.

The officers tried both back and front doors. Locked. "Break it down fellows," yelled Lieutenant Collins. Two policemen kicked at the front door several times before tearing it from its hinges.

"Hurry. That young woman could be dying as we stand here polishing our badges." The lieutenant rushed in, brandishing his revolver, scanning the room from one side to the other.

"Police! We're here, Miss McCormick."

But Miss McCormick, Molly, was far from being able to respond. Her energy had been drained dragging herself to the radio to make the call. She'd lost consciousness and never heard Papa Jack's response.

The lieutenant pulled the closet lock from left to right and the door sprang open. He peered in, hoping to hear a whimper, a cry. Anything to tell him she was alive.

Holding his revolver tightly, he swept the closet with his eyes. There, crumpled in a heap on the floor, was the body of a young woman. He reached down, placed his finger on her neck and was relieved to find a pulse. A strong one.

"She's alive. Medics on the way?"

"Yessir. They'll be here any minute now."

~ ~ ~

Johns Hopkins Hospital
Baltimore

The tall, trim, handsome older gentleman standing at the nurses' station simply reeked of authority. His salt and pepper hair was close-cropped and his lined face was tanned, indicating he spent a lot of time outdoors. His creased slacks and crisp, buttoned-down, collared shirt only enhanced his intimidating look.

Susan Collingsworth, RN, squared her shoulders, hoping to appear confident as she reiterated her statement. "As I said, sir, you can't see her just yet."

"What do you mean I can't see her? Molly McCormick is my granddaughter and I WILL see her!"

Captain Jackson McCormick, United States Navy . . . arriving.

"Sir, if you'll just be calm, I . . ."

"Be calm my ass! Where is she?"

As soon as he heard that heated interchange, Dr. Charlie Watts had no doubt who this gentleman was and he hurried over.

"Captain McCormick? I'm Charlie Watts. A friend of Molly's. I'll take you to her. The staff is only following orders, sir. It's protocol."

The Captain looked Dr. Watts up and down and apparently decided he was worthy of a handshake. Then he began peppering the young physician with questions.

"How's Molly? Where is she?"

This old seaman was short on manners and small talk most of the time, and in situations such as this, had no patience for being told to be calm.

"I believe she's going to be all right, sir. She's sedated, which means she won't be able to talk to you."

"What's her condition? Don't mince words. Tell me straight."

"She's sustained a penetrating wound to her skalp which required several stitches. She has a dislocated shoulder, superficial cuts on both wrists and what appears to be cigarette burns on her breast."

"Is that it? No broken bones?"

"No, sir. No broken bones."

The Captain stared at Dr. Watts . . . waiting . . . as if he knew there must be more information to come.

"As I said, she has a head wound and there's always the possibility of intracranial bleeding. I haven't seen the x-rays, but I'm hopeful the bleeding was from the scalp wound. We'll know more when she awakens."

"That's it?"

"Well, there is one more wound, and this one may be the most serious of all." Dr. Watts took a deep breath and let it out. He knew this next bit of information might not sit too well with Captain McCormick.

"It appears her attacker carved into the side of her cheek. And he carved deeply. A surgeon stitched the wound and suggested Molly contact him a bit later after the wound has had a chance to heal somewhat. It may be she'll need more surgery to reconstruct that area."

Captain McCormick nodded. "You say she'll be all right though?"

"Yes, I believe so."

"Then I'll see her now. Can you take me to her?"

"Yessir. This way."

They walked down a long hallway, turned left at the end and entered a dimly lit area. "This is the ICU. She'll remain here overnight for observation. If all goes well, tomorrow she'll be moved to another room for the remainder of her hospitalization."

"I see."

"Molly talks about you a lot, sir. You appear to be her only family. Well, the only family that matters, anyway. I know she and her mother don't communicate often."

"Uh, huh. That's Molly's business."

Jack never discussed Molly's mother if he could avoid it. He never liked her but did see what Tom had found appealing. A lot of beauty was packed into those five feet, two inches. But, like Molly's wrist wounds, it was all superficial. Only skin deep.

Entering the ICU room, Charlie pulled at the curtain surrounding Molly's bed. She lay there covered with a white blanket that only accentuated her ashen face.

"As I said, she's sedated. It could be several hours before she's alert enough to talk with you."

Captain McCormick, stoic old buzzard that he was, did not comment. He took note of the numerous intravenous lines, medications dripping from glass bottles hanging from poles by her bed, and the constant beeping of the monitor next to her head. Finally, he allowed himself to look at her face. To really see this granddaughter. The light of his life.

Her head was covered in a thick bandage and a few wisps of auburn curls had managed to creep out of their confines as if refusing to follow the rules. Both wrists were bandaged and she'd been outfitted with a sling to keep her shoulder properly positioned.

His eyes traveled up to the left side of her face where a bandage covered most of her cheek and a portion of her temple. Even now blood was oozing around the edges of the wound covering. He took a deep breath and reached for Molly's hand.

Hang on Molly Mac. I'll find the bastard that hurt you and deep-six his sorry ass. Then I'll laugh as the sharks feast on his bloody carcass!

"The police were here earlier but she wasn't in any condition to give them any information. The officer said he'd come by tomorrow. Maybe Molly can tell them something that will help them find the man. Did you talk to her last evening? Before this happened?"

"No. She always calls me on her ham radio . . . every Friday evening around eight o'clock. But it was after nine and I hadn't heard from her. I figured she was out celebrating.

"When I finally did receive her call, I knew something was wrong, so I called the Baltimore police immediately, then caught the next flight. The police sent me here. Still don't know anything about what happened."

Charlie nodded, "Let's go down to the coffee shop. I'll tell you as much as I know, which isn't a lot."

Chapter 6

Cayo Canna

$\mathcal{S}$olana arrived early, just as the sun peeked its brilliant head over the horizon. She left her shoes at the front steps and padded around the lighthouse on her large brown feet, silent as a gecko running across the floor.

She had no trouble going up and down that spiral staircase, even with her large feet, and sometimes the captain had to yell to find her as she was always so quiet.

No matter how early she came, Captain Jack would be up, drinking that strong coffee that Crab somehow still managed to bring him from Cuba.

Getting coffee from Cuba had become difficult since the U.S. government put an embargo on anything coming from that country in 1959. But Crab apparently had connections and Captain Jack was glad.

He'd be listening to his transistor radio, tuned in to station WINK in Fort Myers. Sometimes he'd be bent over his other radio, a ham radio, that noisy machine that was forever squawking. And it was squawking a lot lately.

Today when she entered the downstairs den, Solana knew something was off. Something was missing. The scent of that strong coffee met her every morning, but not today.

She walked through the den, then on to the kitchen. The plates from last night's dinner were stacked on the counter.

That's a good sign. Most of my food's gone. Of course, the good father probably ate most of it. She went to the bottom of the spiral staircase and called up.

"You up there, Captain?" Nothing.

Her bare feet scampered up the spiral. Still no Captain and one more item was missing. Ensign. This particular dog, a young black lab—a water dog—was the latest companion of Captain Jack. He'd always had a dog and he always named them Ensign.

Where is that four-legged monster? Captain Jack must have taken him with him. But he always lets me know when he's going off-island and when he'll be back. Something is wrong here.

She decided to get on about her chores. She was acquainted with some of Captain Jack's history and knew he could take care of himself.

The Captain had spent his life as an Intelligence Officer in the U. S. Navy, planning and executing covert operations. There was even a period when he was attached to the Rice Paddy Navy, a very secret operation that only a few high-ranking officers even knew about.

During this time he'd been given the call sign "Casper" as he was able to infiltrate enemy fortresses without them ever knowing he'd been there . . . like a ghost.

Most of the time he was at sea, stationed on a carrier in the middle of an ocean somewhere. He'd escaped being wounded in any wars or conflicts, even though his work called on him to be in some precarious places. Once he retired, he and Margaret moved to Cayo Canna and he'd lived there ever since.

When Margaret had been diagnosed with cancer, Jack had taken her to the best oncologists at Dana Farber Cancer Center, Sloan Kettering Cancer Center, and M. D.

Anderson Cancer Center in Texas. Her cancer was of such a wicked, aggressive nature that no one could offer any hope. With that, Margaret asked Jack to take her back to Cayo Canna where he and Solana cared for her until that hideous disease finally won the battle.

~ ~ ~

Jack and Margaret met at the wedding of a mutual friend. Margaret was a bridesmaid and, in Jack's opinion, was even more beautiful than the bride. He was a quiet young man and stood in the corner at the reception hall, sipping the champagne that was flowing freely.

He was surprised when a lovely young woman walked over and introduced herself. Her dark hair fell to her shoulders and her sparkling green eyes studied every inch of his face as she held out her hand.

He had seen her earlier, moving about the room, speaking to first one group, then another. She reminded him of Tinkerbell flitting about all over. She just needed a set of wings. Her laughter was infectious and every group she chatted with was laughing by the time she left them.

"I'm Margaret. You appear to be alone over here. Mind if I join you?"

"Would be my pleasure, ma'am."

"Oh, please. No Navy formality."

He was a handsome young officer, resplendent in his Service Dress White uniform and already sporting a few ribbons on his chest. Margaret had no idea what they meant, but they lent a special touch to a most appealing man. He smiled and conversation flowed even more freely than the champagne.

"Are you called Maggie, Molly, or some other nickname?"

"Nope. A couple of cousins call me some other names that I can't repeat." They both laughed again and he loved hearing that tinkling, melodious sound.

"Margaret what?"

"Pardon?"

"Your last name. What's your last name?"

"Knew you'd get around to that."

"Oh? It can't be that bad. Is it Mudd? You know, the doctor that treated the fellow who killed President Lincoln."

"No, it's worse."

"Oh my. Then let's hear it!"

"If you insist. It's Humphrey."

The young officer certainly knew that name.

"Not THE Humphrey family . . . mining magnates?"

"I'm afraid so."

Then she laughed once more. That sound would thrill Jack to her last days. They couldn't have been more different. He, quiet, not given to small talk, and she, gregarious, filled with laughter and mischief to boot. A perfect match.

It took some cajoling for Margaret to convince her father she truly did want to marry this Navy officer. "He's exactly what I'm looking for . . . intelligent, confident, determined, and generous. He never shows up at my door without flowers or a small gift."

"A Navy officer, huh. At least he's got a job. Unlike some of your other beaus," her father commented.

"He's very responsible and I WILL marry him, father."

"What's his name?"

"McCormick. Jackson McCormick."

Her father groaned, "Oh, good heavens, Margaret. A Scot? Every Scot I've ever known was so tight with money he squeaked. That silver spoon you were born with might not like that arrangement." But Margaret being his only daughter, he finally gave in to her wishes.

"I'll have no choice but to leave you a generous trust fund. In case that Scotsman decides to keep you in rags." He would have left her one anyway. It was family tradition. Just the way the Humphreys did things.

Margaret had never taken a dollar from the trust fund, however. The military took care of them quite well, and when Jack retired, they relocated to Cayo Canna where they had spent many vacations over the years. When the lighthouse was offered up for auction, Jack lost no time checking it out.

"We still have my trust fund, Jack. We can use that if we need to."

Jack wouldn't hear of it. Besides, the lighthouse was quite inexpensive as far as real estate went. It needed a lot of work, which was exactly why it was to be auctioned off. The government no longer wanted the expense of taking care of it. In fact, they were glad to let it go for a nominal fee.

The two of them enjoyed their years together there, with Molly coming down at every school break. She thrived on the island and Jack and Margaret looked forward to her visits. Tom had been their only child, and Molly's presence helped them bear their grief upon losing him.

Chapter 7

Oh, for heaven's sake. Do you have to wait 'til you come inside to shake the water off?" Patrick ushered the dripping dog out the door of his bungalow, muttering to himself.

Jack McCormick, you owe me big time. You didn't tell me the dog hadn't been toilet trained yet. And the beast runs into the ocean whenever the mood strikes him. Never had a dog. Don't know anything about taking care of one either.

"C'mon Ensign. Let's take a walk. We'll go to the lighthouse and see if I can find some doggie bones, or whatever it is you eat."

He did have the presence of mind to attach a leash to the dog's collar. Ensign lifted his hind leg, reached up to scratch an itch behind his right ear, then wagged his tail and looked up as if awaiting his next command.

"Don't look at me with those puppy-dog eyes. I've met your kind before," grumbled Patrick. But he bent over and ruffed the small dog behind his ears.

As he did so, he saw a shadow at the periphery of his vision. He looked again. This person was not exactly someone he wanted to see. Ensign pulled at his leash, always anxious to greet anyone.

"Don't you dare make friends with her, mutt."

But the young pup continued to pull at the leash and his tail began to swish like windshield wipers in a rainstorm.

"Queenie, what brings you up this way? Thought you stayed down on the south end, close to your lagoon."

The visitor leaned against the riotous flame tree that abutted the edge of the porch. It was bursting with spectacular color and the ground was covered with long-dead, faded blooms.

Queenie stepped closer, "That dog not yours. Belong to the Cap'n."

"Yeah, he does. I'm looking after him for the Captain."

"Why? The Cap'n . . . he be sick?"

"No. He's off-island taking care of some business."

"I see him in lagoon. Something comin' for him. Something from the sea. Something dark."

Patrick watched the tiny, pygmy-like woman. Her dark skin shone in the sunlight and her long, wavy hair flowed down to her waist. She wore a calf-length, printed dress with a long black scarf wound around her neck, an item she wore no matter how hot it might be. The scarf was littered with fallen leaves, bits of shells and a few flower petals that she picked up from dragging it along behind her. When asked about the scarf, her response was always, "This be holy scarf. Protects those in need."

The locals called her Queenie as she insisted she was a direct descendant of the first king and founder of the Yoruba people, some of the first to be trapped in the Atlantic slave trade horrors. Queenie had been born in Nigeria, and by way of cunning escapades and luck had found her way to Cuba, then to Cayo Canna.

Her ramshackle, tin shack sat on the edge of a lagoon on the south end of the island. Locals were aware she visited the lagoon behind her shack where she practiced some unusual rituals in the water.

Most folks paid her no mind, thought her harmless. But Patrick, Father O'Brien, Catholic priest, believed her to be practicing some kind of *Santeria* religious rituals. He thought she was evil through and through and avoided her whenever possible.

"Go on about your business, Queenie. I suggest you keep your lagoon visions to yourself." He tugged at Ensign's leash and left her standing under the tree, softly singing under her breath.

When they arrived at the lighthouse, Patrick entered, knowing Jack would not be about. He'd forgotten about Solana and jumped three feet high when she appeared in the kitchen doorway. Those bare feet never made a sound.

"Damn it, Solana! You need to let people know when you're about. Scared the daylights out of me." Solana continued with her dusting.

"Captain Jack's not home. I don't know when he'll be back."

"I know. I just came to get some dog food for the mutt. Jack's gone to Baltimore. Something's happened to Molly. Don't know details, but it sounds as if she's in trouble."

Solana dropped her dusting cloth, lifted her hands and put them together beneath her chin in a prayer-like fashion.

"Oh, no. Not his Molly. He worships the ground that child walks on. He's had enough to deal with already. First his son and then Margaret. I'm not much on praying, Father, but I believe you might know about that. Can you send one up for me?"

Patrick smiled. He was under no illusions that Solana particularly liked him. But he was not offended. He knew she was just overly protective of Jack. That's all it was. Give her time. He'd eventually grow on her . . . maybe.

"I'll see what I can do. But, Solana, God hears all prayers from all people."

Or at least I used to think so. Not sure of much of anything in that realm any longer.

Chapter 8

Johns Hopkins Hospital
Baltimore

The coffee shop at Johns Hopkins Hospital was located in the bowels of the old institution. The air smelled of formaldehyde, cleaning solution, and mold. Rumors of a renovation were always floating about but no one had seen any evidence of that yet.

Captain Jack rubbed at his nose but said nothing. Charlie observed this as he observed everything. "Sorry, sir. This place is ancient and odors from the past still haunt many of the old sections."

"No problem. Been on many a ship that smelled worse."

Charlie brought two cups of black coffee to the table. Quickly realizing Captain Jack was a man of few words, he began to tell him what little he knew.

"I spoke with the police officer that escorted Molly's ambulance to the emergency room. They found her in a closet in the foyer of her apartment. She drifted in and out of consciousness, and was only able to talk with them for a few moments now and then. After the ambulance arrived, it was only a few minutes before word got around that the incoming was one of ours.

"Today we celebrated the completion of our Residency Program and it was quite a great day for Molly. She was selected as the recipient of the Nora Johnson Award for Clinical Excellence.

"The award can go a long way in helping her secure employment in a great place . . . like Johns Hopkins or Cleveland Clinic. She deserved it. She's quite a talented woman."

Jack nodded and a half-smile crossed his weathered face. "Couldn't agree with you more. She's special."

"When I heard Molly was in the ER, I hurried over and stayed with her through the procedures. I was saying my goodbyes to the staff. Most of us are leaving tomorrow morning. Gotta find a job."

"Then Molly has to begin to search also, I suppose?"

"Yessir. We all do."

Charlie led the way out of the bowels, back to the creaky elevator. "Let's make a final check on her, then let's get some sleep."

When they entered her room, Molly turned her head in their direction. She was bleary-eyed and her voice was hoarse from all the crying in the closet.

Before she even looked, Molly knew he was here. . . that nostalgic, sweet smell, a bit of floral laced with a hint of honey. His pipe tobacco.

"Papa Jack?" Jack walked to her bedside and looked down into her colorless face.

"I'm here, Molly Mac."

She lifted her hand toward her head and Charlie rushed over and halted it mid-air. "Don't touch anything, Molly. Your head's bandaged and touching it will only make it hurt more."

"Charlie? What are you doing here?"

"Just hanging out, Molly. Hanging out."

Papa Jack reached for her hand and held it. He was not a demonstrative man, but at this moment he needed to touch her.

Charlie stepped out the door, scurried down the hall and grabbed Molly's chart from the nurses' station and began reading.

He walked back in, eyed her monitor, taking note of her mental state, observing her every movement as best he could without alarming her. He then spotted a large envelope on the table behind her bed. Just what he was looking for. X-rays.

He read the report from the radiologist and let out a long breath. "Thanks be to God and all his angels."

Molly looked at him as did Captain Jack. She might still be groggy, but she was aware Charlie was checking her out from head to toe.

"What? What are you reading? And don't make up something that sounds good but doesn't tell the truth, Charlie."

"There doesn't appear to be any internal bleeding. Best news I've had all day." He grinned at her.

"No internal or intra-cranial bleeds?" she asked, her scratchy voice barely audible. Just like Molly to ascertain exactly what was written.

"X-rays only tell us so much, you know that. But everyone on the case believes there's nothing there. No internal bleeding and no intracranial bleeding."

"Let me see my chart." Molly began to try to sit up.

"Nope. You stay in that supine position until I say you can move. You're a patient now. Not the doc."

"What else? Tell me everything, Charlie. You know I'll read it the minute you leave anyway."

"Yeah. I'm sure you will. Apparently, you've sustained a penetrating wound to the cranium, a dislocated shoulder—which has been re-positioned—a couple of flesh wounds to your breast, and superficial cuts on both wrists. That covers it."

Papa Jack had memorized the various wounds Charlie had rattled off earlier.

He's not told her about the carved area on her cheek. He's right. That wound will be more difficult to heal than the others. Perhaps not physically, but emotionally it will take quite a toll. She's never had any confidence in her looks, and this will only set her back again.

He knew Cathy—petite and blond and one who could charm a cobra with her constant chatter—had convinced Molly she was not particularly attractive. That had never been true. Molly was actually very attractive, just in a very different way than Cathy.

Molly had inherited her Scottish grandmothers' auburn hair and soft brown eyes and was about five feet four inches. And, no, she was not one to charm anyone. She preferred standing on the sidelines and watching rather than being in the midst of things.

After boarding school and college, she was off to medical school. That was when she began to come out of her shell . . . if only slightly. Jack was convinced that being away from Cathy for a few years had been beneficial. He'd told her to "let your light shine" on more occasions than he could count and had thought she was doing so.

Becoming more alert by the moment, Molly addressed Charlie. "Read the rest to me."

"What?"

"The neurological report from the ER. I want to know what it says. Exactly, Charlie."

"Not tonight, my dear friend. Tonight you are a patient and that's that. I'll read it to you tomorrow when you're more alert. Right now, I'm going to call your nurse to give you something to help you get some much-needed sleep."

He walked out of the room then, giving Papa Jack a few minutes to say his goodbyes.

"Papa Jack? Do you know what happened? I can only remember bits and pieces. Not everything."

"You're safe and these folks are taking good care of you. That's all we need to think about tonight. Charlie's right. Rest now. I'll be here when you wake up. We'll talk about it then."

"Papa Jack . . . I . . . "

"Hush now. I'll see you in a few hours. Goodnight, Molly Mac."

"Goodnight, Papa Jack."

She tried to smile but discovered it sent a sharp pain along the side of her cheek. Then she closed her eyes and even without more medication she was asleep in moments.

Jack stepped out of the room as Charlie returned from talking with Molly's nurse. "She's asleep already."

"Good. Then we'll walk out together and I'll come by in the morning. I'll want to see her latest labs."

"No. You go on. I'll stand this watch," Jack said.

Charlie allowed a small smile to cross his face. "It's really not necessary for you to stay, sir. They'll take good care of her. And they may not be keen on you being in this ICU room."

"I understand. But I'll be staying just the same." He returned to Molly's room and took a seat in the corner.

Chapter 9

Baltimore

The wind whipped about bringing scattered, icy drops of rain. Sam crept around to the side of the apartment as he had last evening when he'd make his first "house call" on Dr. Molly McCormick. He'd had no choice but to leave her, all snug in the closet. . . with the promise of returning at a more convenient time.

Tonight, in his drug-induced haze and with the darkness, he failed to see the crime-scene tape surrounding Molly's apartment. He tripped over it, cursing when he found himself on his knees, and he was now covered in slush from the snow.

"Dammit. They found her."

The tape meant she'd gotten away and his plan for finishing her off would have to wait. But he'd not give up. She would have needed medical care. And he knew where to start his search. Johns Hopkins Hospital.

"I'll find you. You belong to me." He stumbled away, reaching to his inside coat pocket for another Marlborough.

Chapter 10

Cayo Canna

Patrick stood with Ensign's leash in hand, waiting to board the ferry to the mainland. Not a trip he'd planned, but one he had to make nevertheless.

A few other passengers were waiting at the dock but he didn't recognize anyone he knew. With nothing to occupy his mind, he found it drifting to a time he didn't particularly want to recall very often.

As a young man, he dreamed of becoming a professional golfer and playing the European Circuit. To that end, he was employed as the Assistant Pro at a popular golf club in a picturesque village in the countryside of Ireland.

One afternoon, following eighteen holes of golf in which Patrick had not scored very well, he entered The Druid's Fountain, a local pub where he often met Angus, an older gentleman who mentored him.

The two sat in the far corner of the pub, always at the corner table that had been baptized with many pints of ale over the years. And, just to give it a little personality, numerous folks had carved their initials deep into the top.

Angus listened as Patrick ran through his excuses for playing poorly . . . the greens were too slow . . . the wind had come up . . . he'd hurried through the last few holes.

After witnessing today's disastrous round and hearing Patrick's whining, Angus decided to get on with it. Today. Tell the lad the truth so he could move on.

The wise old mentor reared back in his chair, lifted his pint, cleared his throat, and began to speak in his halting, coarse, voice.

"Ahem, Patrick. My boy. You're a fine golfer, but by now you must realize you're never going to be a great player. Most of us aren't, my lad."

Patrick had heard similar comments from one of his brothers but had decided that was just sibling rivalry. But, in his heart, he knew it was true. Plus, Angus was a friend who always spoke the truth. Even when it was painful. Then Patrick simply had to accept that fact. Had to make some decisions. If not golf, then what was he to do?

A couple of days later a winter storm brought golfing to a halt and he took the step. The necessary one. There was a cold wind tugging at his overcoat as he hurried up the steps to the Lime Kiln, his folks' cottage. Icicles hung from the eaves and he had to bend down to avoid being nailed by one.

"Damn this cold," he muttered as he stomped in and headed for the hearth where a warm fire was keeping the cottage snug.

"The Almighty can hear you, Patrick, even if you mumble under your breath," his mother called out. But he heard a smile in her comment.

"Yeah, I'm sure you're right, Mum," he said as he deposited his large frame in the nearest chair.

"Tell me lad, what brings you out on such a blistering cold evening?" His father was a quiet man with more than his share of intuition and he could always sense when something was up with his oldest.

Patrick shifted in his chair. "I've left the golf club. That's done. Angus was kind enough to give it to me straight. Golfing is not something I can make a living at."

The comfy old armchair he sat in all but embraced him, and he looked down at the floor, never making eye contact with either of them.

"I see. What else are you considering?" his father asked.

Now he did look. At both of them. "I don't rightly know. Not yet anyway. But I'll be gone awhile."

He rose then and came to stand next to his mother. "Don't worry about me, Mum. I can take care of myself."

Then, with a quick hug for each of them, he walked out the door into the bitter, dark night.

His mother looked so forlorn but said nothing. "It's all right, Aibreann. It'll be good for the lad to put some distance between himself and this place. Time for him to become his own man," his father explained.

But even he was dismayed when almost two years passed with only one postcard that simply said, "I am well. No need to worry, Mum. Your loving son, Patrick."

When he did return, with no explanation as to where he had been for two years, he followed the path that many "first sons" turned to. He entered the priesthood.

As a young thirty-year-old, he left Ireland straight out of seminary in Dublin and headed to his first pastoral assignment, St. Mark's, a small coastal parish on the outskirts of Boston, Massachusetts. A parish which had been without a priest for several years.

The parishioners were primarily middle-aged and older. For six years Father Patrick had ministered to them and led a fairly enjoyable, if uneventful, life. He liked people and these older ones didn't require the skills that might have been needed in a large parish, those with lots of children, teenagers, summer bible schools, etc.

Most of his time was spent visiting the sick, administering last rites and officiating at funerals. He'd been in this one parish until one day last spring he simply walked away.

And today, six months later, he was still as confused about the situation that drove him away as he was when he left.

He didn't care much to recall some of these memories, but sometimes they came without invitation. Such as this morning.

Chapter 11

Releasing three short blasts from its horn, the *Calypso* slowly pushed away from her moorings. She'd been making the trip to and from Cayo Canna to Fort Myers so many years she could do it without the aid of a skipper if need be. She was ancient but had been well cared for.

"She's got a lot of life left in her yet. She's one of those old *chicas* who get better with age. Hee, hee," laughed Crab as he climbed the steps to his pilot station.

He'd been her skipper for two years now, having replaced Mick, the former one who, like the *Calypso,* was old but had NOT been well taken care of. He'd pickled his liver with too much booze, and his lungs eventually gave out from his three-pack-a-day smoking habit.

Crab waved when he saw the priest boarding at the last minute. Then the ferry began to slide away from the pier into the open waters.

Patrick loved the feel of the wind blowing through his hair, which he was aware was beginning to gray at the temples. He'd never given much thought to his age, but he'd turn thirty-seven shortly, and for the *second* time in his life had no inkling what he was to do next.

The *Calypso* left her dock early each morning, taking passengers to the mainland. Then, in the late afternoon, she took them back to Cayo Canna and returned to her mooring dock. The trip took about an hour and a half, depending on weather and water conditions.

~ ~ ~

Yesterday had started out well enough. Patrick and Ensign walked about the island, stopped at the vegetable market, then checked his mail at Bailey's Island Grocery where he had a pleasant conversation with Agnes.

Agnes Bailey was an old-maid school teacher who had retired some time back. She now ran Bailey's Island Grocery and was the postmistress as well. Her grocery had been designated as an official post office, and she took her position as postmistress very seriously.

She sorted the mail each morning before she even opened shop. She could be prune-lipped and short, but most knew her tough outer shell protected a soft heart. For some reason, she particularly liked this young priest and welcomed him with a smile she only bestowed on a few people.

After leaving Bailey's, Patrick went for his daily swim in Crabber's Cove, a bay not far from his bungalow. This bay was a favorite place for crabbers to place their traps, but it was not frequented by many people which was exactly why Patrick liked to swim there.

He took Ensign with him and grinned as the pup splashed about the water, chasing the small fiddler crabs as they skittered to and from the water's edge.

He walked into the water, looked all around, scanning the area before diving in. Out of the corner of his eye, he spied Queenie, her long scarf flapping in the wind as she strolled along the beach path . . . with a companion.

That looks like a child. Didn't know Queenie had any children. Can't be hers. She's too old to have a kid.

There was a small cruiser anchored about two hundred yards out in the bay. Patrick liked the lines of it and thought it might be the kind of craft in which he would be interested. That is if he was going to stay on the island. Of course, he hadn't made that decision yet . . . whether to stay or return to St. Marks.

He dived under and felt the refreshing coolness of the saltwater. As soon as he surfaced, he heard Ensign yelping.

The pup had made a mad dash through the crab traps, no doubt chasing some ocean-going critter who moved much faster than he did.

"Oh, you idiot mongrel. What have you done?"

Patrick waded over. The pup's left rear paw was caught in one of the crab traps, and the water was quickly becoming a bloody cloud all around him.

"Jaysus, Mary, and Joseph. You're more trouble than you're worth, mutt."

He worked carefully, trying to avoid causing more damage. Shortly, he'd freed the injured paw and carried the young pup to the shore and on to his bungalow.

"You don't look like much when you're wet, but Jack seems to think you'll be a great dog. Not too sure of that myself."

Today they were aboard the *Calypso,* headed to the vet on the mainland. Ensign was resting at Patrick's feet, his head laying between his front paws.

"That *el Capitán's* dog?" asked Crab as he stepped away from the helm for a few minutes, confident that his new assistant could keep them on a steady course.

"Yeah, I'm taking care of him for a couple of days while Jack's away. Silly mutt got his paw caught in a crab trap yesterday, so we're on our way to the vet. Hope it's not too serious. Jack won't be happy with me if it is."

"No, el *Capitán* has a reputation for being very harsh. Wouldn't want to be on his wrong side."

"Don't believe everything you hear, skipper. He's a fine fellow once you know him."

"Huh." Crab returned to the helm and prepared for docking. Shortly, the ferry slid into the slip at Fort Myers with Crab making only the slightest bump on her port side. He was an excellent skipper but could use some work on his personal appearance.

Patrick held Ensign's leash firmly, letting other passengers depart, then walked toward the exit.

"Alright, flea catcher, let's find that vet's office."

Chapter 12

Patrick and Jack had been friends since Patrick came to St. Marks. Jack was not a religious person, but Margaret, a cradle Catholic, attended Mass regularly at St. Mark's and Jack accompanied her on occasion. He was Anglican and had attended church as a child, but once he left home, he drifted away from all organized religious activities. He knew what he believed and didn't need anyone in a collar—Anglican or Roman Catholic—to impose their thoughts on him.

Father Patrick was well-received at St. Marks and Margaret was one of the first parishioners to invite the new priest to dinner.

"Jack, he's young, maybe twenty-eight or thirty? He's fresh out of seminary and full of energy and life. He's just what our congregation needs."

Margaret was right. Father Patrick was perfect. His sermons were short, never boring, and his excitement about life was contagious. He and Jack struck up an immediate friendship when they discovered they had a mutual interest, or better said, an addiction. Golf.

Jack was surprised to learn the young man had been an assistant golf pro at an ancient and respected club in Ireland. He thought perhaps the young man had "embellished" his stories of playing golf in Ireland. That was until they played a round.

After their first outing at Kissansett Golf Club where Jack was a member, there had been quite a conversation between the two new friends.

"I'd not expected that you know," Jack stated, in his staccato, matter-of-fact fashion.

"What? What were you not expecting?"

"That you'd birdie six and nine. Then make eagle on fifteen. What the hell? Was there some divine intervention?"

"Well, I'd not say it just like that."

"And just how WOULD you say it, Patrick?"

"Oh, perhaps I might say it was just "the luck of the Irish." The priest grinned as he leaned back in the comfy lounge chair.

Jack laughed aloud. This young man was definitely to his liking, in spite of their age difference. He never did call the young man Father. Just didn't feel right. For God's sake, he was old enough to be the priest's father himself.

Patrick cleared his throat, "Umm, I think it would be appropriate for me to ease your pain. Say we have a wee dram of Jameson, my favorite libation?"

"Huh. If you insist on easing my pain, I prefer a bit of Glenfiddich myself."

"Ah, and you would then, wouldn't you. Scotsman through and through."

The two played golf often and most times, after an eighteen-hole day, Patrick would end up making himself useful in Margaret's kitchen. He'd learned to cook at his mother's apron strings. She ran a bed and breakfast called The Lime Kiln, in a quaint village deep in the moors of Ireland. She had a saying: "If you live here, eat here, and sleep here, then you work here." She had no time for anyone who didn't carry their own weight, which meant that Patrick was skilled in many areas.

Dinner was always followed by heady discussions on world affairs, politics, and philosophy. Conversations that sometimes went far into the night. On those long, discussion-filled evenings, Margaret usually bowed out.

"You two are a lost cause. I'll leave you to settle world affairs. Meanwhile, I'll bury myself in my latest Scottish Highland novel. Goodnight, gentlemen."

Six months ago, Patrick had shown up at Jack's door on Cayo Canna, looking a bit ragged around the edges. He needed a shave, his eyes were red-rimmed, and a haircut would definitely be in order. Jack was surprised to see him but took one look and invited him in, no questions asked.

Patrick stammered for a second, searching for words to explain his unexpected visit. "Jack, hope you don't mind my dropping in unannounced. Didn't know I was coming myself until this morning."

"We've invited you many times. Glad to see you found the place. Come in. I'm just about to scoff up Solana's *tapas* and have a little nectar of the gods. Would prefer a taste of Glenfiddich, but my latest shipment seems to have lost its way to the island. Come on. Let's go outside. The breeze is good this late in the day. Maybe the no-see-ums won't carry us off."

Jack led him out to the patio where a couple of canvas-backed beach chairs sat under an ancient banyan tree. He hadn't seen Patrick in some time, but their friendship was one that picked up where it left off, no matter how much time had passed. As soon as they sat, Jack handed his friend a small glass of sangria, Margaret's favorite afternoon drink.

Jack pointed out to the ocean. "See that shrimper out there? That's Eduardo. He'll bring in his catch tomorrow. Think I'll get down to the dock and see what he's got. Solana knows what to do with shrimp."

"Solana still with you?"

"Oh, Solana's still with the lighthouse. It couldn't operate without her. Of course, it doesn't really "operate" now, but when it did, she was here."

"I see. You still painting?"

"Yeah, some. Been working on one for a while now. But still haven't finished it. Lately, I've been spending a lot of time talking with my Navy mates. Some of them are still on active duty, and from their messages, I gather they're busy these days."

"Why? Why now, I mean."

"That damn fool, Castro, down in Cuba. He's stirring up trouble. Could lead to some issues for us, too."

"Huh. Haven't been keeping up very well since you left Boston. Guess I'd better tune in again."

They passed the evening talking politics and world affairs. Patrick never offered any explanation for his being on the island, and Jack didn't question him. That had been several months ago now, and Patrick was still on the island.

Chapter 13

Johns Hopkins Hospital
Baltimore

The nurse quietly entered the dimly lit room. "Miss McCormick, uh, Dr. McCormick? I am sorry to wake you, but Dr. Gentry's ordered another X-ray. I've got to take you down now."

The nurse moved quickly as she didn't want to be on the receiving end of a lecture from Dr. Gentry if he came by and the X-ray hadn't been done.

Molly opened her eyes, yawned, and recognized her surroundings. She knew where she was and why. And, in case she might have forgotten, a pounding headache reminded her. But even this morning, most of the details of her horrifying experience escaped her memory.

"Yes. Of course."

As the nurse raised the head of her bed, Molly saw a familiar face standing at the window—watching her—as he had all night.

"Papa Jack? What are you doing here so early?"

He gave her his usual tight smile.

"You stayed here all night, didn't you? You must be exhausted."

"I'll sleep some other time. It's a highly overrated event in my opinion." He walked closer and looked down at her. It was apparent that she was alert, aware of her surroundings, and able to communicate with no problem— all positives in his book.

"I'll go down to the coffee shop and drink a cup of their swill while you're gone."

"Swill is right, Papa. It's not exactly that special blend you have at home. In fact, you might want to skip it altogether." He was thrilled to hear her making a small joke.

The nurse wheeled her out, the old bed clacking as it warbled along the tile floor. Molly was alert enough to notice something unusual in her grandfather's demeanor.

Something's not right with Papa Jack. What?

But the unrelenting ache in her head demanded her attention at the moment, not allowing her to dwell on Papa's problem.

~ ~ ~

Jack headed down the hallway, his thoughts still on his granddaughter. But other thoughts kept poking at his consciousness, too. Maybe he'd allow them in after some coffee was on board.

He waited for the elevator, and when it opened, Dr. Charlie Watts stepped out carrying two cups of black coffee and a newspaper folded beneath his arm.

"Thought you could use one of these, Captain."

Jack smiled at the young physician. He wondered briefly why Molly couldn't have struck up a relationship with this one. He was intelligent and indeed handsome enough with his neatly trimmed, sandy-colored hair and blue eyes.

"Ah, hot steaming swill. Just the ticket."

"I know you stayed here last night which means you missed the evening news broadcast," Charlie said. He handed the newspaper to Jack, then watched to see what kind of reaction the Captain had as he read the headlines:

AERIAL PHOTOS REVEAL POSSIBLE BUILD-UP OF WEAPONS ON THE ISLAND OF CUBA!

Again, that expressionless, blank face.

"That idiot, Castro, needs his head examined. Or better yet, removed. I hope Kennedy has the balls to stand up to that egotistical maniac. I'll try to catch Walter Cronkite this evening. He's the only one I listen to."

Molly was chatting up a storm as the nurse brought her back into the room where Papa and Charlie were waiting.

"Nurse, would you please get me something for this headache?"

"Right away."

Molly turned her attention to the two men in her room— one a loving grandfather, the other a trustworthy friend.

"Thanks for coming early, Charlie. But it wasn't necessary. Now, first things first. My head hurts but not as bad as yesterday. And this bandage on the side of my cheek is pinching the bejesus out of me. Then I'd like to see my chart, and I want to speak with the ER physician that stitched me up."

Charlie moved closer, "I told you what was in your chart last evening. And you don't need to start giving orders. Relax and let the staff do their work."

"Charlie, I won't stop bugging you until you bring me the chart. Please get it for me."

He retrieved the chart from the nurses' station and handed it over to Molly. She read it from front to back, never saying a word. She looked at the two men.

"It appears I have a penetrating wound to my head, a possible concussion, several contusions, a deep laceration to the cheek, a dislocated shoulder that has been addressed, superficial wounds on my wrists and a couple of cigarette burns on the upper portion of my left breast."

Papa Jack listened as she read aloud the remarks from the chart.

A deep laceration to the cheek? Is that what the physician wrote? Surely, he was more descriptive than that, Jack thought.

Then she repeated the phrase, 'cigarette burns on the left breast.' A quick flash. Vivid memories of the pain when he touched her with the lighted cigarette.

"Oh, Papa, I can almost see his face. But everything about that event is fuzzy."

Regardless of how Papa Jack tried to keep him submerged, the old Naval Intelligence Officer, the covert spy, clawed his way to the surface and couldn't resist asking questions.

"You know him? Are you sure?" Charlie and Papa were all ears. Both leaned in and listened.

"I'm not sure, but there was something familiar about him. I just can't remember. They must catch him. He's evil, Papa."

"Don't think on that right now, Molly Mac. Let it go for a while. We'll have time to piece it all together later."

"What did the police say? Any leads?"

Charlie hesitated, then answered her. "No, not yet. The police lieutenant indicated he would come by this morning. If you're up to it, tell him what you can remember no matter how insignificant it may seem to you. That could give him a place to start."

Molly's hands were shaking and that fact didn't escape Charlie's keen eyes. Nor Papa's either.

"I think we'll let you rest for a while and I'll get a couple hours of sleep."

"Papa? You'll help them, won't you? The police? They might miss something, but I know you won't." He nodded.

"I'll be back in a few hours, Molly Mac. Rest now."

Jack and Charlie waited for the elevator. As soon as they reached the first floor, they headed down the hall to the doorway that would take them outside.

"The part about a 'laceration to the cheek,' was that what the chart stated?" asked Jack.

Charlie nodded. "Actually, yes. Perhaps the physician thought that was sufficient, but it doesn't quite tell the whole story."

"Well, I need to know the whole story and I'd like to see that police officer when he comes."

"I'll give him a call."

"Thanks, Charlie. You're leaving soon? Where you headed?"

"I have an interview at Cleveland Clinic later this week. But it's a couple of days away. I can hang around another day if I need to."

"Cleveland Clinic, huh? That's quite a place, I understand."

"It would be a great place to start my professional career. At least I have an interview."

"What are your concerns about Molly at this point? Do you think she needs to stay in the hospital a few more days?"

"I'm not her attending physician, but he'll tell you a concussion is not something to play around with. Most likely he'll want her to take some time to recover. Perhaps several weeks even. The wrist wounds will heal quickly, as will the cigarette burns."

"And the 'laceration to the cheek?' Did you see it?"

Charlie had hoped to avoid this discussion. He'd learned a lot about Captain McCormick in a few hours with him. There was no way he could use medical jargon to try and soften the impact of this information, so he told him straight, as Jack had asked him to earlier.

"That wound will be difficult to heal. It's considerably deep, about an inch in width and three inches long. There will be a noticeable scar. As I said earlier, Molly may want to consult with a plastic surgeon later for more surgery. But, sir, it may be that there's nothing to be done. It's quite deep."

73

Jack nodded, then started toward the elevator. "I'll be back at 5:00 p.m. I'm staying at the Monaco. If the police lieutenant needs me to come at another time, call me. I'll come at his convenience."

"Yessir. I'll call you."

Charlie began to walk away but Jack called him back. "Wait. You're leaving something out. Don't. What did he carve on her cheek?"

Charlie stared at his feet for a moment, then looked up at Captain McCormick, who stood at least a head taller.

"He carved the letter "S".

Jack made no comment. Just turned and walked on without another word.

He carved the letter "S" in her cheek. Then you can rest assured I'll carve more than a letter on both your che

eks before I'm finished with you, you low-life son of a bitch!

Chapter 14

Baltimore

The walk was a short one . . . one Sam had made several times when he stalked Molly. So after finding the crime scene tape at her apartment, he headed straight for Johns Hopkins Medical Center.

His brain, still muddled with drugs and alcohol, reasoned that he would pretend to be a friend, a visitor. Then he'd take advantage of Molly's injured state and complete his task. Not what he had planned originally, but he had no choice.

A shame I can't take my time with you . . . you're such a sweet little number.

Torturing her had brought Sam great pleasure. But she could identify him. He had to finish her now.

He bounded up the steps to the hospital and hurried across the tiled lobby, glancing only briefly at "Christ the Divine Healer," a ten-and-a-half-foot marble statue that takes center stage.

When he opened the door to the stairway, a guard stepped from behind the stairwell. "Hold there. These stairs are for medical personnel only."

Sam had failed to read the "Hospital Personnel Only" sign above the door and walked right into this problem. He stared at the man, then turned to leave. Before he could reach "The Divine Healer" again, the guard was on his heels. He'd caught the disgusting odor of the man, and after a second look realized he was a street bum, trying to get out of the weather.

"Out you go, buddy. The Salvation Army is two blocks down the street. They'll take you in."

Chapter 15

Johns Hopkins Hospital
Baltimore

After sitting in Molly's room all night, Jack was back at the Monaco. The hotel was quite luxurious, and the cab driver had insisted this was the place to stay.

He entered his room and headed straight to the shower, a long-standing habit when he was worried. He did his best thinking there and the hot water relaxed the tightness in his shoulders. Molly had been right when she said he must be exhausted.

He knew he should order something to eat, but wasn't hungry. He was aware he was thinner than usual and some days he felt every one of his years. But now was not the time to indulge in issues pertaining to himself. There were much more critical events in the making and he was right in the middle of them.

He toweled off, using the thick Turkish towel that smelled like the soap Margaret had always kept in their bath—*Crabtree and Evelyn, Verbena and Lavender de Provence.*

Smelling the familiar scent brought to mind days that were long gone, but still as fresh in his memory as if they had just occurred . . . and this one was a favorite . . .

Margaret looked up at him, her eyes sparkling, full of questions. "The lighthouse? You want to buy the lighthouse on Cayo Canna?"

"Yeah, what do you think? Could you live in a lighthouse?

"Tell me what it would be like. Obviously, you must like the idea." She poured him a small glass of Glenfiddich. She, herself, kept to something lighter . . . a little sauvignon blanc was more to her liking.

"Uhm hmm, well, there would be lots of light as the first floor has windows in every room. Then up high, in the tower itself, the lantern room is glass, all 'round."

Margaret didn't pay a lot of attention to Jack's words but saw such excitement in his face that she'd say yes, no matter what. "That sounds appealing. Smelling the ocean all day . . . feeling the cool tropical breeze . . . go on."

"Oh, I guess every sailor would like to live in a lighthouse and watch the ocean. Kinda like being at sea without really being at sea, you know?"

Margaret knew Jack's love of the sea was ingrained in every cell of his body. He'd retired from the Navy, but that ocean still called to him.

"Then go for it. We have the trust fund if we need it."

"Nope. Got enough retirement funds put aside to cover it. But it does need some work, you understand. The government hasn't kept it up since they stopped its operation some years ago. Only did the minimum. Limited funds, no doubt."

The day Jack took Margaret to see the lighthouse, he parked the golf cart—the most convenient vehicle for getting about the island—beneath the huge banyan tree that hugged the rear corner of the property.

Jack wasn't sure which had come first, the lighthouse or the banyan tree. The tree was exceedingly old as witnessed by its great span of limbs with hundreds of roots streaming down from them . . . like icicles hanging from the eaves of a New England home on an icy, winter day. Somehow, through the years, this magnificent specimen had managed to inch itself close to the lighthouse, its leathery green leaves all but embracing the rounded structure in places.

In addition to its beauty, this tree's most endearing quality was that it provided much-needed shade from the blistering sun that never considered taking a day off.

Situated on the northern tip of Cayo Canna and standing one hundred eight feet high, the white, stone tower stood taller than any other building on the island. Initially, there had been a tiny, square limestone dwelling attached to the front of the lighthouse, where the keeper resided.

In a moment of spectacular creativity, when the lighthouse was rebuilt, the architect removed the rear wall of the limestone dwelling and incorporated the rounded walls of the lighthouse into it. Some thought it made the lighthouse look as if it had been an afterthought.

Whatever the reason, this ingenious idea meant there was space for a keeper to live on the property. Later on, a proper keeper's cottage was built with a breezeway attaching it to the lighthouse. The uniqueness of the place was most appealing to an old seadog like Captain Jack McCormick.

Jack looked up as a lone osprey winged his way toward the top of the tower, then glided effortlessly to the sky. The old lighthouse never looked better to Jack.

"She's still a beauty after all these years."

He took Margaret's hand, and they stepped up on the porch, whose railing needed a bit of repair. Jack lifted his knuckles to knock when the door opened, and they were greeted by a tall, lithe, attractive woman with skin the color of café con leche.

Her warm brown eyes and gracious smile belied the backbone of steel she possessed. Her floor-length, colorful dress skirted the floor as she moved from the door and stepped back into the room.

"Welcome to the lighthouse. I'm Solana, keeper of the place at present." She moved so gracefully she seemed to float across the bare floor.

Jack reached out his large, tanned hand and Solana offered hers in return. "Good morning. I'm Jack McCormick and this is my wife, Margaret. My understanding is the lighthouse is to be auctioned off shortly. That is unless someone buys it first. We're interested in perhaps buying the lighthouse for our permanent residence."

"Yes, that's also my understanding. But I'll remain until a new owner occupies it."

"I see. Then, with your permission, I would like to take my wife through the place. I believe I can guide her well enough."

The woman smiled. "As you wish. Please close the front door when you leave. I'll come by later and lock up."

"Thank you, Ms. Solana."

"Just Solana, please. And I believe it's Captain, isn't it, sir?"

"Yes, that's right."

Captain Jack was well known on the island as he and Margaret had vacationed there for years. Solana had been aware he would be coming by to tour the lighthouse. She could have been absent today, but she'd wanted to check out the prospective buyer. After all, this new owner was about to invade her lighthouse—and she wasn't exactly keen on that idea—someone buying this place, that is.

It wasn't just that she'd be out of a job. She'd become attached to this ancient, towering edifice with its whistling winds and light-flooded rooms. It held secrets that even she knew nothing about.

Solana departed, leaving Jack and Margaret to themselves. As Jack had wanted. He didn't need a guide. He'd already been given the tour a couple of weeks ago by a Coast Guard official. Solana had not been present that day although the official had mentioned there was an attendant who kept the place clean and orderly.

As soon as Solana left, Jack led Margaret through the door to a large room on the first floor. "I think you might call this a den. Very casual."

"Jack, look at the floors. Hardwood. And the beadboard walls. This place is amazing."

"You like it then?"

"Well, yes, so far. Let's see the rest of it."

They then entered a room that opened off the den on the left side of the building. "Could be considered a dining room, I suppose. Looks like the kitchen is next door. Let's check it out."

The kitchen was small with black and white tiled flooring. The top half of the entire back wall—where the sink and stove were positioned—was windows outfitted with Bermuda shutters to shield the room from the sun that could be blinding at times. But what an ideal place to prepare dinner, looking out to the lushness that raged just outside those windows.

Margaret took in the view and smiled when her eyes feasted on the bougainvillea that had been allowed to run wild over the lawn, having its way with the hibiscus bushes and endearing itself to the small patch of canna lilies close by. The only opponent that was strong enough to call halt to her wildness was the even-thornier Madagascar Palm. If its thorns don't get you, its poison just might.

All appliances appeared to be in working order, if somewhat dated. Margaret opened the refrigerator, then turned her head and wrinkled her nose.

"Oh, my. We'd need a new refrigerator. That one really smells."

"Right. New reefer. Aye, madam. Can manage that, I believe."

They exited the kitchen through an arched doorway on the opposite side of the room and found themselves in the den again.

"That's it? But . . . where are the bedrooms?"

"Well, that is a small problem. But it can be overcome. Come on. Follow me."

A curving, spiral staircase with narrow steps dominated the rear corner of the den. Jack saw Margaret pause before she committed herself to such a hike. After a moment, he began to pull her by the hand, knowing she was in store for quite a treat if she would make the effort.

"Jack? The bedrooms are up there? All the way up?"

"Yep. That's right. Let's check it out."

Nothing could have prepared Margaret for the breathtaking view and the feeling that embraced her when she reached the top of the steps and entered the lantern room.

The room was enchanting, awash in sunlight. The windows were open and a cross breeze brought the scent of the ocean . . . salty, pungent, alive. She was entranced with the panorama before her, that vast expanse of clear turquoise sea, white capping while terns and seagulls wheeled against the wind.

"Look, Jack . . . on the window sill . . . a nest. Maybe a tern or a black skimmer. We can't touch the eggs, you know. If you do, the bird will never come back to her nest."

She spotted an old wooden box laying on a small table, a table curved at the back to fit the roundness of the tower. She picked the box up and opened it. Even after opening it, however, she wasn't sure what she held.

"Jack?"

He came closer. "It's a sextant. An ancient one. Very necessary at one time." Margaret carefully placed it back in the box and continued her inspection.

"Look. Some sort of logbook." She held up the tattered leather journal, then returned it to the rounded table.

"Yes, also a needed item in any lighthouse."

Jack was interested in the mariners' maps on the wall and a pair of binoculars hanging from a knob near one of the open windows.

He ran his fingers over the binoculars, feeling the pitted, briny covering that had developed over the years of exposure to the open windows and salt air.

"But Jack . . . I do see one small problem . . . there AREN'T any bedrooms up here! And what about when Molly comes to visit?"

Jack grinned sheepishly, "Couldn't we could squeeze a small bed up here?"

"Jack, that's impossible."

"I see. Then let's go back down. Perhaps we shouldn't buy it after all."

Descending the stairs was much easier than climbing them. Jack took Margaret through the kitchen and out the back door, which led to a covered walkway that joined the lighthouse with Keeper's Cottage next door.

Margaret started laughing when they entered the cozy cottage, which had two large bedrooms and a reasonably modern bath.

"You conniving, old seadog. You liked that, didn't you? Making me think there were no bedrooms."

Jack smiled and shrugged, and Margaret continued, "I suppose we could put a fold-away cot in the lantern room, for napping, if you like. And you can paint in there. Couldn't be any better light than that."

Margaret took both his hands in hers and looked up at him. "I think I've taken a closer step to heaven. This lighthouse is fantastic. Please tell me we can buy it."

Jack grinned, "I think that can be arranged, Madame McCormick." In fact, he'd already made the purchase, but he'd keep that information to himself.

Molly came every school break and they'd made Keeper's Cottage home. After Margaret passed away, Jack slept in the lantern room on his cot. The large bed in Keeper's Cottage was too lonely.

That was a long time ago. The memories were wonderful, but now he brought himself back to the present, and packing those memories away again, he lay down and snuggled beneath the down comforter.

After a couple of hours of fitful sleep he got up and dressed. He fished through his coat pocket and pulled out his pipe, a very fine meerschaum Margaret had given him as a birthday gift one year.

He opened a small pouch of *Cohiba,* his favorite tobacco—imported from Cuba—pinched a few fingers of it, filled the bowl, tamped it down with his forefinger, then lighted up. He didn't smoke it much. Just held it in his hand. The warmth of the pipe was soothing, and he'd often used it to thaw his hands on a raw, cold, day in New England.

Molly had made sure he'd read the recent Surgeon General's report relating to smoking and lung cancer. But a little pipe smoking and a taste of Glenfiddich in the evenings were his only vices. And he didn't plan on giving up either of them.

Having a television in his room was a treat, and only a luxurious place such as the Monaco would have such. He switched the TV on, and for a moment there was only a gray-green screen, then some unintelligible noises. Finally, Walter Cronkite's face splashed across the small screen.

Jack had missed last evening's news but wasn't surprised to hear there was more turmoil in Cuba. Most of the information he knew already. But hearing it again brought its significance to a new level.

President Kennedy was a young man and Jack was apprehensive about his leadership abilities. But he was in agreement with him on some issues, particularly the latest one regarding Cuba's weapons buildup.

Relations with Cuba had been strained since 1959 when Castro took over, which made it difficult to get some items from there. Jack could still get his *Cohiba* tobacco, with help from Crab, but his last order had been late getting to him. And the one he had placed a couple of weeks ago had still not arrived. He'd have a word with Crab when he got home.

Crab's primary job was to keep the ferry going as people used it daily to get to and from the mainland. He also brought the island's mail and a few people, such as Jack, depended on him to bring their special deliveries, such as his *Cohiba* and his whisky that he ordered from his cousins in Scotland.

As the news ended, Jack stood, switched the TV off, emptied his pipe residue in the toilet, and put the pipe back in his coat pocket.

Damn Castro. If this situation continues, I'll have to find another source for my tobacco. I like that Cohiba, but if this situation escalates, that'll be the end of anything coming out of Cuba.

After watching the newscast, he felt compelled to get back to the island. Presently, it was almost five in the afternoon. If he hurried, he'd have time to collect Molly and get to the airport. He grabbed his coat and slammed the door behind him.

She's coming home with me. To Cayo Canna. I'll listen to her protests, but she's coming.

Chapter 16

Cayo Canna

J ack was more informed than the average person about the Cuban situation. His background as an Intelligence Officer meant he had access to information that others did not.

He'd been in contact with some of his former Navy buddies who were still on active duty. In fact, at the moment he was involved in a rather complicated situation on Cayo Canna.

The Cuban problem did warrant some concern. Some weeks back he had taken the Cobra out for an afternoon of drifting the flats, hoping to catch a redfish. Catching them was the easy task. Convincing Solana to prepare them for him was a bit more difficult. She'd make it seem like a lot of work, but then she'd present him with a dinner fit for a king . . . or at least a Captain.

He'd cast his bait out once again and started reeling his line back in when he spotted a boat not far off his port bow. It was a sleek craft, black with a yellow stripe running from bow to stern on both sides and traveling at a rate of speed his old Cobra could only dream about. The name, *El Escorpión,* had been emblazoned on the stern.

Wonder who that could be? Not one of our locals. None of them could afford anything that fancy.

He spotted the craft several more times over the next couple of weeks. One day he pulled his binoculars out and took a closer look.

Being an experienced spy and seaman, he took note of how many men were on board. Three. He also noted that even though the craft was a lightweight one, it rode very low in the water. It should have been skimming across the top of the ocean. Unless it was loaded down with heavy cargo.

It's that boat again. Carrying something heavy. Just like the last few times I saw it. That's not a fishing boat. I don't think you guys are out looking for redfish, or any other kind of fish either. Why are you always at this location? And why is your craft always riding so low in the water? Involved in something illegal?

Jack's finely-tuned brain sent him a resounding YES to that last question and he began calling on his training and skills. They had lain dormant, but with a little prodding they'd saluted him snappily and were now front and center. His years of experience had honed his intuition and he sensed something was not right.

He took out a small pad and made notation of the exact location of the black runner, *El Escorpión*, the time of day, and number of occupants in the craft.

Even after he returned home he couldn't stop thinking about that fast-moving craft. He'd watched through his binoculars for a while and knew they could well have been aware of him, too, so he'd reeled his line in and moved on as if looking for a new place to drop anchor. He'd left the area but his mind kept churning.

After giving it considerable thought, he decided to share his sighting of this watercraft. That evening he raised Drifter on the ham radio.

Following retirement, Jack had remained in touch with several of his mates, primarily through their ham radios as the phone service on Cayo Canna was just as unreliable as the electricity. Plus, these old seadogs loved playing with their radios. A throwback to another time. They'd all started using them when they were teenagers—a hobby. One they still enjoyed.

Drifter was a call sign Jack and a couple of other mates had assigned to their friend. They marveled at his ability to just drift along, never letting much bother him. A great asset for an Intelligence Officer.

Drifter, still a few years from retirement, was assigned to the Naval Station in Key West, just a hop and skip from Cayo Canna.

Jack pounded out his message in their special code. To anyone listening in on the call, the message simply stated:

"Saw five Australian Mao-Maos while bird watching this morning. They were really flying fast, too. Headed south for the winter, I suppose."

He signed off with "Casper," his own call sign. This coded message told his friend a lot more than any casual listener would understand.

Drifter responded immediately.

"K4ELD. K4ELD. Over."

"Go ahead, Drifter."

Drifter sent his coded response.

"Talked to my sister yesterday. She saw an old bear prowling around her back yard. She thought he might be looking for his mate, or more likely, his cubs. Sis is a bird watcher, too. You've got her number. Give her a call. She'd love to hear from you. Be sure to tell her about the Mao-Mao sightings."

This coded message was a directive for Jack to make a phone call to Admiral Theodore (Teddy) Bowen, another retired buddy. Admiral Bowen was "Bear Bowen" to this august group of spies. He growled a lot but was an exceptional leader who knew how to formulate a plan and lead his officers and sailors. These men would follow him anywhere.

This small group of covert operators had been together on a number of assignments and had played a pivotal role in gathering information that had prevented more than one disaster for America and her allies.

Even though retired, the admiral was privy to information due to his rank. He was putting together an intelligence force that would provide information to Navy ships stationed in the waters around Cuba, as well as the Gulf waters on the west coast of the state.

Jack made a call to Bear who convinced him that he and his skills were needed. There were not nearly enough "spies," so some high-level officials had asked the admiral to activate some retired ones he trusted. This Cuban missile crisis was very real. The country was in trouble.

Chapter 17

As the old seaman pulled away in his Cobra, the three occupants of *El Escorpión* were silent. Finally, Carlos spoke up. His long, dark hair was held at the nape with a thin strip of leather and his shirt was open, allowing a view of his smooth chest where his gold chains were on display.

"That old man could make trouble for us. He might not have noticed our cargo, but we can't be sure. I saw that old boat of his several times in the last few weeks. Stands to reason he noticed us, too. We should take him out next time we see him. Old as he is, it shouldn't be difficult."

Roberto, the youngest at twenty-three years of age, shook his head. "No, Carlos. That old man? He's el *Capitán*. He lives in the lighthouse where my *Tia* Solana works. I hear her talk about him. He got a reputation for being a bad *hombre*."

"That old *zopilote* (buzzard)? We could use his body for shark bait. No one would ever know what happened to him," Carlos snorted.

"No. *Tia* Solana would have the police all over this island. She been his housekeeper for years. He's good to her. Pays her good wages. Listen, *Tia* been around a while . . . knows things. ¿*Comprendes*? We best leave him alone."

Elian, the third occupant, sat quietly. Listening. He'd been brought on to this project as he was a top-notch mechanic and their boat had to be in perfect running condition for their particular tasks.

"We should ask *Jefe*. He'll know what we should do," said Roberto.

"We always have to ask *Jefe*! Can't we make a few decisions on our own?" Carlos hated someone else making all the calls. Finally, he conceded, "*Sí*, we'll avoid *el Capitán*. Change our route a bit. Keep out of his sight. But if he gets in our way, his days are over."

They scurried back to their cove, taking great pains to anchor *El Escorpión* deep within the mangroves along the shore. These mangroves concealed their boat and were quick cover if they ever found themselves in need of a place to hide.

The three *hombres* entered the small shanty where their leader was waiting. He'd arrived earlier and was going over his maps and route plans. He had years of experience with gun-running for various groups and was well aware that Carlos disliked having to obey his orders. *Jefe* chose to ignore the impetuous moron. That young man had a lot to learn, and if he were smart, he'd watch and learn a few tricks he didn't know yet.

"*Buenas noches, amigos. Como estan?*"

In his capacity as commander of this "rebel" group, their leader insisted on being called *Jefe,* (boss).

Jefe greeted his crew and passed around *cervezas*. The shanty was equipped with a small table with four chairs, an old ice chest, and half a dozen cots. Its location was known only to a few and *Jefe* wanted to keep it that way.

Carlos took a long swig of his *cerveza* and began to tell about seeing the old seaman. "He's always running about out there. Fishing, he says. But I'm not sure about that. He seemed a bit too nosy in my opinion. I say we eliminate him."

"What old seaman?" asked *Jefe*.

"That old man that runs about in that ancient Chris Craft. He came up to us today, asking about fishing. I don't trust him," responded Carlos.

"You say he has a Chris Craft?"

"*Sí*, an older Cobra model."

"You are right about him. He knows much. That's Capitán Jack. He's a former U.S. Navy *espia* (spy). Some kind of intelligence officer. He's been retired for some time now, but my sources tell me he's always on his radio. Listening in, I suspect."

"That old man is *espia*?"

"Something like that. And he still keeps up with military operations."

"Then we have no choice but to sink him and that old tub of his."

Jefe shook his head, "Carlos, calm yourself. Don't worry. He's not as dangerous as you think. Trust me. He's being taken care of. We've got bigger issues to deal with.

"Our next cargo shipment will be here in less than a week. This shipment is more important than all the others, and it must get to our brothers in *la Habana* quickly.

"This *presidente,* this Kennedy, he is young and stupid. He thinks he can bluff his way out of this conflict. But he doesn't understand us. Our commitment to Fidel. We will wipe his country out. He's in for a big surprise."

Chapter 18

Johns Hopkins Hospital
Baltimore

Jack took a cab from the Monaco and asked to be let off a couple of blocks from Johns Hopkins. He needed to walk a bit, to finalize his plan before he let Molly in on it.

The snowstorm had produced a couple of inches of snow that was now turning to slush. There were puddles along the street, and the snow on the ground was covered in black soot from the constant traffic that whizzed by him even now, splattering his highly polished shoes.

He looked up at the leaden-colored sky and moved on quickly. He'd lived in New England many years. An East coast sailor. The slushy aftermath of the snowstorm and the biting cold nipping at his ears was a reminder that his lighthouse on Cayo Canna was where he'd finish out his days.

His task today was to convince Molly to go home with him to the island. Dr. Charlie said she needed several weeks, if not a couple of months, to recover. But Jack knew how stubborn his granddaughter could be.

He took the elevator to the third floor and strode down the hallway. The place was buzzing with activity; monitors were beeping, breakfast trays were being wheeled in and out of the rooms, and white coats and uniforms were dashing about.

A high-pitched voice came screeching through a speaker: "Code Blue, Code Blue. 313." Jack stepped closer to the wall as several white coats rushed along the corridor.

Molly? No. Molly's in room 316. Not Molly.

When he entered her room, Molly was sitting on the edge of her bed talking with a police officer, a middle-aged man with thinning hair and a threadbare suit. She was speaking in a calm, soothing voice.

"I'm sorry. I can only remember snatches of scenes . . . nothing concrete. My memory is very fuzzy. I can't put everything together."

"I understand. We'll catch him, Miss McCormick. It's just a matter of time. If you think of anything else, give me a call." He handed her his card.

Molly took the card and then touched the officer's arm. "Oh, there is one more thing. He grabbed my necklace and ripped it from my neck."

"Describe the necklace. It might be important."

Molly looked up as Papa Jack entered the room. "It's a gold necklace—a lighthouse actually—and there's a small diamond in the center where the light is. Papa gave it to me a long time ago." She smiled over at Papa Jack and he watched her face as she spoke with the officer. Fear. In her every movement. In her voice. Even as she plastered a smile on her face.

Smiling. As if this is a minor event, instead of the life-changing one it really is. I see through that facade, Molly Mac. You never were good at lying.

The lieutenant made his notes and stood. "We'll talk again, Miss McCormick." He nodded to Jack, then stepped out of the room only to find the older man had followed him.

Reaching his hand toward Jack, the officer gave him a quick "once over" look. He recognized an element of authority and confidence when he saw it.

"Jeffrey Collins. Lieutenant."

Jack stuck his hand out and grasped the lieutenant's.

"Jack McCormick. Captain."

"What's your relationship with Miss McCormick?"

"She's my granddaughter."

"Does she have other family here?"

"No. I'm her only family."

"I see. Then I would suggest Miss McCormick not return to her home just now. Her attacker may still be stalking her place. We're watching it twenty-four-seven, but he's still out there."

"Do you have any leads? Know any more about him?"

"We have a little more information, but not anything I want to share with Miss McCormick. We found a woman's body yesterday . . . an older woman. She'd been tortured much like Miss McCormick. Could be this man was her attacker also. Finding him is priority number one."

"Let's hope you do. Meanwhile, Molly's going home with me to Florida. She'll be safe there."

"Good. We don't need any more bodies."

"I'd like you to call me with any new developments. I'd rather you tell me than Molly," said Jack. He handed the lieutenant a small rectangular card that read Jack McCormick, CAPT, USN (Ret) Ph. Liberty 7-2052.

"Yessir, will do," the lieutenant stated and hurried on. Jack liked this man's style. Compassionate in his dealings with Molly but all business otherwise.

When Jack returned to the room, Molly was on the phone. "I will. I promise. Call me when you get back from your interview. Yes, Charlie, I heard you. Bye now." Jack waited for her to acknowledge his presence and then walked closer.

"Hey, Papa Jack."

"Hey, Molly Mac. Glad to see you sitting up. Got a little better color, too. How you feeling?"

"It's really nothing, Papa. My head is better, my wrists are healing quickly, and the shoulder is less painful this morning. The only area that bothers me is the side of my face. The membranous tissue there is more sensitive than some places."

She still doesn't know about the carving. Might be a good thing. She'll know eventually.

"What are your doctors saying? What happens next?"

"There's not much else to be done. I'm cleared for discharge later today. If you'll hail a cab, we'll stop at the Jiffy Mart, get a dozen cans of chicken soup and a gallon of chocolate ice cream, then we'll get me settled in my apartment. I'll pull out some good books and settle in for a couple of weeks. Not much I can do but rest and let nature takes its course.

"Uhm. So you're planning to rest, eat chicken soup and ice cream and read a few books?"

"I'll be fine, Papa. I'll put this incident behind me and move forward. Mrs. Jenkins will check on me, and as soon as I'm recovered I'll get busy looking for a position, a job. I've got applications ready to submit. And now, with the award, that could help me secure a place in a major institution. You know that's been my goal all along, Papa. To work in a research department in a major institution. I won't give up on that dream."

"I agree. You shouldn't give up your dream. And you should continue submitting your applications. But today, you need to be cared for yourself. That means you'll go back with me to Cayo Canna for a while. You can get back on your feet and be ready to run full-steam ahead."

"But, Papa, I want to stay here in Baltimore. Maybe I can even get a position here at Johns Hopkins. This place is familiar. I have friends here. I know the city."

"You're an adult now, Molly. And I try to remember that. But this is one time when I'm going to insist you listen to your Papa. If you go to work before you've recovered, you'll only have a setback later. You're the doc. You know that."

"Papa, you know how I hate change. And my life is here, in Baltimore. I can't just take off to your island."

"You'll just be taking a short vacation. Getting a little sunshine and letting Solana and me pamper you for a while. She's a great cook, and her *tapas* are mouth-watering."

"Solana. She's still with you, then?"

"Of course. She came with the lighthouse, remember?"

"Doesn't look like you've been eating much yourself. You look a little thin, Papa. Are you still climbing that spiral staircase every day? Might be more than you should be doing at your age."

"My age? Bite your tongue, girl. I'm in the prime of my life and that spiral staircase keeps me in shape."

"But, Papa, I have no clothes for island living. And I'm in no condition to go shopping."

"I'm quite sure we can figure out the small details, Molly. Meanwhile, I'll make reservations for us on the next flight to Fort Myers. Whatever you need we'll be able to get either in Fort Myers or on the island.

"But, I . . ."

"No argument. You're coming with me."

"Aye, Captain."

She knew this was a losing battle and part of her was relieved. Deep down, in that secret place where only truth is allowed, she knew that fear had taken up residence in her mind. And maybe even her soul.

Chapter 19

Cayo Canna

Solana jumped back from the open kitchen window. Once she regained her composure, she let her anger loose, using her tongue as her weapon.

"Get away from this window! You hear me! Get on, now. Get away!"

But Queenie didn't leave. She put her arms on the window sill and leaned in even closer. "Saw the Cap'n in my lagoon. Somethin' comin' for him. Somethin' from the sea. You need to warn him. He listen to you."

Solana slapped her hand down on the window sill, barely missing Queenie's. "Queenie, take your crazy ideas and go home."

"I seen a young *chica* too. Dark shadow follow her." She turned to her left and looked down, then began talking to some unseen person.

"I say be still. You making much noise. Let go my scarf."

As Solana leaned out to close the Bermuda shutters, two small dark hands appeared next to Queenie's on the window sill. Solana peered out and looked down. Those small coffee-colored hands were attached to a little child with shoulder-length, dark hair and saucer-sized black eyes . . . eyes that were staring up at Solana.

Any sane person could tell the child was in distress and pulling at Queenie's scarf to get her attention.

"Stop. You no listen!" Queenie called out. A second later she was hurrying down the path dragging the crying child behind her.

Who does that child belong to? Queenie's too old to have a child that young.

Solana tried to put the incident out of her mind, and that infernal ham radio kept calling out letters and numbers all day long. She had experience operating a ham radio . . . a long time ago. She was sure the letters and numbers were codes but were not any she was privy to.

She finished folding the laundry, gathered her basket, closed up the lighthouse, then started for her bungalow. She hoped the good father had followed up on his promise to send up prayers for the Captain's granddaughter.

Solana had known the girl for some time as Molly had spent school breaks with Captain Jack and Margaret over the years. And Solana couldn't bear to think of the Captain having to face another tragedy. Molly was all he had left now, except her of course. She'd always be here. At least as long as he wished her to be.

Chapter 20

Patrick's ears could have led him to the vet's office near the bayfront. The doors and windows stood wide open and the loud barking of large dogs and the yapping of smaller breeds filled the humid air. Entering the open door, Patrick wrinkled his nose as the combined odors of dogs, dog poop, dog food and medications battled for his attention.

Then, as if to lend his own special touch, Ensign lifted his left hind leg and marked a spot for himself . . . and that spot included Patrick's leather dock shoes as well.

"Christ Almighty!"

Patrick had taken up swearing and smoking in his teenage years when he'd roamed the pubs and villages of Ireland with a gang of older lads. The friendships were short-lived but left some unsavory habits in their wake.

"Patrick, the Almighty is pleased to have you in his flock, but I don't think he'll take kindly to your limited vocabulary," his Mum had admonished when he 'took the collar.'

"I believe HE could care less about what we say and more about how we behave, Mum," he'd responded. He'd given up smoking a couple of years ago, so he figured he was due a little leeway in the swearing area.

The vet, Doc Simpson, was an older gentleman, with a few sprigs of hair like a newly-hatched eaglet . . . and brown as a coconut from all his years in the Florida sun.

"Nah. No charge. I've been treating Captain Jack's dogs for years. This little guy just needs a splint for a few days. He'll heal quickly if you keep him indoors for a short spell.

"Of course, he's a water dog, so he'll run back to the ocean the minute he gets the chance. Won't you?" he laughed, scratching his young patient under the chin.

Patrick lay the pup across his shoulder and headed to the dock. The ferry would be departing in about an hour which gave him time to grab lunch at the Tiki Hut on the south end of the pier.

Taking a seat under a thatched umbrella, he ordered a hamburger and a beer and had just finished his meal when the ferry arrived.

"Let's get you on board, crip. Time to go home." He picked Ensign up and took a seat on a bench up front at the bow. This had been a long day, and he wanted nothing more than to get to his little bungalow, have a taste of his Jameson, and tune his TV to whatever channel it might pick up. Wanted to watch the news.

The crossing was smooth and a short while later he walked into his cozy place and turned on the air conditioner. An old bean bag in the corner made an excellent bed for his house guest, so he eased him down on it. He was stuck with him at least one more day, unless Jack was back already.

Unable to get any TV reception, he decided to walk to the lighthouse, hoping Jack had returned. Dog sitting a puppy that wasn't house-trained wasn't his idea of fun. Plus, he'd had to ditch his dock shoes. That urine odor would never come out of that leather.

He took the path along the shore and was learning that the ocean had its moods. Today it was calm; the waves were barely clawing their way to the shore. Looking out across the bay, he took note of the boat he'd seen for some time now. Most probably a winter resident.

Many northern residents sailed their boats down for the winter, anchored them in a bay and lived on them for months. They would then amble their way back north in late spring.

As he neared the lighthouse, he saw soft lights at the windows, but when he knocked there was no answer. No Solana. Jack wasn't home yet. Maybe tomorrow.

He was beginning to worry. Had Jack's granddaughter been in real trouble? This granddaughter was Jack's only family now. His son was still MIA and Margaret was gone.

Jack would have been back by now unless something was wrong. What?

Patrick returned to his bungalow, and after a few minutes of twisting his antenna every direction possible, he caught the tail end of the newscast from Fort Myers. He almost wished he hadn't. The expression on the face of the young correspondent told Patrick a lot. One word. Fear.

The newscast had again been about the trouble in Cuba. And however disconcerting it was, recognition of the state of affairs of the world gave Patrick a new perspective on his own "problem." He still hadn't spoken about it to anyone, but knew he'd eventually mull it over with Jack.

Early in their relationship he'd found that Jack, that old seadog, gruff as a gorilla most times, had a way of listening that allowed others to express their feelings. An empathetic capacity that only a few people possessed.

Perhaps I'm making too much of 'my problem.' Not much I can do about it anyway.

Chapter 21

Molly always loved going to Cayo Canna. But not today. She was leaving behind her life in Baltimore, where everything was familiar . . . her apartment, the hospital staff, the city. And even though she'd not voiced it, she had hopes that her award may increase her chances of getting a position in the Research Department at Johns Hopkins.

Sitting next to Papa, she breathed in the captivating scent of his pipe tobacco. It spoke of sunny days swimming in the surf, warm evenings with a breeze blowing through the open windows, and star-studded nights high up in the lantern room, Papa pointing out the Milky Way and other constellations. Such sweet memories.

Papa had timed their arrival in Fort Myers perfectly. As soon as their plane landed, he hailed a cab to the ferry dock. Molly had become silent. Exhaustion had set in.

"I came over on the Cobra, but we'll take the ferry across. That'll be more comfortable. I'll ask Crab to let you rest in his cabin below decks. Should be a smooth crossing. No small craft warnings tonight." Molly nodded. The whole event was taking its toll.

Jack watched as Crab brought the ferry in, "crabbing" it sideways the last fifty yards. At the very last moment, he made a quick turn that put it precisely on target for its mooring. Jack smiled at this level of skill.

Guess that was what earned him the name of Crab. He certainly is adept at maneuvering this old tub.

He helped Molly board, found her a seat, and then the pilot himself came strolling towards him.

"Ah, *Capitán* Jack. You return."

"Yes, I'm back." Then he turned to his left.

"Crab, this is Molly. Dr. Molly McCormick, my granddaughter. She'll be making the crossing with us. Visiting with me for a while."

Crab nodded and bowed slightly. "Missy . . . Missy *medico?* No . . . Missy *Doktor? Si.* Inglés word. D*oktor, no?*"

He made no comment but must have observed her head and arms were bandaged, and a sling held her shoulder in place.

Jack turned to Crab, "I wonder if she could go below and rest on your bunk? As you can see, she's pretty beat up. Rather fragile at the moment. Your cabin might be more comfortable than trying to sit up top."

Just as Crab had taken in Molly's condition, she had observed that his right hand was missing the first and second fingers.

At first glance she thought he'd had an accident of some kind. But looking a second longer, she knew exactly what it was: ectrodactyly, a congenital disorder in which the person is born without one or more digits of the hand or foot. The hand or foot is then often described as "crab-like" in appearance. She guessed that must be why he was called Crab.

Crab certainly couldn't say no to the Captain's request. That old seaman had a reputation as a fellow you didn't want to cross. But Crab wasn't real keen on someone going below in his personal space. But this girl, this *doktor,* wasn't in any condition to do anything except lie still and be quiet.

"Of course, *Capitán.* It's my pleasure to help you, sir. But, *Capitán,* I see your boat, the little *serpiente* . . . how you say . . . the Cobra? She is docked here already. You will ride with me . . . not her?"

"Molly will be more comfortable on your ferry I think, Crab. I'll come back with you tomorrow morning and take the Cobra back to the island. She's not going anywhere." He then began to help Molly go below.

Crab's accent was still pronounced even after some years in the United States. Papa Jack got Molly situated and went topside. The cabin was a mess, but Molly wasn't aware of that. She was asleep almost before he left her.

"Thank you, Crab. She's had quite a day. Just need to get her home."

Crab nodded and went about his work. The porpoises played escort, leaping high out of the water and diving back down. Molly would be sorry she missed that. It was a treat for her when she was younger.

Papa Jack took a deep breath and exhaled slowly. It was good to be going back to the island. A few days in Baltimore was more than enough for him.

Chapter 22

Solana, habitually protective of Captain Jack, now included Molly in her nest of those she spread her wings over. Even though she'd not heard from the Captain, she'd taken it upon herself to get a room ready in Keeper's Cottage. If it wasn't needed, then that was all right. But, with the Captain having stayed gone this long, she guessed something was wrong.

Yesterday she'd aired the linens, dusted, and smiled to herself when she found a container filled with Margaret's homemade potpourri—a mixture Margaret concocted of lemon peel, dried rose petals, and lavender. The guestroom in the cottage still carried its delicate scent.

This morning she arrived, removed her shoes at the door, and entered. The rich smell of the Captain's coffee told her he was home. Relief flooded through her.

Captain Jack greeted her. "Good morning, Solana. Everything all right with you?"

"Yes, Captain. And you be okay?"

"Yeah, I'm all right. Finding a room ready for Molly when we got here last night was very helpful. We were both ready to find a bed. Thank you."

"Molly?" Solana lifted an eyebrow, almost fearful of hearing his response.

"She was attacked by some deranged madman. She's going to be all right, but it may take some time. Right now she needs a place to recover and feel safe again."

"That's good news. She'll recover, Captain. I'll see to that. I'll go over there and check on her. See if she needs anything."

"She may still be asleep. But, yeah, see if she's ready for some coffee. I've got to catch the ferry this morning. Gotta bring the Cobra back."

A knock at the door halted their conversation. Solana could see through the window that it was the "good father."

Now why does he have to drop by today? The Captain and Molly need a few days to rest. Don't need any visitors. Especially not one as loud and foul-mouthed as this one. Maybe I won't answer the door. But the Captain will if I don't.

She took her time getting there, her long skirt swaying as she sashayed along.

"Good morning, Solana," Patrick smiled, holding Ensign in his arms as if he were a baby. The pup began struggling, trying his best to get to Solana. She might not care for him, but he knew she was the one that kept his water bowl full and put out his dish of Alpo.

"Father. Come in. The Captain's in the kitchen." She walked away, headed to Keeper's Cottage to see about Molly.

Patrick went on to the kitchen where Jack was already pouring him a cup of coffee. Jack nodded. "Ah, just the man I want to see."

"Me? Come on, Jack. Shouldn't tell lies to a priest, you know." He smiled but couldn't avoid seeing the tired look around his friend's eyes.

Ensign let out a howl and Patrick was happy to hand him over to one who appreciated him more. "I believe this belongs to you." He handed the pup over and Jack grinned.

"And what have you done to him?" Jack asked as he noted the bandaged paw.

"What? You think I did something to that flea catcher?" Patrick couldn't help grinning back. "He gave

112

chase to a fiddler crab on the beach, ran into the water and got his paw caught in a crab trap. I didn't know what the hell to do with him, so I took him to the vet on the mainland. Doc Simpson."

"Good man. Doc Simpson knows his business. What'd he say?"

"Said to keep twinkle toes inside for a few days. He'll heal quickly being he's a young puppy. Here he is. All yours."

Patrick was surprised to see Jack moving over to his comfortable chair. Most often they went upstairs or out to the patio with their coffee.

Must have been some trip. Maybe I'll put my counseling hat on for a few minutes. See if I can at least get him to tell me a few details. Sometimes sharing your troubles makes them not feel as overwhelming.

"You gonna tell me about it, or do I have to dig for it detail by detail?"

Jack shook his head. "She's hurt, Patrick. Some unhinged, perverted, fool attacked her in her apartment. She's had a pretty bad blow to her head, cigarette burns on her breast, and cuts to her wrists. But most damaging of all, he carved his initial in her cheek."

"God Almighty send your angels to watch over her." The prayer had escaped Patrick's lips before he stopped to think about it.

"She's going to need them—the angels, that is. At the moment she doesn't know about the initial carving. She just knows her face was cut and is quite painful.

" She's a bit on the shy side, Patrick. More at ease with books and ideas than people. And thanks to her mother, unsure about her looks. Even so, she was coming out of her shell and finally coming to grips with her talents. But now, after this attack, she's been thrown into a tailspin. She's like a scared little hermit crab, slinking back into its protective shell."

113

Patrick shook his head back and forth in disbelief. "Jaysus. A carved face. That's going to be a hard pill to swallow. I wish I could give you words that might be comforting, but I don't think there are any."

"No. Damn his sorry ass. Obviously, he's crazy. And when they do catch him, he'll get off on some insanity plea. But, you know, there are instances when even those who are institutionalized go missing. Perhaps he just walks away from his "group therapy" setting one day—or fails to return to his assigned room following an outing . . . or . . ."

"Jack, it's not a good idea to be thinking like that." Patrick had no problem envisioning Captain Jack McCormick, former covert operator, making someone disappear—never to be seen again.

"Ah, give it no more thought Patrick. I'm tired and beyond angry. And this Cuban situation is weighing on my mind. I've been in touch with a couple of former mates. I believe we have activity here on Cayo Canna, but can't prove it yet. Soon as I get Molly settled properly, I'll get back to work figuring out a few details that may help my mates."

Chapter 23

The sun slowly inched its way above the horizon, flirted with the ocean for a few short minutes, then finally peeked through Molly's open window. Its warm rays crawled over her face. Like fingers of a blind person seeking to identify some unfamiliar person or object.

The warmth was comforting and Molly didn't want to leave her cocoon of softness with its clean, fresh linen smell. Even before she opened her eyes, she was greeted by the scent of lemons and lavender.

I'm in Keeper's Cottage. Today Mimi and Papa are taking me to the Seminole village on the mainland. We'll go across Alligator Alley . . ."

For the briefest moment Molly was a young girl again, anxious to start her day in Papa's lighthouse. But the instant she moved her head and felt a sharp, stabbing pain rush across her cheek, reality came flooding back.

She sat on the side of the bed and looked about. Memories that she'd stored long ago clamored to be revisited. Mimi's dish of potpourri sat on the night table, photos of the three of them splashing in the surf clustered next to it, and a couple of Molly's drawings hung on the wall. Such happy memories. She began to cry.

If only life were as simple as it had been then.

She was still wearing the clothes she had worn from the hospital . . . the clothes she'd been wearing when she'd been attacked. Papa told her they'd figure out the details when they got to the island. Well, they were here now, and she had nothing else to wear.

Sensing a presence, she looked up. Moving as quietly as a gentle mist, Solana appeared in the doorway. Her silent way of moving about had always intrigued Molly.

"Solana. Papa said you were still here."

"Where else would I be, Molly? My heart and soul reside in this lighthouse. I'm not going anywhere." She knelt by the bed and placed her arms around the young woman. Then the tears really began to flow.

"Oh, my dear child."

"Solana, I woke up thinking I was a little girl. With Mimi and Papa. And we were going to the Seminole Village on the mainland today. And then reality erased that thought."

"Memories have a way of returning when we most need them, Molly. They come back for a reason."

"But today it feels like that's all I'll ever have . . . memories."

"Come now. Let's get you in the tub. I'll pour in some of Margaret's potpourri and your spirits will be lifted."

"A bath would be a treat. But I have no clothes. Papa said we couldn't go to my apartment. Guess I'll just have to wear one of his robes until we can wash these."

"What's in this bag over here? This black one."

"That's my medical bag. The police brought it to me from my apartment. Thought I might like to have it. But they wouldn't let me go back inside as, apparently, my apartment's a crime scene."

"Then you let Solana worry about the clothing. Come with me."

The warm water was therapeutic. Molly wanted to cleanse every place where that man had touched her-to erase all traces of his vileness.

Solana cringed when she saw the cigarette burns on Molly's breast. She helped her towel off, went to find fresh bandages, and to borrow a robe from the Captain's closet. When she returned, however, she didn't bring a robe.

"I think this will suit you better than the Captain's robe." She held up a long, sleeveless dress, a soft shade of coral, with a border of small white shells at the neck and again on the hem.

"I remember that dress. Mimi called it her island muu-muu," Molly murmured as she stroked the dress.

"Yes, she had several. She favored them over all her other clothes."

"I can't believe you still have them."

"I couldn't seem to part with them, so I packed them away. Never thought I would need to pull them out again, though. Here, slip this on. You're thinner than Margaret, but I believe it may work. For the moment, anyway."

Molly let Solana ease the dress over her head. Even with the passage of time, the dress still held a whiff of lavender. Mimi's scent.

"This is perfect. No belt, no sleeves, and it still smells like Mimi."

"Now, about shoes . . . I'll dispose of yours—those stains are too hard to remove. Here, try these."

Molly's feet were smaller than Mimi's, but for the time being these leather sandals would be fine.

"Now let's see what we can do about that hair. I see you've got stitches across the back of your head. But the front still has those luscious curls. We'll comb through those lightly."

Molly nodded, "Good idea. I can remove the stitches in about ten days but might need some help with that. It's difficult to remove stitches on yourself."

"Solana's removed stitches in her time. We'll manage."

"Then maybe you can help me with these other bandages, too. I'll need to change them tomorrow." She stood in front of the mirror and tried not to look away.

The large, full-head bandage had been changed to one that only covered the back of her head. Her wrists had been dressed with small bandages, and the side of her cheek was thickly padded with heavy gauze, several inches thick, to soak up the blood that continued to seep.

As Solana carefully pulled a comb through Molly's thick hair, her soft auburn curls fell into place.

~ ~ ~

Solana drew in her protective wings, stood erect, and waited behind. Molly needed to walk alone through the breezeway and into the kitchen at the lighthouse.

Solana's wings may have been missing, but Molly stood in the kitchen and felt as if she had entered a place of refuge, a place of safety where all thoughts were allowed, tears could stream, disappointments could be voiced, arguments could be made. Home. Yes, this place was home.

"Papa? Are you here?"

She walked through the kitchen into the den and stood there, taking in the scent of the ocean breeze through the open windows and the high-pitched cry of an osprey as he circled overhead. The waves were small this early in the morning, but forever rushing to the shore. Voices from above caught her attention and she looked up as a deep voice continued.

"How the hell you climb this spiral every day is beyond me. My feet are just too damn big. You're gonna find me at the bottom of it one day, bleeding all over Solana's floor. She'll have my arse on a . . . "

Patrick stopped his rant mid-sentence and stood looking down at the woman at the foot of the stairs. Papa Jack stared also, appearing to flounder a moment. But not for lack of words. He was experiencing a moment of *déjà vu*.

That's Margaret's dress. One of her favorites.

He hadn't known Solana had kept Margaret's things. They were just not in her closet one day. Solana had taken care of that. Like she did many other things.

118

Finally, Papa Jack broke the silence.

"Hey, Molly Mac. You're up early. Get any sleep? Sometimes the noise of the ocean can keep you awake."

"Papa, that ocean noise was the best sleeping pill I could have. I usually go to sleep listening to traffic from the freeway," her voice so soft it was almost a whisper.

Patrick continued to stare. *Jaysus, Mary, and Joseph. God, but she's gorgeous.*

"Patrick, this is my granddaughter, Molly McCormick, Dr. Molly McCormick."

No. That can't be Molly. She's supposed to be plain Jane, "bookwormy," and unattractive.

Patrick's brain and tongue appeared to have no connection. And if there was any part of him that retained its "priestly" bearing, it was in hibernation.

"Molly, I . . . I . . . hello. I'm glad to meet you. Jack speaks of you often."

"Molly, this is Father Patrick O'Brien."

"Father O'Brien. Papa also speaks of you frequently."

"Patrick came by to unload his burden on me," Jack looked at his friend.

The young man laughed. Molly took note of the crinkles about his dark eyes and his strong, square jaw. He was far more handsome than any priest she'd ever known.

"Burden?" she asked.

As if he'd understood the conversation, a whimper from the corner had all eyes turning that direction. Jack brought "the burden" over to meet Molly.

"This is Ensign. Patrick's been taking care of him while I was gone. Some care, though. Poor pup has a bum paw, now. Think Patrick was sleeping on the job."

"You ungrateful old . . ." Patrick started and smiled at Molly. She quickly understood these two had a special relationship.

119

"How many Ensigns is this now, Papa? Three?" She rubbed the pup's soft belly, his fuzz of coat, and touched his small, velvet-padded paws. Then she saw his bandaged leg . . . and understood his helplessness.

Patrick asked only questions he felt wouldn't be too difficult or prying. "How you feeling? Need anything? I've got nothing but time and I'm available day or night."

"Thanks. There's nothing to do but sit in the sun and let Mother Nature take over. But thank you." She walked out to the patio where she made herself as comfortable as possible in a lounge chair under the ancient banyan tree.

Patrick took his leave and Papa joined Molly who was inspecting a small tree at the edge of the patio, one she and Mimi had planted long ago.

"I see our tamarind tree is still alive, even if it isn't exactly thriving." She shifted her body several times. It was impossible to get comfortable with the shoulder sling and bandages on her wrists.

"Tamarinds are a pretty hardy species. But this one hasn't produced any seeds yet. Maybe this year," said Papa.

Molly cocked her head, "Did you know the natives in South Asia use the seeds to reduce fever? They make a salve out of them and apply the salve to the forehead. Apparently, it works pretty well."

"No, Molly. Didn't know that. Think I'll stick to aspirin myself," Papa answered as he started back inside.

"I've gotta call some buds. We're working on a project for the Navy. I'll be inside on the radio. If you need anything, call out. Solana's got ears like an elephant. She'll hear you even if I don't."

"Papa, did Lieutenant Collins call this morning? Have they caught him?"

"No, Molly Mac, not yet."

She nodded and looked out to the ocean, wishing she could drift away on the next outgoing wave. Then she'd have no decisions to make, no complicated situations to figure out, and no pain. Emotional or physical.

Chapter 24

It was early evening and Jack poured himself a couple of fingers of Glenfiddich, walked outside and stretched out on the lounge chair near the water.

His transistor radio rested on his lap, and Ensign occupied himself chasing sandpipers as they teased him with their quick darts back and forth to the water's edge.

The radio made its squeals and blasts of static, then the signal righted itself and Walter Cronkite's voice came through clearly, announcing that the news was being preempted by a message from President Kennedy.

After a few moments of imparting unnecessary information, or so Jack thought, President Kennedy informed the nation that the small country of Cuba, which was situated less than two hundred nautical miles south of Jack's home on Cayo Canna, had built some forty ballistic missile sites on the island and had allowed the Russians to place missiles in them.

These missiles were capable of launching nuclear warheads that could hit the United States, the Panama Canal, Mexico City, and as far south as Lima, Peru.

That statement was unnerving even to Jack. But the news was not surprising. He was expecting it. Castro would go to any lengths to take control. Jack just wished it weren't happening this quickly. He'd hoped to have Molly's situation in hand before he'd be needed . . . and he would be . . . to participate in a covert operation that could have impact on this Cuban missile crisis.

The President had limited choices to curtail this disturbing development. The Russians could launch these missiles at any time, which would mean disaster for the country. Thousands of people would be annihilated. He and the Russian Premier, Nikita Khrushchev, were playing a very dangerous game.

The last skirmish between these two—the Bay of Pigs—was one Jack couldn't forget. That whole operation was a disaster from day one. He'd not been in charge, though had played a part in it. Now he'd been called upon again. This time they had no choice but to stop this madness. The alternative was unthinkable.

~ ~ ~

"K6DNB . . . K6DNB . . . over."

Jack waited a few seconds, then his call was answered.

"Casper, where you been? Sister's been asking for you again. She saw that old bear prowling around in her yard yesterday. Looks like he still hasn't found his mate and all his cubs. Maybe if you take a ride up to her place, just talk to her . . . maybe she'll leave me alone."

"Roger that Drifter. Gotta take my Cobra up there anyway. She's in need of a few repairs. Casper out."

That was the call Jack had been waiting for. His instructions, actually. It appeared that Admiral Bowen wanted him in Placida. This Cuba fracas had everyone on alert.

This afternoon he'd take a cruise out to the spot where he had last seen that little black runner, *El Escorpión.* See what he could find out.

Solana brought lunch to the patio. Papa Jack joined Molly there but neither of them ate much. She picked at hers and then closed her eyes. He tried to initiate conversation but she just answered with a yes or no.

He was experienced enough to know she would let him in when she was ready. Not before. After lunch he spoke with Solana.

"I'm going out in the Cobra for a couple of hours. Gonna do a little fishing. Be back before dark. You watch out for Molly?"

Solana gave him a look that needed no words. Molly couldn't be in better hands. Solana had no children, so no grandchildren. Molly was the closest thing she had to that.

Jack departed and had been anchored a half-hour when there it was—*El Escorpión*—again. There were three men aboard, and as before, she was riding low in the water.

Jack waved to them as he would greet any fisherman. He put his line in the water and "fished" for a short while, then pulled up anchor and headed in their direction. There was only one way to see what they were up to. Take a look.

"Hello," he shouted as he pulled up next to their craft. Its two 50 HP Evinrudes looked new, just like the boat. "Hope you're having better luck than I am. Not even a bite yet."

The three men, all with dark hair, dark eyes, and skin like caramel, stared at him. No one answered. Finally, the one with gold chains around his neck spoke up.

"Lo siento, señor. No hablamos Ingles."

Jack saw several fishing rods in their holders, but none of them were baited. A real fisherman would have them ready for casting. He didn't see a bait bucket or an ice chest either. Other items that real fishermen would have had.

What he did see was two large, rectangular plastic boxes, about three feet by eight feet, stacked in the bottom of the boat. One of the boxes had not been closed tightly and a metal rod stuck out the end of it.

The men stood on top of the boxes, trying to cover them with their bodies. Jack was sure the metal rod sticking out of the container was a rifle. Even an inexperienced covert operator would have figured this scenario out. These guys were carrying a boatload of weapons.

He nodded and smiled at them. "And I don't speak Spanish, so I guess we'll have to call it a day. I'll try my luck over near the bird's nest, marker sixteen. Sometimes find a few speckled trout there."

He smiled and pulled away, waving at them as he pretended to head toward the marker. To complete his "play-acting," he anchored there and cast his line. A few seconds later they took off to the open Gulf, headed south.

When he returned to the lighthouse, Solana took supper to the patio. She'd prepared shrimp scampi, Molly's favorite. She set out the food, turned back Molly's bed in Keeper's Cottage, and readied herself to leave.

"I can stay the night if you need me to, Captain."

Jack thought about her offer for a second, then made a decision. "Thanks, Solana. But I think Molly and I have to deal with this ourselves. You and I can help her only so much. The real healing has to come from Molly, from within."

"Yes, Captain."

Once again Jack tried to engage Molly in conversation. About mundane subjects like her friends in Baltimore, what music she might be listening to, what was she reading. But again she gave one-syllable answers.

"Molly, remember what you told me . . . what the speaker at your graduation service said?"

"You mean Dr. Cajina? Yes, I remember. He talked about change being inevitable. And that we should embrace it."

"What you are experiencing is just that. Change. Change in what you believe about life, the world, how things are as opposed to how you wish or thought them to be."

"Yes, Papa," she answered. Then nothing more.

"Our problems and fears don't go away on their own. We have to deal with them and put them to bed ourselves."

Molly nodded. People were attacked every day. But her mind continued to play bits and pieces of the attack and these scenes kept her locked in a place of fear and anxiety.

Chapter 25

J ack sighed. "She's slipping away from us, Solana. There's got to be something we can do."

"Captain, it will take time. I'm going to change her dressings and remove her stitches this morning. That could be painful but some of the wounds will be healed by now. You go on about your business. I'll take care of Molly."

Jack headed to Bailey's Island Grocery to get a couple of batteries for his flashlight. They didn't have storms often, but this time of year one would occasionally form in the Gulf. He wanted to be prepared.

He parked his golf cart and went into Bailey's. The overhead fan was slowly turning, clicking with every rotation, and Agnes was ringing up a customer.

"Mornin' Cap'n Jack. What brings you in at this hour?"

"Need a couple of batteries, Agnes. Flashlight's dead. Can't have that."

Agnes lived several miles south of Jack. Her small, one bedroom cottage fronted on the bay, and she often sat outside late at night watching the sky and listening to the cicadas as they droned out messages to each other.

"You see that light last night? Down on my side of the bay? I watched it for several minutes. First it was off, then on, then off again. I couldn't tell what it was, but that's the third time I've seen it in the last two weeks."

"A light you say? No, I'm usually in bed by eleven. Maybe some fishermen. Some of 'em like to night fish using lanterns and flashlights. Probably something like that."

He picked up his batteries and went out to his cart. *Not night fishing. That's someone sending signals. Better make a couple of calls.*

He returned to the lighthouse and upon arrival heard Solana and Molly talking out on the breezeway.

"I've boiled these utensils for thirty minutes. That long enough?"

"That really wasn't necessary, Solana. Pick up the thread using the suture remover and pull the stitches out slowly."

Solana smiled. "Molly, I've removed stitches many times. You hold still now and we'll get this done."

The stitches came out easily. Molly's head had been shaved in the area where stitches were needed and new hair was already sprouting.

Solana unwrapped the gauze and bandage from Molly's wrists next. They, too, had healed, leaving a thin scar on each wrist.

Solana held her breath as she removed the last bandage, the one on Molly's cheek. The incision had been perfectly executed, and the letter "S" was carved with the precision of a surgeon. But this wound was far from healed.

"Let me look, Solana. That's been the most painful one of all."

Solana stepped back, knowing Molly would look no matter what she said. Molly brought the hand-held mirror closer. Surely what her reflection revealed couldn't be true.

"No! No!" she screamed as she fell to her knees.

"Oh, why would he do that? I'll have this scar the rest of my life! No!" She looked at Solana who fought back tears as she knelt and put her arms around Molly.

The bone-chilling scream had Jack on his feet. Racing to the breezeway. His heart pounded and his mind reeled.

Molly was on the floor leaning into Solana's arms and holding a small mirror in her hand. No words were necessary. Jack understood without her telling him.

"Papa? Oh, Papa!" Her eyes searched his face as if he might have an explanation that would help her comprehend this situation, this unbelievable ordeal.

"We'll deal with it, Molly Mac. We'll deal with it." He pulled her up, held her close, and let her cry on his shoulder . . . until she was done.

Finally. Maybe now we can get somewhere, he thought.

~ ~ ~

This morning Jack didn't feel a whole lot better than he had last night. He was up long before Solana arrived and was on his third cup of Cuban coffee.

Solana took one look at him and before he'd finished his coffee she'd served him scrambled eggs, bacon, toast, and sliced mango.

"And don't tell me you're not hungry. Eat it anyway." And he did eat most of it. He had a lot to do and needed the strength to complete his tasks.

Molly joined him but only wanted coffee. Even Solana's coaxing couldn't get her to eat. After only one cup she announced she was going back to Keeper's Cottage.

"I think I'll read for a while," she said as she walked away.

Jack picked up his pipe, filled it to the brim, tamped it down with a skill developed over many years, then lighted it.

He spoke quietly to Solana as she cleared the table. "Every evening, just before she retires, she asks me three questions: 'Papa Jack, has Lieutenant Collins called yet?

Have they caught him . . .the man who attacked me?' Any mail for me?"

"And every evening I answer: 'Not yet, Molly Mac, not yet.' That answers all three questions."

He sighed and looked out the window at the ocean. Always the ocean. "I think I'll ask Patrick to talk to her. He's had training in this area. Hate to admit I'm at the end of my rope, but I believe I am."

Solana was really concerned now. She'd never known Captain Jack to give up on anything.

He's not himself. Maybe if I can convince Molly to use her medical skills on him he might feel better. She might feel better, too, if she'd stop thinking only about herself and give a little thought to some other folks.

Jack was back on his radio again, this time rattling off numbers and letters so fast Solana took herself back to the kitchen to escape the chatter. Something was happening and she feared what might be coming next.

A knock at the door followed by a booming voice announced Patrick's arrival. "Anybody up and about?"

"Ah, you must have ESP, my boy. I was just about to drop by your place," said Jack.

"Yeah? What's up?" Patrick went to the kitchen, poured himself a cup and joined Jack outside. The ocean was such a draw that everyone migrated there no matter the time of day. Another plus was smelling Jack's tobacco smoke. Patrick had given up cigarettes a few years ago but still enjoyed sniffing Jack's pipe residue.

"You're not gonna ask me to sit with that untrained, wild mutt again are you?"

Jack smiled. "No, but I'm at a loss as to how to help Molly. She's crawled so deep into that shell I can't reach her."

"Jack, I have absolutely no experience with women who've been attacked. I can comfort the oldsters who've lost their mates but I've not dealt with this kind of problem."

"Just give it a try. That's all I'm asking."

"I'll try, but don't expect any miracles."

Molly didn't come out again that day. She stayed in Keeper's Cottage and Solana took her a dinner tray. A tray that remained untouched.

~ ~ ~

Each morning Molly took her place on the lounge close to the water, beneath the banyan tree. She tried to keep her mind off the throbbing ache in her cheek, but it was useless.

Yes, she would see a plastic surgeon. But it would be weeks before he'd be able to make a reasonable assessment, and she knew the possibility of her cheek ever looking normal again was slim.

This morning the loud voices told her Patrick had arrived. Molly wondered if perhaps Patrick filled some of the emptiness Papa felt with the loss of her father, his son, Tom. She'd not thought of that until just now. But then she hadn't thought of anyone but herself for some time.

Patrick came through the door and, as with the spiral staircase, he'd learned to duck his head through the doorways too. That was, after a few hard knocks.

"Something interesting up that tree?" he called.

"Huh? Oh, no. I was just wondering how it continues to grow even though it's quite old."

Patrick lowered his large body down on the nearest rattan chair and continued chatting. "Don't know anything about banyan trees. Having been a priest for some years, I don't know much about anything at all." They both chuckled.

Patrick let his conscience guide his questions. He knew she'd not listen to any "priestly platitudes." He had an inkling he'd been in this same place Molly found herself . . . once upon a time.

"The thing I do know a lot about is wounds. Not in the sense you, a physician, know. But from a different perspective. Some wounds heal quickly. Others take longer. And no amount of medication will speed the process."

Molly smiled at him. "Do you speak from personal experience?"

"Oh, maybe."

"At our graduation ceremony, Dr. Cajina made a statement that I found disturbing. But now I see he must have been speaking from his own experiences."

"Why disturbing?"

"He said, 'Your life will change today and tomorrow. Change is inevitable. Don't fight it, but rather, embrace it. It's how we move forward.'"

Patrick smiled, "Not sure, but I think there's something in the Bible about that. But it's true, you know. Change is inevitable. The key is to embrace the change and make it work for you rather than letting it define you."

"Change is difficult for some. I'm one of those. I feel like I'll never be the same and perhaps my wounds may never heal in the sense you're referring to."

Patrick ran his hands through his hair then stared at his feet as if thinking carefully before speaking.

"What is the one common denominator in wounds that have difficulty healing, Dr. McCormick?" asked the priest.

"Most of the time it's an underlying problem, perhaps an infection. An issue that hasn't been dealt with yet."

Patrick raised an eyebrow to her. "Amen. End of sermon." There was nothing more to be said.

He stood then, indicating he was about to leave. "Jack and I are going over to one of the outer islands on Sunday. Want to come along?"

"Why are you going to the outer islands? Do people live there?"

"Yes, quite a few people live on those islands. I go about once a month and we have a celebration."

"A celebration? You mean a feast of some kind?"

Patrick smiled, "Not that kind. I celebrate the Eucharist with them. Many have immigrated from Catholic countries and the Eucharist has meaning for them. I take it to them as I'm still allowed that privilege even though I'm on sabbatical."

Did she dare take a first step? Try to reengage in life? There was still much fear and anxiety. But she knew she couldn't continue as she had been.

"Yes, I think maybe . . . yes. What time do we leave?"

"Early. Takes most of the day."

"All right. See you early."

Patrick took his leave and walked to his bungalow. But his mind was still back at the lighthouse. Back where he'd left Molly. He was astonished at how attractive he found her.

She gave you her undivided attention when you spoke and intelligence oozed from every pore. When he was talking with her, she had lifted her chin and turned her head sideways. As if deciding whether or not to take his word as gospel, or whether she might challenge him.

Hmm. Interesting. Maybe not as "acquiescing" as Jack seems to think. I'd like to spend more time with her.

A little voice that he hadn't heard in a while whispered in his ear. *Be careful what you wish for, Father O'Brien. You're still a priest. At least at the moment.*

~ ~ ~

When Patrick departed, Molly thought about their conversation. What could he know about wounds? Such an unexpected man. With unexpected ideas. She turned her head then and caught a glimpse of color some distance away.

A small person was walking up from the beach. It was a female from all outward appearances. Wearing a long, island-print dress. Was it a young girl? She was quite small. The closer she came, though, Molly could tell she was an adult, perhaps middle-aged or older. Some yards behind her a small, dark child with long hair followed. Without any fanfare the tiny woman approached Molly.

"You be his granddaughter. I know. I see you in lagoon. Somethin' in water comin' for the Cap'n. Maybe comin' for you too. Dark water . . . dark."

Before Molly could respond, the tiny woman turned back in the direction from which she came, a long scarf billowing in the wind behind her. Grabbing at the child's hand, she dragged him along, mumbling to herself.

Solana hurried out the minute she saw Queenie. "Solana, who was that strange-looking little woman?"

"That's Queenie. Don't pay her any mind. She's not quite right in her head. She's always seeing stuff in that lagoon behind her bungalow. Her visions never amount to anything. Just ignore her."

"That child with her . . . who does he or she belong to?"

"Don't know. He's just appeared lately."

"Oh, it's a boy? I couldn't tell. The long hair made me think of a girl, I guess."

"Yeah, a boy. Queenie came yesterday looking for Captain Jack and that child was with her. I sent her on her way. Don't need her bothering the Captain."

~ ~ ~

Early the next morning Captain Jack left as soon as Solana arrived. "I'll be gone all day. Don't know what else we can do for Molly. Just be with her, I suppose."

"Molly's a smart young woman, Captain. Give her a little time. She'll figure things out. I know you got business to take care of. I hear that radio all day. Go do whatever it is you need to do."

Jack said goodbye, then sped along in his Cobra, arriving at Placida mid-morning. He'd sent a message to Bear Bowen the evening before and the admiral was waiting for him, sitting at the helm of his own craft, a 32-foot Sport

Fisherman which was quite a spectacular specimen with its mahogany and cedar hull.

Jack boarded, taking the cup of coffee Bear handed him. The two old mates talked quickly. No small talk, just business.

"Just what I expected. They're carrying weapons. My bet is they're supplying the rebels in Cuba. But where are the weapons coming from? When I saw them, they'd already loaded the boat, which leads me to believe the weapons must be coming from somewhere close by, maybe from over this way."

"Yeah, but where? Actually, Casper, there's a bigger problem. Rifles and arms are one thing. Chemical weapons are another."

"What? You think they're carrying chemical weapons, too?"

"Intelligence out of Washington indicates that might be the case. There's a lot of activity in the Gulf right now. We've got to find out who's supplying them and where these chemical weapons are being stored."

"Any idea exactly what kind of chemical weapons?"

"There's a warehouse in Tampa. It's where the military stockpiled various chemical weapons that were left over from World War I and World War II. It's not guarded very well as the chemicals stored there are no longer used. They've been banned for use. It seems that the contents of a boxcar of sulfur mustard have disappeared.

"Disappeared. You mean missing?"

"Yep. It's my bet that the rebels have stolen the sulfur mustard from that boxcar and are moving it in small containers to their contacts in Cuba. They can turn it into mustard gas with little trouble and disperse it in many ways."

"Now we do have a problem."

Jack left the dock, headed back to Cayo Canna. He'd been fairly sure there were weapons on *El Escorpión*. But chemical weapons could be hidden much easier than guns and ammo. And the danger they posed was infinitely greater.

He was bone tired by the time he arrived at his dock behind the lighthouse. The trip to Baltimore, the mental stress of the situation with Molly, and this worry now of chemical weapons was taking a toll.

After a hot shower, he sat for a few minutes on the patio. Then he stepped over to Keeper's Cottage where Molly was sleeping soundly in her room . . . with the door ajar.

She's afraid. She never did that even as a child. Keeper's Cottage was a safe refuge for her.

It pained his heart and ignited a renewed promise to find her attacker. He'd wait patiently for the Baltimore police to do their job, but if he hadn't heard from them in a reasonable amount of time the former intelligence "spy" would make his own investigation. *Casper* would re-engage.

After taking Ensign for his last wee, Jack climbed the spiral. The pup had already learned to whine until Jack would pick him up and place him on the foot of the bed.

"So much for instilling discipline early on," Jack grumbled. But they both liked the arrangement.

Chapter 26

Sunday morning rolled around and Jack was pleased Molly was going to accompany him and Patrick to one of the outer islands. It was a big step for her, getting away from the lighthouse and Keeper's Cottage for a day.

With the removal of the sling and the stitches from her head, that only left the bulky bandage on her cheek. That wound was still healing.

Outwardly, she appears to have recovered . . . mostly . . . but I know that girl. She's still fearful and anxious. Damn that idiot who attacked her! She was finally doing what I've been telling her to do all her life. Letting her light shine. But now her light's been extinguished. Like the one in my old lantern. And I don't know how to light it again.

Jack felt a responsibility to help a granddaughter who'd had the rug pulled out from under her. And then there was Patrick. How was he going to help him? The young priest was struggling with a problem and Jack still didn't know what that problem was. He thought it was something to do with the Church, but Patrick still hadn't divulged any information. Why else would he be taking time off? He'd called it a "sabbatical" but Jack knew it was more than that.

The two men readied the boat and Molly, clad in a pair of Mimi's Bermuda shorts and a nautical-looking navy blue blouse, appeared at the dock. Solana had insisted on her taking a sun hat, but Molly quickly jerked it off. Her head was still too sensitive to wear anything.

As soon as Jack turned the ignition switch, the Cobra came to life and they were underway. Molly experienced a moment of delight when her hair began blowing in the wind, the sun glinting on a few blond streaks in the deep auburn. When on duty in the hospital, her hair had to be pinned up off her shoulders. Today there were no hairpins, no starched uniform and no lab coat—just freedom.

They docked at the first island and Patrick dug into a canvas bag he'd brought with him. He pulled his cotton T-shirt over his head, revealing a surprisingly fit, muscular chest. And unlike the hair on his head, the hair on his chest had no grey strands.

Molly was spellbound as she watched Patrick fish out a short-sleeved, black shirt—a shirt without a wrinkle anywhere— and pull it over his head. He then attached a crisp white collar. Reaching back inside the bag, he retrieved a long green stole, brought it to his lips, kissed it gently, then draped it around his neck. Lastly, he brought out a simple gold cross on a long gold chain. He kissed the cross and placed it around his neck along with the stole. The transformation was complete.

Molly was sure her mouth had dropped open. In a matter of minutes, Patrick had gone from a barefoot, disheveled beach bum to a drop-dead, handsome, dignified Catholic priest.

She'd studied anatomy, physiology, genes, and chromosomes, and knew genetics were responsible for these enticing physical characteristics on display in front of her. But there was something incongruous about what she saw here. No priest should look like this.

Papa stepped onto the dock and held out his hand to Molly. "This is how I spend a Sunday now and then. Figure it can't hurt and might help. Margaret would approve." He smiled and stepped aside to let Patrick lead the way. This was his show. Jack was just a lowly seaman in this setting.

Molly followed Patrick and shortly found herself in the middle of a small crowd of people. Some were speaking accented English but there were several other languages thrown into the babel also. That Father Patrick was well-known and received was obvious.

He knelt to speak to a young girl sitting on a makeshift chair, a tree trunk. Her foot had been wrapped with several large, broad leaves, and tied with a fibrous string.

"Hello, CoCo. How's your foot? Better?"

"Better, Father Patrick. Soon I can walk again. Mamacita says so."

Father Patrick made his way through the throng to the platform at the front of the meeting hall—the meeting hall being a thatched roof held up by large poles made from the trunks of palms.

Molly and Papa took seats on two palm stumps at the rear of the room. She was surprised to see such a large group gathered in the hall.

Some oldsters sat together in the front. Molly guessed that was so they could hear better. And the most surprising sight of all was the number of children. Eight or ten youngsters, from infants up to teenagers, were darting here and there, finding a friend to sit with.

Just as he had undergone a transformation with the donning of his black shirt and collar, the moment Patrick stood at the front of the meeting hall a hush fell over the crowd. And the hall became as elegant as any cathedral. A transformation happened here as well. The celebration had begun.

His voice, deep and comforting, faded into the background and became a soothing drone for Molly and she focused her attention on the people.

After she'd made her initial visual tour, she looked more closely. This time Molly, the recovering granddaughter of Papa Jack, stepped aside and Molly McCormick, M.D., stepped in.

In a few short minutes, she had identified one person who'd had a stroke, three oldsters with swollen calves (insufficient cardiac circulation), and two of those had cataracts as well. One small boy limped along as he tried to keep up with the other children who ran to the front and sat on the ground.

One older man had separated himself from the others. Molly thought it odd that he was wearing long sleeves and long pants. She took a look at his face. It was covered in sores. No doubt the others had deemed him contagious and thus he sat apart.

But was he contagious? What was his condition? Molly could hardly keep herself seated. Perhaps it was something as simple as impetigo, common in these islands. She leaned over and whispered to Papa.

"Do these islanders not have any medical care? I see some who need attention."

"Medical care? Here? No. Most have come here to escape a ruthless dictator or trying to find a better life. There are a few who are probably running from the authorities, too. Don't forget about those."

"But, Papa. Look at them. The little boy with the limp, up front on the left side of the room. Is he crippled, or does he just need a brace for his leg? And that young girl Patrick spoke to. Did you see her foot? It was twice it's normal size. It's most likely infected, and if something's not done she could lose it."

Papa nodded. He had no answers to these questions. His mind was still on the Cuban problem. He needed to gather more information, find out more, but he just didn't have the energy. Maybe tomorrow. Today he would let Patrick celebrate with these people and then get back to the lighthouse and listen. Maybe there would be some radio traffic that would tell him something.

Molly watched and listened. She understood now why Patrick would go to this much trouble, coming all the way over and dressing in his "raiment." These people were important to him, and he to them.

Patrick all but whispered his final prayer and the celebration ended. The three walked back to the dock. As Jack started the Cobra and began to pull away from the island, the villagers stood at the water's edge and waved until the boat was out of sight.

As the people waved, the small hermit crab that had taken up residence in that place where Molly had hidden her dreams and wishes, began to send out a few feelers . . . slowly . . . just to make sure nothing dangerous was lurking about before he ventured farther out.

Jack called out, "Here, Patrick. Take the helm. Think I'll sit awhile. If you're serious about getting a boat, then you need to rack up some hours behind the helm."

"Aye, Cap'n" smiled Patrick as he saluted his friend. "Still thinking about it. Not sure yet." They were close to home when he pulled back on the throttle and came to a slow crawl.

He looked over at Molly. "This is Crabber's Cove. I live just a short distance from here. This is the best bay for swimming if you ever feel so inclined. The lighthouse doesn't provide much in the way of privacy."

"I agree. As a kid I never minded people watching, but now I think this might be a better place. Thanks for pointing it out."

Molly turned to Papa Jack. "Papa, do you still keep binoculars on board?"

"What kind of question is that? Of course, I do. Pay attention, Patrick. Binoculars always on board." He reached under the seat and brought out his Steiner, Military/Marine binoculars and handed them to Molly.

"There's a boat in the far corner of the cove. Do you know that man? The one standing on the bow? Looks like he's bringing something up from the water. Some kind of container," Molly said.

"I don't know him, but he's been moored here for a couple of months now. Most likely a snowbird down for the winter," responded Patrick.

Papa motioned for Molly to hand the binoculars to him. He looked carefully, then handed them back to her. "He's got a couple of rods and a huge antenna. And there's a logo of some sort. Can't quite make out what it is. Here, Molly, see if you can see that logo on the port side."

Molly took her time as she scanned the boat. She'd seen this logo before, but couldn't remember what it represented.

"It's a small yellow rectangle. That's it. No letters, no words. Just a rectangle. It looks familiar, but I can't remember where I've seen it."

Jack nodded. Apparently, the man on the boat had seen them as he threw up his hand and waved. Molly, watching through the binoculars, was intrigued by what she saw.

Then she spoke, giving the other two a rundown of what she could see. "Average height, maybe 5 feet 10 inches, deeply tanned, cut off shorts, smooth bare chest, very toned, bandana tied around his forehead . . . and wait . . . yes . . . dark hair fashioned in a long braid down his back!"

She continued to watch another moment. "Wait. There's a name on the stern . . . Endeavor II. And he's writing in a journal or notebook."

Patrick started the engine up slowly. "Maybe he's a Game and Fish Commission employee. I read an article in the local paper about our fisheries being all but fished out. People are catching fish out of season and keeping some that should have been thrown back."

"Since when did you keep up with the fishing reports? The only thing I ever see you read is that newspaper.

What is it? The Boston Sun? You have it sent to you?" Jack inquired.

"Yeah, it's a couple of days old when it finally gets here. But it keeps me informed about happenings on the East coast."

"Do you miss your home and your church?" Molly asked, casually.

"Occasionally." He throttled the Cobra, and they were on their way to the lighthouse, spraying saltwater into the air.

Chapter 27

Solana was about to leave for the day when Molly, Patrick, and Jack came walking up the dock. Patrick was carrying his canvas bag and Molly's windblown hair was evidence she'd not worn the sun hat Solana had given her. But there was a healthy glow about her with a bit of sunburn across her nose and cheeks.

Solana called out, "From the looks of you three I believe a bath and a sit down on the patio might be a good idea. Go in and clean up and I'll serve you the paella I made this afternoon."

She eyed the Captain. The dark circles under his eyes appeared even darker today. She'd watched him as he walked in from the dock. He was lagging behind the good father and Molly. Not his usual place. That man always led the way.

After his second helping of Solana's delicious *paella,* Patrick was satiated. Molly's appetite was still minimal and Jack poked at his plate, but only took a couple of bites. When dinner was over, Solana brought out Captain Jack's tumbler of Glenfiddich and Patrick's Jameson. Molly stuck with sangria, having never acquired a taste for any strong alcoholic beverage.

"Molly, could you come in here for a moment?" Solana called from the doorway. Molly had offered to help with the cleanup but Solana wouldn't hear of it. This was her domain and she wasn't about to give up an inch of it. Not even to the Captain's granddaughter.

They walked to the kitchen where Solana pointed to Ensign's food dish. "See that? The food hasn't been touched. And he's hardly gotten out of his basket all day."

Molly got on her knees and placed her hand on Ensign's head. She was no vet, but there was no doubt the puppy was warmer than he should have been. She gingerly picked up his bandaged paw. He had chewed most of the bandage away and his paw was red and swollen.

"Oh, geez. His paw's infected." She felt along the top of it, then around the edges and finally the bottom. When she touched the bottom he cried out, then whimpered, and lay his head back down.

"We'll have to take him back to the vet. My bet is he's got a piece of foreign matter, a bit of shell, or something, lodged in his paw. I'm a doctor but this is a very small puppy who needs the care of someone who knows more about puppies than I do."

"Hmm. There's one other one that needs some help, too. I know it's not my place, but I'm saying it anyway. Molly, I've done all I can to help with your recovery, but it's time you pulled yourself out of your depression and took a look around.

"The Captain isn't a young man any longer. He's lost weight recently and he's not himself. Watch him walk. Slow as a snail. That's not like him. I also noticed he didn't climb that spiral staircase last night. He was asleep on the sofa down here when I arrived this morning. I don't think he had the energy to climb those steps. Something's wrong.

"You need to put that medical training to use. Find out what's going on with him." She tossed her dishtowel on the counter and walked out, headed to her own place.

Molly was stunned for a moment. She looked down at Ensign. It didn't take much thought to come to a conclusion about Solana's comments.

She's right. That paw didn't just become infected today. It had to have been getting worse every day and I never noticed. And Papa? Yes. He's lost weight and he does seem older somehow. Have I been so self-absorbed that I failed to see that? Yes, Molly, yes you have!

Chapter 28

Shortly after Solana left, Patrick stood, indicating he, too, was going.

"Thanks for taking me today. That was quite an experience. Maybe I can go again?" asked Molly.

"Sure thing." Patrick looked over at Jack, now asleep in his chair. "Tell Jack I'll come by tomorrow. Need to have a talk with him. Been putting it off long enough."

Molly headed to Keeper's Cottage where she retrieved her medical bag, then returned to the den and touched Papa's arm lightly.

"Papa, let's get you over here to the sofa. I want to take a look at you."

"What? Why do you want to look at me? You know what I look like, Molly Mac. Older than Methuselah."

"Right. Tell me then, when was the last time you saw Dr. Burns? Does he know about this weight loss? And how long have you been sleeping on the sofa instead of climbing the stairs at night?"

"What? Damn Solana's big mouth. It was only last night. Just went to sleep early and didn't wake up. Nothing wrong with that, Dr. Mac."

Molly applied the blood pressure cuff, arranged her stethoscope, and listened for several minutes.

"Took you long enough. What did you hear?"

"Your heart. Beating as strong as a horse. It might even have been galloping there for a bit."

"And what does that mean?"

"Your pressure's a little high, but nothing to worry about. We've had a busy morning and afternoon. Probably too much excitement for one day."

Papa smirked, "May I go upstairs now, doctor?"

"Just one more thing."

She reached inside her bag and brought out a couple of vacuum tubes and a syringe.

"What the hell is that gear for?"

"I'm going to take a little blood. I want to see what's going on that we can't tell from observation."

"There's no lab on the island, Molly."

"I know that, Papa. I'm going to the mainland tomorrow, anyway. Pretty sure I can find a lab over there somewhere."

"Going to the mainland? What for? I don't think that's a good idea. You're supposed to be recovering, remember?"

"I do. And I am recovered. Solana called me to the kitchen for a reason. Ensign's paw is very swollen. He won't put any weight on it and cried out when I touched it. He needs to go to the vet. I'll take him and you stay here and let Solana fuss over you while I'm gone."

"I'll go with you if you must go."

"No. Please stay here. Besides, Patrick said he's coming by tomorrow. Something important he wants to talk to you about."

"Did he say what?"

"No, but he borrowed your golf cart. Said he usually walks but it's late and he was ready for bed."

"Borrowed it, huh? Hope he doesn't get caught. It has no lights!" He laughed.

She really did need to get this blood to the lab. She had no idea what was wrong, but his pulse rate was concerning, his blood pressure was elevated, and she didn't like the fact that he fell asleep in his chair. So unlike him.

152

~ ~ ~

Patrick found his way home but it was a struggle. He was sure he was going to run into a tree or shrub. He would talk with Jack about installing some lights on this cart. Of course, consuming a little less Jameson before driving might be a good idea also.

This morning he drove along, staying as close to the edge of the road as possible. Jack had told him some residents were complaining that golf carts were making it dangerous for others traveling on foot.

Patrick looked out over Crabber's Cove. The boat with the yellow rectangle was still anchored out. This morning a small dinghy was puttering to shore, so he slowed to get a glimpse of this snowbird who'd been here for two months.

The dinghy came to a sputtering stop and the driver stepped out, tied the craft to a mangrove shrub and came ashore. Patrick wasn't sure at first if it was a man or a woman. The long dark hair streaming down his back said woman, but the muscled biceps said definitely male.

He wore a t-shirt, shorts, a printed, folded bandanna around his head, and leather boat shoes much like those Patrick wore, that is before he had to trash them after Ensign baptized them with his own version of holy water.

Patrick came to a stop and got off the cart, making his way to greet the stranger. "Good morning. I've been admiring your boat for some time. It's a beauty. What make is it?"

"It's a Mako, 1960 model, re-outfitted for aquatic research."

"Like the looks of it. How does it handle?"

"It moves along quickly and rides on top of the waves. Great for my work."

"I see." Patrick reached out his hand. "Patrick O'Brien." He was just slightly taller than this stranger and a bit heavier.

"Koiko-Tadi Redhawk," replied the man, offering his hand as well.

"Koi?? Ta??"

"Call me Todd. Todd Redhawk."

Patrick looked closer. The man's skin was not just tanned, it was the color of warm taffy, and his eyes were so dark they seemed to lack a pupil. High cheekbones and a nose, thin and straight as a shark fin, completed the picture.

Jaysus. Looks like a tanned Adonis. With long hair.

"Where you headed? On foot, too," Patrick asked.

"Need a few items from the grocery. I usually walk over and get enough to last a few days."

"Hop on. I'll give you a lift."

"Thanks. This thing could come in handy. Where'd you get it?"

"It's not mine. It belongs to Captain Jack, a friend. I usually walk everywhere or ride my bike. But it was late when I left the lighthouse last night, so I borrowed his cart."

"The lighthouse? You know who lives there?"

"Yeah. Captain Jack McCormick and his granddaughter, Molly, live there. He's been a friend some years now and we visit occasionally."

"His granddaughter lives with him?"

"At the moment. She's a physician. She had an accident recently and is down here recovering."

"A physician? Not many of those around these islands."

"No, there's not even one on Cayo Canna. You have to go to the mainland for medical care. Unless you want Queenie to perform one of her magical rituals and say some *voodoo* words over you." He laughed when he saw the expression on Todd's face.

"She's harmless. Just irritating. She shows up without notice and delivers one of her 'visions' from the lagoon."

"Sounds interesting." Todd smiled, revealing perfect, white teeth.

Of course. They're perfect. Like everything else about him.

Patrick wheeled into the sandy, crushed-shell parking lot next to Bailey's Island Grocery.

Agnes smiled when she saw Patrick. "Ah, Father. Good day to you. What do you need today? Mail or groceries?" Agnes then noticed the man next to him.

"And good morning to you, Todd. You need a few things, I gather?"

"Hi, Agnes. Yeah. I'm down to nothing but peanut butter and jam. Don't even have a loaf of bread."

These two were obviously on good terms. Patrick went on about his shopping, picking up a large can of bug spray and a couple of citronella candles.

"This will do me, Agnes." He left money on the counter and was headed out when Agnes called to him. "Father, would you take this letter to the lighthouse? Looks like it's been forwarded from Baltimore. Addressed to Dr. M. McCormick. I assume that's the Captain's granddaughter. He sometimes forgets to check his mail when he comes in."

Patrick pocketed the letter and went outside where Todd joined him shortly and they headed to the cove.

"Thanks for the lift. I'm sure we'll see each other again. I'm still here for a while longer yet."

"My pleasure. Take care now."

Chapter 29

¡ Dios mío! You want us to move that deadly stuff? You know what it can do to a body? No. We can't transport that stuff. Not in a boat. I read about sulfur mustard, how they make it into a gas. If it spills on you it makes blisters and then you can't breathe. No. Moving guns is one thing. Moving that stuff is something else. We can't take that in our boat, *Jefe*." Roberto's fear now overrode his usually quiet, acquiescing manner.

"I travel with it often, Roberto. It's not dangerous in this liquid form. You just gotta pay attention to not spill it on yourself. It's the perfect weapon. It doesn't kill outright but the people will be very sick and won't be able to function. The military personnel at the bases will be unable to do their jobs. The men on the ships. . . they'll all need help. . . the ships won't be able to move about in the Gulf.

"We've got to get it to the rebels, the real fighters. They can then process it and turn it into a sulfur mustard gas, load it into the missiles, or spray it from the planes. That's what makes it so great. It can be used in many ways."

Carlos looked to *Jefe,* then to Elian and back to Roberto, who stood perfectly still. Seeing Roberto was not going to cooperate, Carlos chimed in. "I don't like it either, Roberto. But we'll only have to make this one run with the sulfur stuff."

Roberto held his tongue as long as he could, then spoke up again. "I didn't sign on for this, *Jefe*. You could hurt thousands of people with that stuff. It might not kill them, but it can blind them, eat away at their bodies. Especially old ones and *bambinos*. Do you want that on your conscience? Fighting for the Revolution and our beliefs is good. But this . . . this stuff . . . carrying it in our boat . . . that's not good."

Jefe stared at Roberto, smiled at him, walked over and put an arm around his shoulders. "You have a good point, *amigo*. We can all be of service to our country in many ways, but we should follow our conscience, as you say. You sit this transit out. There are other jobs you can help with."

It appeared Carlos and Elian would make the sulfur mustard run. They weren't keen on performing this task either, but it would only be one time.

"We'll move the sulfur mustard soon. We have to be careful of our timing and it must appear that you are fishing as usual. We don't want the Coast Guard getting too close.

"There's less traffic in the Gulf on weeknights so that might be a good time. With the old man out of the way, no one else will have knowledge of what we're carrying in *El Escorpión*.

"When you've left your cargo, get back here to the shack. Stay hidden until I come for you. And you, Roberto, visit your *Tia* Solana. Who knows, you might learn something about the old seaman that may help us."

Chapter 30

Solana walked up the steps of her bungalow. It was quite cozy, with a few pictures of family back in Cuba—those she would probably never see again—a couple of Captain Jack's paintings she had convinced him would look great in her place, and a few pieces of pottery her great-grandfather had created long ago. Family photos, the Captain's paintings, and her pottery. These were her treasures.

As she started to enter, a voice behind her called out from the dark. "*Tia! Tia* Solana!" Roberto hurried over to her.

"Roberto? What are you doing here this time of night? You have a job to go to tomorrow morning. You ought to be getting yourself ready for bed. You do still have a job at the fish house? A job is hard to find. Tell me you didn't lose it."

"No, *Tia*. I just wanted to talk to you for a few minutes. That's all."

Solana had sent him funds to come to Cayo Canna a few months ago. He was the only son of her sister, Mercedes, who died after a long illness. His father had been long gone, so Solana was his only family.

Castro was getting rid of families right and left, and Solana knew her nephew was not safe there any longer. With her help, he had managed to get himself here.

"Come, we'll chat for a while, then you get yourself back to your place. That fish house opens early." Solana read his body language and was sure he had something to say. She'd spent a lifetime reading what the body said that differed from what the lips might utter.

"Hungry?"

"*Sí, Tia.*"

"Then we'll have some sangria and *tapas*. We'll talk and then you must get yourself home and to bed." She set out two small glasses and a plate of *tapas*.

Roberto took a deep breath, "I need to ask you something, *Tia,*" he said, looking about, unable to make eye contact with her. Solana raised her eyebrows, then gave him a half-smile. "What's bothering you, Roberto?"

"I know it was a long time ago, but Mamá, just before she died, told me the story of how the two of you were with the guerrillas—Fidel, Raul, and Che—when the Revolution first started. She said you were the *corazón* (sweetheart) of Che . . . or was it Fidel? I forget.

"She said you were very brave and helped her get back home when the fighting was terrible and she was too sick to continue. Then you came here to this island. Did you no longer believe in the Revolution? Or Fidel?"

"Roberto, that was a long time ago. Things were different then. I thought Fidel and Che would help our country, save our people. I was wrong. I helped Mercedes because she could never survive in that environment. With help from Che, I managed to get her home.

"As I traveled through the villages, I saw how our people were being treated, their homes taken, their families destroyed by the very rebels I was a part of.

"Once I got Mercedes settled in a place of safety, at least at the time, I knew I must leave Cuba. It was a difficult time for all our people. My story is no different than a thousand others. I was just one of the lucky ones who got out."

"But, the Revolution? Do you no longer believe in it?"

"I believe some men have grand ambitions. Some seek personal glory and their greed leads them to make decisions that prove to be disastrous to many.

"Fidel and Che lost their way. They forgot to put their people first. Instead, they became obsessed with power and position. I no longer wanted to belong to them.

"Mercedes should never have told you. It is the past, my past. It belongs to me only." She rose then, picked up the dishes, and looked directly at Roberto.

"Never speak to me of this again."

"*Sí, Tia.* But, did you not feel you were letting your *compadres* down? By not continuing to support the Revolution?"

Solana returned to the table. "What are you talking about? What are you involved in?" She'd not forgotten how engaging and exciting working with the "revolutionaries" had been. She felt her pulse beating in her temples. What had this foolish young man gotten himself into?

"There are some *hombres. Hombres* that I know. They are helping with the Revolution, *comprendes?*"

Before he got any farther, Solana stopped him.

"Listen to me, Roberto. There is much trouble in our country. Fidel's power has grown. He is very dangerous. You must not participate in any of the Revolution's activities. You hear me?"

"*Sí.* I have helped some, doing small jobs, like taking guns to the rebels. But now I no longer wish to work with them. They are dangerous. And *Jefe?* I think he is planning something big. Something to hurt a lot of people. I told him I would not work with them. But I feel I am letting them down."

Solana went to her bedroom and pulled a small rectangular box from beneath her bed. Opening it up, she brought out a roll of bills. Six hundred dollars to be exact. Her heart ached as she realized this money, this gift, would take her nephew to some unknown place and she may never see him again. But she also knew what would happen if he stayed here on Cayo Canna.

"If you have helped them and now refuse, they will kill you, Roberto. I know how they think. They will no longer trust you. You must listen to me!"

"But, *Tia. Jefe* understood. He was not angry at me."

Solana shook her head. "You must leave as soon as possible. Here, take this money and hire a boat to take you to Fort Myers. Don't take the ferry. Someone might see you. Once you get to Fort Myers, take a bus across to Miami."

Solana pulled him close then, taking care to hold back her tears. Now was not the time for that. That would come later. She must protect him now.

"When you get to Miami, go to Little Habana. Find *Padre* Francis, tell him to send a message to this radio call sign. Just say 'all is well.' I will know what that means. She quickly wrote down K4ELD on a small sheet of paper and stuck it in his shirt pocket.

"Go now, my dear *niño*. Go now."

Roberto walked to the door, looking like a child who didn't understand what was being asked of him. He took one last look at *Tia* Solana then disappeared into the night.

Solana fell to her knees—a long-forgotten gesture—but one she felt a need to assume at this moment.

Chapter 31

Roberto ran all the way to the bungalow he shared with Carlos. It was late, but something about *Tia* Solana's voice, the way it shook when she spoke. She knew about these things. About people like *Jefe.*

Carlos was lying on his bunk, smoking one of his foul-smelling, Cuban cigarettes. Roberto pulled out five twenty-dollar bills and waved them in front of Carlos' face.

"I'll pay you a hundred dollars to take me to the mainland. I'm going to Miami. I don't like this business about the sulfur mustard. Think I'll find another job at another fish house. Probably lots of those in Miami."

Carlos sat up and tried to jerk the bills from Roberto's fingers, but missed. "Where'd you get a hundred dollars?"

"I've got a lot more than that. I've saved it up for a long time. I'll give you a hundred and that leaves me five hundred. Enough to get by until I get a job."

Roberto had stuck the other five hundred under the lining of his tennis shoes. He was savvy enough not to trust Carlos and figured he'd try to take it all if he knew where he'd put it.

Carlos grinned at him. "Let's hurry. We'll take *El Escorpión,* but I need to be back here before Elian comes by tomorrow morning. He's like a mother hen when it comes to "his" boat. It's not his. It belongs to *Jefe's* friend in Placida. He's got more money than *Jefe* has ever seen. C'mon."

They hurried down the dock where *El Scorpión* was moored. Carlos retrieved the key from beneath the seat and had them flying across the water. He loved being behind the helm, which Elian only allowed when absolutely necessary.

The ocean was calm, making their crossing easy. When the outline of the marina could be seen in the distance, Carlos called out, "Here, take the helm. I gotta take a leak."

Roberto stepped forward and put both hands on the wheel. He'd never been allowed to drive the boat. This was a new thrill.

Carlos reached under the canvas cover laying on the stern and pulled out his weapon. Without a moment's hesitation, he pulled the trigger and Roberto's body was riddled in a frenzy of bullets. The young man never made a sound, just slumped forward, his body draping over the wheel.

"Stupid. How can anyone be so stupid?" Carlos rammed his hand into Roberto's right front pocket. A hundred dollars was folded inside. But that was all he found.

"Where did you put the rest?" He searched the other pocket. Nothing. "You lied. You never had any more money," he grumbled as he lifted Roberto's body and heaved it overboard.

"*Lo siento, amigo. Jefe's* instructions were to get rid of you." He gave the throttle a hard push forward and *El Escorpión* was out of sight before Roberto's body even had time to sink.

Carlos kept the throttle wide open and was back on Cayo Canna before anyone knew he'd been gone. He'd followed orders and the task was done. Maybe now *Jefe* would see how dependable he was.

Chapter 32

The sun was barely yawning but Molly was up and about. Papa Jack was making coffee and she was glad to see him up. Last night she wasn't sure what today might bring but was anxious for Solana to show up.

Papa handed her a cup, "doctored" as she liked it, cream with a hint of sugar. "Thanks, and I have a cup for you as well." She handed him a small plastic container with a lid.

"I need a urine sample, please. About four ounces will do," she smiled. Jack took the cup. "Next, you'll want me to parade around in a gown that shows my ass," he grumbled. A few minutes later he brought her a urine sample and she put it on ice with her blood specimens.

"I don't like you going to the mainland by yourself. You've still got some healing to do, Molly Mac."

"Papa, I'm doing fine. It's been a month now. Everything is healing well."

"I wasn't just talking about your physical well-being. Some wounds take their own time about healing."

"Papa, this day-to-day existence, not caring if tomorrow comes, it has to stop. I worked hard to become a physician, and I refuse to let an attack by a madman continue to rule my every waking moment."

Papa Jack nodded. "Then get on with your chore for today. Tell Doc Simpson I'll catch him later. And make sure Ensign gets his next round of shots."

"I believe I can handle one small puppy, Papa Jack. Oh, while you were asleep last evening your radio was busy—a lot of traffic. I heard your call sign but decided to let it go and tell you about it this morning. Probably should have answered it, but I think a female voice might have been a bit strange to them."

Solana arrived, shed her shoes, and came in with her basket in hand.

"Good morning," Molly called out. "I'm going over to the mainland today. Taking Ensign to the vet and dropping off some specimens at a lab, if I can find one."

"Specimens? What kind of specimens?"

"I'm having Papa's blood analyzed. It's possible he may be anemic and may need some iron supplements. Just doing what I've been trained to do." She smiled.

She met Solana's eyes and the two women had a moment of unspoken communication. Solana was relieved. She was afraid she may have been too harsh with Molly yesterday. Well, if so, then so be it. It had gotten the girl's attention off herself and onto someone else.

"Then you'd better get a move on. Crab doesn't wait for anyone."

"I'm taking Rafael's cab to the dock," said Molly as she gathered Ensign and her needed items.

As soon as Rafael's cab arrived, Molly got in and sat with Ensign in his basket, her mind in turmoil.

Why have I sat like a weeping willow, wallowing in self-pity for so long? Why did I allow this incident, horrendous as it was, to bring my life to a standstill?

When they arrived at the dock, Rafael stopped the cab, opened the door, and Molly ran the last few yards to the ferry, just before it was to shove off.

"Ah, Missy D*oktor!* Come aboard!"

Crab was surprised to see the young physician. When he'd last seen her she was in rather poor condition. But here she was along with the *Capitán's* young dog, and the only evidence of trauma was a thick bandage on her left cheek.

"You have a traveling companion, *sí*?"

"Yes, this is Ensign. He's headed to the vet again. Needs to be looked at by someone who knows about dogs."

"The Father, he traveled with him last time."

"Right. But today I'm his appointed keeper. He's no trouble. He'll stay in his basket."

Crab smiled and greeted a couple of other passengers before he took his post in the pilothouse.

Molly stepped up to the front of the ferry where Crab's assistant, *Tomás,* was standing, readying the lines for departure.

"Do you think I could use the restroom? Too much coffee this morning."

"Yes, miss. Follow me."

He led Molly to Crab's cabin and she put Ensign's basket down by the door. The bathroom was a tight space with only a toilet. No sink. The only sink was in the cabin itself.

She decided Crab must cook with garlic as the place reeked of it. Her nose then led her to another scent coming from a small crate. This scent she particularly liked. She knew that smell—Papa's tobacco. The crate also held other items of interest . . . a dozen bottles of Glenfiddich were nestled alongside the tobacco pouches.

These must be the orders Papa's been waiting for.

She made her way topside, taking her basket with her. She walked to the pilothouse, then stuck her head in.

"I see Papa's tobacco and his whisky is on board. He'll be happy about that."

"*Sí,* Missy Do*k*tor. His order will be delivered to the pier this afternoon. I think our port officials are falling down on their job. His items have been sitting in their receiving room for a couple of weeks!"

"I let them know how unsatisfactory that is. My people depend on me for their mail and their special orders. I don't like to disappoint them."

When the ferry docked, Molly stepped off quickly. The vet's office was only a couple of blocks from the dock so she walked, carrying her precious cargo. An attendant greeted her and she was taken back to the examining rooms where Doc Simpson waited.

"Ah, Ensign, you're back. What did you attack this time, eh?" This vet had a way with animals and Molly liked him immediately.

"Hi, I'm Molly. Jack McCormick's granddaughter."

"Ah, yes. Heard about you. Jack never comes without telling me your latest triumph. You were about to finish your residency training last I talked with him."

He smiled at the young woman. She had a bandage on her face, but that didn't distract him from her engaging smile and inquisitive eyes.

"He says to tell you he'll catch you next time. He's resting today so I brought Ensign."

After careful examination and a couple of X-rays, the vet agreed with Molly's diagnosis. The pup had a sharp piece of coral lodged deep within his paw and the vet would have to anesthetize him to remove it.

That meant Molly would either have to spend the night or go back to the island and return tomorrow. After a quick call to Cayo Canna to let Papa know the plan, she found a room for the night at one of the motels on the waterfront.

Before she left the Dr. Simpson's office, she got the name and address of a lab close by. A large hospital served the area, and that being the case, a couple of labs were available. One was primarily for use by physicians at the hospital and the police mostly used the other. It was the Coroner's lab.

She tried the hospital lab first, but they were already overworked and understaffed. She knew she'd never get the tests run any time soon.

She walked a block south and found the Coroner's lab. After explaining her situation and presenting her credentials, they agreed to run the labs later today, and she could pick them up tomorrow.

When they realized Molly was from Cayo Canna, they were willing to speed up the process as they were not very busy at the moment. Presently they were waiting around for the next victim.

The next morning she arrived early. It was a few minutes before the lab opened so she sat on a small bench outside the door. Shortly, a man in hospital scrubs came to the door and invited her in.

He was tall, very blond and suntanned, as everyone down here seemed to be. He smiled broadly and held the door for her to enter.

"Good morning. Come in. My lab assistant will be here shortly. But until then, maybe I can help you. Are you identifying a family member or friend?"

"What? Oh no. I'm here to get lab results from some specimens I dropped off yesterday."

"What was the name?"

"McCormick. Jackson McCormick is the patient."

He walked to another room and returned, holding several sheets of paper. "Yeah, I remember these. Not something we see very often."

"What do you mean?"

"We run labs on victims every day and we see a lot of unusual chemicals in their blood work. But what we found in the blood you brought us is a bit puzzling."

"Show me."

"It's not unusual to see an older patient with a decreased white blood cell count and with hemoglobin that's out of ideal range. But some of these results are disturbing."

169

Several results from the blood analysis got Molly's attention. Serum electrolytes . . . elevated; calcium and magnesium levels . . . elevated; blood glucose . . . elevated. But the urine test was even more telling.

The presence of urinary crystals jumped off the page at her. Her face must have registered her thoughts.

"We thought of kidney stones off the bat, but then we saw some other levels that had us checking further. Look at this."

Molly's eyes glued themselves to the paper, never missing a single word or lab value. She looked again at the various lab results, then back again at the urine results. She stared at the man as if he weren't there. She seemed stunned.

"Let me try to explain then, in layman's terms. That might help," he began.

"That's not necessary. I know what I'm looking at. He's one step away from being in full metabolic acidosis. My God, no wonder he feels so tired and listless."

"Are you a chemist or pharmacist?"

"No, I'm a physician."

"I see. Glad to meet you. I'm David, Dr. David Strickland, coroner for Lee County."

"I'm Molly. Dr. Molly McCormick."

"Are you treating this patient? Where's your office?"

"No, not exactly. The patient is my grandfather, Jack McCormick. He lives on Cayo Canna and I'm visiting him for a while. He's not been feeling well, so I thought I'd run some labs and see if there's anything that would shed some light on the situation. But I didn't expect to find this."

"No, of course not. We've still got one vial of blood. I believe if we run a couple more tests we can determine what might be causing such extreme values. Might be able to zero in on the cause."

"That would be very helpful. I'm a visitor; I don't have an office here. In fact, I've just completed my Internal

Medicine Residency Program at Johns Hopkins and am in search of a job."

"Wow. A great institution in which to do a residency." He gave her that brilliant smile again. It seemed incongruous somehow. Here was someone who dealt with dead bodies all day, and had such an outgoing, warm personality. Very alive.

"Give us a little while. We should be finished by noon."

"Thanks. I'll go check on my other patient in the meantime."

"You have another patient?"

Molly laughed quietly. "Well, sort of. It's my grandfather's puppy. He's got a piece of coral lodged in his paw and Dr. Simpson's removing it. I'm hoping to take him back to the island today. He's just a puppy, a black lab. About four months old."

"I've got a Great Dane. A sweet old girl named Tess. She's on borrowed time but I don't have the heart to put her down. Not just yet."

"Yeah. That would be difficult."

"All right then. Come back at noon. We'll see what we can find out." He took the reports and headed to the back.

Molly killed a little time poking about the boutiques along the waterfront where she bought two pairs of sandals that actually fit. She'd been wearing Mimi's, but they were a full size too big.

Next, she stopped at Carla's and ordered a *cortadito*. That sweet, strong Cuban coffee might give her a rush of energy she needed.

She sat at a table by the window, looking out over the water. And for the first time since she had left the hospital, she allowed her thoughts to return to Baltimore.

As she sat there in the warm sunshine, with a light breeze blowing her hair about, returning to Baltimore didn't seem quite as enticing now. This time of year Baltimore would be cold, raw, and icy. And she still didn't have a job.

Just before noon she headed to the vet's office. Ensign was awake but groggy. Doc Simpson stepped in, "He's ready to go. In a few days he'll be running around, chewing on your shoes and peeing on everything in his path. Take him. Tell Jack it's time for a visit."

Molly gathered up Ensign's leash and placed him in his basket, then headed to the coroner's lab. She had just put Ensign on the floor when an attractive, dark-haired young woman came out from the back.

"You must be Dr. McCormick. I'm Kathi Jowers, Dr. Strickland's rad tech. He said you'd be coming by. Come on back."

Dr. Strickland was sitting at his desk. He raked his long fingers through his thick, blond hair and took a deep breath.

"Dr. McCormick, your diagnosis is correct. Your patient is in a state of metabolic acidosis. He's gotta be feeling pretty lousy.

"We see a lot of poisons, insecticides, and overdoses of medications. But this I don't see very often. Actually, I've only seen it once before. In a homeless individual."

"What did you find?"

"Your grandfather is suffering from ethylene glycol toxicity."

"Ethylene glycol toxicity? Ethylene glycol, ethylene glycol . . . that's used in automobiles . . ."

"That's right. Commonly called anti-freeze. Used to prevent radiators from overheating or freezing, depending on the season."

"Antifreeze? But how? How would it get in his bloodstream?"

"He's either inhaled it or ingested it from food or liquids. There are several ways he could have been exposed to it."

Molly was quiet for a few seconds, then cocked her head to one side, as if "weighing" her thoughts.

"Then this would be something he ate or drank or both?"

"Dr. McCormick, we see victims every day. Their bodies are brought to us and we try to figure out what happened to them. I'm sure you don't deal with these situations, but I believe your grandfather has been "poisoned" for lack of a better word."

"But . . . that makes no sense. Papa doesn't have any enemies. He's a bit gruff at times, but he's a kind, thoughtful man. This can't be right."

"These results are correct. Those calcium oxalate crystals are seen in the urine when acidosis or an increased osmal gap is present in the blood.

"He needs to be hospitalized. If he's not treated immediately, it could kill him. My guess is that he's been getting the poison over a long period of time in minimal amounts and that's why it has taken this long to cause problems. Perhaps it's not done so much damage that he can't recover, but it should be taken care of immediately."

"I'm unfamiliar with the treatment for ethylene glycol poisoning. Tell me about it," Molly said.

"Early treatment increases the chance of a good outcome. You have to stabilize the person and give them an antidote. The preferred one is fomepizole. Hemodialysis may also be necessary in those patients where there's organ damage or a high degree of acidosis. Sometimes they're given sodium bicarbonate, thiamine, and magnesium. This isn't a tremendously high degree of acidosis, but any amount is not good."

"Of course not. I'll bring him over tomorrow morning on the ferry, or maybe Patrick can bring us over on the Cobra. That's faster."

Dr. Strickland nodded, "If you like, I'll make arrangements with the hospital. I know most of the docs there."

"Thanks. I'll take Papa to the ER as soon as we get here. I'll be in touch." She gathered Ensign and headed to the door.

"Where are you off to now?"

"Going to get some lunch and catch the ferry back. My patient here still can't ambulate on his own, so I have to carry him."

"How about I buy you a hot dog at the Tiki Hut?"

She almost said no thank you, recalling her earlier experiences with men . . . when she clammed up and looked like an idiot. But he was quite engaging. Maybe they could have a short discussion. Medical issues, of course.

"Don't care for hot dogs but I would relish a great big juicy burger," Molly replied.

"Burger it is." He turned to Kathi and held up one finger. "Be back in an hour."

Leading the way, David started talking as if he'd known Molly for a long time. "We received a body this morning. Kathi's doing a panel of X-rays. We need to know as much about this victim as we can. He can't be more than twenty to twenty-five. Such a waste."

"Do you know what caused his death?"

"Yeah, gunshot. In the back. Which reminds me, I need to call the police and give them a couple of details."

"Such as?"

"Most victims don't show up with a few hundred dollars stuffed in their shoes. They'll be minus anything of value, watch, rings, whatever. But whoever killed him must not have known about the money."

The Tiki Hut was busy. Some people were having a margarita, the specialty of the house, and others were content to have beer. For Molly, a Coke was sufficient and David kept to water.

"How long are you staying on Cayo Canna?"

"I'm not sure. I'll be here a few more weeks at least. It will depend on how Papa does. I've never had a patient with this kind of poisoning. I hope it's not damaged his kidneys or liver."

"He'll be in good hands at Memorial. As I said, the level of poisoning is not extreme. I believe there's a good chance he'll recover.

"Getting your grandfather taken care of is your first priority, certainly. But I don't believe he just decided to drink a little anti-freeze. Someone's been poisoning him for some time. You'll need help finding out who this person is. I don't deal with the criminals, but I do see their victims. This is a matter for the police."

Molly sighed, "I don't even know where to start. It's just so ironic—the situation I find myself in. Having to deal with criminals two times in such a short period."

"How's that?"

"It's complicated. About a month ago I was attacked in Baltimore. In my apartment. That's what brought me to Cayo Canna. Papa insisted I come back with him to recover. And I have, mostly. Still have this facial wound that's taking its time about healing. Other than that, I'm all right." She didn't think she needed to discuss that other wound—abject fear—the one that couldn't be seen.

David said nothing. He'd noticed the bandage on her cheek, but more than that, he'd been drawn to her alabaster skin, the tilted corners of her soft brown eyes, and the small dimple in her right cheek that winked at him when she smiled. She was quite a striking woman. Not beautiful in the usual sense. No, her beauty was unique. And he was quite sure she was unaware of it.

"This attacker, is he warming a prison cell somewhere by now?"

"No. Last time Papa talked with the Baltimore police they hadn't found him. He's still out there."

"At least you're here now, in a safe place."

"Yes. I'm safe here. Papa has always been my refuge. Still is. But now it doesn't look like he's safe."

"As I said, the police will step in now. We have a top-notch investigative team here in Lee County."

He looked down at his watch. "Looks like my hour's up. Kathi will come looking for me if I don't hurry back."

Molly stood and held out her hand. "Again, thank you. Maybe this nightmare will end quickly."

"I'm sure it will. I'll see you again. For sure."

Molly watched him walk away. Something about seeing a man in scrubs was comforting. Perhaps that's why she felt free to talk with him. And that little hermit crab—the one that resided in her brain—sent out a couple more feelers. Even the crab was aware of a certain magnetism that had drifted across the table when David looked at Molly.

The ferry's whistle screamed and Molly boarded, sitting on the forward bench, her mind whirling in every direction.

Papa is ill. Maybe dying! What have I done? I came here to recover from a brutal attack and all the while a much more subtle attack was taking place on him. I failed to see his symptoms. Some physician you are, Molly McCormick.

She prided herself on the fact that she could assess and diagnose patients, perhaps better than most. But she'd never thought of herself as a sleuth. Today, however, that was what she needed to be. Just as she sometimes dug deep to find the cause of a particular disease process, she'd need to turn those skills to finding who was trying to kill Papa.

Chapter 33

Baltimore

The harsh wind blowing off the harbor cut through Sam like a scalpel. He huddled beneath his elegant tweed coat—one he'd found in his father's closet—then hurried inside the back door into the warmth of the kitchen. It was his now, this lovely place that had been his parents' home. Or at least he was taking possession. He'd been unable to get in for a couple of weeks as it had been labeled a "crime scene." But once the police removed the tape, he'd sneaked in after dark and taken up residence.

He was quite set now, financially, with the cash he'd taken from his mother's safe shortly after he killed her. That is, if his drug habit didn't eat it away.

His mother had been his first kill. Very satisfying. Then he'd moved on to Dr. McCormick, a still unfinished piece of business. The next two victims were a piece of cake. But killing them had not been nearly as enjoyable as the time he'd spent with Dr. McCormick.

His last trip to Johns Hopkins had taught him a lesson. Today he cleaned himself up and donned a white physician's jacket borrowed from his late father, along with his name tag. He just needed to ask a few questions, or better yet, find the files on Dr. McCormick. He had waited patiently for several weeks now and she'd not returned to her apartment. Where had she gone?

Today he walked the halls at Johns Hospkins, held a stethoscope in his hands and flipped through a file, then looked up when a young nurse came walking past.

"Ah, Nurse Adams, have you seen Dr. Molly McCormick? I wanted to congratulate her on her graduation but can't find her. Did she move away?"

"Well, sort of. She's gone to Florida, lucky girl. You may not have heard, but she was attacked in her apartment the day she graduated. She was injured and unable to return home so she went to her grandfather's place."

"Florida, you say?"

"Yes, to an island . . . Cayo something. Somewhere near Fort Myers, I think."

"I'm sorry to hear that. She was a good friend. Well, may she heal quickly. I'll see her when she comes back. Thanks." He closed the file and walked toward the stairwell. He now had the information he needed to complete his task. Finishing off the one who had caused him such pain and humiliation.

Chapter 34

Cayo Canna

When Molly left for the ferry, Solana poured Captain Jack another cup of coffee and one for herself. Then she took a seat across from him.

She told him about Roberto's visit, not leaving out any details. She knew if she did Captain Jack would keep at it until he got them all anyway.

"Did he give any names? Rebels he was working with?"

Solana shook her head. "He said his *jefe* was planning something big . . . something he wanted no part of. He was frightened, Captain.

"He's gone. I gave him some money and told him to leave last night. Told him to find someone to take him to the mainland and then to make his way to Miami, to the Cuban section. Father Francis is a priest there. He will help Roberto become a ghost."

Jack nodded. "Apparently you felt it necessary for him to leave immediately."

"Yes, Captain. They will kill him. These young men are committed to the cause. They will not let Roberto live. He was too young to understand how this game is played. He had to leave last night."

"But he didn't tell you anything more. What they are planning or when?"

"No, Captain. I should have asked him questions, but I was frightened when he told me of his involvement with the revolutionaries. I haven't forgotten how ruthless they can be. He probably wouldn't have told me even if he knew what they are planning. He feels he has let his *jefe* down. He still feels some attachment to the other men. They are all young and taken with the "Revolution."

"You're right, Solana. They would kill Roberto if he decided not to go along with them. That was an indication he's not as committed to the cause as they are. Then let's hope he makes it to Little Havana and becomes a ghost. I know a little about that process," he smiled.

She nodded and stood. The best thing for her was to stay busy and ask the good father to pray for Roberto. She'd do so herself, but thought her prayers might not be heard. She'd committed her own transgressions . . . in another life.

As soon as Solana left the room, Jack was on the radio. Her information confirmed what Bear Bowen had told him. This "something big" was probably the chemical weapons that were to be transported.

"K6DNB . . . K6DNB . . . Drifter you there? Over."

The radio was busier than ever. Jack had to take precautions now. Every word would be carefully weighed.

"Drifter here, Casper. You seen my sister yet? Over."

"K6DNB, she's well. Said that old bear found his cubs and she's sure he's gone now. Over."

"Thanks, K4ELD. That's good. She planning on a visit anytime soon? Over."

"Not yet. Said she'd see you sooner than you might think. Says to take care of yourself. Maybe she'll see you at the market. Over."

The static grew noisier.

"K4ELD. K4ELD. You still there?"

"Still here, K6DNB.

180

"Tell her I'll be there. And, Casper, I know I'll only see you if you want me to. Ha Ha! Drifter out."

~ ~ ~

It was late afternoon when Solana heard the golf cart drive up. Sounded like a lawnmower, though not as loud. Today she was glad to open the door to the good father. She needed his help.

"Solana? You still here? It's almost dark. I know I should have brought the cart earlier, but I needed to run several errands and I forgot about the time."

"Come in, Father. Your evening libation is waiting for you. But don't keep the Captain long. He needs to get some rest."

"Everything all right?"

This priest recognized a worried face when he saw one. She was still her quiet, elegant self, but there was an edge to her that was unusual.

"I would ask you to intervene for me, if you will. Please send some prayers for my nephew, Roberto. He needs them."

That was all she said. Then she went to the den where Captain Jack was signing off on his radio. He looked so haggard that Solana felt the first real fingers of fear crawling up her spine.

"Father Patrick's here. I'll lay out supper for you two. On the patio. Then I want you to take these two aspirins and take yourself off to Keeper's Cottage. You stay over there where I can keep an eye on you. You don't need to be climbing that spiral tonight."

"Stop your fussing, Solana. I'm fine. Just bring me those aspirins. Now, you need to be going. It's almost dark. Molly's due any minute."

Jack was too tired to argue with her. For once she was right. He didn't feel like climbing the spiral tonight.

Maybe Molly's right. Might be a little anemic. Iron supplements will take care of that.

He took his aspirin, downing them with a glass of water.

Solana finished the shrimp casserole, made some fresh orange juice for breakfast, and tidied the den. She heard the beating on the front door and before she could answer it, Queenie walked in.

"Where *doktor?* The Captn's girl. She *doktor.* I see her in water. I know she here."

Jack and Patrick had been outside, but came in when they heard Solana's voice raised to a louder decibel than usual.

Solana was accustomed to Queenie's strange ways, but she'd never seen her as agitated as this. She pulled at her hair and kept wrapping that long scarf around her neck, taking it away, then wrapping it again.

"Queenie? What's wrong with you?"

"The boy. He hurt. Need *doktor*. The Captn's girl. She help Bem."

Captain Jack spoke up then. "Molly's not here. She'll be back soon. Who are you talking about? What boy?"

"Bem. Grandson. He stay with Queenie. Bem."

"Where is this boy, Queenie?"

"He come. He walk slow. But he here."

The next moment the sound of the cab as it pulled up at the lighthouse got everyone's attention. Molly came in and deposited her "patient" and his basket on the floor inside the door. Rafael followed her in and placed the crate with Jack's tobacco and Glenfiddich next to the basket.

He nodded to Jack. "Captain. Crab sends his apologies for your shipment being late. He's raised holy hell . . . uh, sorry Father . . . he raised cane at the port on the mainland. Said he'd keep track of your order himself next time."

Molly was glad to be home. She was about to fill everyone in on her day when she noticed that strange woman over next to Solana, the one that looked like a small pigmy from some African nation.

Molly stood quietly when Queenie walked up to her and pulled at her hand, trying to get her to follow her outside.

"You *doktor*. I see you in lagoon. Bem hurt. You fix him, yes?"

Molly looked at Solana, who just shook her head. She didn't understand any more than Molly did.

"Bem. You fix Bem. Bem hurt."

"Who's Bem? Molly looked around again. No one seemed to know who she was referring to.

"Grandboy. Bem. He stay my house."

She tugged again on Molly's hand and headed out the back door of the kitchen. She pulled Molly along and there, sitting behind the overgrown bougainvillea bush with its petals strewn all about, sat a small boy.

Molly recognized him. The first time she'd seen him he wore only a pair of shorts and no shirt. Today he was wearing a long, dirty t-shirt. Perhaps one that belonged to Queenie.

Molly got on her knees at eye level with the child and he watched her every move. She spoke softly and before she touched him made a head-to-toe assessment, looking for any apparent injury or wound.

"Bem? I'm Dr. McCormick. I want to hold your hand now." She reached out to the young child who offered no resistance but said nothing.

Taking his small hand she turned it over, looking up and down his arm and hand. Other than the fact that his arm was dirty and sticky, it didn't appear to be hurt. She took the other hand and repeated the process.

Moving slowly in order to not frighten him, she lifted his chin and looked closely at his eyes. No dilation of pupils, but the puffiness around his eyes told her he'd been crying.

"I'm going to lift your shirt now. Have a look at your tummy. He remained still and quiet. But when she started to lift the shirt, he began to squirm and cry. When she got the shirt over his head, she gasped before she could stop herself. The child had a first-degree burn that covered his chest, his stomach, and a portion of his abdomen.

All right, Dr. McCormick. You know what to do here. Now get your act together and be the physician you've been trained to be.

She moved closer and spoke slowly and quietly, never taking her eyes from his. "I can make this all better. We need to clean you up a bit, and then I'll put some medicine on your tummy. Let's go to the bath."

The child still said nothing but didn't protest when she reached for his hand.

"Solana, you take care of Queenie. I'll clean Bem up and put some antibiotic creme on this burn. And I'll try to find something that will ease his pain."

Jack and Patrick stood by helplessly. Patrick finally found his tongue and verbalized a few observations.

"Well, then. 'Dr. McCormick' is quite impressive. A very different woman than the weepy, disinterested, self-absorbed, frightened wisp of a girl I've been seeing. Quite a transformation."

Papa let out a long sigh. "That's the real Molly. She's afraid to come out of that shell she's hiding in. Perhaps she's beginning to need some air though, so maybe she'll eventually leave that shell behind. It took her a long time to find her own inner light, but it's there. I hope she'll eventually want it to shine again."

~ ~ ~

Molly took great pains when bathing Bem. He stood in the tub and the only movement he made was to reach out and touch the bandage on her face. She guessed him to be about four years old but it was difficult to know.

"Yes. I've got a hurt place, too. His dark eyes watched her as she washed him, dried him off, and lay him on her bed. She had a few medications in her bag, including

184

a large tube of Silvadene, a sulfa antibiotic medication used for burns. She gave him the smallest amount of pain reliever as he had to be hurting. Of course, she knew this would put him to sleep. But that was probably a good thing.

"Stay here. I'll get one of my t-shirts and you can wear it home. She looked through several dresser drawers before she found a t-shirt that would do. When she returned, the child was sound asleep, so she went to the kitchen.

"Queenie, I've put some medication on Bem's burn. I think you should leave him here tonight. I'll change his dressing again in the morning. He'll be fine but he's going to need care for some time."

"Bem. He okay now, *Doktor* Mac. You make well."

"What happened, Queenie? How did he get this burn?"

Molly needed to know this. If Queenie was as unbalanced as she appeared, did she do this to the child?

"Queenie make plantain food. In fry pan. Bem pull pan. Fall on him. Queenie put magic powder on him, but he cry and cry. But he okay now?"

"Come back in the morning and I'll be able to tell you more," said Molly.

Solana handed the woman several containers of food, enough to last her several days, then ushered her out the door.

"I'm sure he was frightened, Solana. But he never said a word to me."

"Yes, and you look a bit tired out yourself."

"It was a full day. Ensign's going to be fine in a couple of days. Papa's another story."

"What? Tell me."

She closed her hands, digging her fingernails into them to keep herself from shaking Molly and demanding to know more.

"It's complicated. I'll tell him first. You know how private he is. Better let him tell you what he wants you to know."

"Yes, he is very private. I'll go on home now if there's nothing more you need." She pulled herself together and resumed her calm demeanor.

"I'll need your help, Solana. I will tell you that he must go to the hospital. Tomorrow. Can you be here early? I may need some help convincing him to do so."

"Of course. I've made up the bed in the second bedroom in Keeper's Cottage. I already told him to sleep in there and not climb those stairs.

"Actually, why don't I sleep on the cot in the lantern room tonight? That way I can be here to help you with your task. You're right. He'll fight you over this."

Patrick was about to call it a night. Molly asked him to check on Ensign and give her a private moment with Papa.

"Sure thing," said Patrick. "Then I'll be on my way."

"No, please wait around for a bit. I need to talk with you, also."

Jack didn't beat about the bush. "All right. Out with it, Dr. Mac. What did you learn? Anemia like you thought?"

Molly was very direct. As he would want her to be. "No, Papa. It's not anemia. You're suffering from ethylene glycol poisoning."

"Ethylene glycol? But, that's anti-freeze . . . isn't it?"

"That's right. Anti-freeze. It appears you've been either ingesting it, inhaling it, or both for some time. Your body is in a state of metabolic acidosis."

"What the hell is that?"

"It means your blood chemistries are way out of balance, not nearly in the ranges they should be. That explains why you've been feeling rotten and lost weight."

"And what medication are you going to treat me with?"

186

"This is not something I can give you a pill for Papa. You've got to go into the hospital for a couple of days. You need to have several intravenous medications and the doctors need to run more tests. They've got to do whatever it takes to get rid of this poison."

"I can't go into the hospital right now, Molly. There's a lot going on. Stuff I haven't told you about. It's crucial that I be here, on the island, for the next days or weeks."

"Papa, there's nothing as important as getting this poison out of your system. We can't wait another day. I don't like saying it in such a harsh manner, but you must understand. This is a matter of life and death."

"And so is my task. The reason I must be here," Jack replied.

Molly's frustration was evident. "What can possibly be so important as to require you to be here when you are very ill? It could mean your life!"

"Thousands of peoples' lives are more important than one, Molly. That's what's at stake."

"Tell me. I'm not a child, Papa. Just tell me."

Papa Jack stared out the window, perhaps seeking an easy way to relay his information. "I'm sure you know there are problems with Cuba at the moment."

"I know that Castro's turned the island into a Russian stronghold. I also know that many of the people on Cayo Canna came from there, trying to get away from his dictatorial demands."

"Yes, and there's more. Russia has installed some missile pads on Cuba. And they're pointed directly at the United States. As far as the military can tell, they're unarmed at the moment. But that can change in a heartbeat."

"Oh, Papa, no. What can the United States do?"

"Many military types are working on this situation. Suffice it to say that I'm playing a part in this Kabuki dance. I've been in touch with some former Navy buds. We're getting information and sending it to the folks who need to know."

"And why does that make it imperative for you to be here?"

"I've learned there are some men here on Cayo Canna supplying weapons and arms to the rebels in Cuba. I know how they're being transported. I just don't know where they're coming from yet and I don't know who their leader is."

"How do you know this, Papa? Oh, forget that question. What is it that you must do that keeps you here?"

"As you said, you are no longer a child. But I wanted to shield you from this as long as I could. But now there's no choice. I must tell you."

"What? What must you tell me? Papa?" Molly leaned forward, placing her hands gently on his knees, that place where she had sat many times telling him her problems. She looked up and gave him her undivided attention.

"I've just learned, this day, that the rebels are planning to take another shipment to Cuba. And this time it won't be rifles and arms. This time it will be containers of sulfur mustard." He waited a moment for that information to sink in.

"Sulfur mustard was used to make mustard gas in World War I. Oh, Papa, it's a wicked weapon. It will hurt many and even kill some. And those that survive? They'll be so miserable and disfigured they'll wish they had died as well."

She stood then as if sitting was too confining. She walked about, then sat again, not sure she wanted to hear the rest of the nightmare.

Papa continued. "I need to learn the identity of the leader, figure out where he's getting his weapons, and most importantly, learn when they're planning to transport the sulfur mustard."

Molly stood once more and began to pace back and forth, running her fingers through her curls and rubbing her hand along the edges of the bandage on her cheek.

"We have to figure this out, Papa. You must go to the hospital in the morning. That's not negotiable. We have to solve these other problems, learn the leader's name, his source. All that stuff."

"Yes, Molly, I'm working on it. Most of the information I've already transmitted to the proper authorities. But I don't know when this sulfur mustard shipment is going to take place. I must get this information."

"How? How do you do that?"

"Most of my sources contact me on the ham. We communicate in code, and so far we've not been discovered. But that, too, could change quickly."

"Is that why the radio's been so noisy lately? Solana threatened to throw it into the Gulf. I convinced her that wouldn't go over well with you. There's certainly a place for them. I wouldn't be alive today if Nancy hadn't been in my closet. She saved my life."

The two of them shared a smile, both remembering the days of Molly reading her Nancy Drew mysteries, learning how to operate the radio and send Morse Code. Such simple times. Nancy and Drew, names only a quick-witted child would come up with for ham radios.

"Papa, you must listen to me now. You're wiser than anyone I know, but in this instance you must let me lead the way. Please."

Patrick joined them and Papa Jack stood up, leaning on his chair. "Fill Patrick in. We'll talk again in the morning. I'm too tired to think about it tonight."

"You're sleeping in Keeper's Cottage tonight, Papa. Solana's upstairs for the evening and I'll be along soon. Goodnight."

Papa nodded and went through the kitchen to the cottage. He'd feel right at home there . . . maybe pretend Margaret was next to him.

Molly gave Patrick a synopsis of the story. Things had gotten worse in a short amount of time in his opinion. As he started out the door, he turned back, "Oh, almost forgot. Agnes sent some mail. Asked me to drop it off."

Patrick took off and Molly stared at the envelope for a moment. The return address was a familiar one . . . Johns Hopkins Hospital, Baltimore, Maryland. Did she dare open it?

After another moment of sheer frustration with herself, she tore into it. She re-read it again . . . the important part:

The Research Department at Johns Hopkins is pleased to inform you that your application for employment has been accepted. Please sign the enclosed forms and return them at your earliest convenience. Further details will be forwarded upon receipt of your acceptance signature.

~ ~ ~

The next morning Solana was up before anyone, had coffee brewing and stuck a pan of empanadas in the oven. Breakfast. She was ready to do battle if called upon. She'd done so before. But she'd never fought with the Captain. This was not going to be easy.

Molly surfaced next with a sleepy-eyed Bem on her hip. He didn't appear to be frightened but clung to Molly.

"He's feeling better but still hasn't spoken. I've put together a small packet of medications and bandages. Hopefully, Queenie can change them.

"Patrick and I are going to take Papa to the hospital on the mainland whether he likes it or not. He said we'd talk this morning, but there's nothing more to talk about. He's going."

190

When they entered the Captain's room, it was apparent to all that he was not in any condition to argue with them. He was dressed, but his movements were even slower than last night and being the old warrior he was, he'd figured out he must follow the doctor's orders.

"Molly, if you'll excuse us, I need a private moment with Solana."

"What? Oh, yes, Papa," Molly said, then left the room.

"Solana, I don't have time to discuss the details, but I know you have skills that we may need in the coming days. We don't need to talk about them, but I'm asking you to use them if the time comes.

"When we leave, go up to the lantern room and look inside the telescope. You'll find a small sheet of paper rolled up inside there. It's a code Drifter and I use when we need to communicate private information. It's not terribly difficult. Molly learned it as a young teenager, and I expect you'll have it down pat in a few hours. You may not have to use it, but there are many unknowns at the point. Do you understand?"

"Of course, Captain. That you know about my former life does not surprise me. You know much about many people. It's what you do.

"Fidel's movement started long before 1959. That coup was the culmination of years of strategy, when he finally overtook Batista. My involvement with him was over long before that event. I saw first-hand his ruthlessness, his oppressive nature, his thirst for power, and detached myself before that time. Yes, I'll use whatever skills I have to keep all of us safe."

Captain Jack nodded and called to Molly. "Get this done as quickly as possible. I've told you the situation. Days could make a difference. Solana, the radio will drive you crazy. But don't turn it off. You and Molly will be manning it while I'm gone. Let it squawk."

"I'm well acquainted with a ham radio, Captain."

"But I'll be staying at the hospital with you, Papa," interjected Molly.

"No. I need you to be here, Molly. You'll take my place. Drifter knows about you. Send him a brief, coded message. Solana can help you with that. Tell him I'll be back soon. Until then, you're my eyes and ears. Where's Patrick? I thought he was coming."

"I'm here, Jack."

Patrick had been leaning in the doorway, listening. It was difficult to see his friend in such a weakened condition. Why hadn't he noticed earlier? Like Molly, he'd given no thought to anyone's problems but his own.

He still hadn't told Jack why he had come to Cayo Canna. Perhaps it wasn't even important anymore. He'd always told his parishioners to make the most of each day. "Rejoice and be glad in it" he would say. Perhaps he should take his own advice.

Chapter 35

(W)hat is this? Let me help you, *Capitán.*" Crab watched as Captain Jack leaned on Patrick for support.

"You are ill. *Sí.* You are ill." The ferry skipper escorted them to the front row and helped them get seated.

"Now, I must attend my duties. If you need anything my assistant will be standing by to help you." He ducked inside, climbed up to the pilothouse and manned his station.

Molly joined them in the front row. Papa opted for the wind blowing in his face over smelling the diesel fumes coming from the stern. The water was beginning to whitecap which meant the crossing might be a bit rough.

Molly had considered coming over on the Cobra as that would have been faster. But Patrick was only just learning to navigate the craft and she was afraid that may have been too uncomfortable.

They were about thirty minutes from arrival time when Molly noticed Papa slumping in his seat. She touched his hand and squeezed it gently.

"What? Are we there already?"

"No, Papa. Here, lean on me. It's not much longer."

The whistle announced their arrival. Molly aroused Papa and Patrick helped him to his feet. As soon as he had maneuvered the ferry to its mooring, Crab came over to Molly.

"*El Capitán* does not look so good, Missy D*óktor*. He looks ill to me. But, then, I'm just a ferryman. What do I know about sickness?"

Molly turned to Crab, "He's not feeling well. He's going to spend a couple of days in the hospital. Just checking him out. Most likely he's anemic."

"It is good you are with him. He speaks of you always."

They took a cab to Lee Memorial Hospital Emergency Entrance. Molly entered the name Jack McCormick on the registration sheet and handed it to the triage nurse. But she'd not filled in the section that asked for the patient's primary complaint.

"You haven't completed the form, miss. We need the form to be completely filled out." The nurse handed the form back to Molly and resumed reading a stack of papers on her desk.

"That's not necessary, Janie. He's with me," called a deep voice behind Molly.

"Yes, Dr. Strickland," the nurse replied. She'd not question this order. All the nurses knew Dr. Strickland. And some wished they knew him even better.

"I didn't expect an escort but I won't turn it down either." Molly was surprised to see David, but glad also.

"Dr. Strickland, this is Jack McCormick, my grandfather."

Papa reached out his hand and Molly couldn't' miss seeing the tremble as he did so.

"I believe it's Captain McCormick, isn't it, sir?" Dr. Strickland took the Captain's hand and shook it.

"Your name is known around here. I seem to recall we have a cancer ward named in honor of Margaret McCormick. Apparently, she was quite a lady."

"Thank you. She was that and more," replied the Captain.

Jack had followed Margaret's wishes and funded this ward as she had requested. Her trust fund had never been touched, and Margaret thought this was an excellent place to use some of those funds.

Molly looked at Papa. She knew nothing about any of this. But really wasn't surprised. That was his way . . . keeping his business to himself.

"I'll get him settled and then you two can come on back. I've spoken with Dr. Blake, our staff Medical Toxicologist. I work with him frequently. He's the best."

He pushed the wheelchair away before Molly could get a word in. Perhaps that was best. Let someone else take charge. She was mentally exhausted what with trying to figure out how to deal with her many new problems. Her head ached just thinking about them.

Papa's ill. My attacker is still out there. Is little Bem safe with Queenie? Crazy rebels are about to transport sulfur mustard to Cuba and Papa wants—no, insists—that I man his ham radio in his absence. And, oh yes, the police will have to be contacted shortly. Whoever has been poisoning Papa has to be found.

Molly McCormick, even Agatha Christie couldn't figure this one out. You'll have to use every ounce of brainpower you can dig up. And, as much as you prefer doing things alone, you must let others help you. Better ask Patrick to intervene also.

Chapter 36

Tu eres un imbécil! His body washed up under the fuel dock on the mainland! How difficult can it be to kill one small boy? He wouldn't have even put up a fight! But now the authorities on the mainland will be asking a thousand questions, looking for clues as to what happened to him.

"You could have simply hit him over the head. But no. You shot him with a rapid-fire pistol! They'll be searching everything on the water now. From now on, do EXACTLY what I tell you! People are counting on us to get our shipments to them!"

Carlos kept quiet. That was a good thing as he was not the brightest of young men and often spoke when he should have listened. There was no doubt in his mind that *Jefe* would think nothing of getting rid of him, too.

The leader droned on. "We'll get the last containers of the sulfur mustard soon. Once we receive them, we'll decide the day for delivery to our *compadres*. This stuff has to be handled with care. We can't have any slip-ups."

Elian cleared his throat. "We've got to bring the boat dockside for a day at least. There's a problem with the port engine. She's got a leaking valve cover and spews out oil with every thrust of the throttle. I need to check it out before we run her again."

Jefe nodded. "As I said, we can't have any slip-ups. No errors. Get that engine repaired. Let me know when it's ready.

"One more thing. I've learned that the old seaman, the one you encountered out fishing, is not feeling well. You can stop worrying about him.

"We'll meet here again on Friday. I want that engine repaired by then."

"I will do my best," said Elian.

"I'm not interested in your best. I want it done," barked *Jefe*.

Jefe left then, leaving the two at the shack as he got into his runabout. It was quite small but allowed him to get in and out of tight places when he needed to. He could handle most any watercraft, but this little number darted about like a sportscar.

Chapter 37

Dr. Blake and a team of nurses were in and out of Jack's room all night, checking labs every hour and keeping intravenous drips running. Molly desperately wanted to read their notes and see his chart.

She was familiar with most of the medications, but there were several she did not recognize. But then, as she'd told David, she'd never had a patient with ethylene glycol poisoning.

Less than twenty-four hours later the Captain was more alert than he'd been when he arrived yesterday. Dr. Strickland stopped by on his way to his lab. Jack was sleeping so he talked with Molly and Patrick.

"I understand Captain McCormick's improving. That's good news."

"It's been a busy night. He's certainly getting a lot of attention," Molly responded.

"I'm sure Dr. Blake will be by shortly. Better run. Got several cases today."

"Thanks again. You've been a great help."

David waved goodbye and disappeared down the hallway just as Dr. Blake entered the room. The toxicologist nodded to Molly and lightly touched Jack's arm.

"Good morning, Captain McCormick. You're responding well to the fomepizole. That's what we were hoping for. You also need at least one round of dialysis. We don't want any leftover poison hanging out in your kidneys."

"Just get it done. I need to get home."

"I can't hurry the process. Poison has a way of hiding in various places. We must make sure we've got it all."

Molly walked down the hall with Dr. Blake, hoping to learn a little more. "Do you think he will be here a couple of more days then?"

"Yes. He's doing well but his age is a factor. All processes take longer in a geriatric patient. I'm sure you're aware of that."

"Of course. I'm just glad to see him responding so well already. Do whatever you must. I'll tie him to the bed if I have to."

She returned to the room and Papa had Patrick pulling up a chair for her, closer to his bed. "Molly Mac, sit here. I'm ill. I don't deny that. But so far my brain's not been compromised. At least I don't think it has been. There are some tasks that must be done and you two are going to be the ones to do them. Now, listen carefully as you both have to take part in this project. He stopped short of calling it a black ops mission, but that's what it was.

"But, Papa. I'm a physician and Patrick is a priest. Neither of us is a "covert spy."

"I'm aware of that. But I know you both are capable of doing everything I will ask of you and more. You've just never been faced with this kind of situation. Hear me now.

"Drifter knows about the sulfur mustard. He needs to know when it's going to be transported. That's what we've got to find out."

"We?" Patrick could see Jack's wheels turning and was afraid what that statement meant.

"You'll both go back to the island today. Patrick, you'll take the Cobra and go fishing tomorrow. See if *El Escorpión* is still running about. It appears to make one run a week, best I can tell.

"Molly, you'll get on the radio and chat with Drifter. Stay close and answer all my incoming calls. You know the call signals and my call sign, Casper.

"I've assigned you the call sign, Mac. My buds know who you are and they know you can send Morse as well as I can. Just say Casper's out haunting houses somewhere. They won't question that.

"The rebels are sending messages, too. Bear Bowen is listening, I'm listening, and Drifter's listening. With you manning the radio, one of us is bound to learn when the transport is taking place.

"Someone uses the call sign *Padre*. *Padre* sends messages to *Niño*. But this could be anyone in the chain, not necessarily the leader. The leader would be less likely to use the radio unless absolutely necessary. He'd call on his minions to do that.

"Most of the time they speak in Spanish and that takes a bit of unraveling. Drifter speaks Spanish. Better than I do for sure. I know you studied it at boarding school, Molly. Just do your best. And don't forget, Solana speaks several dialects fluently.

"I spoke with the three 'fishermen' on *El Escorpión* recently. Don't think any of them are sophisticated enough to use Morse Code, so that's in our favor."

"But, Papa. What if I don't get them right?"

"Get what right?"

"The messages. What if I can't understand them, decipher correctly? I know how to help people with their health problems, not this."

"Molly Mac, what you do—at the basic level—is save lives. You can save perhaps thousands of lives if you will. Stop questioning yourself. Trust your instincts. Your skills and abilities are needed.

"Patrick, the rebels run about the Gulf close to Crabber's Cove. When *El Escorpión* is loaded she sits low in the water. If she's riding high then they either haven't picked up their cargo yet or have already delivered it."

"So what am I supposed to do? Look busy fishing?"

"Exactly. They know the Cobra. They say they don't speak English, but I know better. Take note. The Cobra will run hot if you keep her wide open. Give her a little rest occasionally. She'll get you where you need to go."

"And what happens when she runs hot?"

"You'll know if it happens. Shut her down. Let her rest a while. Then she'll start up again."

"Jaysus, Mary, and Joseph, Jack. This sounds like a suicide mission." Jack ignored the comment.

"The military must stop this sulfur mustard from getting to Cuba. We cannot fail in this operation. Now, one last instruction. You two are to observe and report only. You are not to engage in any heroics. Understood?" His instructions were very specific, but instructions were one thing. Carrying them out was another.

~ ~ ~

Molly and Patrick stood at the dock waiting for Crab to bring the ferry in. When they boarded, he greeted them. "Ah, Missy D*oktor*, and Father. *El Capitán* is not with you?"

Molly was aware of Papa's preference for keeping his business private, but Crab would know he was in the hospital. She'd told him that's where they were headed.

"Papa's resting in the hospital. He's feeling much better. He'll be home in a few days."

Crab nodded his head, "That is good. Good. He is lucky you are his granddaughter. Anyone else may not have seen he was having difficulty."

Molly looked out towards the ocean. "He's a tough old seadog. He'll be fine.

Chapter 38

The question Solana refrained from asking was written on her face. "He's going to be all right, Solana. He's better already."

Molly was aware Papa Jack was an essential part of Solana's life. They'd been together a long time. Her quiet elegance was felt throughout the lighthouse, and Molly hoped she'd stay for many more years, especially now that Papa was getting older.

"Thanks be to *Dios* and to you, Father. Your prayers must have helped."

Patrick acknowledged the comment with a nod. Solana made no bones about not caring much for him. He wasn't exactly sure why that was but was glad to be in her "better" graces.

"What about Bem? How was he today?" Molly asked. She'd thought of nothing else on the trip back. That child needed someone to care for him and Molly didn't think Queenie was capable of that.

"Queenie came by mid-day. Bem went with her. I told her to bring him by tomorrow. Let you take another look at him. Perhaps she will, but she may forget."

"Did he speak to you?"

"No. He just pointed when he needed something. Not sure what that means," said Solana as she gathered her basket.

"It's time for me to go. Supper's waiting on the stove and there's a pitcher of sangria in the Frigidaire. Father, your Jameson is in the cabinet."

Molly sighed, "Thanks, Solana. I couldn't do this without you."

Solana went to the porch, slipped her sandals on, and quietly went her way.

Patrick watched as Solana left. "You're right. We couldn't do much around here without her. She takes good care of Jack. And me, too, now that I think about it. As much as she feeds me, I should offer to pay the grocery bill occasionally." They both chuckled at that.

Patrick continued, "I heard on the radio that President Kennedy is addressing the nation again tonight. I'll give a listen but the TV reception at my place is not the best."

"What's the reason for the address?" asked Molly.

"Another update on the Cuban situation, I believe."

Molly looked thoughtful. "I had no idea Papa was involved in these military activities. Just like him to keep this to himself. I wish he'd stay in his ivory tower and work on his paintings. Keep away from such dangerous projects."

"Once a spy, always a spy?" Patrick wondered if that logic might apply to himself. Once a priest always a priest?

They finished dinner and Patrick was ready for his bed, too. He took a second to check in on Ensign, bent down and spoke softly to him. Molly stood by watching him interact with the pup. He really did have a way of communicating, even with animals. Not her strong point.

Patrick stood, "I think I'll take the golf cart. Be back early and go fishing I suppose."

"And I'll sit by the radio. My Spanish classes were a long time ago. Papa Jack expects too much from me. I hope I won't disappoint him."

Just as she headed out the kitchen door to Keeper's Cottage, the radio squawked.

"K4ELD, K4ELD. Casper you there? Over."

She hurried to the radio and sat down. She repeated the sign and answered.

"K4ELD. Here. Casper's out haunting houses. I'm Mac. Taking his place. Over."

"Mac, Drifter here. Checking in. Gonna see what Johnny's got to say tonight. Check back with you tomorrow. Drifter out."

"Goodnight, Drifter. Mac out."

It took her a couple of seconds to understand that message. Johnny? Who was that? She didn't know anyone named Johnny. A few more seconds passed and she put two and two together. 'Gonna see what Johnny's got to say to us tonight.' Of course. President Kennedy's address—Johnny.

For a brief moment she thought of Nancy, her own radio in the closet in Baltimore. Would she ever be able to go back to that apartment? Would it always represent fear? Maybe she'd call the lieutenant herself now that Papa was out of commission.

Chapter 39

Jefe paced about the shack then stuck his hands into his pockets. His flushed face and the staccato rhythm and pitch of his voice told Carlos and Elian that listening might be the best idea for them.

"The old seaman is in the hospital. On the mainland. He's very ill. But he should have been dead by now!" Rubbing his hands together again, he stalked from one end of the small shack to the other.

"He was one of the U. S. Navy's top Intelligence Officers back in his day. He still works for the Navy in some capacity. He's been on the radio lately, talking to some *amigos.* I'm sure they're listening to us as well.

"He uses the call sign Casper—and talks to someone called Drifter. Even so, I don't think we need to worry much about him anymore. Yesterday someone named Mac was using his call sign. A female. I assume this is his *corazón,* someone he trusts, or she wouldn't know his call sign."

Carlos snickered, "You think that old man has a *chica?*" *Jefe* made no comment but gave Carlos a long look of disgust.

"With him out of the picture we can relax. Don't think he'll be intercepting any messages. But, to be safe, I'll use Fidel's code to alert our Cuban contact. So even though the old man is well trained, he can't break this code. No one can.

"Fidel was smart, years ago, when he had his own special code developed. That, Carlos, is an example of how a true leader works. That was long ago and the code is still useful today. He was able to plan for the future. That's what a real leader does."

Carlos squirmed in his seat. "I don't know this code but I can do other work. Would you like me to take care of the old *hombre*? Like I did Roberto?"

"You fool! You botched that assignment! You must learn to think things through before you act. Thanks to your blunder, I now have to be more careful than ever. So far the authorities have no knowledge of me, and I've been able to come and go with ease. But since Roberto's body was found, the police are everywhere.

"And, now, the U. S. Navy is watching every vessel moving in any direction. That makes it difficult for us to take the sulfur mustard directly to our *compadres*. We'll have to rethink our plan and I'm already working on that.

"No, don't bother with the old *hombre*. He won't survive anyway."

Then Carlos added more fuel to the flame. "When Roberto's *Tia* Solana learns of his death, we may have a new problem."

"Maybe, but that could take a while. The police on the mainland don't have a clue about Roberto's death. They only know he was killed with an automatic weapon. It'll be weeks before they begin figuring out details of that case."

"I don't know, *Jefe*. If Roberto told his *Tia* Solana anything about us, she might be trouble. And, if Roberto's story is true, then we might have to deal with her, too."

"What story? What are you talking about?"

"Roberto told us his *madre*, and his *Tia* Solana ran with Fidel and Che in the old days."

"Bah! Every woman in Cuba will tell you she "ran" with Fidel and Che. It's a tale they all like to spin. Fidel had many women. This Solana, she is a beautiful woman, even today. She may have shared his bed a few times, but nothing more.

"Listen now. I've been working on a new plan. Still have a few items to sort out, but basically, it's a good plan.

"In any case, my superior wants us to move the stuff on Oct. 24. A passenger ship, the Royal Caribbean Princess, will be making its way from Cancún, heading to its home port of Miami. It will make a stop in Key West where the U. S. Navy has a base. A lot of military types are gathered at that base, trying to find out what's going on in our country.

"When the ship makes anchor in Key West, we'll deposit the sulfur mustard in her cargo hold. She'll stay in port for a day or so, and it's unlikely any inspecting agencies will board her, a tour ship. Our rebels will go aboard, retrieve the liquid, and take it to be processed into gas.

"Fidel's pilots will use crop-duster planes as they can fly under the radar. They'll make a pass over Key West and spread that mustard gas throughout the area. Many Americans will be injured and some of the older ones killed outright. That event will bring all military operations on Key West to a standstill.

"Elian, make sure *El Escorpión* is in condition to transport the sulfur mustard on my command. When we're ready, I'll bring the containers to you during the early morning hours when it's still dark. You'll follow that passenger ship to Key West, then board her."

"But, how will we get it aboard the cruise ship?" asked Carlos.

"Carlos, think, if you can manage that. The skipper of the ship is an *hombre* I went to school with. This man has worked with Fidel. He is a trusted aide. This is a minor job for him. He will make sure the sulfur mustard containers get put into the cargo hold."

Elian let the two talk. When they had completed their conversation and *Jefe* had given his orders, he decided it was time to say a few words.

"*Jefe*, I agree with you regarding Roberto's *tia*. She is not a concern. And *el Capitán* will probably not live. I do not worry about him.

"But I do worry about how we are to receive our compensation once we have made our delivery. You will be here on Cayo Canna and we will be in Cuba.

"Is there a contact there that will see that we receive our money? Once the mustard gas is spread there will be a great deal of chaos and activity on both sides. I would like to know I have my money so I can get my family and myself to Nicaragua as soon as I deliver the stuff."

"Nicaragua? Hmm. You will go there to live, *amigo?*"

"*Sí*. It is a beautiful country."

"Not to worry. I will make arrangements with my contact in Cuba, Vicenté Fernando. You know him. He can be trusted. He will have an envelope waiting for you when you arrive at his dock.

"Tomorrow you two will take this load of rifles and ammo. This may be our last. As for the important shipment, the containers of sulfur mustard, once I get my orders from my superior in Placida, I'll bring them to you for delivery.

"You'll go your usual route, but this time you'll continue on directly to the ship. I'll notify the skipper using Fidel's code. The skipper will know when to expect you. You can count on him.

"It won't be long now. My superior is anxious to get this behind him, too. We are all believers in the cause. In Fidel. This will be our shining moment. We will succeed and Fidel will be pleased with us."

Jefe sped off, leaving rooster tails in his wake. He had much work to do and time was getting short. And he still had a few problems he needed to work out.

~ ~ ~

A couple of hours later Carlos was antsy, downing one *cerveza* after the other. "I'm tired of living in this pigsty.

210

Eating whatever *Jefe* decides to leave for us and never knowing what tomorrow will bring. When I get my money, I'm heading south to the islands. There are many *chicas bonitas* in those islands."

"*Chicas,* always the *chicas* with you." Elian grabbed a *cerveza* from the ice chest and dug down into the ice, bringing out a package of cold cuts, then found some stale tortillas in a plastic container on the counter.

Elian eyed Carlos. "You could have let Roberto go. *Jefe* wouldn't have even known about it. Now you have Roberto's soul on your conscience, no?"

"He would have gotten us killed, Elian. We could no longer trust him. He had to disappear."

"And what about me, *amigo*? Do you trust me? Or are you going to make me disappear also? Eh?"

"We need each other, Elian. It takes both of us to run the guns and if the boat has problems, only you can fix it. I would never think of harming you." He lighted a cigarette and reached for another *cerveza,* tossing his uneaten cold cuts into the mangroves.

Elian watched but did not comment. He ate his cold cuts and finished his *cerveza.*

"All right. We'll make this arms run early tomorrow, just before sunrise. Crank up that radio and we'll let our *amigos* know we're coming."

Elian was the number one radio communicator, primarily because he and *Jefe* were the only ones who could speak the old dialect and use Fidel's code. Elian found a clear signal and began his message.

"K9CBA . . . K9CBA. *Niño? Padre* here. We are set to deliver the packages tomorrow morning. See you then.

Chapter 40

Solana rose early. She slipped on a long, turquoise skirt and pulled a floral printed top over her head. Then she tied her long hair back with her satin ribbon. Red today. This scrap of satin completed her look. It was her "signature" piece and she had a strip of it in every color. Its purpose was to pull her abundant hair back and put all focus on her face. Which was exquisite.

She was hopeful Captain Jack would return soon and prayed that whatever was ailing him would be done with. Last evening she'd not asked any questions, but today she would insist on specifics. As she stepped out the door, she stumbled over something at her feet.

"Oh, what is th. . . "

She looked down. The child, Bem, was lying at her feet, curled up like a small kitten, looking as if he had no bones whatsoever.

"Bem? What are you doing here?" Even her voice didn't wake him. Had he been here all night? Where was Queenie? Solana got to her knees and shook him lightly, but still he slept.

"Bem, wake up, child. Bem!"

She put her fingers on his small wrist, feeling for a pulse. Yes, he had a pulse, but she thought it was weak.

"Bem! Wake up now!"

She lifted him and started running down the path. She never stopped, arriving at the lighthouse out of breath. She slipped her shoes off and called out the minute she got inside.

"Molly! Molly, I need you!"

~ ~ ~

Molly had awakened early, anxious as to what this day might bring. She had tuned in to President Kennedy's address last evening and wished Papa was here. He would have been able to reassure her that all was well. Wouldn't he?

She poured herself a cup of his Cuban coffee and went up to the lantern room to watch the sunrise. She sat for a short while, peering out the open window, marveling at the way every day on Cayo Canna began . . . with a promise from the sun that this day would be glorious, as the day before had been, and as the day after would be.

Papa's old brass lantern was laying on the table by his easel. It appeared to be disassembled, the pieces laid out in an orderly fashion. She held one section of the glass panes up to the window, seeing the prism of colors that was always visible if you held it just right. She decided Papa must be working on it so she laid the piece back in the exact spot where it had been.

When she was young, Papa always told her that if she looked hard enough she could see his lantern from her window in Connecticut. One more fond memory that she'd tucked away for safekeeping.

When she heard Solana calling, she fled down the spiral staircase.

"What? What's wrong?"

"It's Bem. I found him on my porch. He won't wake up!"

"Put him on the sofa," Molly instructed. Then she poked and prodded, looked and assessed. He was oblivious to any of her ministrations.

214

She lifted the front of his shirt and checked his abdomen and chest. His burn was healing. There were no bruises or cuts of any kind. His pulse was slow, but not erratic.

"Where's Queenie? Is she not with him?"

"I haven't seen her. I don't know how long he'd been on my porch. I didn't hear anything during the night. He was just lying there when I came out. What do you think?"

"I believe he's been drugged. There's no way of knowing what the drug was. All we can do is watch him closely. I suppose we could call the police, but they couldn't do much else. Let's keep him here on the sofa. That way I can keep checking him and listen to the radio, too."

A few minutes later Patrick showed up and Solana greeted him with a steaming cup of coffee. His stock had definitely gone up.

Thanks be to God, he thought. He wasn't sure what had brought about this change of attitude, but was thankful.

"Morning, ladies. What's this? A patient so early in the day?"

"It's Bem. Solana found him on her porch. He appears to have been drugged. There's nothing I can do but keep checking him. Let's hope he'll sleep it off."

Patrick ran his fingers through his thick hair, then stared at Molly. "Maybe this is a situation for . . . "

"I know. You'll tell me to call the police. But if I do, they'll alert Child Welfare Services and put Bem with someone he doesn't know. He's been through enough already."

"Drugged? A child?" asked Patrick.

"That's all I know. Queenie's not shown up yet. Maybe she can tell us something."

"Yeah, and maybe she's the one who drugged him. That woman needs to be seen by a psychiatrist, or somebody. She's dangerous. Can I do anything?"

"There's nothing to do but wait for him to wake. You need to get on about your own chores. I believe you're going fishing today, right?"

"Yeah, those were my orders."

Molly gave him a half-smile and shook her head. She knew exactly how he felt. Like he'd been sent to the moon to bring back a lunar specimen.

"Did you hear President Kennedy last night?" she asked.

"Yeah, my TV lost the picture a few times, but I heard him."

"Papa Jack has known a lot that we haven't. I can't believe Castro would let the Soviets put nuclear weapons on his island."

Solana brought in a plate of hot cinnamon buns and passed them around. Patrick was talking about going fishing.

"If you're going fishing then be home before dark. It's not good to be caught out in the Gulf in the middle of the night," admonished Solana.

"I'll be back late afternoon, early evening."

Molly added her own concerns. "Then be careful. I'll bring Solana up to date on Papa's condition while you fish."

Patrick downed a couple of buns and a few minutes later pulled away from the dock with the wind at his back and a prayer on his lips.

Molly hesitated and fidgeted with the bandage on her cheek. As if reading her mind, Solana lay her hand over Molly's.

"Just tell Solana the story."

Molly took a deep breath. "Papa's been poisoned."

Solana remained calm, waiting for Molly to continue.

"The lab reports reveal he's been ingesting a kind of poison—ethylene glycol—for an extended period. Ingestion can cause organ damage, primarily the kidneys, and may lead to death.

"Dr. Strickland, the coroner, has brought in an excellent toxicologist, Dr. Blake, to help care for Papa. When I left him, he was weak but improving. Dr. Blake wants to give him a round or two of dialysis to make sure there are no traces of the poison left in his body."

Solana had not moved a muscle.

"Both Dr. Blake and Dr. Strickland believe he has a good chance of pulling through. But he's got to stay in the hospital another day or so."

The relief that washed over Solana's face nearly brought Molly to tears. "Then I gather he's given you both specific orders and expects you to carry them out?"

"Yes, but Solana, I'm in way over my head."

"Yes and the Captain taught you to swim, Molly. And you swim quite well as I recall."

She stood, glided across the room, her long skirt swishing as she swayed her hips. Then she turned back.

"And Molly? I can swim too.

Chapter 41

Patrick gathered up a couple of rods and a bait bucket, then threw in a gaff and a small hand-held net. Figured that ought to be sufficient for his 'props.'

He started the Cobra and checked the gas gauge. Almost a full tank. That was good but he thought a short prayer might be in order also.

Holy Mary, protect this foolish priest.

He pulled away from the dock and began to motor down to Crabber's Cove. From there he'd go out to the area Jack told him about. The Captain had tried to give him navigation coordinates, but he'd balked.

"Jack, just tell me the general vicinity I should be "fishing." I don't know one damn thing about reading a chart or understanding coordinates. I know how to get to Crabber's Cove, and I know how to get to the outer islands. Don't confuse me with all that latitude, longitude, shit."

Jack smiled. He was remembering how Margaret had forever nagged Patrick about his salty language. *"Patrick, you sound more like a drunken sailor than a priest. Jack was trainable, but I'm not so sure about you."*

He pushed the throttle forward. Surely this thing wouldn't run hot on him today. Would it?

The winds were about five knots, coming from the southwest. He began to think about what this day might bring, which was not a comforting thought.

And if El Escorpión is out there? What the hell am I to do? Wave to those guys? Jaysus, Jack.

As he got closer to the cove he spotted the Endeavor II, Todd Redhawk's craft. He didn't even hesitate when a really brilliant thought crossed his mind. He made a quick turn and headed in a new direction.

Why don't I ask him to join me? He obviously knows a lot about boats or he wouldn't be living out there on that beauty.

The handsome young man was standing in the stern, wearing a pair of black swim trunks, having his morning coffee. He came to the side of the boat.

"Patrick, what's got you up this early?"

"Going fishing. Want to tag along? I don't know a damn thing about fishing and even less about a boat."

Todd laughed aloud. "Sure, why not? Let me get a couple of things together. Be right with you." He tied a bandana around his forehead and the long, dark braid hung down his back. He grabbed a t-shirt, threw in a pair of diver's fins, a mask and a snorkel, and held a couple of mesh bags in his hand.

"Might need these."

Patrick nodded. The relief he felt just having Todd on board was palpable. They pulled away from Crabber's Cove toward the open Gulf.

"What you hoping to catch?"

"To tell you the truth, I'm hoping I don't even get a bite." He laughed as did Todd. Before long, they were out of the cove and in the area where Jack had told him to anchor up.

"I heard the President last night. Don't have a TV, but I do have a good radio. Did you hear it?" Todd asked.

"Yeah, and if I wasn't scared before, I am now. His first address to the nation told us about possibly nuclear-armed, Soviet missiles pointed at us. Now, a blockade?"

"Looks like it. While you fish, I'm going to snorkel about."

"Snorkel? Haven't done that in years. You ever see anything interesting down there?"

"Sometimes, but mostly, it's my job."

"What? Snorkeling?"

"Not snorkeling, exactly. But combing the water, looking for particular aquatic life, searching for species that may not have been found here before. Doing my work."

"Somebody pays you to do that?"

"Yep. Pays pretty well, too. Keeps me busy and it's what I want to do. My career."

"Who do you work for?"

"You notice the yellow rectangle on my boat?"

"I didn't but Molly did. Said she'd seen it before but couldn't remember where."

"It's a logo for National Geographic. I work for them. Studying aquatic life, habitats, water conditions. Many things."

"Are you a scientist, or what?"

"I'm an oceanographer. I study the physical and biological aspects of the ocean."

"I see. Do you go from place to place then? Studying the ocean?"

"I move about some. But I'll be here for a while. I have family close by, so I'll stay as long as I can."

"Family? On Cayo Canna?"

"No, on the reservation."

"What reservation?

"The Seminole reservation."

"There's a Seminole reservation close by?"

"That's right. My mother and sister live there. Some distant cousins, too. That's where I grew up."

"That's quite a leap . . . from the reservation to National Geographic."

"A long story. I was good at science, received an award for my science project in high school, then got a scholarship to the University of Miami where I majored in Marine Biology."

Their conversation was cut short by the sound of another boat. Cruising at high speed. Patrick was mindful to not mention the real reason he was fishing. Jack may not want that information given out. But it was only a few minutes before he spotted *El Escorpión about* a two hundred yards off his starboard bow.

Good. I can report to Jack that those guys are still about.

He watched as the slimline boat sped across the open Gulf, headed south, south-east. To Cuban waters. Then, at the last minute, they turned back towards the cove.

Chapter 42

"K4ELD . . . K4ELD, Drifter here. Over."
"Mac here, Drifter. Over."
"Casper said you were visiting. He still out haunting houses? Over."

"Yep. It's October. He's practicing for Halloween night. Over."

"Ha! Let me know when he's done haunting. Over."
"Will do. Could be a few days. Over."
"Take care, Mac. Casper's not the only ghost out there.
Over."

"Understood Drifter. Will give you a fishing report shortly. Out."

Solana watched Molly as she placed the call to Captain Jack's friend. No doubt the young woman was at ease with the ham radio.

Solana had turned her ears to listening closely to the radio, an instrument she'd learned to use long ago. It was a vital piece of equipment when she traveled with Fidel and Che.

She had hoped she'd never have to use the skills she'd learned back then, but perhaps she'd been wrong about that. Whatever she needed to do to help the Captain would be what she would do. Nothing was more important than that.

Molly sat down next to a sleeping Bem. "Solana, what do you know about Queenie?"

"She says she comes from Africa. Came here a few years after I did. Just showed up on the beach one morning, dragging that scarf behind her.

"She lives in a shack on the south end of the island, near the lagoon. One minute she makes sense, the next she's telling you about her latest vision. You can't trust anything she says. She mentioned a daughter a couple of times so I guess she was telling the truth about her."

Bem opened his eyes and stared up at Molly. He reached his hands up toward her. "Bem, hey. Feeling better?" He said nothing but held on to her hand when she took his.

"Maybe something to drink, Solana?"

Solana brought a glass of orange juice. Bem took the glass with both hands and gulped the entire contents down.

"I believe he's feeling much better."

"I'll get a cinnamon bun. See if he can eat that."

Solana headed to the kitchen. As she did so, she heard someone on the radio. Someone speaking Spanish.

"Molly, listen. That's someone calling *Padre*. Isn't that the name you said the Captain said to listen for?"

"Yes, *Padre and* Niño. Can you understand what's being said?"

"Something about needing another man to help with something. Didn't get it all."

"Solana, you stay here and listen. My Spanish is weak at best. I'll get the bun. You're better at languages than I'll ever be."

Solana felt those old, familiar feelings—anxiety, danger lurking nearby, violence just waiting for a time and place. But this time she'd be on the opposite side. This time she'd not be one of the rebels. This time she'd oppose them.

Molly brought the bun and Bem scoffed it down.

"I believe he's hungry. Don't know what he was drugged with, but I think he's recovering. Bem, can you talk to me? Tell me where Queenie is?"

The boy looked up at Molly then all around the room, finally settling on Solana.

"Solana. That's Solana. Remember her?"

He sat quietly. Still staring at Solana.

Solana listened to the radio but looked back at Bem. Then, without preamble, she walked over to him and took his hand in hers.

"*¿Bem, comprendes Español? Si?*"

For a long moment nothing happened. He continued to stare. Then he nodded to Solana.

"*¿Si? Dónde está Queenie?*"

He stared at her face again, then reached down inside the pocket of his shorts. He pulled out a piece of paper that had been torn from a grocery bag. He handed it to Solana.

"Take Bem. Queenie go home. It coming for Queenie. From the water."

Solana read the words the best she could. It was written in a dialect somewhat close to one of her Cuban ones, but not exactly. She didn't need to understand it exactly. The meaning was clear. Queenie was gone and had left Bem with her.

"Queenie's gone. She's left Bem here. It appears she's gone home. She says something is coming from the water for her. She's left him with us. Probably the only people she thought might take care of him. That means he's an orphan now, like many others, passed from one person to another. It's a common situation in my country."

Bem reached for another bun. Before he took it, he looked to Solana again as if asking permission.

"*Si, Bem. Es para ti.*" He watched her face carefully, then took the bun.

"Solana, he understands you. I thought he was just ignoring me but I don't think he can understand English."

"Bem, would you like more orange juice?" Molly spoke slowly in a moderate tone. He immediately looked to Solana.

Solana repeated in Spanish. He watched her face again and nodded. "Yes. He only understands Spanish."

"I think it's more than that," Molly said as she walked behind the sofa where Bem sat. She called out loudly, "Bem, look at me." Then even louder, "Bem!"

Bem continued to eat. Never responded in any way. "He can't hear me. I think he's reading your lips. That's why he watches you so closely."

Reaching inside her medical bag, she brought out her otoscope and handed it to Solana. "Give it to Bem. Let him hold it a moment to see it's nothing to be afraid of."

Solana placed it in Bem's hand. He turned it over, then handed it to Molly. He sat still while she looked in both ears. "His left ear is infected, but the real problem is the right one. The eardrum has ruptured. I'm sure he hears nothing on that side. He needs an antibiotic to treat the infection and may need repair of his eardrum. He needs to be seen by an ear specialist."

Solana nodded. "Then I'll keep him close and talk to him. He's just a little boy. He's not had much of a chance in this world."

"He's just our latest complication. Our more pressing problem is figuring out how Papa's been poisoned. And maybe we could be getting it, too," Molly suggested.

"I don't know, but if someone was trying to poison us, I think we'd all be sick like the Captain. Somehow, they've singled him out and managed to get the poison only to him. There has to be something unique to him," suggested Solana.

"That makes sense. Something unique to Papa. But what?"

Solana ran through a litany of the Captain's daily habits. "He eats the food we eat and drinks the same fresh orange juice. Occasionally he goes to The Temptation, a restaurant and bar over on the bay side. He and Father Patrick sometimes go there to eat their fill of oysters.

"Here, at home, they have a pitcher of sangria on a hot day. In the evenings the Captain will have his Glenfiddich and the good father will drink his Jameson. Oh, and he drinks that strong coffee every day."

"His coffee. Yes, perhaps that's how he gets it," remarked Molly.

Solana cocked her head sideways, "That coffee comes in sealed bags. I suppose it could be tampered with but it would be difficult."

"Yes, and Patrick and I both drink Papa's coffee every morning. No. It's got to be something else."

Molly scratched about the edges of the bandage on her cheek, plopped down on the nearest chair, held her hands at her temples and let out a long sigh. "Oh, my head hurts so. I've got to rest a short while, Solana."

"You go take a nap. I'll watch over Bem."

"When I was small and had a problem, Papa Jack would tell me to 'sleep on it.' He thought sleep cleared the mind for solutions that may have escaped it during the heat of the moment."

While Molly rested, Solana's brain ran rampant. Her days of "running" with Fidel and Che were long ago. But, as she well knew, some experiences, especially those you regret, have a way of hiding in your memory and surfacing when you least expect them. And hers were slithering out from their hidey-hole.

An hour later Molly came rushing through the kitchen door, leaving it ajar as she whizzed through. "Solana! What does Papa drink every night? Every night!"

"He drinks his whisky. Only Glenfiddich. You know that, surely."

"Just so. And does Patrick drink Glenfiddich, as well?"

"No, he's as adamant about his Jameson as Captain Jack is about his Glenfiddich."

"That's it. The whisky. Has to be. Couldn't be anything else."

She hurried to the liquor cabinet and peered inside. There were various bottles of alcoholic beverages—vodka, bourbon, wine. A large bottle of Glenfiddich, about half full, stood in the front. There were six more bottles but only this one was open.

"This has to be it. He imports it from Scotland. Has done so for as long as I remember. I must take this to the mainland. Have it tested," exclaimed Molly.

"But how would someone poison it?" asked Solana. "It comes from the distillery in Scotland to the mainland, then over to the island on the ferry. Just like the mail and other special deliveries.

"If it's being delivered through his whisky, how is it possible to get it into a bottle that's been sealed at the distillery?

"The crate is opened by customs for inspection. But the bottles themselves are not opened. They've been corked and sealed to ensure protection of the contents."

"Does Papa pick them up at the dock? Or does someone deliver them?"

"Crab delivers them to the dock and Captain Jack takes the golf cart, loads them and brings them here. Occasionally, Rafael drops them off. I place them in the liquor cabinet, then line them up neatly as the Captain likes them," explained Solana.

Molly paced the room, listening half-heartedly to the static on the radio. Her brain was in its element—figuring out a difficult problem.

"Then maybe it's not the Glenfiddich. It would be impossible to get poison in a sealed bottle, but I can't think of anything else that's unique to Papa."

Molly sat down on the floor next to Bem. He and Ensign were enjoying a game of tug with a Doggie Bone.

She appeared to be looking at Bem, but Solana watched her face. She was working through this complex scenario.

Molly darted out the kitchen, through the breezeway, to Keeper's Cottage. She was back in an instant, carrying a small magnifying glass in her hand.

"Let's take a closer look at this bottle."

She placed the Glenfiddich on the coffee table. Holding the magnifying glass on the top of the bottle, she looked for a long moment.

"Take a look."

Solana leaned down and peered through the glass.

"Do you see it?"

"Yes, I see it. The pinprick is tiny, but I see it. *¡Dios!* What do we do now?"

"I'll take the bottle to Dr. Strickland's lab. He'll be able to tell us if there's poison inside the bottle."

"But even if there is, we still don't know who put it there."

"No, but we're one step closer. That whisky is being 'doctored' before it gets to Papa."

Solana took a deep breath, "Perhaps the police should handle this. We might be opening ourselves up for even more trouble.

"Someone is trying to kill Captain Jack. It must have something to do with this Cuban situation. He's known for some time about the rebels and recently spotted them out in the Gulf. They may know about his involvement. They may think he's a threat in some way, and will not stop their attempts if they know the poisoning scheme has failed.

"Yes, Molly. Take the bottle to the mainland. Get it analyzed and come back as quickly as you can. I believe it's better if we all stay together. Being alone is not a good idea. It would make any one of us an easy target."

The radio burst into high gear, squawking and squealing. Several people talking at once. Molly shook her head. "I can't understand any of that. My Spanish was a long time ago."

Solana listened for a few moments. "That's not the Spanish you would have learned. That's an ancient dialect that only a few people know. People from my country."

"Papa says to send messages using Morse Code. He doesn't feel those fishermen he saw would be sophisticated enough to know Morse Code."

"The Captain is right about that. Those fishermen probably do not know Morse Code. But I assure you their leaders do. Not only that, Fidel and Che were cautious and inventive. They brought coders in from Europe, people who translated codes for many others, through several wars over time. These specialists created a code for Fidel and I'm sure it's still being used today for high-level communications."

Molly frowned, "But that means that even if I listen all day I won't be able to understand what *Padre* and *Niño* are saying if they use this code."

"Yes, if they resort to using Fidel's code it can only be understood by his top-level leaders."

"Papa doesn't know about that. He would have told me."

"No, he couldn't have known about it. Only a few of Fidel's closest associates know about the code."

"Then I can't do what Papa has asked. I'll have to tell Drifter I can't help him."

Solana stared at her feet for a moment. "No. Don't tell him that." She stood then and took a deep breath.

"Do you think Captain Jack will be home tomorrow?"

"No . . . I don't know. He was doing much better, but his age makes detoxing more of a challenge."

"Then, until you talk with him, don't tell Drifter anything. This situation is complicated. We must speak with the Captain before we make any more moves."

She looked directly at Molly. "I know Fidel's code. I can decipher their messages. We must do what the Captain has asked."

"You know Fidel's code? But how?"

"That's a story only a few know. I will tell it to the Captain when he returns. Until then I'll stay close by this radio. Please don't question me on this, Molly."

Chapter 43

Patrick's booming voice carried on the wind blowing in from the ocean through the open lighthouse windows. "Molly! Molly! Get down here!"

"Was that Patrick?" Molly asked.

"Yes. Something's wrong. Hurry, Molly," prompted Solana. "He wouldn't be yelling unless he was in trouble." Molly fled down the dock and met Patrick halfway.

"It's Todd. He's been shot."

"What? Who's Todd? Shot? Who's been shot?"

Rather than answer her questions, Patrick grabbed her hand and dragged her down the dock to the Cobra.

"This is Koi . . . something . . . Todd Redhawk."

Molly nodded briefly but her attention was on the blood streaming down the side of the man's face. "What's happened?" She climbed aboard and knelt next to a very dazed Redhawk.

"The fishermen—the gunrunners—they took a shot at us. Todd was hit. Can you help him?"

"Get him inside. To the sofa."

Solana ran on ahead and had Molly's medical bag waiting for her. Patrick helped Todd to stand and they made their way to the sofa where the injured man collapsed.

What in the hell am I going to tell Jack? If he hears about this, he'll be climbing the hospital walls trying to get back over here. Jaysus!

Patrick stood back. Molly spoke softly to Redhawk, explaining everything she was doing. She cleaned the wound with Solana handing her whatever she needed. Her voice was calm, soothing. Full of confidence.

Ah, so this is where she excels, where she thrives, thought Patrick. *Not what I was expecting.*

"You've had a close call, but if you lie quietly we can get the bleeding under control."

"Then do whatever you need to do. It hurts like hell. That much I can tell you."

"As soon as the bleeding stops, I'll give you a small amount of lidocaine, then I've got to put a few stitches in your temple area and another couple a little farther down on your cheek."

Patrick came closer and squatted down next to the sofa.

Molly continued, "The bullet grazed his temple and cheek. At least it didn't lodge in his face. I'll have to put some stitches in a couple of areas. I'll make them as small as I can, but they'll leave a scar."

So. Adonis will have a couple of scars now. That will only add to his interesting looks, thought Patrick.

"But he'll be all right? Huh?"

"He'll need to rest and let his body recover from the trauma. But, yes, he'll be all right. You might want to go to the kitchen, Patrick. Watching someone get stitched up may not be a pleasant experience."

"Good point. I'll check on Bem and Ensign."

He heard the giggles before he got to the kitchen. Bem was on his knees playing tug with Ensign. The pup's paw didn't appear to be giving him any pain at the moment.

"You two don't look sick to me. Guess you'll be expelled from Molly's wounded ward shortly." The small boy looked directly at him so Patrick was sure he had heard him.

"Want some ice cream? Solana keeps a stash in the top of the Frigidaire." Still no response.

Placing the dish of ice cream in front of Bem, Patrick sat down on the floor. Communicating was one of his better skills, but this little boy still wasn't coming around.

"Where's Queenie? She coming back later?"

Bem said nothing but attacked the ice cream. Patrick had to smile. Most of the ice cream made it into Bem's mouth, but the front of his shirt was quickly covered in chocolate dribbles and somehow, he'd managed to smear it on his cheeks as well.

When Patrick returned to the sofa, he found Todd sitting up, the stitching completed, and his face bandaged. He'd come in on a conversation. "You work for National Geographic? Wow. What a great job that would be," stated Molly.

"I can't think of any other work that I would find as satisfying," her patient replied.

"How long will this project last, this research you're doing here in the Gulf?"

"Some projects take years. Some are completed in a matter of months." Patrick stood in the doorway. They had yet to acknowledge his presence if they were even aware of it.

The bandage on Molly's cheek had been removed recently. The wound was healing and a scab had formed over the carved area. She reached up and stroked the "S" on her cheek. Patrick had seen her do this several times. It was becoming part of her behavior.

"Did you say your name is Todd?"

"That's close enough. My Seminole name is a twister for most tongues."

"Tell me."

"Koiko-Tadi Redhawk."

She stared off in space for a second,

"Redhawk. Redhawk."

She finally saw Patrick, then broke into a grin as she turned back to Todd.

"Not T. Redhawk, PhD?"

"Uh, yep. That's me."

"Of course. I knew I'd seen that name somewhere. T. Redhawk. I read an article in National Geographic a few months ago. It caught my attention because it was about the findings of an oceanographer studying the aquatic life in the Gulf waters near Cayo Canna."

"Yeah, that's part of the job, too. You have to report, publish, document. Not my favorite part."

Patrick watched. Not wanting to interrupt their conversation. *Looks like Adonis and Dr. Mac have a lot in common. I've never seen her this animated.*

He pushed those thoughts aside. They weren't especially comforting. Then he joined the conversation whether it was appropriate or not.

"And here I thought I'd find you in need of last rites, but apparently, I'll have to wait to deliver those. Looks like you're gonna live."

"Think so. Now, you want to enlighten me about what went on out there? I thought you were going fishing. Guess it was a bit more than that. I hadn't expected to get shot when I agreed to go with you."

Patrick sighed, "Jaysus, Todd. I didn't expect anything to happen. I was doing what Jack asked me to do." He explained the situation as best he could and Todd listened without asking any questions.

"Sounds like Castro is ramping up trouble. I had no idea we had a covert spy on the island. But it sounds like he may be just what we need."

"Todd, I'm truly sorry. I would never have asked you along if I had thought there was any danger."

"Not to worry. It seems I'll survive, and I'm ready to get back to Crabber's Cove if I can talk you into helping me get there."

"You'll need an order from Dr. McCormick before I can do that. She's the attending physician on the case."

Molly smiled at the two men. "You're going to have a headache for sure. The stitches will begin to irritate and you'll have to sleep on your right side. There'll be some pain, too. Let me see if I can find something to help you in that department. As it is, I'm down to the bare bones in my medical supplies."

"I've got aspirin and I'll fill my ice chest and keep an ice pack on it as you suggested. Let's not make any more of it than it is."

"No, not aspirin. Could cause more bleeding. I'll give you something that will work better than that. But, yes, you are cleared to go to the Endeavor."

Patrick knew he'd better speak up now. It was time the three of them had a serious conversation.

"Sure, then. I'll get you to the Endeavor. First, though, we need a short discussion about whether or not we should report this incident. How do we know those 'fishermen' won't come looking for us? I'd just as soon not be shot at again. I'm sure you agree with me on that."

Todd did have a question now. "Who would we tell? How do we know the fishermen aren't working for someone on Cayo Canna?"

Molly spoke up, "Papa says they're running guns and ammunition to the rebels in Cuba. And his latest information is that they're planning on moving a shipment of sulfur mustard as well."

Todd stared for a moment. "Whoa. Being shot at. And now chemical weapons? That's troubling. I guess I'm saying we don't know who to trust."

Patrick nodded. "I agree. My gut tells me to keep quiet until we have a chance to talk with Jack. He keeps a lot to himself and only tells it when and if he needs to."

Solana moved about the room quietly, clearing the dishes and taking a moment to wipe at Bem's ice-cream-laden face. "I would like to make a suggestion if I may."

"Of course, Solana. I believe you've had more experience in this kind of thing than any of us," said Patrick.

Solana gave him a long stare. "You're right. We shouldn't report this until Captain Jack has been told. There is more going on than we know. Even if the Captain can't be here, he'll know who to contact and give us some direction.

"We keep quiet until the Captain gives his orders. Molly, you take the whisky to the lab, then go to the hospital and see the Captain. If he's better as you say, he'll have already drawn up a plan."

"We're all in agreement, then?" Molly asked.

Patrick summarized, "Solana's right. Jack will have a plan. Meanwhile, I'll get Adon . . . uh, Redhawk to his boat, get him settled and get to my bungalow.

"You take the early ferry to the mainland and check on Jack. Todd, I'll come by tomorrow morning and see if you need anything. Molly, you think Jack may be released tomorrow?"

"Dr. Blake said it could be a couple of days. I don't want him released until he's totally recovered."

She turned then to Todd, "Do you think you're safe on the boat? I mean, it's anchored in Crabber's Cove. Those fishermen could come back."

"I'm not worried. I've got a pistol on board and I know how to use it."

"What? No bow and arrow?" Patrick joked. Redhawk smiled. "My bet is they were just trying to scare us off."

"Then I'd say they did a good job of that," Patrick countered.

Chapter 44

Solana insisted on staying at the lighthouse. "I'd like that, Solana," Molly said. "To say I'm scared would be an understatement. Papa's been my protector as long as I can remember. And it appears he's getting better, but we're all in danger."

"Molly, go to him in the morning. He'll know what to do. He's told me stories about his time in the Navy. This is just another exercise. He's a competent man."

"But, Solana. If this sulfur mustard gets in the wrong hands, the results are unthinkable."

"I know. And one more thing. Lieutenant Collins called this morning."

Molly's heart pounded. "They found him? My attacker?"

"No, but they're searching night and day."

Molly sighed, "Then he's still out there. Looking for me."

Solana rose. "Go to bed. Get some sleep. I'll take Bem upstairs with me."

Molly was exhausted but her brain was working overtime. When she did drift off, it was a fitful sleep and she kept waking up. Eventually, she settled down into a dream that became a disturbing nightmare.

Solana, likewise, couldn't rest. She tucked Bem in the small cot up in Captain Jack's lantern room, then came downstairs. She went to the radio hoping she hadn't missed anything.

If she did hear something, then what? Her time with Fidel and Che had been an exciting time for a young woman who saw the need for reform in her country. She followed Fidel. Believed in him. But after some time, it became apparent he was just like Batista, the dictator he had overthrown. Power hungry.

That she'd been able to escape had been only due to his feelings for her. If he'd wanted to find her, or kill her, it could have been arranged. The fact that he didn't showed he still had a small threat of decency somewhere deep inside.

She lay down on the sofa, keeping one ear open toward the radio. Her thoughts turned to the child. Even if Queenie came back, was that a solution? No. She didn't think so.

And what about Roberto? Would she know if he made it to Miami? Oh, why had he gotten involved with the rebels? But she knew the answer. Youth. The call of excitement. The need to belong.

She closed her eyes and fell into a restful sleep. No dreams, just rest and quiet. Too good to last, though. No sooner had she drifted into this peaceful place, then she was awakened.

"No! Papa! Help me! Papa!" The scream slashed through the darkness. Solana jumped up, taking a moment to remember where she was.

Molly. That's Molly.

She dashed out the kitchen door to Keeper's Cottage, into Molly's room. She grabbed her with both arms and held her tight.

"Oh, Solana," Molly sobbed. "He came to me in a dream. It was so real. The whole event happening all over again."

"I know, child. I know."

Molly took a couple of deep breaths, willing her heart rate to regulate itself and her brain to function. "But as horrible as the dream was, it brought answers I've been looking for."

"What kind of answers?"

"I know who he is."

"Would you recognize him?"

"Yes. When his face flashed across my memory, I could hear his voice, smell that beef jerky on his breath. I remember every agonizing moment."

"Then you must call the lieutenant first thing in the morning."

"Yes. Right now, though, I'll stay up. The dream may come back again if I go back to sleep."

Solana brought two cups of tea and they sat on the patio in the dark, sipping the brew, listening to the soft whispering of the ocean as it sent silver tongues to lap at the shore.

A full moon shone above the lighthouse, the lingering scent of the night jasmine floated on the air, and Molly was at peace, even following the disturbing dream.

"There's something about this island, this lighthouse, that makes me feel grounded. Safe. As if I belong."

Solana smiled in the dark. Those were the very reasons she had stayed here. There could be another one or two as well, but some thoughts were hers only.

"Cayo Canna is a refuge for many, including me."

"But I have a job waiting for me in Baltimore. If I don't return the signed forms soon, the job will be given to another new graduate."

Solana was not surprised to learn that. "You have some decisions to make, but let a little more time pass before you turn your mind to that matter."

"I'll call Lieutenant Collins early, then catch the ferry to the mainland. I hope Papa's ready to be discharged, but if he's not, then I'll insist he stay until Dr. Blake says he's ready."

"Hmm. That may be a struggle. He'll be running everyone on that ward ragged by now, especially if he heard President Kennedy's message," Solana said with a sly smile.

"Hospitals don't allow radios and none of them have televisions," replied Molly.

"Uh-huh. But Captain Jack seems to have a way of keeping up with what's happening wherever he is."

Molly smiled. "You know him very well."

At 8:00 a.m. Molly lifted the phone receiver, hoping the fickle instrument would work. The dream last night had been disturbing and she felt fragile this morning.

"Are you sure your dream was accurate?" Lieutenant Collins asked, afraid to hope for any real information that could help in his search.

"I'm positive. I can't remember everything, but I know he was a patient in the Psychiatric Unit at Johns Hopkins a couple of weeks before graduation. I treated him for cuts on his wrists. Obviously a suicide attempt. I suggested he be held for further observation. For his own safety. And the psychiatrist on call issued the order."

Molly provided a detailed description, which was what the lieutenant needed most of all. "I'll get over to the hospital. Records will be on file."

The information Molly presented was critical. In a matter of seconds after hanging up, Lieutenant Collins's brain began to piece together several facts that fit perfectly. He had a new direction to go in. Beginning at Johns Hopkins.

Chapter 45

Solana took the coffee cup from Molly's hand. "Better get a move on. You know Crab. Doesn't wait for anyone. I'll take care of Bem and Ensign. I've been listening closely to the radio. *Padre* and *Niño* have been busy, so I'll stay close by."

"Right, then I'm off. Patrick will come by to check on you two. He's like a mother hen. Sorta like Papa."

"Yes, I suppose he is. Hope the other one, the Seminole, is better this morning."

"Yeah, well, he'll have a few days before he's back to his usual routine. He's quite an interesting man."

Molly hurried out the door where Rafael's cab was waiting. She was surprised when she got to the ferry, however. Even though the ferry was docked, a large chain was stretched across the entry to the dock and a notice was tacked to the sign that gave the ferry's schedule.

"Ferry in for Maintenance and Repair. No Passenger or Automobile service today. Service will resume tomorrow." Molly looked about. In the small shack where the attendants kept their supplies, she saw several people milling about.

"Hello?"

"Ah, Missy *Doktor.* Good morning." Crab greeted her as he made some notations on his sheaf of papers.

"Good morning, Crab. What's wrong with the ferry?"

"Eh? Oh, nothing's wrong. It's time for her regular maintenance. The company has very specific rules and regulations about their ferry. I think it must have something to do with liability and those kinds of issues."

"But I've got to get to the mainland. It's very important."

"Is it *el Capitán*? Is he not doing well?"

"No. I mean yes, he's doing well, but I must go see him today. It's an emergency, of sorts."

"Oh, I see. Well, you can travel over with me. But I'm not sure if the ferry will be ready to come back this afternoon. Sometimes it takes only a couple of hours, but it could take longer. It might even be night before I come back to Cayo Canna."

"Oh, Crab, thank you. I don't care when we get back. I just need to go today. You're a lifesaver."

He nodded, "Come with me then. Let's get her underway."

Molly went up front to watch for the dolphins but when a quick coastal rain shower appeared overhead she hurried down to Crab's cabin. By now she knew the smell would run her out quickly, but at the moment it was better than getting soaked to the bone.

She looked about the cabin, noting several framed certificates. Crab's piloting licenses and documentation, a license for his assistant, Tomás, and a couple of award notices.

As before, there were ropes, boxes of mail, his safe— locked as before—and containers with letters and numbers embossed on the side of the large jug. $C?2OH$? Or was that $CH3OH$? Difficult to tell.

Neatness was not Crab's forte. But he kept the ferry in good condition and you could depend on him to have it running on time.

The rain stopped and she went topside. Attendants were standing on the dock ready to assist Crab with his docking procedure. Molly waited for the signal from Crab then walked off the ferry.

"I'll come as soon as I've finished my visit with Papa."

"Yes, Missy D*oktor*. But, again, I do not know how long this maintenance will take. But I'll be here."

"Thanks, Crab. See you later."

Chapter 46

Molly walked the few blocks to Memorial Hospital and took the elevator to the third floor. She spoke to a couple of nurses, watched as a housekeeping employee entered Papa's room, and followed her in.

The room was empty. The bed had been stripped and the housekeeper was about to begin her cleaning routine.

"Where's my grandfather?"

"What's that?"

"My grandfather. He was in this room. Where did they move him to? Do you know?"

The woman checked her schedule, then looked up at Molly. "I'm sorry. I don't know. I was called to clean the room."

Molly walked down the hall, turned the corner, and headed to the nurses' station.

"Where did you move the patient in room 313?"

The nurse took a glance at her roster. "Room 313? Oh, Mr. McCormick."

"Yes. That's right."

"Are you family, miss?"

"Yes. I'm his granddaughter."

The nurse stood and came around the counter to stand next to Molly. "I'm so sorry. Mr. McCormick expired this morning about 2:15 a.m. We looked in his chart, but there was no number to call and we had no choice but to wait until some of the family came in."

"Expired? You mean died? Papa died?"

"Yes. I am so very sorry." The nurse placed an arm about Molly's shoulder.

"But he was getting better. Dr. Blake said he was going to make a full recovery."

"We're never prepared to accept an outcome like this. Is there anything we can do?"

"I . . . I . . . what . . . where is he . . . where is his body?" Molly was finding it difficult to hold back her tears.

"He was taken to the morgue across the street. Dr. Strickland will take care of him for you. If you'd like to go over there, they have a very nice waiting room for family members."

Molly stared at the nurse. *This can't be true. Papa was better. I know he was. He can't be dead. No.*

The nurse escorted Molly to the elevator and pushed the button for the ground floor. "Dr. Strickland's staff will take care of you."

Molly walked out of the elevator and continued through the doors that took her outside. She'd never experienced this feeling—this total inability to think—this inability to put one foot in front of the other. She stood rooted to the sidewalk.

A fast-moving body sprinting across the parking lot got her attention as it came closer. Dr. Strickland was running so fast he almost fell trying to get to her.

Molly wanted to say something but no words came out. She wasn't even sure her lips were moving, but as soon as David took her hands she crumpled to the ground and wracking sobs escaped her lips when words would not.

"He's . . . Papa's . . . "

David went down on his knees and took her chin in his hand, lifting it so that she had to look at him.

"No. No, Molly. He's not dead. Hear me. He is NOT DEAD!"

Molly stared into his blue eyes, taking note of his freshly shaved face, his blond hair falling over his forehead.

"What? What did you say?"

"Captain Jack is NOT dead. I was planning to be in his room when you got here, but the ferry came earlier than usual. I am so sorry. I had hoped to spare you this experience."

"What are you saying?"

Molly tried to get her mind around his words. She wanted them to be true. David pulled her up and held her by her shoulders in case she started to fall again.

"Come to my office. I'll fill you in on what's going on.

Molly stared at him. "He's not dead. Not dead. That is what you said, isn't it?"

"Yes. Jack is NOT dead."

David took her to his office and poured her a cup of black coffee. She was still shaken.

"But they told me you have his body."

"As far as they know, I do have his body. The only other person who knows what is happening is Dr. Blake and his lips are sealed.

"Jack is fully recovered. Dr. Blake was releasing him today. But after he talked with Jack, the two of them decided on a course of action that is most unusual."

"What?"

"Jack knows he's been poisoned and how. The only thing he doesn't know is who. At his request, Dr. Blake agreed to let him 'die' so that whoever has been poisoning him will think he's out of the picture. That will allow Jack to be operating 'undercover.' I believe that was how he put it."

"He's alive. You're sure?"

"Yes, quite sure. In fact, his 'body' is right back here in my autopsy room. He was complaining about my 'God-awful excuse for coffee' when I left him. Maybe seeing you will put him in a better mood." He smiled and led the way.

David opened the door to the autopsy room. "Jack, your favorite person is . . ."

Another empty room.

"Maybe he's in the bathroom."

He came back shaking his head. Then he walked over to the bedside table where Molly stood, reading a note that had been placed beneath a beautiful, ornately carved urn. Papa's ashes, apparently.

Molly Mac, I'm doing fine. Dr. Blake worked wonders on me. Back to my old self. I'll be home soon. At the moment, I've got to be a ghost again. Tell Solana to stay on the radio. I'll contact you when the time is right. Meanwhile, tell Patrick to be very careful when he's fishing. I've a few hunches I have to play out. Don't worry. I know what I'm doing.

Be sure to post my obituary in the local paper. Have Patrick don that black and white outfit, say a few words over my ashes and spread them in the Gulf, close to Crabber's Cove. I want the rebels to know I'm dead. You may tell Solana and Patrick the truth, but NO ONE else. And, Molly Mac? Please mourn appropriately. Love, Papa Jack."

"He's already gone underground. There's a lot I need to tell him. Now I have no idea where to start."

"Start with having a quick breakfast with me. We'll talk some things out. Maybe that will help."

Kathi Jowers walked in as Molly and David came out. "Morning, Dr. McCormick."

"Good morning, Kathi."

Kathi smiled and went on about getting her day organized. She'd heard on the radio about a crash at a small, local racetrack and knew there were casualties. Probably be getting work from that for sure.

Chapter 47

Solana checked her notes once again. Had she decoded the message correctly? A second check confirmed she had. "FINAL SHIPMENT DELIVERY DATE: 24 OCT."

That was the message. Short, but specific. I've not forgotten how to transcribe Fidel's code. Something big is planned for Oct. 24. Does "final shipment" mean more guns and ammo? Or does it mean sulfur mustard? It was of utmost importance, or they wouldn't have resorted to Fidel's code.

Loud rapping at the door had her hurrying to answer.

It can only be the good father.

These days Solana uttered those words with sincere respect for Patrick. He'd stepped in just as Captain Jack would have done had the situation been reversed. But he did need to clean up his irreverent mouth and get himself back on course with his life. Perhaps she'd spread her wings a little farther. To include this most unusual priest.

"Solana? You here?"

"Of course I'm here, Father. Come in. Coffee's ready and Bem left one cinnamon bun for you. The other four he consumed   rather quickly."

"Good heavens, Solana. The boy will look like a piglet if you keep feeding him like that."

"He's missed more than one meal, of that I'm sure. But he does need some attention and I don't know where that's going to come from.

"Molly's convinced he's partially deaf and thinks ear surgery might help him. But that's not available on Cayo Canna, and right now it's rather difficult for any of us to go to the mainland to seek help."

"Yeah, and I have to tell you, Solana. This poisoning business with Jack is baffling. Why would anyone want to harm that old seadog?"

"That part's easy enough. Whoever wants him out of the picture knows about his background, his intelligence work, and knows he's working with the Navy on this Cuban problem."

Patrick smirked, "And I thought he was down here, enjoying life and soaking up the sun. He's never actually retired, has he?"

"Maybe officially, but he always keeps his fingers in the military pie somewhere. It's what drives him, Father. It's part of who he is."

"Uhm." He leaned forward, elbows on his knees. "Do you think we ever truly know anyone completely?"

"How do you mean?"

"Oh, I don't know. It's just that I've always taken people at face value. Respected them as seemed appropriate. But recently I've learned a few of them aren't worthy of my respect and never had been."

Solana smiled, "That's a lesson we all must learn. But don't let a few unworthy ones destroy your trust in the goodness that is inherent in most of us."

"I thought I was the priest here." Patrick grinned at her as she walked over to the radio as it had begun to awaken.

"Something's being planned for Oct. 24. I've listened all night. *Padre* and *Niño* are using Fidel's code for every transmission now. I can hardly leave for a moment."

"Maybe Molly will have some good news when she returns today," Patrick offered.

"That's my prayer also. At the moment, I have an immediate need that I could use your help with."

"I'm at your disposal, dear Solana. The only chore I have today is to check on Redhawk."

"That may not be a pleasant visit. He's going to be one hurting fellow this morning."

"You got that right. What was it you needed? Groceries, fresh vegetables from the market? What?"

"I need clothes for Bem. He's been wearing those shorts and that dirty t-shirt for two days now. It's covered with ice cream, chocolate, and cinnamon.

"Could you go to Queenie's place and see if you can find any clothes for the boy? And shoes."

Patrick groaned, "Queenie's place is kinda spooky, if you know what I mean. Dried animal skins and odd-looking ornaments hanging in the trees at the front of the shack. Don't know what else is there, but it can't be good."

Solana smiled. "She's harmless, Father. Whatever she's hung in those trees can't hurt you. But be sure to make the sign of the cross before you enter." Solana grinned at the look on his face.

"Absolutely. Thanks for reminding me. All right. I'll check on Redhawk and look for the clothes. Anything else?"

"No, I'll keep my regular schedule. If someone is watching us, as they may well be, we need to go about our business as usual.

"And don't go fishing today, Father. The Captain would tell you to stay close by. He may even be coming back with Molly on the afternoon ferry. He'll have new instructions once he knows what happened to Redhawk."

"I agree. No fishing today. Then I'm gone. I'm getting spoiled by Jack's golf cart. Beats walking any day of the week."

Chapter 48

Baltimore

Lieutenant Collins combed through the hospital records at Johns Hopkins Hospital. As Molly had reported, a young man fitting her description had been a patient in their Psychiatric Unit a couple of weeks before her attack.

"Winchester, Samuel G. DOB 03/08/1935. No known address." He read quickly, scanning the physician's notes. The name Winchester jumped out at him. He recalled that the body of an older woman, Dr. Catherine Winchester, had been discovered the day after Molly's attack. That would be the first place he'd go.

~ ~ ~

The Winchester home was a grand place and the lieutenant and another officer entered with weapons drawn. The interior was furnished eloquently. Antiques in every room. But the kitchen was in a state of disarray with leftover slices of pizza, empty beer bottles, and an ashtray spilling over with Marlboro butts. Clearly, someone was living here.

After a thorough search, they found only two items of interest. Scattered on the kitchen table was a brochure advertising a reduced price on airfare to Paris with a list of suggested hotels and restaurants. There were airline schedules listing departure and arrival times for all airports on the East coast. Had their suspect already left the country?

Gone to France? The next step would be to put out a BOLO (be on the lookout for) on Samuel G. Winchester.

Chapter 49

Cayo Canna

For a dead man, Captain Jack McCormick, aka Casper, was getting about quite well. "This coffee is no better than what you served me last time. Pure swill, Bear. I'll bring you some of mine next trip."

"Didn't know you were such a coffee snob, Casper. Here, add a little of this Bailey's Irish Cream to it. Might make it more palatable."

Jack poured the smooth, creamy liquid in. Anything to disguise the bitterness of this brew would be helpful.

"All right. Tell me you're well enough to be participating in this operation," Admiral Bowen commented.

"I am. Wouldn't be here otherwise. And time is of the essence. Things are moving quickly."

"You hear Kennedy's speech?"

"No. I was flat on my back in a hospital bed, but I got briefed by Julian. He was quite adept at reporting what was said."

"Julian?"

"Yeah, Dr. Julian Blake, the toxicologist at Memorial. He's the one who brought me back from the brink, and he's gone out on a limb to help me 'die' to assist our operation. He could be in a bit of legal trouble for that little lie."

"Have to meet him sometime. Now, I know how your labyrinthine mind works, Casper. Talk to me."

"I've had nothing but time in which to think through every scenario that could be possible regarding my poisoning. Dr. Blake thinks I've been getting a minute amount of ethylene glycol for months now."

"Ethylene glycol? That's antifreeze. I thought that stuff would kill you immediately."

"It will unless it's given in minute portions as I've been given. Apparently, someone wanted me to die of what would appear to be "natural" causes. So that was the reason for the long period.

"Molly discovered a pinprick in the top of my Glenfiddich whisky bottles. She and Dr. Blake think the glycol has been put into the whisky using a syringe, a needle, pushing it through sealed corks. The lab analysis confirmed her suspicions.

"That would mean someone close to you. Or someone who knows about your Glenfiddich indulgence."

"Agreed. My labyrinthine brain, as you call it, has been running through various scenarios that might lead us to the perpetrator."

"Who knows you drink Glenfiddich?"

"Probably everyone on Cayo Canna. I keep it in my liquor cabinet but only a few people come into my home. None of them go into my liquor cabinet. Except for Patrick.

"Patrick? Who's that?"

"Father Patrick O'Brien, a friend for some years now. Just so you know, you can check his name off the 'suspects' list."

"Casper, I won't take any names off the 'list' until we discover the culprit. Go on. Who else?"

"Solana, my housekeeper. She knows it's there. She's beyond reproach also. When you do decide to start taking names off the list, takes hers off, too."

"Uh-huh. Any others?"

"Molly lives with me now. But this poisoning was taking place long before she came. You can mark her off as well."

"If you take all those names off, Casper, who does it leave you with?"

"Simple. It means that the poison is put into the Glenfiddich before it gets to me. Which means I have to begin at the beginning. In Scotland."

"Scotland? How so?"

"The Glenfiddich is distilled in Dufftown, a quaint village in Scotland. It's still bottled by the family that began producing it in 1887. The family is distant cousins of mine. Margaret and I went over there some years ago and met some of them. Fine folks. Make great Glenfiddich malt whisky. Can't think of any reason they'd want to do me in. That special malt is not available in the U.S. and I pay my cousins quite well to send it to me."

"All right. The whisky is sent from Scotland. Where do the Scots send it?"

"It comes directly to the mainland where it's kept in a warehouse on the docks. It's then loaded onto the ferry with any other items marked for Cayo Canna. Crab never charges anything for delivery, which makes it easy enough."

"Then where do you think the 'doctoring' of the Glenfiddich takes place?"

"It has to be someone in the warehouse on the mainland. Drifter heard some radio buzz. Someone knows I'm former intelligence and wants to get me out of the way. I'm certain there's a connection with my poisoning and the rebels running guns. Those fishermen carrying the weapons may be *compadres* of the warehouse fiend.

"Someone named *Padre* talks with *Niño* several times a day. Drifter can decipher some of it, but they sometimes switch to a code he doesn't know. But he's heard enough to know they're aware of me and my history.

"Anyway, it'll shortly be known that Captain Jackson McCormick passed away of a heart attack. The grieving granddaughter was seen sprinkling his ashes in Crabber's Cove, one of his favorite fishing spots."

"Bet Molly will really like that part," said Bear.

"Yeah, well, she's had a couple of difficult hits herself recently. And her brain is even more labyrinthine than mine."

"What now?"

"Now I borrow your flashy Sport Fisherman, make a trip to the mainland, and see what I can find out about the warehouse personnel."

"That could be dangerous. Think I'll tag along with you."

"Not a bad idea. After all, I'm dead. Might not get around as well as I use to." Bear guffawed at that and began readying the cruiser to depart.

Chapter 50

Patrick took the golf cart and headed to Crabber's Cove. He parked it close to the beach, shed his shoes and shirt and swam out to the Endeavor II.

Todd was on deck, writing in a notebook. These notes were as important as the research itself. It was from these carefully written notations that he formulated his research theories and observations relating to the aquatic life he was studying.

"Hey, come aboard. Could use a bit of conversation."

Patrick used the steps on the transom and pulled himself out of the water. One look at Todd answered his first question.

"How are you?"

"Don't ask. This hurts like holy hell. Molly said today would be difficult. She was right."

"The stitches bothering you?"

"No, they still feel a bit numb, but I've got a hell of a headache. She said no aspirin and I've used the medications she gave me. Now I'm rather up the creek for this pain."

"You got any coffee?"

"Sure. Can't start the day without it."

"Lemons?"

"Got a bottle of lemon juice, no fresh ones."

"That'll do. What about ginger or cayenne pepper?"

"Actually, I have both. My sister stocked the boat for me. A shame I'm not a good cook, but the kitchen's one place I'd just as soon avoid."

Patrick grabbed a towel hanging over the rail and wrapped it around himself as he was creating a puddle standing there. "Now, then. I know a couple of old Irish remedies that work for headache. Give me a minute."

He entered the tiny galley which was a tight space for his large body. He found the coffee and made a fresh pot, using three times the amount of coffee he would normally use. When it was brewed he added three tablespoons of lemon juice and a generous amount of ginger.

"Here. Drink this. Slowly. Let it have time to start working as you drink it."

Todd took a sip. The expression on his face said more than any words he might have come up with. "Good God, that's the worse drink I've ever tasted. Even worse than my gran's button-snakeroot tea concoction."

"I didn't say it tasted good. I just said it worked. Drink some more."

When Todd finished the cup Patrick handed him the small tin of cayenne pepper. "Here. Take your finger and dab a small amount of this in your nose. Or, if you prefer, you can place it on your tongue. Your choice."

"Pepper in my nose? I think we both know what that will produce."

"Try it. Can't hurt. Well, probably not."

Todd touched a fingertip to the pepper and inserted it up his nose. He was surprised to find that he didn't immediately have a sneezing fit as he had expected. It didn't burn much either.

"Have you used these remedies, Patrick?"

"Me? Absolutely not. Just thought they might help you."

Todd burst out laughing as did Patrick.

"Well, at least you've still got your sense of humor along with the headache."

Patrick wanted to dislike this Adonis but couldn't seem to find anything objectionable about him. Except for being aware that the Seminole was attracted to Molly.

"What do you think we should do now? Don't think fishing is a great idea."

"No, me either. I'm hoping Jack will be on the ferry with Molly. There's a lot of activity on the radio according to Solana. She's not told me everything, but she's able to transcribe a code, Fidel's code, the one the rebels are using. She thinks something is scheduled to happen on Oct. 24 but can't make heads nor tails about what exactly. Only Jack can figure that out."

"Sounds scary. Makes me think I may need to make a short trip. To the reservation. To check on my mother and sister. What about the small boy I saw at the lighthouse? Is Molly his mother?"

"That's Bem. He's Queenie's grandson. You know. The woman who lives in the shack next to the lagoon . . . the one with the animal skins hanging in the trees? She was taking care of him, but she left him on Solana's porch a few nights ago. She's disappeared and Solana and Molly are looking after him."

"Strange. He was so quiet. He stood in the corner while Molly was stitching my face. Never made a sound."

"Yeah. Well, we're not sure he can talk. He seems to be able to communicate with Solana, or at least understand her, but not with Molly or me."

"He's lucky to be taken in by Molly and Solana. Not all children are that fortunate," said Todd.

"Sounds like you may know something about those situations?"

"Some."

"Do you need anything? Food, alcohol, batteries?"

"No. I'm good."

"All right then. I'm off. No snorkeling for you for a few days, I gather?"

"Right. But I've got plenty of notes that need to be organized and ready for submission to my employer. They don't just let me hang out on this great boat and swim about. They expect detailed reports and articles that are interesting enough to be published."

"Now I know why I became a priest," Patrick laughed.

"Thanks for checking on me. See you later."

Chapter 51

The animal skins Patrick had observed earlier were still hanging from the jacaranda trees. He knocked, but his sixth sense told him the place was deserted. When he knocked the second time the door opened of its own accord.

"Hello? Queenie?" It was so dark he could barely see inside. When he could, however, it wasn't a pleasant sight.

Holy Mother of God. What has that woman been up to?

Queenie professed to be some sort of Santeria priestess, and Patrick now thought that may be true. The animal skins were hanging in the trees outside . . . and their dried heads were here, inside.

Animal sacrifice. Jaysus, Mary, and Joseph!

He'd studied religious proceedings and traditions of many peoples and countries. But no matter how much he had studied these various religions, what he saw here could only be called *voodoo,* a word that conjured up a spine-tingling sensation that unnerved him.

The room was small, with a twin-sized bed and several tables. He walked through a doorway covered with a curtain of shells and colored beads strung on thick, heavy strings. Dirty dishes were scattered on the counter and an army of ants had taken up residence.

The most disturbing items, however, were in the center of the room. There was an overturned table in a circle of candles. Dark stains on the wooden floor led from the center of the circle to the wall where they'd splattered up several inches.

That's blood. Something hideous and repulsive has happened here.

He looked about again. A threadbare valise sat in the far corner of the room. Patrick was surprised to find it was filled with items of clothing for a small child. It also held an old newspaper clipping and a large unsealed, manila envelope with several folded papers inside.

As he dug deeper into the valise, his fingers latched onto a small, red satin bag embellished with fine stitchery and drawn together with a bit of yarn. He peeked inside the bag and stared at the object it held, deciding whether he should touch it. A few seconds later, he took it in his hands. The object was irregularly shaped and measured about three inches long and two inches in diameter.

Amber. Used to create jewelry.

When he held it up to the light, it sparkled and held a surprise. A fossilized sea creature had been trapped inside this bit of amber, and someone had created a tiny hole in the top of the piece and run a thin string of hemp through it.

A necklace. An amber necklace. I've seen fossils before, but never one like this. Wonder what Adonis would make of this specimen?

He returned the amber necklace to the satin bag, placed it in the valise with the clothes, and started to leave.

Across the room he caught sight of something under a chair—something long and dark. He retrieved the item, and when he touched it a cold shiver ran through his body.

Queenie's scarf. She'd never leave that behind. Something tells me she didn't just go away on her own. Should I take it? Oh, to hell with it.

He shook his head, tossed the scarf in the valise with the clothes and the satin bag, and headed to the lighthouse.

Chapter 52

Molly and David, Dr. Strickland, took a seat under an umbrella at the Tiki Hut and he placed the small bag containing the urn on the table.

"I know you're worried. I spent quite a bit of time with Jack over the past few days. Believe me, he's in great shape for someone recovering from metabolic acidosis. You got him here in time. No permanent damage has been done to his organs.

"As for his mental capabilities, those are in even better working order. He made mincemeat of every objection I made to him 'dying' and going undercover. He's in his element here and his commitment to this mission is total. Had you been here, you'd not have been able to keep him from 'dying' either."

"I have no doubt about that. He's stubborn as a jackass and when he's made a decision you can't change his mind," said Molly.

"Then you must follow his instructions and put on your 'grieving granddaughter' face before we leave this restaurant. Since we don't know who's been poisoning him, it could well be someone right here. They may be watching us even now."

Molly shook her head back and forth. "It's just so unbelievable. The more I think about it, I'm not at all sure Papa did retire. There was an official ceremony, but Solana says he's always kept his finger in the military operations in this area. He still talks to his former mates on the radio. But then he always has. That's nothing new."

"Let's see a few tears now and I'll put my arms around you. To console you, of course," suggested David.

She smiled.

"No. No smiling. You're supposed to be grieving."

It was almost more than he could do to keep from smiling himself. But he stood and came to stand next to her chair. She leaned into him, taking in and enjoying the familiar smell of antiseptic on his green scrubs. She took a tissue from her purse and wiped her eyes.

"That's the spirit. Let them see what anguish they've caused a beautiful granddaughter. Come. I'll walk you to the ferry dock."

"Thanks." She picked up the urn and held it in her arms as if it were a child. Cherished.

"Crab wasn't sure what time he would be returning to the island. The ferry was in for maintenance. Just walk me to the dock, and I'll take it from there. Something tells me we'll see each other again before this play is finished."

"Certainly hope so."

"You've been a great help, David. And I thought coroners only dealt with dead people. But you've helped Papa stay alive and I thank you for being such a friend."

He cocked his head to one side, "Actually, I helped him die. But go now. See you soon."

Molly waited at the edge of the ferry dock, then Crab motioned her to come closer. "Ah, Missy D*oktor*. You're back. Good. The ferry, she is ready. We'll get underway shortly. And e*l Capitán*? He is coming with us?"

Molly shook her head and turned away, wiping at her eyes as if she were crying.

"What? What is the matter, Missy?"

"Papa's already here with us, Crab."

She reached inside her bag and brought out the ornate urn.

"What is this?" Crab reached for the urn, then quickly pulled his hands away.

"What is this?"

"Papa's ashes. He passed away early this morning. I'm taking his ashes to Cayo Canna where they'll be spread over his favorite fishing places near Crabber's Cove."

She turned away and dabbed at her eyes again.

"¡*Dios*! No! He was getting better, no?"

"I thought so. But he had a heart attack. It happened so quickly there was nothing to be done."

Crab shook his head in disbelief. "Cayo Canna will not be the same without e*l Capitán*. He was respected by many. He will be missed."

Molly nodded. Then she took her seat at the front.

So far, so good. But this play-acting might get tedious before it gets finished.

"I'll have you home shortly, Missy D*oktor*. If you need to rest, my cabin is always available to you."

"Thanks, Crab. I think I'll sit up here for the time being."

Crab radioed the office at the Cayo Canna dock to have Tomás meet him. The wind was pushing twenty knots. He'd have to 'crab' the ferry in and needed Tomás there to grab lines and help him secure the craft for the evening. Those winds most likely meant a storm brewing somewhere.

After they docked, Molly gathered her bag, the urn, and her purse. Crab helped her disembark and again offered his condolences.

"I will remember e*l Capitán* with much respect and fondness. He was a true gentleman."

"Thank you, Crab. I hardly know how to break the news to Solana and Patrick. They'll be heartbroken."

"Of course. Life can be difficult, Missy D*oktor*. I am truly sorry you have lost your *abuelo*."

She went to the ferry office and called for Rafael to pick her up. Ten minutes later the familiar cab was dockside.

269

"Dr. Mac," Rosco nodded. "To the lighthouse?"

"Yes, Rafael. To the lighthouse." And off he went.

"Captain Jack is better, I hope?"

Molly waited a moment before answering him. It was very difficult to say those words, "*he's passed away*," even knowing it wasn't true.

Rafael slammed the brakes, causing Molly's items to fall to the floor. Thank goodness the urn had been sealed.

"What? The Captain?"

"Yes, he died early this morning. A heart attack."

"Oh, my. What? But . . . Oh, what a terrible loss for you. For all of us."

Molly dabbed at her eyes again, detesting this charade she was forced to participate in. She was sure, though, that having told Crab and Rafael the entire island would know of Papa's death shortly. Which was exactly what he wanted.

Molly paid Rafael and approached the front door where Solana stood quietly. Her stoic appearance belied the anxiety sizzling just below the surface.

"Captain Jack's not doing well?"

"No . . . I mean, yes. Actually, he's doing very well. So well, in fact, he's become a ghost again. Casper is on the loose."

"What? But we need to talk to him."

After listening to Molly's long explanation of why Papa was now 'dead', Solana went to the radio.

"I don't know if this is the right thing or not, but I believe Drifter needs to know about Captain Jack's death. I hope he was in on the plan and understands this is a scenario we're playing out. I can only imagine how disturbing it would be to him to think Captain Jack is truly dead."

Molly was amazed at how quickly Solana could process the communications. It had only taken her a short time to learn the code Drifter and Jack used. That had been the skill Solana brought to Fidel. She could learn code quicker than anyone else, and he used her abilities frequently.

Chapter 53

"Quiet, Carlos. I can't think when you're running your trap." *Jefe* rubbed his forehead, a gesture that was familiar to Carlos and Elian.

"I was saying the pathway is clear now that the old *hombre* is gone. We can come and go as we please. Maybe even take a couple of more shipments of weapons. The more we take, the more money they pay us. *Sí?*" Carlos asked.

"I pay you, Carlos. I decide what weapons we take and when. If I left the planning to you, we'd all end up in a U.S. military prison. Quiet. Let me think."

Carlos grabbed a *cerveza* and stormed out the door. Elian stood beneath a palm tree sipping his own brew, swatting at the no-see-ums that were swarming just before nightfall.

"Elian, what say we *scram? Jefe's* getting more bossy every day. I've got enough money to get to the islands. You probably got enough to get to Nicaragua, huh?"

"Maybe. But if we make that final run to Key West, to the cruise ship, we'll both have a lot of money. No, Carlos. We have to stick this out. Now that *el Capitán* is no longer a problem, it will be easier."

"But those other two, the ones I fired a warning at. Do you think they'll be looking for us?"

Elian shrugged his shoulders. "I don't know. Maybe. But you may have scared them off."

Carlos snickered, "Yeah. I bet they never come back."

Jefe was listening from the darkened doorway, and then he walked over. "Scared who off? What are you talking about?"

Elian looked to Carlos then went back inside the shack. He didn't want to hear this explanation.

"It's nothing, *Jefe*. We were just talking about seeing the others, the two fishermen who came without *el Capitán.*"

"The other two? What other two?"

"I don't know. They just showed up in the Cobra, the one the old seaman owns. But he wasn't with them."

"Did they see you?"

"Yeah, but not to worry. I sent a warning shot across their bow. They won't be back. That's for sure."

"What? You fired at them?"

"It was nothing. Just trying to scare them off. Must have worked too. They haven't been out for a couple of days now."

Jefe stared at the young man, turned his back to him, then whirled around and slammed his fist into Carlos' mouth, causing him to fall to the ground, groaning as blood spurted and ran down his chin. *Jefe* then planted his booted foot square in the middle of Carlos' stomach. Besides being painful, it knocked the breath out of him.

"You are the most stupid *hombre* I have ever known! Do you ever think before you act? How can anyone be so dense?" He rammed his foot in Carlos's abdomen again, then kicked at the sand, sending it flying into the young man's face.

At that juncture he went inside, leaving Carlos bleeding from the mouth, blinded from the sand, and unable to move a finger or catch a breath.

Elian was lying on his bunk, flipping through one of his *World of Wrestling* magazines. He wasn't going to take the blame for Carlos' stupidity this time.

Jefe glanced over and made eye contact with him. "Take care of the problem." Then he walked out, started his runabout, and headed back to his place, his thoughts running wild.

I just have to hang on now. This project will be over soon, and I will join my superiors in Cuba. My star is rising. Now Fidel will take notice of me for sure.

Chapter 54

Jack ran his hand across the teak gunwale and nodded approvingly. "*Admiral's Lady*, huh? Very appropriate. She's quite impressive. Puts my old Cobra to shame." He gave the throttle the slightest touch and she responded in a heartbeat.

"Could get used to that. Of course, my Cobra is aptly named too. She's slow to rai her head, but once she does she'll strike out and show you what she's got."

"Not thinking of trading her, are you?"

"Well, she runs hot occasionally, but nah, I'll not trade her. Too many memories. She and I are going to grow old together," he smiled.

Admiral Bowen nodded in agreement. "My *Lady* will get us where we need to be in a hurry. Let's hope we're not faced with that situation, though. We're not exactly young men anymore, Casper."

"Bah! Youth has its advantages, but the older I get the better I like it. Age allows you a better perspective on things. Lets you see the bigger picture rather than just what's right in front of your eyes."

"I don't mind getting older either, but could do without this arthritis in my knees and back."

"Arthritis?"

"Yeah. Why do you think I'm letting you skipper the *Lady*?"

Jack grinned, enjoying the feel of the saltwater spray coming from the brisk wind off the Gulf. It had been some time since he'd carried out a "night-ops," but had no doubt of his ability to do so.

Bear leaned back in his chair, using his foot to push aside the snorkel and fins laying on the floor. He'd brought those as Casper would need them to swim ashore. He lighted a Cuban cigar and let out a deep sigh. Both men were dressed in black from head to toe. Appropriate attire when on a mission.

"Tell me about Molly. How's she doing? Wounds healing?"

"Ah, you know. Physical wounds usually heal given enough time. Emotional ones, not so easily."

"She afraid her attacker is still out there . . . looking for her?"

"Maybe. She doesn't tell me much. Not like she did when she was younger. Knowing her, I expect she's trying to figure out a few things on her own."

"Have the Baltimore police made any progress toward finding the guy?"

"None. I've kept in touch with them weekly. Until Molly can recall some details from that evening, they don't have much to go on."

"Uhm. What are you planning to do? There's no way in hell you're going to let a guy who hurt your granddaughter not pay for his crime."

"Are you suggesting I might interfere in police business?"

"It wouldn't be the first time."

Casper smiled, "I'm biding my time and have my hands full at the moment trying to keep up with your demands. But, yes. I'll be heading to Baltimore as soon as this business with Fidel is over. And I pray it will be over soon. This is one mission at which we must succeed."

"As I recall, Casper, most of our missions were successful."

"Yes, but the few that weren't are still with me, and I'm sure those memories haunt you as well."

Bear didn't respond, just changed positions in his chair and blew out a puff of smoke that was snatched away on the wind.

Casper brought *Admiral's Lady* to a stop about a half-mile out from the marina on the mainland. The small talk now came to a halt. Any talking from this time until the end of the mission would relate only to what was needed for clarification of details.

Bear handed Casper a small item about the size of a pack of Juicy Fruit gum. "You're gonna like this little toy."

"Enlighten me. What am I going to do with this?"

"Feel along the ends of it."

Casper ran his fingers along both ends of the small item, discovering that one end had a slightly raised button.

"Let's see. Small button on left end. Missing on the right."

"This is the latest gadget the Navy is issuing to intelligence types. It's a transmitter and receiver in one. Makes no sounds. Vibrates only. The military is using some very sophisticated equipment these days, Casper. But this little baby can transmit or receive and not be detected by most internal security systems."

"And how are we to make use of it?"

"You'll put this in your pocket. I'll have one like it in mine. We'll run this op just like always. I'll be the watchdog, and you'll be the ghost. I'll alert you if I see anyone looking around or going into the building. You go about your business and become the ghost you are so capable of being, get your information, and make your way back out here. I'll

279

be watching. I'll have my *Lady* ready to make for the open ocean."

Jack nodded. "Then unless I get a signal from you, I'm to assume all is well. When I'm finished, I'll send you a transmission—one touch of the button—to let you know I'm headed your way."

"Aye, sir. And one more thing."

"What's that?"

"If you should find yourself in a 'compromising' position, don't be a fool. Being caught would only be a temporary problem. We'd be able to explain ourselves. Eventually. It wouldn't be our first choice, but could be done."

Casper sighed. "Bear, you can't see a ghost. If you can't see him, you can't catch him. Now douse that cigar and observe silence."

Bear went below to retrieve his night binoculars. When he returned he looked about. Casper was nowhere to be seen. Fins and snorkel were gone. The ghost had disappeared.

"Damned old fool. Didn't have to sneak off like that.

Chapter 55

What did Drifter say? Did he understand your message?"

"I'm sure he got it. But I'm not sure I understand his response. It makes no sense to me."

"What did he say?"

"I checked it twice. I'm sure I've interpreted it correctly. He said: 'Jem, things are never as bad as they at first seem.' Does that make any sense to you?"

Molly racked her brain. The words were familiar. Where had she read them? Or had she just heard them?

"I know that sentence. I'm sure I've read that somewhere."

She stood at the open window breathing in the scent of the moonflower, a night-blooming plant Mimi was fond of. The undulating waves spewed white foam into the air, sure sign of a storm brewing somewhere off their coast.

She then turned to Solana with a grin on her face. "Oh, Solana. Papa's already been in touch with Drifter. That's a message to me . . . to us."

"I don't understand."

"Papa and I keep in touch about books we're reading. I've not had much time for reading in the last couple of years, but there is one book I did take time to read simply because it was getting such rave reviews. I told Papa about it and he read it, too. It has become one of our favorites."

"What book is this?"

"*To Kill a Mockingbird.* That passage is in the novel: 'Jem, nothing is ever as bad as it at first seems.' Papa particularly thought it was worth putting to memory. It's his way of letting Drifter know he's well and still operating undercover. Papa would know I would remember that passage. It's his way of letting us know he is well."

"Drifter knows about this story? And that Captain Jack is pretending he's dead?"

"I think so. But that still doesn't help us know what our next actions should be."

"I know what our next actions should be," Solana declared.

"You do? What? I have no idea."

"If Captain Jack were here and knew about Father Patrick and Todd getting shot at, he'd have us keep some kind of weapon handy. If those who want the Captain dead come looking for us, we have no way to defend ourselves."

"I never thought of that. But we don't have any weapons. I wouldn't even know where to buy a gun."

"We don't need to buy anything. Captain Jack has a closet with several pistols that will work."

"Really? But even so, I've never shot a gun before. I probably couldn't hit anything if my life depended on it," Molly laughed.

"Don't laugh. It may. But I can show you how to use a pistol."

Bem came running through then, Ensign on his heels.

Molly shook her head back and forth. "He's still not speaking. He makes noises but not words. When all this settles down I'll take him to the mainland. See what can be done."

"Molly, you must realize you can't take care of every child you see who has problems. Children such as Bem are common in these islands."

"I know, Solana. But I can help this one. Besides, it's time I put my medical skills to use. I've wallowed in self-pity long enough."

Solana nodded in agreement. "Let's take a look at the Captain's weapons. They're locked away in a closet in the lantern room."

As they were taking a peek at Papa's gun collection, the front door opened and Patrick stuck his head in.

"Solana? Molly?"

Molly yelled down, "We're coming down. Be right there."

As the two women were coming down the stairs, Patrick rattled off his thoughts about his trip to Queenie's.

"That shack is not the best place for a child. She's got dead animal heads on every surface. Gave me the willies. Anyway, this is all I could find," he said, handing the valise to Solana.

"There are several t-shirts and a couple of pairs of the smallest shorts I've ever seen. But no shoes. There's an old newspaper clipping and a large manila envelope, too."

"At least he has a few changes of clothing," said Solana.

"I found one other thing, too," said Patrick as he dug into the valise and brought out the red, satin pouch and fished around inside it.

"This."

He held up the amber necklace and Molly reached for it. "That's a fossilized creature. But what is it? I don't think I've ever seen such an animal. Maybe Todd would know something about fossils."

She held it up to the light and was almost knocked off her feet as Bem ran to her and grabbed at the necklace.

"Mamee, Mamee, Mamee!" Bem jerked the necklace from Molly's hand and put it around his neck. He caressed the amber piece, rubbing it against his cheek.

"A remnant of his past, I'd guess," said Molly. "We may never know what it is exactly, but it's meaningful to him."

Patrick nodded. "I see Jack's not here. What did the doctor say?"

Molly sent a look to Solana. "He's been released from the hospital. According to Dr. Blake, he's made a fantastic recovery, and no major damage has been done to any organs."

"Thanks be to God. Then why isn't he here?"

"That's quite a story. I'll give you as many details as I can, but it's a rather fantastic tale."

Patrick chuckled, "Hell, everything Jack does is fantastic. Nothing would surprise me."

"Don't be too sure about that. His latest instructions are for you to 'don that black and white outfit and say a few words' over his ashes as I sprinkle them in Crabber's Cove."

"What? What does that mean?"

"He's become Casper again for the time being."

"Casper? Oh, you mean his persona when he was operating in the intelligence business?"

"Right. He's gone underground. Wants the world to think he's dead. He thinks that if whoever is trying to kill him believes he is dead, then they'll make a mistake, leading him to discover their identity."

"Jaysus, Mary, and Joseph. Did you tell him about the fishermen shooting and wounding Redhawk?"

"No. I never saw him. He disappeared before I had a chance to talk to him. But Solana sent a radio message to Drifter and his response leads us to believe Papa's been in touch with him."

"What do you think, Solana?" Patrick asked.

"I believe Captain Jack would want us to continue as we usually do. We should post his obituary in the newspaper as he requested and follow his instructions about sprinkling his ashes.

"Someone will be watching us, so life should appear to be as normal as we can make it. Only then will this criminal make a move. A mistake. None of us know the Captain's plan, but I assure you he has one. He'll be in touch when the time is right. Until then, we stay calm."

"Speaking of staying calm, did you get a chance to check on Todd today?" Molly asked.

"Yeah, he was complaining of a terrific headache and said the stitches were irritating. But other than that he seemed to be weathering the ordeal fairly well."

"Headache. That was to be expected."

"I fixed him up with a rather nasty, Irish remedy. He said he owed me one for that. But it did relieve his headache."

Molly looked up at Patrick. "He's very interesting. Do you know he has relatives on the Seminole reservation over on the mainland?"

"Yeah, he mentioned it. He's concerned about the Cuban situation too. Talked about needing to make a trip to check on his people on the reservation. I told him he'd better get clearance from his doctor before taking any trips."

"Patrick, I'm not his doctor. I simply stitched him up from a slight wound."

"Don't think he's of the opinion it's a slight wound. He's concerned enough to have his handgun up on deck next to him."

"Good for him." Solana stepped in. "That's exactly what the three of us must do."

"What? Strap on a .45?" Patrick grinned. His effort at levity met with stern looks from both women.

"Father, this is serious. Captain Jack has several pistols and I believe he'd want us all to have one handy. We have no idea who to trust and until he's here again, we have to take precautions."

"Do you have ammunition as well?"

"Yes. The Captain is well-prepared for an event such as this. There's plenty of ammunition."

"Good God. A pistol-wielding priest. What next?" chimed Patrick.

Solana then spoke up, "I think it would seem appropriate for me to stay with you for a few days, Molly. To comfort a grieving granddaughter. That would be expected. That way I can listen to the radio along with you. If the 24th is a special date, then we only have a few days to figure out who's harboring the sulfur mustard."

Patrick ran his fingers through his hair. His long legs, now suntanned, crossed the room in half a dozen steps. Back and forth. Back and forth. He let out a long sigh and stared out the window.

"I'm no great strategist, but we three must pool our thoughts, make any connections about people we know. Brainstorm our ideas."

"Let's have some food first. We'll all think better on a full stomach," Solana suggested as she brought out a platter of cold cuts and a pitcher of sangria.

"The lab reports verified that the Glenfiddich was tampered with. That's the one fact that's indisputable. By whom? Don't know. Who has access to the Glenfiddich?"

"The distillery in Scotland handles it first. Then it's sent to the U.S. Customs Office on the mainland. The Customs Office inspects all incoming merchandise before it's released to the addressee."

"And you believe the poison was put into the Glenfiddich using a syringe?"

"Yes. Solana and I saw the minute hole in the cork."

"Maybe the distillery staff in Scotland played a part?" asked Patrick.

"I don't think that's a possibility. The family is distant cousins of Papa. Why would they try to poison someone, a family member, who imports their special malt at a very high price?"

"Got it. Let's cross them off. Next?"

"I'm not sure exactly how the process works at the Customs Office. Solana, do you know anything about that end?"

"Not really. When the Glenfiddich is delivered to the lighthouse, the crate has been unpackaged and the bottles are all individually wrapped in brown paper."

"Who delivers the crate?"

Crab brings it over on the ferry and leaves it on the dock for the Captain or Rafael to pick up."

Patrick let out a long sigh, "Then we've not figured out anything. I've been here several months now, and from what I know of Crab and Rafael, I don't think either of them would have any wish to kill Jack. And how do we know someone doesn't tamper with it when it's sitting on the dock before Rafael picks it up?"

"If we don't suspect Crab or Rafael, who does that leave?" Molly asked.

"No one. We're back where we started."

Patrick shook his head. In his few months here, the rhythm of the island, its unique scents, its lush beauty, and most of all its people had begun to seep into his soul. Would he find it difficult to leave if he decided to return to his Church?

Chapter 56

Elian lay on his bunk staring at the ceiling, which was nothing but a few strips of tin grown over with sawgrass. *Jefe's* message was clear. Get rid of Carlos before he compromises the entire operation.

Elian had been taken aback earlier when the order to "take care of Roberto" had been given. In his eyes Roberto was still just a kid. Elian, himself, had a child only a few years younger than Roberto. The fact that Carlos killed Roberto without even talking it over with him was unsettling.

But now his orders were to 'take care of the problem' as *Jefe* apparently thought Carlos was becoming just that. Elian had signed on to this project for one reason. He needed to amass as much money as he could in a short time.

Last week he'd sent most of his money to his wife. She and their two children were to go to Nicaragua to stay with his brother and his family until Elian could get there. He needed to complete this project. Get the money *Jefe* had promised.

Running guns was one thing; killing a *compadre* was another. He didn't want to be a murderer, but he did not doubt that if the shoe were on the other foot, Carlos would kill him just as he had Roberto. That left him only two choices. He'd either have to kill Carlos as ordered, or he'd have to disappear himself.

Once his decision was made, he climbed down from the bunk and went outside. Carlos was sitting on the ground leaning against a large Australian pine, finishing off his latest *cerveza*. This had become his nightly habit. Drinking to the point he finally passed out. Of course, his mornings were rather painful and he was slow to get moving.

Elian sat down next to him. "Don't fret over *Jefe*. He's under a lot of pressure. This is his one chance to prove himself to Fidel, and that's his goal over all else."

Carlos's was swollen and bruised. He had taken a brutal beating and felt the effects of it still. He tossed the empty *cerveza* bottle into the mangroves and reached into his shirt pocket for his cigarettes. The pack was empty.

"He'll get what's coming to him. Trust me. I'll see to that," he murmured.

"Ah, don't waste your time. When this is all over, *Jefe* will be long gone and you'll be in the islands with a *chica* on each arm."

"I'm sick of him and his orders. He's not nearly as smart as he thinks he is." He stood, a bit unsteady on his feet.

"Gotta get some cigarettes." He stumbled on toward the shack.

When he hadn't returned a few minutes later, Elian went inside. Carlos was lying face down on his bunk, having drunk enough *cervezas* to put him out until the next morning. That made Elian's plan easier to execute. He knew what his future would be if he followed *Jefe's* orders. It was quite simple. After delivering the sulfur mustard, *Jefe* would have his Habana *hombres* 'take care' of him, too.

He picked up the small canvas bag that held his few items of clothing and a picture of Juanita and his *niños*. He walked out and closed the door to the shack, then made his way to the mangroves where they kept *El Escorpión* hidden.

He shoved the boat out of the thick mangroves and climbed aboard. He'd filled the tank earlier that morning, readying the boat for the run they were scheduled to make tomorrow. The engine purred softly, and he eased his way to the opening in the mangroves that would give him access to the open Gulf.

Juanita and his *niños* would be waiting for him. That was the thought that he kept foremost in his mind. He smiled, allowing himself a moment of satisfaction thinking how angry *Jefe* would be when he discovered that not only was his mechanic gone, but had taken *El Escorpión* with him. As for Carlos? He was *Jefe's* problem.

A whipping, spume-filled wind blew from the northeast and Elian pointed the bow of *El Escorpión* due south. Nicaragua wasn't that far in a vessel as fast as this. It was made to run wide open. So wide open it would be.

"*Adios amigos*," he laughed.

Chapter 57

Solana, I'm not so sure about this idea of yours. Keeping a pistol handy. I've never used a firearm of any sort. I heal people, not harm them."

"Captain Jack would wish this. He'd want us to be prepared."

"Prepared for what?"

"These people, these rebels, they will not hesitate to kill any of us, Molly. You must believe me."

"I do, but . . . "

"No more buts. Let's go through this once again." She picked up the pistol, a .45 caliber Browning M1911A1 and placed it in Molly's hands. Then she repeated her instructions.

Molly lifted the pistol and pointed it toward the door. She pulled the trigger and heard a loud click as she did so. But she found the pistol very heavy and unsteady in her hand.

There was one knock at the door, and Patrick stepped in, followed by Todd.

"Bloody Hell!" Patrick yelled as he found himself staring down the barrel of a very lethal-looking weapon. He rushed forward and pushed Molly's hand up in the air. Todd took a quick step backward and banged his already-aching head on the wall.

"What in God's name are you two doing?" The tone of Patrick's voice matched the fear on his flushed Irish face.

"I'm teaching Molly to use a pistol. She may need to have that skill, Father."

Patrick relaxed his grip on Molly's hand and lowered the pistol. He swallowed hard, then shook his head. "All right. I agree. We need to be prepared. But let's work together in instructing Molly to use this weapon.

"I, uh, realize you know how to use this weapon, Solana, but for a newbie like Molly, there's a better way of holding it that may help."

Patrick looked back at Todd, who was still plastered to the wall. "Hey, Tonto, why don't you take a seat. Molly needs to check out those stitches. Solana, I really could use a cup of your delicious coffee."

"Of course, Father."

"Any chance of a cinnamon roll?"

Solana smiled then. Patrick was relieved she hadn't taken offense at his remarks. He didn't know details, but he was sure Solana had an interesting history.

"How are the stitches? Itching by now?" Molly asked.

"Not too bad. A couple of 'em are pulling. But the headache's not quite as bad this morning."

Patrick piped up, "I told you my Irish remedy would work wonders."

"Huh, maybe. But I think I'll only use it when I'm desperate and have nothing else around."

Molly motioned to Todd. "Here, sit on the sofa. Let me take a look." The stitches were holding and his face was healing. But he would have a scar.

As Molly was cleaning the area around Todd's stitches, she had to stand near him. When she bent over to get a closer look, he reached up to touch her face.

"What happened here?" he asked, as his fingers stroked her wounded cheek which had now become thickly scabbed over, the "S" well defined.

She jerked back. She wasn't expecting that touch. She also wasn't sure how much she should tell him.

"Just a wound from a recent event. It's healing, but somewhat slowly. Yours will heal much sooner and though you'll have a scar, it won't be very noticeable."

But mine will be.

Todd reached up again and traced the "S" with his finger.

"My people believe a scar such as this means you have been chosen for a special task. It's called a *poia*. It is something one wears with pride. Sort of a badge of honor. There are many legends regarding the *poia*. I like the one about a young boy called Star Boy. Many tribes have similar beliefs and my tribe considers it a thing of beauty.

"It means one has gone through a trial of fire, like a rite of passage. Some believe it was put there so that the great spirits may recognize the chosen ones. If you read the myths and beliefs, you discover they all have one message: you are chosen, and your destiny has been planned."

Molly was ever so conscious of the wound, which was still far from being healed. "I see. Then maybe I'll spend some time reading Native American myths and legends about scars."

Todd smiled at her. "Looks like I've been chosen as well. We have something in common."

Patrick listened to this exchange and had watched the expression on Molly's face as Todd traced the scar. What he told her had taken root.

Perhaps that was a good thing. She was already in the habit of turning her face so that the scarred side was away from those near her. It bothered Patrick when she did this. In his opinion, her beauty went much deeper than any scar could touch.

He walked over to the table where the ham radio was buzzing away. "Anything new on this contraption?"

Solana shook her head. "There's a lot of chatter, but nothing from *Padre* and *Niño.*"

"Then let's get this pistol instruction underway. Molly, stand close here. Todd, I know you have a .38 Colt Special. I assume you can use it?"

"I can. Can use a bow and arrow, too, paleface."

They all laughed, which helped ease the tension in the room. But even so, fear was beginning to worm its way into the lighthouse.

"Now, first things first. Always assume that any weapon is loaded. And yours will be."

Solana watched as Patrick taught Molly how to check the firearm, how to load it, and most importantly for Molly, how to hold it with two hands. That certainly made it easier to manage.

He explained every detail with precision and patience, and his entire persona changed in a matter of moments. That he was knowledgeable about firearms was apparent. It was also evident to Solana that he was experienced. Apparently, she wasn't the only one who had secrets from the past.

Solana raised an eyebrow. "Father, you appear to know something about firearms."

He shrugged his shoulders. "A bit. Cuba's not the only country to have difficulties. Ireland has her own problems. And rebels as well."

"We'll work more on this tomorrow," he said as he took the gun from Molly's hand.

Bem came into the room rubbing his eyes. With the innocence that only a child can exhibit, he walked over to the sofa where Todd was sitting. He reached up and stroked Todd's long hair as it fell behind his shoulders.

"Mamee? Mamee?" Bem looked into Todd's face as if trying to remember if this were someone he should know. Todd sat still until the child walked away.

"He's quite alone, isn't he?"

"Yes. Queenie's disappeared. We still haven't seen her."

"Have you talked to the authorities? Perhaps they can help you find her."

Molly blurted out a quick response.

"I'm obligated to inform authorities about an orphaned child. But not just yet. They'll place him in a foster home of some kind. That's a cruel thing to do to such a small child, in my opinion. And Queenie may return for him."

Patrick hesitated, but only for a moment.

"Queenie's not coming back, Molly. Something happened at her shack. Her scarf was laying on the floor behind the door, and from other evidence in the room, I believe there was a skirmish or fight there. I don't think we'll see her again."

"Then we'll wait a while to make a decision. After Papa's back. He may have some ideas," Molly stated.

Silence. Molly felt Patrick staring at her. She let out a sigh. "I suppose you'll tell me it's not only unethical and likely to cost me my license, but it's also a sin of omission?"

Patrick gave her a small smile. "No, I was thinking perhaps Bem's coming here was an act of divine intervention. And Molly? We all have secrets."

Solana nodded. "I've thought about this situation as well. Bem needs help, but we may be putting him in harm's way just by keeping him here. But I don't see any other way."

Molly decided to change the subject. "Later today, just before sunset, we should have our "sprinkling of the ashes" ceremony. I posted the obituary yesterday; the entire island will know about Papa's death by now."

"Have you done this before, Father?"

"What? Sprinkled ashes? Yes, of course. But the other times I did so the person was actually dead. Makes me wonder who or what is in that urn."

"Oh, David said it was just beach sand. Nothing to worry over."

"I believe it should be just the two of us, Molly. The grieving granddaughter and the priest in his "black and white outfit," as Jack calls it. We'll take the Cobra and sprinkle him in Crabber's Cove. Todd can be observing through his binoculars. If anyone is watching us, he'll see them."

"All right. I suppose we must follow Papa's instructions. But I do wish he would get back here."

"He'll come at the proper time. He knows what he's doing." Solana reminded them. Her faith in Jack never wavered.

Chapter 58

It was after 2:00 a.m. and Bear thought Casper would have returned by now. That was the nature of any night-ops mission. It always took longer than you anticipated, and your nerves would be frayed before it was over.

He was startled when blinded by a bright light shining in his face. He held his breath and halted all movement. His training had taught him to stay quiet and look for an opportunity to get the upper hand if it presented itself.

The light wavered for a short moment, then was extinguished. Total blackness returned, the moon providing the only source of light. He planted his feet apart and drew his weapon, ready to respond to the attack he knew was imminent.

The light struck his face again, blinding him to anything nearby. Then it went dark again. The hair on his neck stood on end, and he listened so hard his ears ached.

Coming from the stern, a gravelly voice called out, "Can you give a ghost a hand? Take the speargun. Didn't use it, so be careful. It's still loaded."

Bear released his breath and cursed like the devil himself. "Dammit Casper, you didn't have to scare the shit out of me. Just a friendly hello would have been enough." He offered his hand and pulled Casper up.

"Just keeping you on your toes."

"Was getting worried. And I really need a cigar."

"Those things will kill you, according to Molly. Says they cause lung cancer."

"That may be. But right now I'm going to light one up unless you tell me not to."

"We're good. No one knows we've been here. The Customs Office is deserted and the guard at the dock was asleep at his station."

Bear took the wheel and when they had put some miles between them and the mainland, he pulled the throttle back and came to a full stop.

"I just happen to have your favorite beverage on board. Care for a taste?"

"Very thoughtful, admiral."

Bear listened as Casper gave him a rundown on what he found in the Customs Office warehouse. The items that were marked for delivery to Cayo Canna were all staged in a particular area, and all were in their original packing from whatever port and country they had originated.

"It finally dawned on me that my Glenfiddich always arrives at the lighthouse in a tightly wrapped packing crate. That is, until the last couple of shipments. In these shipments there was an open crate and each bottle was wrapped individually with a thin, brown paper covering.

"I figured the distillery had changed their shipping methods. Never occurred to me someone had removed the original packaging in order to have access to the individual bottles."

"That eliminates the Customs Office. Which means it got tampered with after leaving them. It leaves Customs and is loaded on to the *Calypso* for transport. Maybe someone on the ferry tampered with it?" asked Bear.

"I doubt it. Crab runs a pretty tight operation there. That old tub leaves on time and he keeps his dockhands in line. I've seen him chewing out a couple now and then. I think it'd be hard to get that kind of activity past him."

Casper leaned back in his seat. His mind was still extremely keen, but he did have to admit the long swim back to the *Admiral's Lady* had tired him. Just a bit.

"What else do you know about this fellow, Crab? Does he have a family? Where's he from? How long's he been here?"

Bear could drill you with questions until you wanted to smack him. But Casper understood the reason for such.

"Let's see. He's been piloting the ferry since old Mick died. Probably three or four years now. As far as family, I know a little but not everything. They were among some of the first to leave Cuba. His father was an educated man and served in Batista's inner circle. Some kind of Minister of Finance or Economics. Something like that.

"Crab brought them to Tampa, to Ybor City where many Cubanos live. They were aging and Crab feared Castro's henchmen might come for the Minister. I suppose they're still there unless they've passed away.

"Crab got a job at the cigar factory in Ybor City. A job that he detested. He'd worked on the water all his life. When the opportunity to skipper the *Calypso* came up, he jumped on it."

"Sounds like he passes the smell test. So what happens when he unloads the Glenfiddich on the island?"

"He has one of the dockhands give me a call that it arrived and he leaves it on the dock. Most of the time I take the golf cart down and retrieve it, but occasionally Rafael picks it up and drops it at the lighthouse."

"Rafael? What do you know about him?"

"He's been on the island a couple of years now. We're all glad to have him as he operates the only taxi service. He calls it "Rafael's Enterprises," which is rather humorous. He only has the one cab."

"What else do you know about him?"

"He came here from Fort Lauderdale."

"Anything else?"

"Yep. He's got a criminal record in Fort Lauderdale. But he was a kid when those charges were filed. It was for some petty stuff, selling contraband, verbal assault on a police officer, and a breaking and entering case.

"He had a short stay in a minimum penal facility, but he's never given me any reason to suspect he was engaging in anything unlawful or illegal on the island."

"Maybe he's not making enough money driving his cab to suit him. Where's his family?"

Casper thought for a long moment before answering that. His thoughts were churning fast and he was having trouble keeping them in order. Taking a long swallow of his drink, he looked at Bear.

"They live in Miami, Little Havana."

He looked down at his feet, rubbed the back of his neck, then looked back up to Bear. "They immigrated from Cuba years ago."

Bear nodded but said nothing.

"I must be slipping, Bear. I've had no reason to suspect Rafael. Maybe he's returned to his past behavior and aiding and abetting criminals is just in his blood." He stood then and took a deep breath.

"Let's head to your place in Placida. I need to make use of your radio and get a message to Solana and Molly. Then I could use a little sleep." He sighed deeply and shook his head.

"But something about this doesn't smell right. Rafael's not a leader. He's a follower if anything. If he's involved, then someone else is pulling the strings. He's just a puppet. Let's find him and "suggest" he give us some information about the weapons and sulfur mustard."

They headed toward Placida, each with his own thoughts of what might come next. Bear and Casper could be fairly convincing with their "suggestions" if need be.

Chapter 59

As had happened the day they took the Eucharist to the outer island, the moment Patrick affixed his white collar to his black clerical shirt he stepped into another realm. He became whole, warmth emanated from him, and his voice took on a tenor that held Molly captive when he read the biblical passage.

She was beginning to understand that Father O'Brien had many sides to him, and she was fascinated each time she discovered a new one.

The day couldn't have been more ideal—for sprinkling ashes, that is. Patrick held his worn, weathered Bible in one hand and made the sign of the cross with the other. Molly followed his cues as to when to sprinkle the ashes and bowed her head when he issued the final prayer.

The gentle breeze tugged at Papa's "remains" as Molly released them from her fingers, and they drifted out with the undulating motion of the warm Gulf waters.

"I believe that'll suffice. Don't think the Almighty will strike me for that bit of play-acting. Was done for a good reason. Quite sure he'll understand," Patrick stated.

And I might have to do this again. For real. Molly thought.

Patrick began to make preparations to start the engine and return to the lighthouse. He kept stepping over a small box on the floor so Molly picked it up and moved it out of the way.

The box held a couple of pruning tools and a small bottle of fluid. Molly decided it must have been in Papa's storage room as it was splattered with bits of oil paint he used for his seascapes. There was a notation on the bottle that got her attention: $C_2H_6O_2$. She thought for a moment, knowing it looked familiar.

"What's in the box?" asked Molly.

"Stuff I'm to deliver to Agnes. Jack asked me to take it to her last week, but I forgot about it until this morning. We'll drop it off as we go by her place on our way home."

Patrick made a sharp turn then, and Molly grabbed the edge of her seat. "Sorry. Still learning how to drive this thing."

Molly kept staring at the letters and numbers on the bottle of fluid. *$C_2H_6O_2$. A chemical notation. Where have I seen that before?*

The thought disappeared as quickly as it had come. They dropped the items off at Agnes's dock and had now arrived at the lighthouse.

Numerous floral arrangements were sitting along the porch railings—no doubt sent by islanders to express their condolences. Molly hadn't thought about that, the fact that Papa's 'death' would be painful to many locals.

"Ah, flowers. The age-old ritual is still appropriate. Today they're used to express love, respect, and admiration for the deceased. But originally they were used to camouflage the odor coming from the deteriorating bodies," rattled off Patrick.

"Thank you, Father O'Brien, for that edifying information. Unless you have more illuminating thoughts to pass on, I'll bring the flowers inside and enjoy their beauty and fragrance." Molly shook her head and smiled at this unlikely priest.

Solana was always affected by Patrick's priestly attire. She'd only seen him wear it a few times, and the effect was as moving as when Captain Jack wore his tropical-white uniform, with four-striped shoulder boards and ribbons galore on his chest. Of course, he only dressed in uniform on special occasions. But there was something about their 'uniforms' that brought out the best in both these men.

"Father Patrick, did the service go well?" Solana asked with a quirky smile.

"He's been sprinkled and prayed over. That's all any of us can ask."

She brought their evening refreshments to the patio. This had become a ritual that was apparently to everyone's liking. The ocean provided a backdrop of relaxing sounds, scents, and lulling movement that aided in their conversation. But even the ocean couldn't calm the environment tonight.

Patrick picked up the newspaper Solana had brought in that morning. "The paper says President Kennedy will address the nation again this evening. Believe it's an update on the Cuban business. Guess we better try to catch it."

Solana went inside and shortly came back to the patio. "I'm unable to raise Drifter. I've tried several times, but he doesn't answer. There's a storm in the Gulf and I suspect it's interfering with reception. I'll keep trying."

Molly began to gather up the remains of their meal and clear the table. "Todd's invited me to go to the Seminole reservation with him tomorrow. He needs to check on his family. They're probably as worried as we are about this Cuban situation.

"Since we're going to the mainland anyway, I'm going to take Bem with us. He needs to be examined by an ear-nose-throat specialist."

"The ferry leaves early. But how are you going to get to the reservation?" Patrick asked.

"We're not taking the ferry. Todd's taking his boat to the mainland then renting a car. The reservation is only about an hour from there. We can take Bem to the doctor and go to the reservation after that.

"Papa and Mimi took me to the reservation a couple of times when I visited them. As a child, I found it fascinating. Wonder what I'll think as an adult?"

Patrick turned his attention back to the newspaper, but his thoughts were not on the news articles.

Adonis isn't wasting any time.

Chapter 60

*J*efe arrived at his bungalow and walked up the rickety dock, his head spinning with so many conflicting thoughts he couldn't keep them straight.

He strode in the back door, tossed his keys on the cluttered counter and reached inside his ancient Frigidaire for a cold *cerveza*. He had electricity but no air conditioning, so he switched on the overhead fan and listened to its hum as he sat at the small kitchen table.

He would put off calling his superiors as long as possible. This project was to have been his entree to serve with Fidel's closest comrades. But because the three *hombres* he'd chosen to be his assistants were exceedingly stupid, the entire operation was in jeopardy.

He'd just returned from the mangrove shack where he'd found an empty room. No Carlos, no Elian. *El Escorpión* was nowhere in sight, and the rifles were still standing where he left them. It only took a minute for *Jefe* to understand this situation.

"Damn you both to hell! You're no better than Roberto—afraid of your shadow. And you took *El Escorpión*? That boat belongs to a very highly placed person . . . Fidel's right hand. He has *hombres* everywhere. You will be found!"

He had stomped about the grounds, then followed a trail of empty *cerveza* bottles that brought him to a patch of dense mangroves where he discovered Carlos. Crouched down. Far back in the brush.

"A*migo, w*hy are you hiding in the mangroves? Come out now. *Jefe* is here."

Carlos crawled out slowly, clearly afraid of *Jefe's* reaction to finding his mechanic and boat gone.

"I had nothing to do with Elian . . . him taking *El Escorpión.* I swear, *Jefe.*"

"Not to worry. Elian is gone. I will take care of you."

He put his arm about Carlos' shoulder and they headed to the shack. Moments later, sea birds screeched and scattered in all directions when the shot rang out.

"Rest in peace, idiot!"

El Escorpión had been the key to, getting the sulfur mustard to Key West, and now it was gone. *Jefe* would have to find a couple of men to help him. Immediately. If he failed in this mission, this delivery, his chances of survival were zero.

Chapter 61

Go. There's no reason both of us have to stay cooped up in this lighthouse. Take Bem to the doctor and enjoy a trip to the reservation. I'll take care of any radio business," instructed Solana.

Patrick picked Molly up at 8:00 a.m. and dropped her and Bem at the path close to Crabber's Cove where the Endeavor was anchored. Todd watched them from the boat, then scooted over to the water's edge on the dingy. Patrick waved and went on.

"Right on time. Bem? You ready for a boat ride?"

Bem looked at Todd, then back to Molly, but said nothing. He took Molly's hand as she began walking toward the dinghy.

Todd helped them board and pulled up the anchor. This craft was quite a step up from Papa's old Cobra. If Molly had any qualms about traveling with Todd, they were quickly allayed. He handled the boat with the skill of an experienced seaman, which he was. Again, she was reminded that he was a most unusual man with many talents.

When they arrived on the mainland, Molly took Bem's hand. "I'm anxious to see what the specialist says about his ears. Solana can communicate with him. She believes he only understands Spanish. And the doctor's office isn't far. I can walk back to the dock from there."

"No need. I've arranged a rental car. I'll take you and then when you're done, we'll take out across Alligator Alley and be at the reservation shortly after lunch."

"Alligator Alley. Is it still called that?"

"Yep."

"I remember Papa telling me we were traveling on Alligator Alley, and I thought that meant we would see alligators every minute. I was fascinated with the village. And I thought there would be teepees." She giggled at her memories.

"Nope. Not a teepee anywhere. Today most of my people live in plain old, regular stucco and brick houses. Sorry to disappoint you. There are still a few chickee huts about though. Some of the older tribal members prefer them, especially in the summertime.

"My grandmother refused to sleep in the new stucco and brick houses. She believed there were healing factors in nature and that we should live out of doors as much as possible."

"She may be right about that, you know," Molly stated.

"Well, she only lived to be eighty-nine years old. So I guess not." He exchanged a smile with Molly that warmed her to the core. Being with Todd was like being with Charlie Watts—so easy. No pretenses, no attempts to impress each other with their various degrees and skills. Just easy conversation as if they had been friends for a long time.

Todd dropped Molly and Bem off and waited close by. He'd grown up in this deep-south part of the state. His work had him traveling around but his heart was here. It was only a short while before he spied Molly and Bem coming out of the doctor's office. Waving to him.

"What's the bottom line? Is he deaf?"

"No. Not deaf, but definitely hard of hearing. He hears well in his left ear. The right one is the real problem. His eardrum is perforated and that'll take six to eight weeks to heal.

"Dr. Langley gave me some antibiotics that should speed up the process. He agrees with Solana about Bem not understanding English. His nurse spoke Spanish and when she engaged Bem, he nodded his head when she asked him questions."

"He's not had a lot of care."

"No, Queenie can hardly care for herself. Certainly can't care for a child."

"What are you going to do with him now?"

"Do with him?"

"You must make some plan for him, don't you think?"

"I'm professionally and ethically required to alert the authorities . . . and I will . . . but not yet."

When they arrived at the reservation, Todd led Molly and Bem through a crowd of people that had gathered as soon as he stepped out of the car.

Molly heard English, but she also heard the language of Todd's people. It pleased her to know the language was still alive and being passed on to the younger generations.

Todd's mother held him close and whispered something in his ear that must have pleased him as he put his forehead against hers and spoke quietly to her. She touched his bandaged face.

"Molly, this is my *aneheh*, my mother. Molly nodded to the attractive older woman.

"*Aneheh,* this is my friend, Dr. Molly McCormick." The woman smiled but said nothing more.

"Koiko-Tadi!" a voice called loudly. Then a young woman ran to Todd, placing a kiss on both his cheeks. There was much concern regarding the bandage on his face and the only word Molly understood was "*poia.*"

"We were wondering if you were ever coming to visit."

This beautiful woman was a female version of Todd. Tall, thin, with long dark hair that was worn loose and being blown across her face by the breeze.

"Molly, this is Cocheetah, my sister."

311

The young woman reached out and took both Molly's hands in hers. She pulled her close and touched her cheeks to Molly's.

"Tadi, you have found this beautiful woman and have not brought her to us before now?" Todd looked uncomfortable for a moment.

"No . . . I mean ·.. . Molly is a friend. Just a friend."

"Of course."

Then Cocheetah spotted Bem, who'd stayed well-hidden behind Molly. She went down on her knees and reached out her hands to him as she had done with Molly. Bem hesitated, then slowly reached out his small hands.

"And who are you?" He said nothing.

"His name is Bem," said Molly.

Cocheetah then made a most unexpected gesture. She spoke to him in Miccosukee, one of the two Seminole languages, and made movements with her hands. Molly had no idea what the movements meant, but Bem's eyes followed each movement. He still didn't respond but did offer a half-smile.

As the young woman continued to talk to Bem, a small girl walked over to them and stood close to Cocheetah, clinging to her skirt. Soon two more girls and a young boy gathered 'round. They appeared to be listening, just as Bem was. The next moment, they all giggled, including Bem.

Molly looked at Todd. "Do you understand what's going on?"

"I do. Cocheetah speaks English and both our Seminole languages. She also speaks the language of children. She never meets one she can't communicate with.

"She's telling them a story of a small bird with long wings that allow it to fly higher than most birds, so it can see the children as it flies overhead. If you noticed, they looked up to the sky to see if they could spot one."

"That's amazing. She seems to have them in a trance."

"She has a special gift."

"Are any of these children hers?"

"They are all hers-in a manner of speaking. These children are orphans of one sort or another. Some of them were born to mothers who couldn't or wouldn't care for them.

"The small girl clinging to Cocheetah's skirt is Keva. Her parents deserted her the day she was born. They've never returned."

"But none of them are her own?"

"No. For reasons of her own, Cocheetah has chosen to be a woman who takes care of children who have no one else. She believes it to be her calling."

Molly watched as the children followed Cocheetah as she sang a song and led them on a dance, weaving like a serpent through the palmetto shrub and palm trees. Bem was smiling and he ran alongside the other small boy.

"I don't know what to say. Bem went with her without question. He never even looked back to me."

"As I said. She has a gift."

At dinner time the children were seated at a table with a long bench. They all talked at once and Bem smiled, as though he understood every word.

Cocheetah and Todd's mother sat with the two of them at a small table inside. Todd's mother was quiet, but falling into conversation with Cocheetah was like slipping into a warm bath.

At the end of a very long day, Todd said his goodbyes and Molly went to claim Bem. Cocheetah took his hand and led him to the car. She kissed him on the cheek, said something in her language, and he smiled as she closed the door.

As agreed, Patrick was waiting when they arrived at Crabber's Cove. "Ah, the lost sheep have returned. Glad you're home safely."

"Thanks for waiting. We've had quite a day, and we're all ready for bed," Molly responded, shifting a sleeping Bem on her shoulder.

"Looks like Bem's already found his."

"Yeah. He had a great day. I'll tell you all about it." Molly turned her attention to Todd. "Thank you for taking me to meet your people. It was even better than my first visit to the reservation."

"It was my pleasure. We'll do it again."

"Goodnight, then. We'll see you tomorrow?"

"Yeah, sure. Patrick, any news?"

"No. Talked with Solana this morning. She says the radio is busy, but nothing from Jack or Drifter. She did hear some chatter between *Padre* and *Niño,* however. More about a delivery on Oct. 24. Nothing else."

"You hear President Kennedy last night?" Patrick asked.

"Yeah, sounds like he's going to blockade the island of Cuba. I was hoping cooler heads would be able to work through this."

"Maybe they will yet. I'll stop by and pick you up tomorrow. Hopefully, Jack will call us or radio us or something. It's getting on my nerves now," Patrick said.

Molly spoke up. "He can't call. The phone's out again. The line was dead this morning."

"The damn telephone system on this island is as ornery as my grandmum," Patrick complained.

314

Chapter 62

As soon as they arrived at the admiral's place in Placida, Jack went to the radio. He was anxious to know what Patrick had seen on his 'fishing' trip.

He tried several frequencies before he found a clear one.

"K4ELD. Casper here." No answer. "K4ELD. Casper here." Static. "K4ELD. Come in."

A moment of silence, then an answer.

"K4ELD here. Switch to Drifter's code please."

That's Solana. If she wants me to go to code, she's got something important to tell me.

It didn't surprise him that she had already mastered Drifter's code. The coded message read: Fishing expedition halted. Cobra was fired upon. No serious injuries. Molly required to stitch up Patrick's friend. Patrick OK. Ashes sprinkled yesterday. No sighting of *El Escorpión* during ceremony. *Padre* and *Niño* communicating. "Final" delivery to be made on OCT 24. Over.

"Did you get that Bear?"

"Yeah. Oct 24 appears to be the delivery date for the sulfur mustard. If they're shooting at the Cobra, they must be scared."

"K4ELD. Stay close to lighthouse. No more fishing. All is well here. Will pay visit soon. Stay close to radio. Repeat: No more fishing. Will be in touch. Stay with Drifter Code at all times. Casper out."

"OCT 24. That's only three days from now. We've got to move our asses, Bear. With a little prompting from us, Rafael will tell us what we need to know."

"What you got in mind?"

"Let's get some sleep. It's too late to do more thinking tonight. Tomorrow evening we'll catch up with Rafael. He may be the key."

"You know where to find him?"

"Yeah. Tomorrow's Wednesday. He'll be at prayer meeting in the evening."

"He's a religious fellow?"

"Not exactly. He goes to Timmy's Nook. Timmy makes one of his back rooms available for the Prayer Group. The group prays over every hand of stud poker before they play it."

Bear smiled, "Good explanation."

"I've been to prayer meeting myself a few times. Never have cared much for throwing money away, so don't make it a habit. Took Patrick once. I told him we were going to prayer meeting and he showed up in his clerical collar and shirt. He was quite a hit at the poker table. He's a good player and can drink all of 'em under the table to boot."

Bear shook his head, grinning. "We'll get ourselves to Timmy's Nook and ask Rafael to come out and 'talk' to us on the *Lady*?"

"Timmy's got a dock; we can berth the *Lady* there. You'll have to go inside. I'm 'dead' remember?"

"Uh-huh. I'll ask Rafael to come out for a brief chat on the *Lady*, and once he's on board the two of us can convince him to spill the beans?"

"Something like that."

"Let's get a shower and go to bed. I'm getting too old for this spy shit, Casper."

"Understood. Have to admit I'll be glad to get this mission over. Of course, then I have to head to Baltimore for the next one. Want to come along? Could use some help."

"Sure. Got nothing else to do. But we rest after that one.

Chapter 63

When Molly arrived home from the reservation, Solana took Bem upstairs and Molly found herself sitting alone on the patio, in the dark, recalling the events of the day.

No matter how many times she reviewed the scenes running through her mind, one kept coming again and again—the one where Bem's face lighted up when Cocheetah kissed him goodbye. Something had transpired between those two. Something unexplainable.

This morning she awoke to the scent of Japanese honeysuckle, a cool breeze on her skin, and the raucous racket from a pack of laughing gulls as they made their way across the island.

She arose and headed to the kitchen for Solana's coffee. After a cup perhaps she could think about their situations . . . Papa, Bem, Castro. Somehow, they would all be resolved. Surely.

Solana was peeling fruit for breakfast. Molly took her coffee in hand, "Come outside with me. I want to tell you about the trip to the reservation."

They took a seat under the banyan tree and Molly began to tell her story. She was more animated than Solana had ever seen her, careful to give pertinent details. Solana listened to every word, then Molly made an astounding suggestion.

"Are you sure, Molly?"

"If you could have seen Bem interacting with Cocheetah and the other children, you'd understand. There was no language barrier. I can't explain it but it was something to behold."

"And you think this Cocheetah would be willing to let Bem live on the reservation?"

"I don't know. I need to talk to Todd. Get his input. But first I want to know what you think. As I said, I have a professional responsibility to let the authorities know about Bem. But I don't think that's the best thing for him."

Solana agreed, "No, neither do I. We could care for him, but he needs more than care. He needs to feel part of a family, to live in a home where he can interact with other children and grow up knowing he's wanted."

Molly stared out toward the ocean, "I could lose my physician's license for not reporting an orphaned child."

"What is that thing, that saying you physicians have? Something about not hurting anyone?" Molly was surprised Solana knew of this.

"*First, do no harm*. It's from the Hippocratic Oath. Perhaps that's how I justify my actions. At least to myself."

"Yes, perhaps. Talk with Todd. He might be able to discuss it with his sister. He and Patrick will come by later."

"And maybe we'll hear from Papa, too," Molly hoped.

"Oh, where is my mind! He called on the radio last evening. He reports he's fine and will be in touch soon. Says to tell Patrick no more fishing and we are to stay close to the lighthouse. He thinks someone may be listening and says to use Drifter Code only."

"He's all right then. Will he call again today?"

"No. Only when necessary. No news is good news, Molly."

~ ~ ~

Patrick collected Todd and they headed to Bailey's Island Grocery. "I'm out of bread and peanut butter. And looking for a package at the post office. Won't be a minute."

"No problem. I've got to pick up a couple of items, too. I'm also expecting some mail."

As they arrived at the grocery, Agnes greeted them from the back corner. "Hey, you two. Be with you in a sec. Hold on."

A couple of minutes later she came forward. "Father, I understand our friend, Captain Jack, passed away. I'm very sorry to hear that. It's a loss for all of us."

"Yes. He was a true friend. I miss him already."

"And his granddaughter, I forget her name, how is she coping?"

"Molly. She's grieving, but doing as well as can be expected. She has no other family and is a bit unsettled at the moment. We sprinkled his ashes as he requested and Molly will have to find a way to make her life without him. But I agree with you. It will be difficult for all of us."

"Perhaps I could visit with her. Another woman to talk to may be helpful."

"Perhaps a little later. Give her some time."

"I understand. I have several pieces of mail for you. And a small package for you, Todd. Here you are." She handed the letters to Patrick and the package to Todd.

"Father, I haven't seen that little woman, Queenie, for some time. She came by occasionally, usually needing to buy candles. Maybe she didn't have electricity in her bungalow. Don't know. But I always have some candles about. Never know when a storm might be brewing."

"Queenie's left the island, I believe. We haven't seen her either. No telling where that woman could be off too."

"She was a strange one." Agnes went back to her counter and began organizing the canned goods.

"Thanks, Agnes. See you later."

321

Agnes stepped forward again, "Oh, Father. Perhaps you can take another letter to the granddaughter? Looks like from the same place in Baltimore."

Patrick stuck it in his pocket and they headed to the lighthouse. "Better get a move on. Molly's itching to do surgery on you."

"What?"

"Just kidding. She did say she'd remove your stitches today, remember?"

"Oh, yeah. I'm ready to have them out, too. They're a pain."

Patrick knocked this time and waited before opening the door. He'd not forgotten staring down the barrel of the pistol in Molly's hand yesterday.

Solana smiled and greeted them. "Father Patrick. Todd. We've been expecting you."

"What? No guns pointing at us?"

Molly grinned. "Not today. But we've been practicing. At least I can hold it now."

"Good thing. I just hope you never have to use it." He started to sit, then reached in his pocket and pulled out the envelope.

"Oh, Agnes sent another letter. It seems she keeps up with where everyone's mail comes from," he smiled as he handed her the thick envelope. He, too, had noticed the same return address as the letter a couple of weeks ago: Johns Hopkins Hospital, Baltimore, Maryland.

Molly placed the letter on the table next to the ham radio and walked over to Todd. "Let's see about your stitches. Bet you're ready to have them out."

"Today would be fine with me."

"Good. Sit here on the sofa. I'll get my bag." She returned momentarily and began the process.

"Hold still. This might pinch, but won't really hurt."

"Uh-huh. Who removed your stitches?"

"A very competent woman who has many other talents as well."

"Maybe I should have her remove mine, in that case."

"No way. I put them in. I take them out." Molly proceeded to remove the stitches without more discussion.

"There. Not bad if I say so myself."

Todd felt the area on his cheek. Without looking, he could feel the scar, and his expression showed his unspoken concern.

Molly smiled slightly, "No. The scar is not terrible. It's noticeable. Gives you a rather 'rakish, experienced-warrior' look. Nothing to concern yourself about."

Todd grinned, "My *poia*. My mother was most impressed with it. She believes it was meant to be and says I'm to wear it with pride. It increases her standing in the tribe to have a son who has been chosen."

Molly wondered if she would she be able to feel that way about her *poia*? Her face was healing, but her scar would be considerably larger and much more noticeable than Todd's. Even if she learned to accept it, it would forever be a reminder of that horrendous attack.

"Any word from Jack?" Patrick asked.

"Solana talked to him last evening. He's well and says no more fishing for you, and we are to stay close to the lighthouse. He didn't elaborate on anything, but Solana says he wants us to use Drifter's Code on all communications."

"Drifter's Code?"

"A modified Morse Code. Something he and Drifter came up with years ago. When they served together in the intelligence world. He taught it to me when I was in my teens. It's really quite simple."

"If you say so. Never could grasp Morse Code myself. Too many dots and dashes for my comprehension," laughed Patrick.

Todd listened. If you believed everything Patrick said, you'd think he was a totally incompetent man. Todd knew that was far from the truth. He was sure this man had history they may never know.

Molly put her medical bag away and sat down on the sofa next to Todd. "I have something to ask. If it's an impossible request, please say so."

"Sounds ominous. Can't be that bad, can it?" He flashed that heart-melting smile at her. She allowed herself one quick, closer glance at his face.

No, that scar isn't going to be a detriment to his looks. If anything, it adds a bit of excitement to his otherwise perfect features.

"It's about Bem. I have great concerns about him and it appears Queenie's not coming back. Solana and I talked about the situation. We both feel the authorities would put him in a foster home. Or worse, in an orphanage if we turn him over to them. But he needs more than we can give him."

"What's your question?"

"I don't know if you noticed, but Bem was so happy at the reservation. Playing with the other children. He seemed to have a connection with Cocheetah. She was able to touch something in Bem that I haven't been able to. He responded to her touch, to her voice. Does this make any sense to you?"

"Go on."

"Well, I was wondering if you would consider asking her if he could join her group of orphaned ones?"

Todd leaned his head back, as if considering the matter. He then looked directly at Molly and shook his head.

"No. There's no point in asking her. I know what she would say."

Molly's disappointment was so great she was on the verge of tears. "I see."

"As I said, there's no point in asking Cocheetah. She's already told me she thinks Bem should be with her and the other children. She felt the connection just as you are describing. It's her belief the spirits find a way to help those who are unable to help themselves. Perhaps Bem was led to her. She would be delighted to have him."

Molly's joy was as keen as her disappointment had been. She called out, "Solana, come in here!"

Solana dashed in, "What? What is it?"

"Todd says Cocheetah would be delighted to take Bem. She believes he should be with her."

"Then our prayers have been answered," said Solana. "We should take him tomorrow. The reservation may be a safer place than the lighthouse at the moment."

Patrick and Todd left shortly and Solana began preparing fruit for the next day's breakfast. Captain Jack was particularly fond of mangoes and papayas, and she kept them on hand.

Molly watched as Solana sliced the firm mango, carefully detaching each piece from the pit.

"I wish you would teach me how to do that. Every time I try to do it, I end up making a mess of the mango and have juice and pulp all over me."

"Not much to slicing a mango, Molly. The key is a sharp knife—like this one. I keep it in the drawer here, away from little fingers like Bem's. Next time I prepare mangos, I'll let you try your hand."

Chapter 64

Prayer meeting will be well underway by now. Rafael's a good player, and if he's holding a winning hand it may not be easy to get him to step outside with you."

"I'll have to be very persuasive then, I suppose. I can still manage to do that, Casper."

"Never doubted you could."

Jack eased the *Admiral's Lady* up next to the dock behind Timmy's Nook. "Being dead has some drawbacks. Rafael would come with me easily enough, but he doesn't know you."

Jack was chagrined that Rafael had pulled the wool over his eyes. For a long time, apparently. "Guess I'm slipping, Bear. Should have thought of Rafael long ago."

"No way of knowing he would resort to his previous behavior, Casper. But we're on to him now. We'll get his story soon enough.

"You're right. Rafael doesn't know me, but I could drop your name at the appropriate time and that would have some bearing on him stepping outside for a quick chat."

"You'll need him to come aboard your *Lady*. If we do have to 'convince' him to give us information, we'll have to take her out to sea. No need for everyone to know where Rafael's gone. We'll keep her dark, no lights on deck anywhere."

~ ~ ~

Bear crossed the dock and entered the bar at Timmy's Nook. He ordered a beer and wandered through the dining area to the back room. So far no one had stopped to question him.

Casper had described the room and the men. By his descriptions alone, Bear knew each of the four players at the table. Regulars, according to Casper.

The men were well into their game. And their beer. Cards were being slapped down on the table and a groan was heard from the one called Skeeter. Skeeter Johnson. Casper had said he'd be wearing a navy ball cap with an emblem of a giant insect on it. He was the local exterminator who kept busy fumigating the blood-sucking mosquitoes and no-see-ums everyone complained about, hence his name, Skeeter.

"That's the third time you've thrown an ace out at the last minute, Pete. Where you keeping 'em? Up your sleeve?"

But his comment was met with laughter and Skeeter excused himself for the men's room. That was the perfect opportunity for Bear to corner Rafael. The only problem was he didn't see anyone who met the description Casper had given him.

Jack had said he'd be easy to recognize as he always wore a shirt with "Rafael's Enterprises" stitched above his right pocket. No one here was wearing such. Finally, with no other option, Bear spoke to Skeeter as he came from the men's room.

"Looking for Rafael. Need to ask him to pick me up tomorrow. I came over to pay respects to Jack McCormick's granddaughter, and I'll need a ride to the ferry dock tomorrow morning."

Skeeter eyed Bear a long moment before answering. He wouldn't give out any more information than necessary, but Rafael had a lot of acquaintances and needed all the business he could get.

"He had to skip prayer meeting tonight. Had some engine problem with his cab and took it to the mainland for repair this morning. He'd hoped to be back today, but since he's not here, he probably had to stay overnight. You staying at the Gasparilla Inn?"

"Yeah, that's right."

"If you float a fiver in front of Jimmy, the gardener at the hotel, he'll give you a ride. He comes in early and could get you there on time."

"Thanks. I'll do that."

Bear walked out and hurried down the dock where Casper was getting antsy. "Well, hell. Then we don't know where he is. Might be on the mainland. Might not be."

"Sounds suspicious to me. You say he never misses prayer meeting?"

"No, he's a good player. Usually wins a bit of pocket money." Casper rubbed at the back of his neck. This was not what he was expecting.

"There's one person who'll know if Rafael stayed on the mainland. Crab. We'll ask him," Jack said.

"It's kind of late, Jack. Crab may not be too pleased to have us dropping in on him at this hour."

"Crab? He's an old seaman. Not as old as we are, but if he is asleep, he'll let us in. I've known him quite some time now. He's a bit on the scruffy side, but he's intelligent and has shown Molly some kindness. He won't mind us stopping by."

~ ~ ~

Crab's ham radio was squealing and squawking with so much static he couldn't catch any call signs, and all messages were garbled. He depended on this equipment to keep abreast of the weather at all times.

The *Admiral's Lady* came alongside his dock, and Jack jumped off, grabbed a line, and secured them. He looked up as Crab stepped under the light at the dock.

"*¡Dios! Capitán* Jack! The Missy Doktor says you are dead. But you are here!" he said as he made the sign of the cross.

Jack smiled, "Yeah, I'm still around, Crab. Give us a beer, and I'll tell you all about it."

"Of course. Come. Come inside. This must be some story, no?" Jack introduced the admiral and the three entered the bungalow at the back door to the kitchen.

"Here. Sit. Sit. I always have *cerveza*. And you are in luck. I have my specialty, Crab dip and crackers."

They all laughed and Jack and Bear took a seat at the kitchen table. Crab went to his radio and turned the volume down, but not so low he couldn't hear it.

"You must excuse this noise, this static. But I try to keep up with the weather report. And the storm is headed our way, but perhaps it will turn north, or better yet, head back out to sea."

Jack laid out the details of his 'being dead,' explaining about the poisoning with anti-freeze, seeing the rebels on *El Escorpión,* and the reasons they suspected Rafael.

"And they're planning to transport chemical weapons sometime soon," Jack continued.

"What? What madness is this? *Capitán* Jack, do you think someone will take chemical weapons to the rebels? My family and I left that place to escape Fidel's wrath. He can't be trusted. He is an animal."

"Our intelligence tells us someone is supplying them with arms. But sulfur mustard is a whole different ball game. It's imperative that we find Rafael. He's a suspect . . . what with his past criminal record. We've got to see if he's involved."

"Rafael? I would never have thought of him in that manner. Of course, I did not know he had a criminal record. He runs packages for me, but I know nothing of him."

"Did he take the ferry this morning?"

"Sí. He told me his cab needed engine work. He thought maybe a new water pump would take care of his problem."

"Did he come back over this afternoon? Back to Cayo Canna?"

"No, *Capitán*. He was not at the dock when it was time for me to make my return trip. He's aware of my schedule. He said he might have to stay overnight. I think he must have done so."

"Then we've got to get back to Placida. Father Patrick's been keeping an eye on *El Escorpión*, which we believe the rebels are using to transport weapons.

"Crab, could I use your radio? Need to try to raise the lighthouse. Patrick may have information that can help us, too.

"When we get back to Placida, we'll talk to Drifter, one of our Navy pals. He's been monitoring his ham, and he's aware of a couple of *amigos* who are arranging the weapons exchange. He's quite adept at using and deciphering code, as is Solana. Now we just need to find that sulfur mustard before it's moved again."

"*Sí, Capitán*. The radio, she is not usually this noisy, but the storm has her agitated."

Jack took his *cerveza* to the corner and sat at the radio. Someone was calling for "Dorsal Fin," another for "Mama Jensen," and a young man's voice calling for "*Jefe*."

Jack tried numerous frequencies but was unable to find a clear one. He'd have to wait until they got to Placida. Bear's radio was newer than Crab's and reception would be better.

Crab and Bear were deep into a conversation about Castro and Cuba, Crab's former home. "Castro will not stop. Some of the people in Cuba believe in him. I am glad my family and I escaped before this latest problem. He is a dangerous man," Crab was saying.

"Yeah, and we won't stop either. We'll find Rafael and he WILL tell us what we need to know," said Bear.

Jack returned to the table. "Couldn't get through. You're right; the radio's not working very well. Must be the storm. Sorry to have bothered you, Crab. We'll keep in touch. Keep your eyes and ears open.

Chapter 65

S olana held Bem close for a moment, then kissed him on both cheeks. "*Sé buen chico, Bem.*" (Be a good boy.) He smiled at her as he nodded. He had understood her and appeared to be excited about the day's plans. Molly took his hand and picked up the small bag Solana had packed for him.

Bem sat on Patrick's lap and steered the golf cart as they headed to Crabber's Cove where Todd was waiting. They'd all become attached to the child but agreed with Molly and Todd's plan.

Molly had made them swear—on Patrick's Bible—that they'd never breathe a word of this. Patrick was personally confident there had been divine intervention in this case.

Todd turned to Patrick, "We'll be back late. My mother will insist on feeding us before we can even think of leaving. Can't be sure of the time, but Molly will be ready to get to the lighthouse for sure."

"I'll be waiting." No matter how late, he'd wait for Molly.

Molly glanced at Patrick. He always seemed available to do whatever needed doing. When did he plan on returning to his parish? Perhaps he was in the position she was finding herself . . . in limbo.

She'd admitted to herself that Baltimore wasn't nearly as exciting as Cayo Canna and she knew she'd have to make a decision soon. Her dream of becoming a physician, being a staff member of a reputable healthcare institution, had been a difficult one to pursue. And she had been presented with an opportunity to make that dream come true. Now, as much as she might like, she could no longer put off answering the latest letter from Johns Hopkins.

Tomorrow. I'll think about that tomorrow. Today I have a more important task.

~ ~ ~

Molly's keen sense of smell told her they were close to the reservation. She had noticed the scent last week and wondered if it was a type of gardenia.

Todd laughed when she ask about the scent. "No, that's wild coffee. The berries were once used as a coffee substitute. It also has hallucinogenic properties. In the early days my people brewed it for ceremonies and medicinal purposes. I'd not suggest trying it though. It's pretty bitter. Tried it once."

Molly laughed. "It does have a nice scent, though."

"Maybe I should take some to Patrick. He'll like it as much as I liked his headache remedy," he laughed.

As soon as they parked their car and entered the grounds, Bem started making noises Molly had never heard him utter. As they walked along, a giant osprey dipped down and glided just above their heads.

Cocheetah was waiting at the chickee hut with her arms outheld. Bem ran into them, chatting away in his language.

"Bem, I am glad you're here. I have missed you every day. Come, we're making clay pots today."

Cocheetah greeted Molly with an embrace as well. "Thank you for bringing Bem. He will bring happiness to us. Did you see the osprey that flew just overhead? That was an omen from the spirits. A sign that Bem has found his home."

Molly looked to Todd who stood there with a smile playing at his lips. "As I told you, Cocheetah has a gift. In fact, she has many gifts."

They spent the afternoon with Todd's family discussing the troubles with Cuba and what it might mean to all of them. As they were about to leave, an old woman wandered over to their table. She was quite small with wiry, gray hair fashioned in a long braid down her back and wearing her tribal dress with strands of colored beads and shells at her neck.

Todd stood and bowed his head. Obviously a gesture of respect, Molly decided. She, too, stood and bowed as it seemed appropriate.

The old woman traced Todd's *poia* with her fingers. Then she ran them over the *poia* on Molly's face. In her native language she uttered words. As if she were praying.

Todd waited and when she finished, she touched her cheek to his and then to Molly's. Then, using her long walking stick to keep her balance, moved on.

"What did she say?"

"That was Ayana, our oldest medicine woman. She congratulated us on being chosen ones. She says our souls are intertwined and our destinies will keep us close."

It was time to leave. Molly reached into the bag Solana had packed and brought out the amber necklace with the fossilized sea creature. She placed it around Bem's neck and he touched it, then turned to Cocheetah.

"Mamee, Mamee," said Bem.

Cocheetah nodded and Todd got on one knee and took a closer look at the piece.

"I don't believe it. Molly? Do you know what this is?"

"It appears to be a fossilized sea creature of some kind."

"Yes, but it's more than just a sea creature. It's an Anolis fossil, a lizard of sorts, trapped in amber. They're found in the Caribbean and date back millions of years.

"The reason amber is critical is that most fossils are two dimensional, but fossils in amber are three dimensional.

Amber lets us see even the minute hairs of the animal that was trapped. Where did this come from? It's invaluable."

As Todd lifted the necklace again, Bem squirmed and pulled away.

"The necklace is something that must have belonged to his mother. It now belongs to him." Cocheetah made the statement with such authority that neither Molly nor Todd questioned her.

Molly pulled Bem close. "I will miss you Bem, but I know this is where you belong." Bem smiled at her and ran to Cocheetah's side.

Todd and Molly said their goodbyes and started for home. The trip back was quiet. Bem was precisely where he should be and Molly did not question that decision. At least he was safe. But were they?

~ ~ ~

Patrick strolled along the shore kicking at some shells. Shortly, he heard the engine of the Endeavor in the distance. That was his cue to take the dinghy out to meet them.

As Todd anchored, Patrick pulled the dinghy closer to Endeavor. "Good. You're back safely. Both of you appear to have survived the day. How did Bem take it?"

Molly grinned, "He's never been so happy in his young life. We did a fine thing this day, Patrick."

"What do you think, Todd? Bem will be all right with Cocheetah?"

"If I never do anything right again, I know that this day I have. Bem is safe and will be cared for. I never believed much in omens and such, but perhaps there's much I don't know."

"Yeah. Some things can only be learned through experience. At least that's my belief," said Patrick.

Todd took the two of them to the shore and waved them off as Patrick started the golf cart. "It went well then?" he asked.

"It was unbelievable. Bem and Cocheetah were meant to be together. The spirits were definitely in agreement about that."

"The spirits? Didn't know you were inclined to believe in such."

"Neither did I. But after today I might be. Right now, though, my bed will be very inviting. At least we don't have to worry about Bem if anything should happen at the lighthouse."

Patrick sighed, "Don't worry so. Nothing's going to happen at the lighthouse. Casper is out there frightening the daylights out of someone. He'll come through and stop this insanity."

Chapter 66

In a few minutes, Patrick and Molly were back at the lighthouse. It had been a long day for everyone. "Come on. I'll walk you to your door as a proper gentleman should. Not that I'm a proper gentleman, but I can give it a try."

Molly smiled up at him. He couldn't be more different than Todd and she found both interesting.

Patrick reached for the doorknob and his fingers ran across something metal. He looked closer. Something was suspended from the knob. He removed the item and turned to Molly.

"Hmm. A beautiful necklace. Yours? Someone must have found it and left it here."

Molly looked at the necklace. She continued to stare for a long moment but didn't reach for it.

"What? It's not yours?"

Molly was immobilized. She looked up at Patrick. The terror in her eyes was overwhelming. He'd seen this kind of terror once before. In another woman's eyes.

"What's wrong?"

He put his hands on her shoulders. She tried to speak, but no words would come.

"Come inside. Tell me what's wrong." He gathered her inside and pushed her down on the sofa.

"Hold on. I'll get a dash of my Jameson. It'll loosen your tongue. Trust me." One minute later he was back with a small glass of his Irish whiskey.

"Here. Drink this."

Molly downed it in one gulp. She had a coughing spasm but finally caught her breath. "It's mine. The necklace."

"All right. What's frightening about a necklace that belongs to you?"

"The man who attacked me. He tore it from my neck the day he attacked me. Took it with him." Patrick was then the one left to stare.

"Jaysus, Mary, and Joseph. No wonder you turned white as a ghost."

"That means he's here, Patrick. He's here on the island!"

Patrick struggled to find the right words. This situation called for clear thinking over mouthing words of comfort and repeating platitudes. This called for the thinking of a different man. A man he'd been a long time ago.

"Molly, listen to me. Perhaps the Baltimore police found him and left the necklace on your door. That's a logical explanation."

"No, Patrick. I talked with Lieutenant Collins yesterday. He took the information I gave him and said he'd be in touch when they had any leads. He would have called or come if that were so. This is a message from Sam. He said he'd come back for me. I guess he has."

"Then he'll have more than a young, defenseless woman to deal with this time. I'll stay here and be on watch. You get yourself ready for bed. Like any other night. If he's close by he'll be watching. I'll pretend to leave, but I'll be back shortly. Lock all the doors. I have Jack's keys and I'll find my way back in.

"First, though, let's awaken Solana and tell her. She'll sleep in Keeper's Cottage in the master's room, and I'll stay on the sofa here. Solana's no stranger to using a weapon. She'll be watching too."

Molly nodded. She couldn't think and was finding it difficult to move her feet.

Solana was flabbergasted to learn of the necklace on the door. "I didn't hear a thing. But the radio's been full of static and noise. He's not been in the house, though. I would have sensed his presence."

Patrick nodded. "Sit tight. I've got an item in the cart for you, Molly. Just a moment."

He was back quickly. "Solana, you have the Sig Sauer from Jack's collection. I believe you know how to use it."

"I do."

"And Molly, I found this 2-shot derringer in Margaret's evening bag. Take it. I was going to school you on how to use it before I left it with you, but now you've just got to wing it.

"All you have to do is point it in the right direction. It's a small gun and it may not kill with one shot, but it'll slow an attacker down while you run. And it's loaded as we speak."

Molly took the derringer and held it in her palm. So small. So lethal. She had trouble picturing Mimi keeping it in her evening bag. Papa must have insisted.

"I want you both to keep your weapon on your person at all times. And keep it loaded. Don't hesitate to use them, either of you. We'll sort out what else to do in the morning.

"Right now I'll leave as we discussed. I've got Jack's keys and in a few minutes I'll be back inside. Keeping this sofa warm. Try to get some sleep, Molly. He won't get past me."

~ ~ ~

The next couple of nights were uneventful and Molly wondered if perhaps Patrick had been right. Perhaps the police had placed the necklace on the doorknob. The phone was still not working and the radio wasn't telling them anything new. Well, except the fact that the storm had not changed direction. But it was still a tropical storm and could do damage.

They went about their activities. More flower arrangements arrived and Molly brought them in and arranged them in a vase, discarding the earlier ones.

Two days had now passed since they discovered the necklace hanging from the doorknob. Each night Molly and Solana went to bed and Patrick left as their scheme called for. In a short while, he would sneak back through the kitchen door.

Tonight they'd followed the set pattern. After tossing and turning for several hours, Molly got up in the wee hours of the morning, put on one of Mimi's caftans and as Patrick had instructed, put the loaded derringer in her pocket.

She needed to occupy her mind so she thought she'd try her hand at making cinnamon buns and fresh fruit. She'd prepare breakfast and give Solana a break.

The approaching storm had already dispatched a couple of early showers and a thin, silvery rain fell quietly. Molly hurried across the breezeway and entered the lighthouse through the kitchen door, then closed the door that opened to the den where Patrick was sleeping.

She turned on a small light over the kitchen sink and began organizing the items she needed to make the cinnamon buns. The Bahama shutters on the windows were open and she caught the rich, earthy scent coming from the newly planted hibiscus and the sharper scent of wet ginger that grew beneath the window.

She found a packaged mix in the small pantry and combined the ingredients as indicated on the package, then arranged the buns in the pan. Next, she checked the refrigerator to see what kind of fruit Solana had. Mango and Papaya. Papa's favorites.

Well, now is a good time to try my hand at preparing them.

She stuck the buns in the oven, set the timer, and located Solana's sharp knife in the first drawer on the left. She took it out, amazed at how small it was. She'd have thought you would need a larger knife to slice the fruit. That was before she touched the blade. It was razor-sharp and she nicked a finger, then stuck her finger in her mouth and licked away the small droplets of blood.

Ouch. That's sharp. Like a scalpel.

She began to pare the mango, carefully pulling the skin away from the fruit. So far, so good. She lifted the fruit to her nose and sniffed. The mango had a distinctive scent that was mouth-watering. But something was off. She brought the fruit closer to her nose again. Perhaps it had ripened too much, and she needed to discard it.

She sniffed once more and then abruptly pulled her nose away, dropping the fruit to the floor.

Beef jerky.

The smell of beef jerky turned her stomach and her heart skipped a beat. The next instant her body was jammed against the counter. Two strong, hairy arms surrounded her and something hard and metal was pressed into her lower back.

Panic rose as she felt his hot breath down her neck, and the odor of beef jerky had nausea knocking on her door.

He whispered into her ear then . . . softly . . . as a lover might. "Ah, Dr. McCormick. How nice to see you again. I promised you I'd be back. And I always keep my promises."

Molly's tongue felt glued to her palate. Her feet refused to move and even though she was screaming in her head, no sound was coming out of her mouth.

Sam pressed his body even closer. "We've got unfinished business, you and I. But we'll take our time. Make every minute count. Make each one memorable for both of us."

He took her by the shoulders and turned her to face him, then put his arms on either side, entrapping her again. A pistol was stuck in his waistband. He obviously wasn't worried about her overpowering him, or he would have drawn it already.

No. This can't be happening again!

That disgusting, paralyzing feeling was back—that feeling of being totally helpless, without a way to defend herself.

Papa, you can't save me this time. But I so wish you were here!

Papa was not coming to her rescue. If she were going to survive, it would be because she figured out a way to get away from Sam. Or kill him before he could kill her.

She watched him closely. His breath was coming quickly now and his eyes glittered when he looked at her.

He's aroused. This is a sexual adventure for him.

He was now holding her by her arms, staring down at her, taking in each feature of her face.

"Ah, the tropical air and sunshine agree with you. You're the perfect picture of health. Island living has put roses in your cheeks. But you had lovely cheeks already."

He took his forefinger and lightly traced the "S" that he had deeply carved in her face. It was now scabbed over and still not completely healed.

"That is quite a work of art, you know. In fact, yours looks better than the other two. It's a shame I didn't have more time; I could have made it even more exquisite."

Molly couldn't control her trembling body. She lifted her face and looked him in the eye. He was even more frightening now. His pupils were dilated and in addition to the beef jerky, he also reeked of alcohol.

"Now, if you remain quiet, I won't hurt anyone else in the house. Oh yes, I know that island woman stays in the lighthouse with you. I also know your grandfather passed away recently. So he's out of the picture. And the tall, well-built fellow that left earlier? Well, he's probably sleeping like a baby somewhere.

"Now you and I are going to leave here and find a place that will better suit our needs."

He put a hand under her chin and lifted it. With adrenaline flooding her limbs, Molly lunged at him, holding the paring knife tightly in her hand. When the sharp blade entered his abdomen he grabbed at the knife, now embedded in his body.

"Ahh. . . what . . . you've cut me!" He looked in disbelief at the long knife blade when he pulled it from his body. A trail of blood followed the blade and he stared at it as if he couldn't understand what had happened. Then he smiled as if he enjoyed the pain she'd inflicted on him.

Oh, God. He's even more aroused now!

She'd studied about such people—those who enjoy giving and receiving pain—but this was her first experience with such a person.

He threw his head back and cackled.

"You're insane!" Molly yelled as she backed up, trying to get to the closed door leading to the den. To Patrick.

Sam was loving every minute of this macabre play. It appeared he was only slightly wounded and grinned as Molly continued to move slowly backward. When her back was against the door she looked up at him. If he was in pain, it was not stopping him.

"Stop! I'll shoot you if you come any closer!" she screamed.

"Shoot me? You're going to shoot me? With what?"

Molly reached into the pocket of her caftan and pointed the derringer toward him.

He laughed. "That's the oldest trick in the book, Dr. McCormick. A finger in your pocket?" He laughed again.

"Now, this is a gun. A real gun," he said and moved closer, pulling the pistol from his waistband.

Molly remembered Patrick's words.

'Don't hesitate to use your weapon. Not even for a second.'

345

She wrapped her finger around the trigger and squeezed it. It was amazing how easy it was to pull compared to the heavier pistol she'd practiced with.

POW!

The sound echoed through the lighthouse. Molly thought it strange that this small weapon could make such a loud sound.

Sam grabbed at his thigh. Blood was flowing down his leg, quickly soaking his pants and beginning to drip on the tile floor.

Oh, God. I must have hit his femoral artery!

The expression on his face was one of awe. He was amazed. As if pleased that she'd shot him. That she'd been an exciting and capable opponent. Then she fired the second shot, hitting him square in the abdomen, adjacent to the knife wound. But still Sam stood, grabbing at his thigh with one hand and holding his pistol in the other.

The next instant the kitchen door burst open and Patrick's large frame filled the doorway. Before Molly could take another breath, he stepped forward and grabbed Sam around the neck with his right arm. With his left hand, he leveled his Walther PPK to that sensitive, intimate, space just behind Sam's left ear. As he pulled the trigger, he whispered, "God's speed."

BLAM!

One life ended. One life saved. May Almighty God forgive this sinful priest, prayed Patrick.

The lighthouse once again reverberated with a sound that was incongruous in this normally serene setting. This sound, this blast, was ear-shattering . . . drowning the earlier noise from Molly's derringer.

One shot. Lethal . . . whereas those from the small derringer had bought Molly another second, an important second in which Patrick called upon skills that had lain dormant, but that responded without hesitation.

The entry wound was one thing . . . the exit wound something else. It removed portions of Sam's right temporal and occipital lobes and his body slid to the floor at Patrick's feet.

Molly sank to her knees and pulled the derringer from her pocket. She stared at it as if wondering what its purpose was, and why was she holding it.

Patrick took one look at her face, then kneeled and pulled her to him. She trembled and he wrapped his arms tightly about her.

"What a brave girl you are. This ordeal's over now. Jack will be proud of you."

She looked into his eyes and the expression on her face was one of gratitude. He'd finished what she'd started. And she'd never felt as safe as she did at this moment with his arms holding her close.

His deep soothing voice, the one he used when he was worshipping, was the one he used now. It was exactly what she needed. She rested her head against his chest and the tears came of their own accord.

"Come on. Let's get you to Solana. I'll take care of this disgusting bit of shite."

Molly looked down at Sam, his lifeless body lying in a large pool of blood. Her whole body shivered. The only consolation she could find was in knowing he could no longer hurt another person.

Solana stood at the kitchen door. She had witnessed the horrifying event. "Come, Molly. Let's go to the patio. I'll bring you some brandy. Father Patrick will take care of everything else." Solana nodded to Patrick as if to say "you were here when she needed you."

Chapter 67

At least we know Rafael's not on the island. According to Solana, the sulfur mustard is to be delivered on the twenty-fourth. That's not much time."

"We'll find him, Casper. Let's get the *Lady* moving. I'm ready for my bed. Drifter will have the radio buzzing from one end of Florida to the other."

Jack pushed the throttle forward. Bear was enjoying letting someone else be the skipper and he sat back, taking in the salty scent of the ocean, recalling other adventures with Casper.

He was deep in thought when Jack jerked back on the throttle. They came to an abrupt stop and Bear lunged forward.

"Holy shit, Casper. I almost fell in the drink. What the hell you doing?"

Casper turned, stared, and said nothing for the longest moment. When he did speak, Bear was all ears.

"We've got it wrong, Bear. All wrong."

"Got what wrong?"

"Rafael. He's not the man we're looking for. Crab. It's got to be Crab."

"And just how did you come to that conclusion?"

"The radio. In his bungalow."

"Crab's radio?"

"I tried to call the lighthouse. But the static was so heavy I couldn't get through.

"Yeah. So?"

"I couldn't transmit, but I could hear the incoming calls. They were for three call signs."

"Three call signs. I still don't get what you're trying to say."

"The call signs, the three I heard. Two of them I'm familiar with."

"Ok, tell me more."

"The first call was for Dorsal Fin. I know him. He's a skipper on a charter boat. Uses the name of his boat as his call sign."

Bear listened.

"The second call was trying to raise "Mama Jensen." That's the call sign for a woman who owns several rentals over on Sanibel. Fishermen's cottages, that kind of thing. I talk to her occasionally. She's quite an old girl."

"That leaves one more. Give it to me," said Bear.

"That last call . . .one that was repeated several times . . . was trying to reach *Jefe.*"

"Should I know that word?"

"It's a Spanish word. Means "boss, or leader.""

"Someone was calling for his boss?"

"It wasn't just the word. Whoever was on that radio was desperately needing to talk to *Jefe* . . . there was fear in his voice."

"All right. So someone, someone who's scared, is trying to reach *Jefe.* You gotta help me out here, Casper. Still not tracking."

"Well, it's about what I didn't hear, too. I never heard a call trying to reach Dancer."

"Is that fact important?" Bear asked.

"Yeah, very. Dancer is Rafael's call sign. He's on the radio often. We even radio each other sometimes if the phones aren't working.

"Dancer, you say?"

"Yep. He's quite a show on the dance floor. If he's in with the rebels, surely his radio would be hot right now."

"Yeah, unless he's using someone else's," Bear added.

"Hold on. There's something else. Something important. Solana had a visit from her nephew, Roberto, a couple of weeks ago. He'd been working with the group of men who are supplying the rebels. He was game for helping run weapons, but when he learned about 'something big' being planned, he wanted no part of the operation."

"How does that connect with Crab?" Bear asked.

"Roberto told Solana that '*Jefe* is planning something big. I don't want to be a part of that.' Solana was so shaken she didn't ask questions, just gave him some cash and insisted he leave the island that night."

"And . . .?"

"Think with me for a moment. We didn't find anything amiss at the warehouse, so that eliminates them. If we rule out Rafael, that only leaves one person who had access to the Glenfiddich. Crab.

And where did I hear the call sign *Jefe*? Crab's place. Who has a place to store anything without it being seen? Crab. Where does he store it? The *Calypso*. She's the ideal vehicle to transport anything, and none be the wiser." And . . ."

"Enough. I get the picture. You have some valid points."

"I'd bet my ass on this, Bear. If I'm wrong, so be it. But it's too dangerous to not follow up on our suspicions. Agree?"

"You paint a convincing picture, Casper. I'm in."

"Then we'd better make tracks back to his bungalow. He'll be trying to make his delivery and finding a place to hide out.

Chapter 68

Capitán Jack is alive! How can that be? That changes my plan. When he does find Rafael, he'll learn he's not involved. So his Navy pal is intercepting messages. Then he'll know about Padre and Niño. And that housekeeper, Solana, how much did Roberto tell her? Does she even know he's dead?

It won't take Capitán Jack long to find me in the chain of players. He's no fool. Damnation, why couldn't he be dead! I have no choice. I'll move the sulfur mustard myself. Tonight.

Too many things had gone wrong with *Jefe's* original plan. But just now he felt his brain was on fire, churning out new ideas, looking for a way out of this predicament. After all, if he was going to become part of Fidel's inner circle, then he'd better make this delivery as planned.

He tossed the empty *cerveza* bottle into the sink where it burst into a thousand pieces—as had his original plan. As soon as the *Admiral's Lady* was out of sight he went to his bedroom, a small alcove off the kitchen, and pulled out a battered suitcase that might have one more trip left in her before she disintegrated.

He hurried to the front yard where an old crab trap rested, filled with floats, a few shells, and a short length of nylon rope. He lifted a flat stone underneath the trap and reached down into a small hole, bringing out a sealed plastic bag. He'd need the contents of this bag, the last of his funds, to tide him over until he could deliver the sulfur mustard.

After the delivery he'd find his way to the mainland. Go up the coast. Perhaps to the Sarasota area. There were a couple of *hombres* up there that would give him a place to hide out for a while. For a certain amount of money, of course.

Jefe knew his small runabout would never travel fast enough to get the sulfur mustard delivered tonight. What to do? After a few minutes of desperate thought, he made a decision.

Several of the cruisers at the marina were moored permanently. The owners were still in their homes in the Northeast and some of them wouldn't come down to Florida until after Christmas. He had one final *cerveza* and was pleased with his decision.

All keys for the cruisers are kept in the marina office and since I have a key to the office, I'll borrow one of the faster vessels. I can deliver the containers and have the boat back in its slip before daylight. If a dockhand happens to see me, he'll recognize me and know I must have permission from the owner. Yes. This plan is better than the original one.

If the use of sulfur mustard was successful, he would stay on the west coast, then work his way down to Cuba after things on the island settled down. Fidel would learn of his part in the execution of the plan and take notice. Fidel needed men like him.

He'd leave this place, this United States, and return to his real home. To Cuba. Yes, he could do whatever he wished once Fidel recognized his importance.

Chapter 69

The *Admiral's Lady* made a quick turn, leaving a trail of fluorescent stars glittering in the dark. It only took a short while for Casper and Bear to get back to Crab's bungalow, but even that amount of time had been enough for him to make his move. His runabout was gone and him with it.

"Let's check the place. He's got to have the stuff stashed somewhere." But a quick search turned up nothing. Casper shook his head as if the thought that just passed through was too much to consider.

"What? What are you thinking?"

"If you were Crab, where would you stash the stuff?"

"Well, first of all, it's not very combustible, which means it's fairly safe to have around. But he must have a goodly amount to go to the trouble of taking it to the rebels."

"I agree. It's not here. That only leaves one place. The *Calypso*. She has storage rooms, compartments in the deck, many places he could keep it from prying eyes."

"You think he would keep it there, even with taking the ferry back and forth to the mainland every day?"

"As you said, it's not very combustible, so he'd likely not feel it was unsafe. But he'd have to have someone taking it to the rebels. Probably the 'fishermen' I saw."

"We'd better get to the ferry dock. Hopefully, he's not left. We gotta stop him."

"He wouldn't be using the ferry for the transport. It's too slow. He needs something that can make a speedy departure. Like El *Escorpión*. No. He's got to have someone coming to the ferry to get it. We gotta get to Crab before they do."

Bear took the wheel. Casper was busy once again digging out diving gear. It had been a while since Bear had been called on to suit up and be in the water on a mission.

"You think we're going to need that gear?" he asked.

"Yeah. We should use our wetsuits. Not for warmth. For protection. If there's some unforeseen action and that sulfur mustard touches any part of our body, we've got problems. I don't have to remind you what it can do to your body, your lungs. It can be lethal.

"And we may have a better chance of coming aboard from the water, unseen. We'll strap on a blade and a firearm as well. You still have yours?"

"Never leave home without it."

They stayed in the channel where the water was deep enough for the *Admiral's Lady* to travel but still kept them some distance away from the ferry dock.

From their vantage point on the upper deck, they used their night binoculars to scout out the dock. Most slips were occupied this time of year. Then they spotted Crab's runabout tied up next to the Calypso.

"He's already here. Didn't take him long to make a move," muttered Bear.

"Yeah, we as much as told him we were on to him." They continued to watch for a few minutes.

"Don't see anyone but Crab. Looks like he's transferring the sulfur mustard from the ferry to that cruiser. I happen to know it belongs to Chris Anderson, an artist who lives in Connecticut. He comes down every year after New Year's Day. We sometimes get together for coffee and discuss our art."

"You think he's going to make the run himself? Time's running out for him. Wonder how many containers he has?"

"Does it matter? Even one is too many."

Bear was in full admiral mode now. The audacity of someone like Crab planning to cause a catastrophic event in the United States infuriated him.

"I wish we could have gotten in touch with Drifter," Jack commented. "He could send backup. But the Navy is everywhere out here right now, as is the Coast Guard. All we need to do is alert them that we need help. Can you get Drifter on the ham?"

Bear shook his head. "Probably not, but I can get the Coast Guard on the ship-to-shore. Meanwhile, I'll drop you off here. I like to think I'm as good as ever, but we'd better scrap me being in the water. This knee is going to slow me down. You always were better in the water anyway. I'll find my way onto the ferry from dockside. We'll be coming from two directions that way. He might manage to stop one of us, but not both."

They both suited up and Casper gathered his fins. Then he turned to Bear, "Sulfur mustard is stable at ambient temperatures, but containers may explode when heated. Personally, I'd rather not get too close to it. I've seen the results of it. In Korea. Most times the victims were not even aware they'd been exposed. But about twelve hours later, their skin begins to blister, their eyes are burned—which leads to blindness—and it damages the cells inside the bones. Internal and external bleeding also occurs. And the worse part of all? It can take up to five weeks before death comes to their rescue. It's a nasty weapon."

Chapter 70

Solana led Molly to the patio, away from the morbid scene in the kitchen. A large puddle of blood covered the kitchen floor and was beginning to stream through to the dining area. Solana had the presence of mind to throw a large beach towel on the floor to stop its pathway.

Patrick gave up on the phone and drove the golf cart to the local police station on the north end of the island, just a few miles from the lighthouse.

Deputy Sheriff Harrison, presently dozing on the rickety, rattan sofa in the office, was awakened by pounding on the door.

"Damned if I'm going to go settle another argument between a bunch of drunks at Timmy's Nook. Let him deal with them."

When he pulled the door open, he was taken aback. It was that fellow who was supposed to be a priest. "Father Patrick? What are you doing here this time of the morning?"

"There's been an accident. No, not an accident. There's been a death. A shooting. At the lighthouse. I need you to call the Sheriff's Office on the mainland and have them send their people over."

"What? Who's been shot? When? What are you talking about?"

Deputy Harrison's days were spent writing parking tickets and rounding up the occasional drunk from one of several bars on the island. He'd never been involved in a shooting, and certainly never handled this kind of situation—one involving a death. Anything of that nature was always handled by the Sheriff's Office on the mainland.

"Come in. Tell me what you know."

"I just shot a man. His body is lying in the kitchen at the lighthouse."

"You? You shot him?"

"That's right. Call the Sheriff and have him send a patrol boat for the body. You should ask him to send the coroner and a forensics team also. And a call should be made to the Baltimore Police Department, too. The dead man is wanted by them."

Deputy Harrison was visibly shaken as he sat at his desk, trying to decide how to proceed. "Oh, what a mess. I don't know all the procedures for this. I'll call the mainland right now. You just sit here."

"No, I'm needed at the lighthouse. You come as soon as you can. I'll make sure no one touches the body or anything in the room." With that statement, Patrick left. Molly needed him more than this deputy did.

Solana had given Molly a large brandy to calm her nerves. Her hands had shaken uncontrollably at first, but now she was quiet and her thoughts coherent.

"He's been watching me, Solana. How long has he been here? If Patrick hadn't come in, I think he would have killed me."

"But Patrick did come in, Molly. As I see it, you were taking care of the situation pretty well yourself. A knife puncture and a shot in his leg and abdomen? You did exactly what you were instructed to do. You didn't wait. You acted."

Patrick parked the golf cart and went to the patio. One glance at Molly and he took a seat next to her and put an arm around her shoulder.

"That's exactly right. You kept him from killing you and I just put the finishing touches on that evil spawn of Satan. He's no longer a threat to you or anyone. My conscience is at peace. He deserved what he got. God rest his soul."

Patrick's arm was warm and offered a feeling of security. Something Molly hadn't felt in a long while. She leaned into him and let his presence bring comfort.

"I've alerted the local police. They'll have the mainland office dispatch a forensics team, the coroner, and someone to retrieve the body."

"I hope they get here soon. I want his body out of here. I want to put this whole affair behind me," Molly whispered.

Chapter 71

Bear brought the *Lady* to idle speed and Casper slipped over the side, his entry deathly quiet. Not even a ripple spread across the water. He might have been the young frogman he'd been forty-plus years ago.

Moving about without running lights, Bear headed the vessel toward the dock, then pulled into the last berth on the north end. Crab's ferry was at the far south end where he was moving yet another container from the *Calypso* to the cruiser.

Bear tied up to the nearest piling, stepped onto the dock and began to make his way to the ferry. He would have crawled, but his knee wouldn't entertain that thought. As he reached the piling about twenty-five yards from the *Calypso,* he spotted Crab struggling to lift a box containing several containers.

As Crab continued to pull at his heavy load, Bear crept closer and raised his 9mm Sig Saur, pointing it at Crab. Shortly, he was closing in on his target. He raised his Sig and called out.

"That's far enough Crab. Your little adventure is over. Put those containers down and step away."

Crab jerked his head up and eyed the admiral. "Ah, *Señor Admeeral.* And *el Capitán*? He is with you, also?"

"He'll be along. He knows your plan and the two of us will put a stop to it."

"Ah, but *Señor Admeeral*. You're mistaken. My *compadres* are close by. They will not like this change of plans."

"I repeat. Put the box down," said the admiral.

Crab got to his knees, placed the box on the deck and flipped open one of the containers in the process. When he raised his body to stand, he kicked the container over in the direction of the admiral, flooding the pier with a thick coating of sulfur mustard.

"I don't believe you would like to step in that sulfur mustard, *Admeeral*. If it gets on you . . . well . . . I am sure you know what it can do to a body."

Bear saw the thick dark liquid running down the pier and jumped back with lightning speed, a quick move far too demanding for his weak knee. It crumpled beneath him and he landed on his left side, lying on the deck.

When Admiral Bowen fell, Crab pulled his pistol from his waistband, releasing a shot that pierced the quiet night. Crab's shot failed to hit its target, the admiral's heart, but did manage to strike him in his upper right thigh. Ironically, this knee that Bear had cursed had saved him from a direct hit.

"Ah, God Almighty!" Bear yelled as he reached out, grabbing the nearest piling. His crippled knee was screaming at him and the blood flowing from his thigh was as slippery as an eel. With a great deal of effort he rolled off the dock and plunged into the water below.

Crab watched as the admiral disappeared beneath the dock. "Let the *tiburones* (sharks) get a whiff of that bleeding knee. They'll finish you off. So much for ending my plans, *Señor Admeeral,*" Crab muttered. He stuck his gun back in his waistband and turned back to his canisters, determined to get the last two onboard the cruiser.

Being careful to step away from the spilled liquid, he picked up two canisters, one in each hand, and headed to the cruiser. He'd only taken a couple of steps when a voice behind him halted his progress. The voice was deep and firm. As icy as the coldest *cerveza* Crab had ever drunk.

"Put them down, Crab. Place them on the dock."

Crab stopped and turned to face his adversary. Captain Jack stood a few yards away, clad in a wetsuit with fins laying on the dock where he'd removed them a few moments earlier.

"Ah, *Capitán* Jack. Perhaps you should be searching for the *Admeeral*. He had an unfortunate accident and fell into the water. Just moments ago. You may be able to save him from the *tiburones* if you hurry."

"Put the canisters down."

"*Sí, Sí, Capitán.* I'm putting them down." He bent over and when he stood, he again reached into his waistband for his weapon.

Before he could pull it out, he felt a sharp, excruciating pain rushing up from his abdomen. His weapon thudded to the deck and he grabbed his stomach.

He looked down, quiet for a long moment. Blood gushed from his abdomen where Jack's 12 ½ inch long diving knife was embedded to the hilt. Crab toppled forward, falling face down into the spilled sulfur mustard.

"*¡Dios!*" He yelled as he tried to lift his face from the deck, still holding his abdomen with both hands. Blood was pouring from his body, flowing freely, mixing with the sulfur mustard on the deck. Blood and sulfur mustard. One fluid used for saving lives, the other for taking them.

Jack came closer, careful to avoid the liquid. "Stay down, Crab. I'll call the Coast Guard to send an emergency team. If we get that stuff off you quickly you won't die, but you will spend many years in a Navy brig."

Crab's breath was coming in short bursts. He blinked, trying to clear the sulfur mustard from his eyes. He no longer tried to stop the flow from his abdomen. It was useless. Blood seeping out, sulfur mustard seeping in.

"I know what this sulfur mustard will do. And I'll not go to any prison. No, not again." He appeared to be struggling to sit upright when the second blast of the evening had sea birds and gulls scattering to safe harbor elsewhere.

Jack came closer. The clouds overhead drifted away and the moon shone brightly on Crab's face. A gaping hole in his right temple made way for more blood to add to that already pouring from his abdomen. He appeared to be staring back at Jack with eyes devoid of any life, with his pistol laying next to his body. Crab had ended this adventure himself.

Jack breathed deeply, then sighed, "I suppose this seemed a better option to you. Perhaps it was. Perhaps it was." He stood. He felt no pleasure in watching Crab die.

The admiral was still in the water, hanging on to the pilings, managing to keep afloat. Once Jack had him back on the dock they called the Coast Guard to send detachments to the area to clean up the hazardous material. And most importantly, to alert the military that all was well.

The Coast Guard emergency team arrived shortly and began to administer care to Admiral Bowen. He lay on the gurney, wondering what would have happened if they'd not been able to stop Crab. It was too horrible to contemplate. But, now, with his knee sending out SOS signals to his brain, he was past tired.

"Casper, this is the last operation I'm going to participate in. The final one, you hear?"

"Of course, Bear. And I agree. The final one. I'm off to see Molly, now. We'll both visit you in the hospital tomorrow. She'll want to know every detail, so be prepared to tell her the story."

Bear smirked, "I'll tell her some lies. Some things she doesn't need to know, Casper."

Casper smiled at his old shipmate as the team lifted the gurney and placed the admiral in the Coast Guard patrol boat. Then he started for the lighthouse.

Chapter 72

Solana's brandy had done the trick. Molly sat quietly, staring at her feet. Thinking. Suddenly she bolted from her chair. "Patrick! Patrick!"

The panic in Molly's voice had Patrick running from the kitchen to the patio. "What? What's wrong?"

Molly grabbed him by the arms. She was trembling. Holding on to him as if she might fall were he to move. "Patrick, I know who's been poisoning Papa."

"What? Who?"

"I remember where I saw that notation . . . $C_2H_6O_2$."

"Saw what? Molly, slow down. What did you see?"

"That chemical notation. I saw it on that bottle in the box you took to Agnes."

"Yeah, we took some stuff to Agnes."

"The number on the bottle, $C_2H_6O_2$. That's the chemical notation for anti-freeze."

"Yeah. I took a bottle of anti-freeze to Agnes. Jack said her car was running hot and asked me to take some to her."

"That's it, Patrick. I know where I've seen that notation before. In Crab's cabin. On the ferry. There was a large container with that notation."

"Crab would have anti-freeze on board, Molly. He

keeps many fluids on board. Stuff for the ferry."

"One of the numbers was missing, but I know it must have been a six. There was nothing on the container but those letters and numbers."

"You mean because Crab had anti-freeze on the ferry you think he poisoned Jack?"

Molly nodded.

Patrick frowned, "I can't think of any reason he would do such a thing. of

"Think for a minute. Crab brings the Glenfiddich over on his ferry. He has access to it and could infuse the bottles without anyone knowing."

"We can't prove that, Molly. That's a serious charge to lay on someone without proof." She grabbed his shirt and jerked him closer.

"We've got to warn Papa! He may be planning to take the ferry back to the island. He could be . . ."

Using his soothing, comforting priestly voice, Patrick reached out and took her hands in his.

"Jack can take care of himself. He's no fool. Neither is Crab. He wouldn't be stupid enough to try something on the ferry. If he is the culprit, he'd go after Jack some other way, like the poison. Something less dangerous than hand-to-hand combat with a former spy."

"I think former is not correct. He's still a spy," Molly commented. Her heart pounded and her pulse throbbed in her scarred face.

"We've got to get a message to him right away."

The nauseating fear she'd felt during the attack in Baltimore crawled out from its hiding place and began to slither into her body. Fear was more paralyzing than any anesthesia and she'd just been given a large dose.

Patrick pulled her close, hoping an embrace would ease her trembling body. Her head came only to his chest. Then as he looked out over her head, he received his final shock of the day.

Jack came walking up the lane to the lighthouse. Barefoot, carrying his fins, and dressed in his diving gear.

Captain Jackson McCormick, USN, Arriving . . .

Patrick grinned, "We have a visitor, Molly. Take a look." He took her by the shoulders and turned her around.

Jack slowly walked up the steps and was assailed by flailing arms from every direction. "Oh, Papa. I thought you were dead . . . for real!" Molly wrapped her arms around his waist and buried her face in his neck, crying and laughing at once.

"Glad you made it home, Jack. You're needed around here." Patrick waited for a second, then joined Molly in a warm hug for his friend.

"Captain. May I serve you a small tumbler of Glenfiddich?" Solana wanted nothing more than to throw her arms about him also. But she kept her emotions in bound. As Captain Jack would have wanted.

Jack hardly expected this scene and certainly not the one that greeted him in the kitchen. A dead body. Dead body or not, other more important issues took precedence at this time.

He got on his ham radio and made his report to Drifter and the commander in charge of Naval Station Key West. Bear Bowen would take care of informing his superiors. The chain of command dictated the proper protocol for such information as this.

Jack would review the events of the evening. Later. It was all still too raw now. He'd feared the worst—the sulfur mustard being delivered to the rebels—but had prayed for the best. Might be something he'd tell Patrick about.

He moved from the radio to speak with the police who were knee-deep working this crime scene, making frantic notes as they did so.

Even the old spy was bothered by the gruesome scene. An enormous amount of blood. And much of the right side of the man's head was missing. He felt the emotion he always felt in such a situation. Sadness that a life had ended.

Dr. Strickland was never so glad to get a call. He dropped what he was working on and took a team to Cayo Canna, courtesy of a Sheriff's Office patrol boat. He spoke briefly to Molly and Patrick, then began his work.

A while later, his team had completed their work. "Let's wrap it up, fellows. Load him up. Get him to the morgue. We'll touch base with Baltimore. Send them a copy of the autopsy report and ship the body to them. Let them take things from there." He said goodbye to Molly, knowing he'd see her again. Of that he was positive.

Sam's body was removed, the crime-scene tape torn away, and a cleanup crew mopped down the entire area. In a short time, it was as if nothing had ever happened. The breeze came through the open kitchen shutters and the scent from the night jasmine drifted in. Molly was the only one who could detect a faint smell of blood even after a thorough cleaning.

Any stains from this event would be those left in the minds and emotions of Molly, Patrick, and Solana. This event would bind the three whether they wished it or not.

Dr. Strickland completed his paperwork, then turned back and nodded toward Patrick. This seasoned coroner had not failed to recognize the role this man had played in tonight's happening. In saving Molly's life. The shot that took Sam out had been delivered with the intent of killing him . . . with the precision of a sniper. Dr. Strickland also hadn't missed how the priest followed Molly's every move with his eyes.

Chapter 73

When the last police vehicle pulled away, an eerie quietness fell over the lighthouse. The moon wormed its way from behind the dark clouds, but only for a brief period as the storm wasn't far off the coast now.

Papa Jack sat next to Molly as if afraid to let her get too far away. This night was one he would like to erase from memory.

Jack had given only the briefest of accounts regarding the sulfur mustard and Crab's involvement. Molly might wish for more details, but like Bear Bowen, he'd lie to her if need be.

"Let's just say the sulfur mustard has been contained by the U.S. Navy and is no longer in rebel hands. Crab had been an integral part of the plan from the beginning. No telling how long he's been working for them, using his position as a ferryman to keep under the radar. There's more to his story than we know, but he's no longer a problem for any of us."

"But . . . you're not going to tell us anything more, Papa Jack? Like how did you discover it was him, where did you apprehend him, how did you do it? Were there others involved? People here on the island?"

Jack smiled at his granddaughter. She'd always had more questions than anyone could answer. She'd have made a great Navy Intelligence Officer.

"Molly Mac, you still ask too many questions."

He smiled at her. She'd been right. It had been Crab. She'd just gotten to that conclusion in a different manner than he had. Perhaps she was part spy herself.

"I would like to make a proposal if I may," Patrick announced.

"And what would that be, Patrick?" Jack looked at his friend, the one who had saved his granddaughter's life.

"I believe a 'resurrection' party is in order. As you see from the floral arrangements on the patio, many folks on this island are very fond of you and will be delighted to know you've returned from the abyss."

"What a great idea, Patrick." Molly smiled at him and looked at Papa.

"Papa? What do you think?"

Jack laughed and turned to Solana. "What do *you* think, Solana? We'd need your help to pull this off."

"I think a celebration would be perfect, Captain Jack." She went in to gather her things. Time for her to head home, also.

"Father Patrick, I wonder if you would drop me at my bungalow. This day has been a long one."

"My pleasure, Solana."

Papa Jack and Molly waved them off and entered the lighthouse. "Now, I have a most important question," Jack said.

"What's that, Papa Jack?"

"Where's Ensign?"

Molly laughed. "I believe he's up in the lantern room, his favorite place. Slept through the entire affair."

Chapter 74

Life at the lighthouse was resuming some semblance of normalcy. The day before the "resurrection" party was to take place, Patrick showed up just as twilight came calling.

He was unexpected, which was not a problem as Solana now accepted him as readily as the Captain. Which greatly pleased Patrick.

Today he came with a purpose. The same purpose he'd come with some months ago. So much had happened since then, but his "problem," the one that had driven him from his Church and possibly from his priestly calling, was still with him.

Solana greeted him and pointed to the banyan tree. Jack was pouring over the report from Admiral Bowen, who was always exact in his details. They had prevented a catastrophe and this was one mission Jack was relieved to be done with.

He looked over his half-glasses and saw Patrick, slowly coming his way, his head down, looking as if his thoughts were a thousand miles away. As they were.

"Ah, Patrick. Join me."

Solana showed up with a tumbler of Jameson and handed it to Patrick. "Thanks, Solana. I might need this." She left as quietly as she had come.

He took a small sip and leaned back in the canvas chair. Jack remained quiet. He knew Patrick would begin when the moment was right.

"Jack . . . I . . ." He ran his hands through his hair.

"It's like I've fallen through Alice's looking glass. Nothing is as it was. Nothing is as it seemed to be."

"You don't have to choose your words with me, Patrick. Let them come as they will."

"It's difficult. This problem, my problem, has me questioning everything I've ever believed in." An hour later, he had laid out his problem in a very haphazard way that was reflective of his confused feelings and thoughts.

Jack waited a moment before he spoke. "You know Church history better than I, Patrick. That being the case, I don't have to tell you that sexual abuse began long ago with the very first popes and bishops.

"That doesn't excuse the abuse you've described. In fact, I'd say evidence of abuse in this day makes it even more important that it be exposed for what it is. A cruel and abominable act that robs children of their innocence and leaves a wound. A wound that never heals."

"I know. It's just . . . Jack . . . I'm speaking of my friend, Paul. We share everything. The difficulties in our parishes, our problems with our bishops. We even tell each other about our desires for women . . . occasionally. But this, his admittance to abusing young boys . . . this is unforgivable.

"I thought about reporting him, but my bishop insists I keep this to myself. Apparently, Church authorities are aware of it already and Paul's not the only one.

"And it makes me think. Do I want to be part of something—the Church—that fails to bring these acts to light? I'm struggling to keep my faith, my beliefs."

Jack leaned closer and made eye contact with Patrick.

"Problems that at first seem unsurmountable seldom are. A week ago I was afraid our island would be destroyed. Today I'm sitting here with a friend. One who has a heart that is even bigger than his feet.

"Take your time. You don't have to make any permanent decisions regarding the Church. At least not today. What you do with this information could have lasting consequences. For you and others. Whatever you decide, make peace with yourself first. That will pave the way for peace with others."

Patrick nodded. *Yes. I'll make peace with myself regarding this problem. Then I'll find a way to make peace with other problems that I buried long ago.*

Chapter 75

The sound of stirring, upbeat music coming from the island band greeted guests as they began to arrive at the lighthouse. Some residents walked and others came by golf cart or took Rafael's cab.

Molly had posted invitations in The Temptation, Timmy's Nook, The Gasparilla Inn, and Bailey's Island Grocery. That pretty much ensured everyone would be aware of the event and know they were welcome.

She and Solana had hung "fairy lights" all about the lighthouse, the patio, and in the palm trees. All doors and windows were flung open and a soft breeze had the palm fronds creating their own music.

"A resurrection celebration for Captain Jack! Great idea," giggled Isobel, the barmaid from the Temptation, as she reached for a glass of champagne from Solana's tray.

Molly was passing out more *tapas* when she heard a voice behind her, "Need any help?"

She turned to see Todd Redhawk smiling across the room at her. He'd left his hair streaming down his back and every woman in the place was envious of such tresses.

"Todd, I didn't know if you would come. I know you're making up lost time on your research." She hugged him and handed him a tray of snacks. "Here, pass these around."

Captain Jack greeted the guests and was thoroughly enjoying the evening, particularly seeing how Molly appeared to be engaged in life again, lighting up the room with her smile.

Admiral Bowen had arrived, sporting a cast on his leg and commandeering a wheelchair. He was holding court at a table in the corner of the patio, telling "sea stories," albeit embellishing them somewhat.

Molly was interrupted again when she felt a tap on her shoulder. She looked around and was greeted with a grin that had her smiling in return.

"Dr. Strickland . . . David! What a surprise. I thought about calling you but I know any coroner's schedule is quite full."

"Since I was the one who declared Jack dead, I thought the least I could do was attend his resurrection. Wouldn't have missed this for the world."

"You were the one who made this possible. Papa Jack would never have been able to complete his "covert ops" without your help. He played a crucial role in preventing some terrifying events from happening. That's about all I can tell you as that's about all I know. Papa doesn't tell anyone much about his "covert" work. Come, let me take you over there so he can thank you himself."

By the time Patrick showed up the party was in full swing. He'd thought it appropriate that he, a priest, say a few words at this 'resurrection' party, and he'd spent considerable time preparing a speech for the event.

He held his speech in hand when Solana walked up to him, "Since when have you needed a written speech, Father Patrick? I've never known you to be without words for most anything. Just say what needs to be said. The right words will come to you. Then I'll serve you a chilled glass of champagne."

Patrick walked to the table where Captain Jack and Admiral Bowen were sharing their escapades. Jack greeted him and offered him a chair.

"No, I've got a few words to say first, then I'll chat with you two." He stood tall, pulled his shoulders back, and clinked a spoon on his glass to get the attention of the guests. After a couple more clinks, they yielded him the floor.

"Uh . . . I'd prepared a very eloquent speech, regaling the feats of Captain Jack, telling you how special he is, what a gentleman he is, and telling of his many talents and abilities. But, as Solana reminded me, he needs no words from me. All of you are here because you are thankful he's "returned from the dead" and is with us again. Then let us lift our glasses to him, Captain Jack McCormick, our dear friend. Long may he live . . . again!"

There was cheering and applause and then the crowd went back to celebrating. Patrick started toward Molly's table, the table where Todd Redhawk and Dr. Strickland were gathered. Molly was grinning and making animated gestures with her hands as she talked with them.

As Patrick reached the table the "fairy lights" went out, leaving the dance floor in darkness. "Oh, no. We were having such fun," Isobel called out.

Patrick darted up the stairs, trusting that his big feet wouldn't trip him up. When he returned, he went to Molly's table. "Here you go. This will put a little light on the situation."

He placed Papa's old brass lantern in the middle of the table and lighted it. The flame rose high and the glass panes sent shimmers of light throughout the room.

"Patrick, what a great idea. You are amazing. I thought that lantern was broken. Didn't think it would ever work again. I should have known Papa would fix it." The merrymakers cheered and quickly returned to celebrating.

"Good move on the Father's part. This party could go on all night, Jack," Rafael called as he took Isobel by the hand and led her to the dancefloor again.

Admiral Bowen shifted his leg. "This damn cast is driving me crazy. And my knee itches like hell!"

Jack laughed. "Yep. Bet it does. Have another glass of champagne. It'll ease that itch."

The admiral groaned and shook his head. "If it's not one problem it's another. Speaking of problems, I thought you told me Molly had difficulty dealing with men. Never had much luck with them. That's what you told me."

"Yeah, seems to be the way it is."

"Well, my old friend, take a look over there. She's got the attention of not one, but three young men. Look at 'em. They're entranced."

Jack lifted his head slightly. Todd Redhawk and David Strickland were gathered around Molly, each giving her their undivided attention, appearing to hang on to her every word. And Patrick stood a short distance behind her. Perhaps waiting for an invitation to join them?

Jack took a deep breath. "Huh. Perhaps I stand corrected. Now what the hell am I to do with that information?"

"Looks like Molly can handle her affairs—without your help, Casper." Bear laughed when he saw the look that crossed Jack's face.

"That lantern hasn't worked for some time now. I've been working on it but never could get it going again. Looks like someone's brought it to life again," commented Jack. He had no doubt who had repaired the lantern.

And maybe someone's brought life to Molly again.

Chapter 76

Next morning Solana appeared at the front steps, her long skirt swishing as she climbed them. Her hair had been left loose today and the breeze lifted it as she moved about.

She removed her shoes and entered, then headed to the kitchen where she would get breakfast ready for Captain Jack. She was surprised to see him coming down the staircase, Ensign at his heels.

"Ah, good morning, Solana."

"Good morning, Captain. Early riser today?"

"Yeah, it always takes me a few days to get back to my routine when I've been away for a while. Thought I'd take Ensign for a quick walk. See what's been going on while I was gone."

"Then I'll wait to do breakfast when you return." She placed her basket in the corner and removed an envelope from it.

"This was on the steps when I came in. It's addressed to both you and Molly."

"Oh?" He took the envelope from Solana's hand, sat on the last stairstep, and began to read. It was a note and a short one at that. He read it, then got up and put it in his pocket.

"I'll give it to Molly when I return. Won't be gone long." Solana never questioned him and went about getting the kitchen in order.

Over in Keeper's Cottage, Molly awoke and pulled on one of Mimi's caftans. She brushed her hair and hurried over to the lighthouse. Solana's coffee would get her day started right and then she was to go with Patrick to check out Todd's latest aquatic specimens.

As she entered the kitchen, Papa and Ensign came in. "Morning, Papa. You're out and about early."

"Too much sleep isn't good for you." He grinned and took the cup she thrust at him. He didn't quite know what to say to her, so he didn't say anything, but rather, handed her the note from Patrick. Then he went out to the patio where he would listen to the waves as they ushered in the incoming tide.

Molly opened the note.

Jack and Molly. I have some unfinished business in Baltimore. And Ireland, as well. I must attend to this business as my life is at a standstill. Please accept my thanks for your friendship. I treasure it, and you are both dear to me. I don't know what my future holds, but if it brings me closer to you then I will have been truly blessed. Take care of yourselves and each other.

Patrick

Molly folded the note and returned it to the envelope. She joined Papa on the patio where he was staring out at the open ocean. She sat down next to him. "Papa?"

He shook his head. "I don't know any more than you, Molly Mac. Patrick is a complicated fellow. He's been conflicted for some time and his issues are like everyone's— personal—and he keeps them inside. But he's not one to run from trouble, so I expect we may see him. Perhaps sooner than you think."

Molly sighed, "Yes, that would be like him. To keep everything inside. That's a trait we share, I guess."

"Not a bad trait, Molly. It's a good idea to keep your own counsel until you're ready to share your thoughts."

"Then perhaps I should share my thoughts with you now. I, like Patrick, have some unresolved issues. But in my case, I don't need to go anywhere to resolve them.

"In fact, going anywhere is the antithesis of what I need to do. It's become clear to me that the life I want, one where I can help others, is right here on Cayo Canna.

"After spending time with Patrick visiting the outer island and seeing the condition of those people living there, then working with Bem, I know where my talents could serve the most. Not in a research department somewhere and not in Baltimore. But here. I'm not going anywhere. My destiny lies here. This is my home. This is where I belong."

Papa Jack leaned forward and smiled at her. "I agree. Your talents and skills are needed right here on this island."

He stood and looked out at the ocean. "Stay here. Just a minute." He returned shortly with an envelope in his hand. "Before she passed away, Margaret asked that this be given to you as a gift upon completion of your medical training. I think now is the appropriate time."

Molly looked at the handwriting on the envelope . . . beautiful letters, evenly spaced, feminine. Mimi's. She took the envelope, opened it, and read the document inside. It was a short document. Most unexpected.

"Papa? Do you know what this means?"

"Of course. But do you?"

She reread the document. The important part, that is.

"*Margaret Humphrey McCormick bequeaths the remainder of her Trust Fund to her granddaughter, Margaret Elizabeth McCormick to be used as she so desires. . . etc., etc.,*"

"It means I can have a proper office with proper equipment, and supplies, and medications, and I can go to the outer islands as Patrick does, and, and . . ."

Papa grinned, "Finally, that damned Trust Fund will go to good use."

~ ~ ~

When evening came the electricity had gone on the blink again and the island was awash in darkness. Molly walked along the water's edge. The ebb and flow of the ocean were never ending. As if it had a purpose that never changed. It could be counted on to continue no matter what. Much like Papa Jack. That thought had her smiling as she dipped her toes in the warm water and marveled at the phosphorus winking at her as it rode the waves to shore.

She waded out farther into the water, immersing herself in its healing properties. She raised her eyes to the lantern room of that ivory tower that stood like a great knight protecting his castle.

There, sitting on the edge of the window sill, was Papa's old lantern. It was the only light on the island tonight and it glowed in the velvet darkness, sending out a glittering beam of light that danced across the water. Molly smiled. She was sure the beam could be seen in Connecticut as it shone brighter than ever.

"...just one more thing..."

I hope you enjoyed reading this novel as much as I enjoyed writing it. So, if I could ask for "just one more thing," I'd like to hear from you and hope that you could take the time to post a review on Amazon. Your feedback and support will help me improve my future writing projects.

Follow this link

www.amazon.com/review/create-review?&isbn=1943369151

to take you directly to the Amazon review page.

Thanks so much for reading this book and I hope you will check out my other works nearby.

Other Books by Florence Love Karsner

The Highland Healer Series

Highland Healer (Book 1)
Highland Circle of Stones (Book 2)
Highland Bloodline (Book 3)
The Wolf, The Wizard, and The Woad (Book 4)

The Dr. Molly McCormick Series

We All Have Secrets (Book 1)

Tobacco Rose

Tobacco Rose

About the Author

Florence Love Karsner is the author of several published novels, including Amazon #1 Best Seller, *Tobacco Rose.* She also authored four novels in *The Highland Healer Series: The Highland Healer, Highland Circle of Stones, Highland Bloodline, and The Wolf, The Wizard, and The Woad. We All Have Secrets,* a period piece set during the time of the Cuban Missile Crisis, is a personal favorite. When not engaged by her muse, she enjoys playing golf and creating pottery. She lives with her husband, Garry, in North Central Florida, her home state.

Made in the USA
Columbia, SC
17 July 2023

20181037R00236